Seivarden Vendaai was no concern of mine anymore,

wasn't my responsibility. And she had never been one of my favorite officers. I had obeyed her orders, of course, and she had never abused any ancillaries, never harmed any of my segments (as the occasional officer did). I had no reason to think badly of her. On the contrary, her manners were those of an educated, well-bred person of good family. Not towards me, of course—I wasn't a person, I was a piece of equipment, a part of the ship. But I had never particularly cared for her.

I rose and went into the tavern. The place was dark, the white of the ice walls long since covered over with grime or worse. The air smelled of alcohol and vomit. A barkeep stood behind a high bench. She was a native—short and fat, pale and wide-eyed. Three patrons sprawled in seats at a dirty table. Despite the cold they wore only trousers and quilted shirts—it was spring in this hemisphere of Nilt and they were enjoying the warm spell. They pretended not to see me, though they had certainly noticed me in the street and knew what motivated my entrance. Likely one or more of them had been involved; Seivarden hadn't been out there long, or she'd have been dead.

"I'll rent a sledge," I said, "and buy a hypothermia kit."

Behind me one of the patrons chuckled and said, voice mocking, "Aren't you a tough little girl."

ANCILLARY JUSTICE

ANN LECKIE

www.orbitbooks.net

Orbit
Hachette Book Group
1290 Avenue of the Americas, New York, NY 10104
HachetteBookGroup.com

First Edition: October 2013

Orbit is an imprint of Hachette Book Group, Inc. The Orbit name and logo are trademarks of Little, Brown Book Group Limited.

The Hachette Speakers Bureau provides a wide range of authors for speaking events. To find out more, go to www.hachettespeakersbureau.com or call (866) 376-6591.

The publisher is not responsible for websites (or their content) that are not owned by the publisher.

The characters and events in this book are fictitious. Any similarity to real persons, living or dead, is coincidental and not intended by the author.

Library of Congress Cataloging-in-Publication Data

Leckie, Ann.
   Ancillary Justice / Ann Leckie. — First edition
      pages cm
   ISBN 978-0-316-24662-0 (trade pbk.) — ISBN 978-0-316-24663-7 (ebook)   1. Science fiction.   I. Title.
   PS3612.E3353A83 2013
   813'.6—dc23
                              2012051135

10

RRD-C

Printed in the United States of America

For my parents, Mary P. and David N. Dietzler,
who didn't live to see this book but were
always sure it would exist.

1

The body lay naked and facedown, a deathly gray, spatters of blood staining the snow around it. It was minus fifteen degrees Celsius and a storm had passed just hours before. The snow stretched smooth in the wan sunrise, only a few tracks leading into a nearby ice-block building. A tavern. Or what passed for a tavern in this town.

There was something itchingly familiar about that out-thrown arm, the line from shoulder down to hip. But it was hardly possible I knew this person. I didn't know anyone here. This was the icy back end of a cold and isolated planet, as far from Radchaai ideas of civilization as it was possible to be. I was only here, on this planet, in this town, because I had urgent business of my own. Bodies in the street were none of my concern.

Sometimes I don't know why I do the things I do. Even after all this time it's still a new thing for me not to know, not to have orders to follow from one moment to the next. So I can't explain to you why I stopped and with one foot lifted the naked shoulder so I could see the person's face.

Frozen, bruised, and bloody as she was, I knew her. Her name was Seivarden Vendaai, and a long time ago she had been one of my officers, a young lieutenant, eventually promoted to her own command, another ship. I had thought her a thousand years dead, but she was, undeniably, here. I crouched down and felt for a pulse, for the faintest stir of breath.

Still alive.

Seivarden Vendaai was no concern of mine anymore, wasn't my responsibility. And she had never been one of my favorite officers. I had obeyed her orders, of course, and she had never abused any ancillaries, never harmed any of my segments (as the occasional officer did). I had no reason to think badly of her. On the contrary, her manners were those of an educated, well-bred person of good family. Not toward me, of course—I wasn't a person, I was a piece of equipment, a part of the ship. But I had never particularly cared for her.

I rose and went into the tavern. The place was dark, the white of the ice walls long since covered over with grime or worse. The air smelled of alcohol and vomit. A barkeep stood behind a high bench. She was a native—short and fat, pale and wide-eyed. Three patrons sprawled in seats at a dirty table. Despite the cold they wore only trousers and quilted shirts—it was spring in this hemisphere of Nilt and they were enjoying the warm spell. They pretended not to see me, though they had certainly noticed me in the street and knew what motivated my entrance. Likely one or more of them had been involved; Seivarden hadn't been out there long, or she'd have been dead.

"I'll rent a sledge," I said, "and buy a hypothermia kit."

Behind me one of the patrons chuckled and said, voice mocking, "Aren't you a tough little girl."

2

I turned to look at her, to study her face. She was taller than most Nilters, but fat and pale as any of them. She outbulked me, but I was taller, and I was also considerably stronger than I looked. She didn't realize what she was playing with. She was probably male, to judge from the angular mazelike patterns quilting her shirt. I wasn't entirely certain. It wouldn't have mattered, if I had been in Radch space. Radchaai don't care much about gender, and the language they speak—my own first language—doesn't mark gender in any way. This language we were speaking now did, and I could make trouble for myself if I used the wrong forms. It didn't help that cues meant to distinguish gender changed from place to place, sometimes radically, and rarely made much sense to me.

I decided to say nothing. After a couple of seconds she suddenly found something interesting in the tabletop. I could have killed her, right there, without much effort. I found the idea attractive. But right now Seivarden was my first priority. I turned back to the barkeep.

Slouching negligently she said, as though there had been no interruption, "What kind of place you think this is?"

"The kind of place," I said, still safely in linguistic territory that needed no gender marking, "that will rent me a sledge and sell me a hypothermia kit. How much?"

"Two hundred shen." At least twice the going rate, I was sure. "For the sledge. Out back. You'll have to get it yourself. Another hundred for the kit."

"Complete," I said. "Not used."

She pulled one out from under the bench, and the seal looked undamaged. "Your buddy out there had a tab."

Maybe a lie. Maybe not. Either way the number would be pure fiction. "How much?"

3

"Three hundred fifty."

I could find a way to keep avoiding referring to the bar-keep's gender. Or I could guess. It was, at worst, a fifty-fifty chance. "You're very trusting," I said, guessing *male*, "to let such an indigent"—I knew Seivarden was male, that one was easy—"run up such a debt." The barkeep said nothing. "Six hundred and fifty covers all of it?"

"Yeah," said the barkeep. "Pretty much."

"No, all of it. We will agree now. And if anyone comes after me later demanding more, or tries to rob me, they die."

Silence. Then the sound behind me of someone spitting. "Radchaai scum."

"I'm not Radchaai." Which was true. You have to be human to be Radchaai.

"*He* is," said the barkeep, with the smallest shrug toward the door. "You don't have the accent but you stink like Rad-chaai."

"That's the swill you serve your customers." Hoots from the patrons behind me. I reached into a pocket, pulled out a handful of chits, and tossed them on the bench. "Keep the change." I turned to leave.

"Your money better be good."

"Your sledge had better be out back where you said." And I left.

The hypothermia kit first. I rolled Seivarden over. Then I tore the seal on the kit, snapped an internal off the card, and pushed it into her bloody, half-frozen mouth. Once the indicator on the card showed green I unfolded the thin wrap, made sure of the charge, wound it around her, and switched it on. Then I went around back for the sledge.

No one was waiting for me, which was fortunate. I didn't want to leave bodies behind just yet, I hadn't come here to cause trouble. I towed the sledge around front, loaded Seivarden onto it, and considered taking my outer coat off and laying it on her, but in the end I decided it wouldn't be that much of an improvement over the hypothermia wrap alone. I powered up the sledge and was off.

I rented a room at the edge of town, one of a dozen two-meter cubes of grimy, gray-green prefab plastic. No bedding, and blankets cost extra, as did heat. I paid—I had already wasted a ridiculous amount of money bringing Seivarden out of the snow.

I cleaned the blood off her as best I could, checked her pulse (still there) and temperature (rising). Once I would have known her core temperature without even thinking, her heart rate, blood oxygen, hormone levels. I would have seen any and every injury merely by wishing it. Now I was blind. Clearly she'd been beaten—her face was swollen, her torso bruised.

The hypothermia kit came with a very basic corrective, but only one, and only suitable for first aid. Seivarden might have internal injuries or severe head trauma, and I was only capable of fixing cuts or sprains. With any luck, the cold and the bruises were all I had to deal with. But I didn't have much medical knowledge, not anymore. Any diagnosis I could make would be of the most basic sort.

I pushed another internal down her throat. Another check—her skin was no more chill than one would expect, considering, and she didn't seem clammy. Her color, given the bruises, was returning to a more normal brown. I brought in a container of snow to melt, set it in a corner where I hoped she wouldn't kick it over if she woke, and then went out, locking the door behind me.

The sun had risen higher in the sky, but the light was

hardly any stronger. By now more tracks marred the even snow of last night's storm, and one or two Nilters were about. I hauled the sledge back to the tavern, parked it behind. No one accosted me, no sounds came from the dark doorway. I headed for the center of town.

People were abroad, doing business. Fat, pale children in trousers and quilted shirts kicked snow at each other, and then stopped and stared with large surprised-looking eyes when they saw me. The adults pretended I didn't exist, but their eyes turned toward me as they passed. I went into a shop, going from what passed for daylight here to dimness, into a chill just barely five degrees warmer than outside.

A dozen people stood around talking, but instant silence descended as soon as I entered. I realized that I had no expression on my face, and set my facial muscles to something pleasant and noncommittal.

"What do you want?" growled the shopkeeper.

"Surely these others are before me." Hoping as I spoke that it was a mixed-gender group, as my sentence indicated. I received only silence in response. "I would like four loaves of bread and a slab of fat. Also two hypothermia kits and two general-purpose correctives, if such a thing is available."

"I've got tens, twenties, and thirties."

"Thirties, please."

She stacked my purchases on the counter. "Three hundred seventy-five." There was a cough from someone behind me— I was being overcharged again.

I paid and left. The children were still huddled, laughing, in the street. The adults still passed me as though I weren't there. I made one more stop—Seivarden would need clothes. Then I returned to the room.

Seivarden was still unconscious, and there were still no

signs of shock as far as I could see. The snow in the container had mostly melted, and I put half of one brick-hard loaf of bread in it to soak.

A head injury and internal organ damage were the most dangerous possibilities. I broke open the two correctives I'd just bought and lifted the blanket to lay one across Seivarden's abdomen, watched it puddle and stretch and then harden into a clear shell. The other I held to the side of her face that seemed the most bruised. When that one had hardened, I took off my outer coat and lay down and slept.

Slightly more than seven and a half hours later, Seivarden stirred and I woke. "Are you awake?" I asked. The corrective I'd applied held one eye closed, and one half of her mouth, but the bruising and the swelling all over her face was much reduced. I considered for a moment what would be the right facial expression, and made it. "I found you in the snow, in front of a tavern. You looked like you needed help." She gave a faint rasp of breath but didn't turn her head toward me. "Are you hungry?" No answer, just a vacant stare. "Did you hit your head?"

"No," she said, quiet, her face relaxed and slack.

"Are you hungry?"

"No."

"When did you eat last?"

"I don't know." Her voice was calm, without inflection.

I pulled her upright and propped her against the gray-green wall, gingerly, not wanting to cause more injury, wary of her slumping over. She stayed sitting, so I slowly spooned some bread-and-water mush into her mouth, working cautiously around the corrective. "Swallow," I said, and she did. I gave her half of what was in the bowl that way and then I ate the rest myself, and brought in another pan of snow.

She watched me put another half-loaf of hard bread in the pan, but said nothing, her face still placid. "What's your name?" I asked. No answer.

She'd taken kef, I guessed. Most people will tell you that kef suppresses emotion, which it does, but that's not all it does. There was a time when I could have explained exactly what kef does, and how, but I'm not what I once was.

As far as I knew, people took kef so they could stop feeling something. Or because they believed that, emotions out of the way, supreme rationality would result, utter logic, true enlightenment. But it doesn't work that way.

Pulling Seivarden out of the snow had cost me time and money that I could ill afford, and for what? Left to her own devices she would find herself another hit or three of kef, and she would find her way into another place like that grimy tavern and get herself well and truly killed. If that was what she wanted I had no right to prevent her. But if she had wanted to die, why hadn't she done the thing cleanly, registered her intention and gone to the medic as anyone would? I didn't understand.

There was a good deal I didn't understand, and nineteen years pretending to be human hadn't taught me as much as I'd thought.

2

Nineteen years, three months, and one week before I found Seivarden in the snow, I was a troop carrier orbiting the planet Shis'urna. Troop carriers are the most massive of Radchaai ships, sixteen decks stacked one on top of the other. Command, Administrative, Medical, Hydroponics, Engineering, Central Access, and a deck for each decade, living and working space for my officers, whose every breath, every twitch of every muscle, was known to me.

Troop carriers rarely move. I sat, as I had sat for most of my two-thousand-year existence in one system or another, feeling the bitter chill of vacuum outside my hull, the planet Shis'urna like a blue-and-white glass counter, its orbiting station coming and going around, a steady stream of ships arriving, docking, undocking, departing toward one or the other of the buoy- and beacon-surrounded gates. From my vantage the boundaries of Shis'urna's various nations and territories weren't visible, though on its night side the planet's cities glowed bright here and there, and webs of roads between them, where they'd been restored since the annexation.

I felt and heard—though didn't always see—the presence of my companion ships—the smaller, faster Swords and Mercies, and most numerous at that time, the Justices, troop carriers like me. The oldest of us was nearly three thousand years old. We had known each other for a long time, and by now we had little to say to each other that had not already been said many times. We were, by and large, companionably silent, not counting routine communications.

As I still had ancillaries, I could be in more than one place at a time. I was also on detached duty in the city of Ors, on the planet Shis'urna, under the command of Esk Decade Lieutenant Awn.

Ors sat half on waterlogged land, half in marshy lake, the lakeward side built on slabs atop foundations sunk deep in the marsh mud. Green slime grew in the canals and joints between slabs, along the lower edges of building columns, on anything stationary the water reached, which varied with the season. The constant stink of hydrogen sulfide only cleared occasionally, when summer storms made the lakeward half of the city tremble and shudder and walkways were knee-deep in water blown in from beyond the barrier islands. Occasionally. Usually the storms made the smell worse. They turned the air temporarily cooler, but the relief generally lasted no more than a few days. Otherwise, it was always humid and hot.

I couldn't see Ors from orbit. It was more village than city, though it had once sat at the mouth of a river, and been the capital of a country that stretched along the coastline. Trade had come up and down the river, and flat-bottomed boats had plied the coastal marsh, bringing people from one town to the next. The river had shifted away over the centuries, and now Ors was half ruins. What had once been miles of rectangular islands within a grid of channels was now a much smaller place, surrounded by and interspersed with broken, half-sunken slabs, sometimes with roofs and pillars, that emerged from the muddy green water in the dry season. It had once been home to millions. Only 6,318 people had lived here when Radchaai forces annexed Shis'urna five years earlier, and of course the annexation had reduced that number. In Ors less than in some other places: as soon as we had appeared—myself in the form of my Esk cohorts along with their decade lieutenants lined up in the streets of the town, armed and armored—the head priest of Ikkt had approached the most senior officer present—Lieutenant Awn, as I said—and offered immediate surrender. The head priest had told her followers what they needed to do to survive the annexation, and for the most part those followers did indeed survive. This wasn't as common as one might think—we always made it clear from the beginning that even breathing trouble during an annexation could mean death, and from the instant an annexation began we made demonstrations of just what that meant widely available, but there was always someone who couldn't resist trying us.

Still, the head priest's influence was impressive. The city's small size was to some degree deceptive—during pilgrimage season hundreds of thousands of visitors streamed through the plaza in front of the temple, camped on the slabs of abandoned streets. For worshippers of Ikkt this was the second holiest place on the planet, and the head priest a divine presence.

Usually a civilian police force was in place by the time an annexation was officially complete, something that often took fifty years or more. This annexation was different— citizenship had been granted to the surviving Shis'urnans

11

much earlier than normal. No one in system administration quite trusted the idea of local civilians working security just yet, and military presence was still quite heavy. So when the annexation of Shis'urna was officially complete, most of *Justice of Toren* Esk went back to the ship, but Lieutenant Awn stayed, and I stayed with her as the twenty-ancillary unit *Justice of Toren* One Esk.

The head priest lived in a house near the temple, one of the few intact buildings from the days when Ors had been a city—four-storied, with a single-sloped roof and open on all sides, though dividers could be raised whenever an occupant wished privacy, and shutters could be rolled down on the outsides during storms. The head priest received Lieutenant Awn in a partition some five meters square, light peering in over the tops of the dark walls.

"You don't," said the priest, an old person with gray hair and a close-cut gray beard, "find serving in Ors a hardship?" Both she and Lieutenant Awn had settled onto cushions— damp, like everything in Ors, and fungal-smelling. The priest wore a length of yellow cloth twisted around her waist, her shoulders inked with shapes, some curling, some angular, that changed depending on the liturgical significance of the day. In deference to Radchaai propriety, she wore gloves.

"Of course not," said Lieutenant Awn, pleasantly—though, I thought, not entirely truthfully. She had dark brown eyes and close-clipped dark hair. Her skin was dark enough that she wouldn't be considered pale, but not so dark as to be fashionable—she could have changed it, hair and eyes as well, but she never had. Instead of her uniform—long brown coat with its scattering of jeweled pins, shirt and trousers, boots and gloves—she wore the same sort of skirt the head priest did, and a thin shirt and the lightest of gloves. Still, she was sweating. I stood at the entrance, silent and straight, as a junior priest laid cups and bowls in between Lieutenant Awn and the Divine.

I also stood some forty meters away, in the temple itself— an atypically enclosed space 43.5 meters high, 65.7 meters long, and 29.9 meters wide. At one end were doors nearly as tall as the roof was high, and at the other, towering over the people on the floor below, a representation of a mountain-side cliff somewhere else on Shis'urna, worked in painstaking detail. At the foot of this sat a dais, wide steps leading down to a floor of gray-and-green stone. Light streamed in through dozens of green skylights, onto walls painted with scenes from the lives of the saints of the cult of Ikkt. It was unlike any other building in Ors. The architecture, like the cult of Ikkt itself, had been imported from elsewhere on Shis'urna. During pilgrimage season this space would be jammed tight with worshippers. There were other holy sites, but if an Orsian said "pilgrimage" she meant the annual pilgrimage to this place. But that was some weeks away. For now the air of the temple susurrated faintly in one corner with the whispered prayers of a dozen devotees.

The head priest laughed. "You are a diplomat, Lieutenant Awn."

"I am a soldier, Divine," answered Lieutenant Awn. They were speaking Radchaai, and she spoke slowly and precisely, careful of her accent. "I don't find my duty a hardship."

The head priest did not smile in response. In the brief silence that followed, the junior priest set down a lipped bowl of what Shis'urnans call tea, a thick liquid, lukewarm and sweet, that bears almost no relationship to the actual thing.

Outside the doors of the temple I also stood in the cyanophyte-stained plaza, watching people as they passed. Most wore the same simple, bright-colored skirting the head priest did, though only very small children and the very devout had much in the way of markings, and only a few wore gloves. Some of those passing were transplants, Radchaai assigned to jobs or given property here in Ors after the annexation. Most of them had adopted the simple skirt and added a light, loose shirt, as Lieutenant Awn had. Some stuck stubbornly to trousers and jacket, and sweated their way across the plaza. All wore the jewelry that few Radchaai would ever give up—gifts from friends or lovers, memorials to the dead, marks of family or clientage associations.

To the north, past a rectangular stretch of water called the Fore-Temple after the neighborhood it had once been, Ors rose slightly where the city sat on actual ground during the dry season, an area still called, politely, the upper city. I patrolled there as well. When I walked the edge of the water I could see myself standing in the plaza.

Boats poled slowly across the marshy lake, and up and down channels between groupings of slabs. The water was scummy with swaths of algae, here and there bristling with the tips of water-grasses. Away from the town, east and west, buoys marked prohibited stretches of water, and within their confines the iridescent wings of marshflies shimmered over the water weeds floating thick and tangled there. Around them larger boats floated, and the big dredgers, now silent and still, that before the annexation had hauled up the stinking mud that lay beneath the water.

The view to the south was similar, except for the barest hint on the horizon of the actual sea, past the soggy spit that bounded the swamp. I saw all of this, standing as I did at various points surrounding the temple, and walking the streets of the town itself. It was twenty-seven degrees C, and humid as always.

That accounted for almost half of my twenty bodies. The remainder slept or worked in the house Lieutenant Awn occupied—three-storied and spacious, it had once housed a large extended family and a boat rental. One side opened on a broad, muddy green canal, and the opposite onto the largest of local streets.

Three of the segments in the house were awake, performing administrative duties (I sat on a mat on a low platform in the center of the first floor of the house and listened to an Orsian complain to me about the allocation of fishing rights) and keeping watch. "You should bring this to the district magistrate, citizen," I told the Orsian, in the local dialect. Because I knew everyone here, I knew she was female, and a grandparent, both of which had to be acknowledged if I were to speak to her not only grammatically but also courteously.

"I don't know the district magistrate!" she protested, indignant. The magistrate was in a large, populous city well upriver from Ors and nearby Kould Ves. Far enough upriver that the air was often cool and dry, and things didn't smell of mildew all the time. "What does the district magistrate know about Ors? For all I know the district magistrate doesn't exist!" She continued, explaining to me the long history of her house's association with the buoy-enclosed area, which was off-limits and certainly closed to fishing for the next three years.

And as always, in the back of my mind, a constant awareness of being in orbit overhead.

"Come now, Lieutenant," said the head priest. "No one likes Ors except those of us unfortunate enough to be born here. Most Shis'urnans I know, let alone Radchaai, would rather be in a city, with dry land and actual seasons besides rainy and not rainy."

Lieutenant Awn, still sweating, accepted a cup of so-called tea, and drank without grimacing—a matter of practice and determination. "My superiors are asking for my return."

On the relatively dry northern edge of the town, two brown-uniformed soldiers passing in an open runabout saw me, raised hands in greeting. I raised my own, briefly. "One Esk!" one of them called. They were common soldiers, from *Justice of Ente*'s Seven Issa unit, under Lieutenant Skaaiat. They patrolled the stretch of land between Ors and the far southwestern edge of Kould Ves, the city that had grown up around the river's newer mouth. The *Justice of Ente* Seven Issas were human, and knew I was not. They always treated me with slightly guarded friendliness.

"I would prefer you stay," said the head priest, to Lieutenant Awn. Though Lieutenant Awn had already known that. We'd have been back on *Justice of Toren* two years before, but for the Divine's continued request that we stay.

"You understand," said Lieutenant Awn, "they would much prefer to replace One Esk with a human unit. Ancillaries can stay in suspension indefinitely. Humans..." She set down her tea, took a flat, yellow-brown cake. "Humans have families they want to see again, they have lives. They can't stay frozen for centuries, the way ancillaries sometimes do. It doesn't make sense to have ancillaries out of the holds doing work when there are human soldiers who could do it." Though Lieutenant Awn had been here five years, and routinely met with the head priest, it was the first time the topic had been broached so plainly. She frowned, and changes in her respiration and hormone levels told me she'd thought of something dismaying. "You haven't had problems with *Justice of Ente* Seven Issa, have you?"

"No," said the head priest. She looked at Lieutenant Awn

with a wry twist to her mouth. "I know you. I know One Esk. Whoever they'll send me—I won't know. Neither will my parishioners."

"Annexations are messy," said Lieutenant Awn. The head priest winced slightly at the word *annexation* and I thought I saw Lieutenant Awn notice, but she continued. "Seven Issa wasn't here for that. The *Justice of Ente* Issa battalions didn't do anything during that time that One Esk didn't also do."

"No, Lieutenant." The priest put down her own cup, seeming disturbed, but I didn't have access to any of her internal data and so could not be certain. "*Justice of Ente* Issa did many things One Esk did not. It's true, One Esk killed as many people as the soldiers of *Justice of Ente*'s Issa. Likely more." She looked at me, still standing silent by the enclosure's entrance. "No offense, but I think it was more."

"I take no offense, Divine," I replied. The head priest frequently spoke to me as though I were a person. "And you are correct."

"Divine," said Lieutenant Awn, worry clear in her voice. "If the soldiers of *Justice of Ente* Seven Issa—or anyone else—have been abusing citizens…"

"No, no!" protested the head priest, her voice bitter. "Radchaai are so very careful about how citizens are treated!"

Lieutenant Awn's face heated, her distress and anger plain to me. I couldn't read her mind, but I could read every twitch of her every muscle, so her emotions were as transparent to me as glass.

"Forgive me," said the head priest, though Lieutenant Awn's expression had not changed, and her skin was too dark to show the flush of her anger. "Since the Radchaai have bestowed citizenship on us…" She stopped, seemed to reconsider her words. "Since their arrival, Seven Issa has given me nothing to complain of. But I've seen what your human troops did during what you call *the annexation*. The citizenship you granted may be as easily taken back, and…"

"We wouldn't…" protested Lieutenant Awn.

The head priest stopped her with a raised hand. "I know what Seven Issa, or at least those like them, do to people they find on the wrong side of a dividing line. Five years ago it was noncitizen. In the future, who knows? Perhaps not-citizen-enough?" She waved a hand, a gesture of surrender. "It won't matter. Such boundaries are too easy to create."

"I can't blame you for thinking in such terms," said Lieutenant Awn. "It was a difficult time."

"And I can't help but think you inexplicably, unexpectedly naive," said the head priest. "One Esk will shoot me if you order it. Without hesitation. But One Esk would never beat me or humiliate me, or rape me, for no purpose but to show its power over me, or to satisfy some sick amusement." She looked at me. "Would you?"

"No, Divine," I said.

"The soldiers of *Justice of Ente* Issa did all of those things. Not to me, it's true, and not to many in Ors itself. But they did them nonetheless. Would Seven Issa have been any different, if it had been them here instead?"

Lieutenant Awn sat, distressed, looking down at her unappetizing tea, unable to answer.

"It's strange. You hear stories about ancillaries, and it seems like the most awful thing, the most viscerally appalling thing the Radchaai have done. Garsedd—well, yes, Garsedd, but that was a thousand years ago. This—to invade and take, what, half the adult population? And turn them into walking corpses, slaved to your ships' AIs. Turned against their own people. If you'd asked me before you…*annexed* us, I'd have said it was a fate worse than death." She turned to me. "Is it?"

"None of my bodies is dead, Divine," I said. "And your estimate of the typical percentage of annexed populations who were made into ancillaries is excessive."

"You used to horrify me," said the head priest to me. "The very thought of you near was terrifying, your dead faces, those expressionless voices. But today I am more horrified at the thought of a unit of living human beings who serve voluntarily. Because I don't think I could trust them."

"Divine," said Lieutenant Awn, mouth tight. "I serve voluntarily. I make no excuses for it."

"I believe you are a good person, Lieutenant Awn, despite that." She picked up her cup of tea and sipped it, as though she had not just said what she had said.

Lieutenant Awn's throat tightened, and her lips. She had thought of something she wanted to say, but was unsure if she should. "You've heard about Ime," she said, deciding. Still tense and wary despite having chosen to speak.

The head priest seemed bleakly, bitterly amused. "News from Ime is meant to inspire confidence in Radch administration?"

This is what had happened: Ime Station, and the smaller stations and moons in the system, were the farthest one could be from a provincial palace and still be in Radch space. For years the governor of Ime used this distance to her own advantage—embezzling, collecting bribes and protection fees, selling assignments. Thousands of citizens had been unjustly executed or (what was essentially the same thing) forced into service as ancillary bodies, even though the manufacture of ancillaries was no longer legal. The governor controlled all communications and travel permits, and normally a station AI would report such activity to the authorities, but Ime Station had been somehow prevented from doing so, and the corruption grew, and spread unchecked.

Until a ship entered the system, came out of gate space only a few hundred kilometers from the patrol ship *Mercy of Sarrse*. The strange ship didn't answer demands that it identify itself. When *Mercy of Sarrse*'s crew attacked and boarded it, they found dozens of humans, as well as the alien Rrrrrr. The captain of *Mercy of Sarrse* ordered her soldiers to take captive any humans that seemed suitable for use as ancillaries, and kill the rest, along with all the aliens. The ship would be turned over to the system governor.

Mercy of Sarrse was not the only human-crewed warship in that system. Until that moment human soldiers stationed there had been kept in line by a program of bribes, flattery, and, when those failed, threats and even executions. All very effective, until the moment the soldier *Mercy of Sarrse* One Amaat One decided she wasn't willing to kill those people, or the Rrrrrr. And convinced the rest of her unit to follow her.

That had all happened five years before. The results of it were still playing themselves out.

Lieutenant Awn shifted on her cushion. "That business was all uncovered because a single human soldier refused an order. And led a mutiny. If it hadn't been for her...well. Ancillaries won't do that. They can't."

"That business was all uncovered," replied the head priest, "because the ship that human soldier boarded, she and the rest of her unit, had aliens on it. Radchaai have few qualms about killing humans, especially noncitizen humans, but you're very cautious about starting wars with aliens."

Only because wars with aliens might run up against the terms of the treaty with the alien Presger. Violating that agreement would have extremely serious consequences. And even so, plenty of high-ranking Radchaai disagreed on that topic. I saw Lieutenant Awn's desire to argue the point. Instead she said, "The governor of Ime was not cautious about it. And would have started that war, if not for this one person."

"Have they executed that person yet?" the head priest asked, pointedly. It was the summary fate of any soldier who refused an order, let alone mutinied.

"Last I heard," said Lieutenant Awn, breath tight and turning shallow, "the Rrrrrr had agreed to turn her over to Radch authorities." She swallowed. "I don't know what's going to happen." Of course, it had probably already happened, whatever it was. News could take a year or more to reach Shis'urna from as far away as Ime.

The head priest didn't answer for a moment. She poured more tea, and spooned fish paste into a small bowl. "Does my continued request for your presence present any sort of disadvantage for you?"

"No," said Lieutenant Awn. "Actually, the other Esk lieutenants are a bit envious. There's no chance for action on *Justice of Toren*." She picked up her own cup, outwardly calm, inwardly angry. Disturbed. Talking about the news from Ime had increased her unease. "Action means commendations, and possibly promotions." And this was the last annexation. The last chance for an officer to enrich her house through connections to new citizens, or even through outright appropriation.

"Yet another reason I would prefer you," said the head priest.

I followed Lieutenant Awn home. And watched inside the temple, and overlooked the people crisscrossing the plaza as they always did, avoiding the children playing kau in the center of the plaza, kicking the ball back and forth, shouting and laughing. On the edge of the Fore-Temple water, a teenager from the upper city sat sullen and listless watching half a dozen little children hopping from stone to stone, singing:

> *One, two, my aunt told me*
> *Three, four, the corpse soldier*
> *Five, six, it'll shoot you in the eye*
> *Seven, eight, kill you dead*
> *Nine, ten, break it apart and put it back together.*

As I walked the streets people greeted me, and I greeted them in return. Lieutenant Awn was tense and angry, and only nodded absently at the people in the street, who greeted her as she passed.

The person with the fishing-rights complaint left, unsatisfied. Two children rounded the divider after she had gone, and sat cross-legged on the cushion she had vacated. They both wore lengths of fabric wrapped around their waists, clean but faded, though no gloves. The elder was about nine, and the symbols inked on the younger one's chest and shoulders—slightly smudged—indicated she was no more than six. She looked at me, frowning.

In Orsian addressing children properly was easier than addressing adults. One used a simple, ungendered form. "Hello, citizens," I said, in the local dialect. I recognized them both—they lived on the south edge of Ors and I had spoken to them quite frequently, but they had never visited the house before. "How can I help you?"

"You aren't One Esk," said the smaller child, and the older made an abortive motion as if to hush her.

"I am," I said, and pointed to the insignia on my uniform jacket. "See? Only this is my number Fourteen segment."

"I *told* you," said the older child.

The younger considered this for a moment, and then said, "I have a song." I waited in silence, and she took a deep breath, as though about to begin, and then halted, perplexed-seeming. "Do you want to hear it?" she asked, still doubtful of my identity, likely.

"Yes, citizen," I said. I—that is, I–One Esk—first sang to amuse one of my lieutenants, when *Justice of Toren* had hardly been commissioned a hundred years. She enjoyed music, and had brought an instrument with her as part of her luggage allowance. She could never interest the other officers in her hobby and so she taught me the parts to the songs she played. I filed those away and went looking for more, to please her. By the time she was captain of her own ship I had collected a large library of vocal music—no one was going to give me an instrument, but I could sing anytime—and it was a matter of rumor and some indulgent smiles that *Justice of Toren* had an interest in singing. Which it didn't—I—I–*Justice of Toren*—tolerated the habit because it was harmless, and because it was quite possible that one of my captains would appreciate it. Otherwise it would have been prevented.

If these children had stopped me on the street, they would have had no hesitation, but here in the house, seated as though for a formal conference, things were different. And I suspected this was an exploratory visit, that the youngest child meant to eventually ask for a chance to serve in the house's makeshift temple—the prestige of being appointed flower-bearer to Amaat wasn't a question here, in the stronghold of Ikkt, but the customary term-end gift of fruit and clothing was. And this child's best friend was currently a flower-bearer, doubtless making the prospect more interesting.

No Orsian would make such a request immediately or directly, so likely the child had chosen this oblique approach, turning a casual encounter into something formal and intimidating. I reached into my jacket pocket and pulled out a handful of sweets and laid them on the floor between us.

The littler girl made an affirmative gesture, as though I had resolved all her doubts, and then took a breath and began.

> *My heart is a fish*
> *Hiding in the water-grass*
> *In the green, in the green.*

The tune was an odd amalgam of a Radchaai song that played occasionally on broadcast and an Orsian one I already knew. The words were unfamiliar to me. She sang four verses in a clear, slightly wavering voice, and seemed ready to launch into a fifth, but stopped abruptly when Lieutenant Awn's steps sounded outside the divider.

The smaller girl leaned forward and scooped up her payment. Both children bowed, still half-seated, and then rose and ran out the entranceway into the wider house, past Lieutenant Awn, past me following Lieutenant Awn.

"Thank you, citizens," Lieutenant Awn said to their retreating backs, and they started, and then managed with a single movement to both bow slightly in her direction and continue running, out into the street.

"Anything new?" asked Lieutenant Awn, though she didn't pay much attention to music, herself, not beyond what most people do.

"Sort of," I said. Farther down the street I saw the two children, still running as they turned a corner around another house. They slowed to a halt, breathing hard. The littler girl opened her hand to show the older one her fistful of sweets. Surprisingly, she seemed not to have dropped any, small as her hand was, as quick as their flight had been. The older child took a sweet and put it in her mouth.

Five years ago I would have offered something more nutritious, before repairs had begun to the planet's infrastructure, when supplies were chancy. Now every citizen was guaranteed enough to eat, but the rations were not luxurious, and often as not were unappealing.

Inside the temple all was green-lit silence. The head priest did not emerge from behind the screens in the temple residence, though junior priests came and went. Lieutenant Awn went to the second floor of her house and sat brooding on an Ors-style cushion, screened from the street, shirt thrown off. She refused the (genuine) tea I brought her. I transmitted a steady stream of information to her—everything normal, everything routine—and to *Justice of Toren*. "She should take that to the district magistrate," Lieutenant Awn said of the citizen with the fishing dispute, slightly annoyed, eyes closed, the afternoon's reports in her vision. "We don't have jurisdiction over that." I didn't answer. No answer was required, or expected. She approved, with a quick twitch of her fingers, the message I had composed for the district magistrate, and then opened the most recent message from her young sister. Lieutenant Awn sent a percentage of her earnings home to her parents, who used it to buy their younger child poetry lessons. Poetry was a valuable, civilized accomplishment. I couldn't judge if Lieutenant Awn's sister had any particular talent, but then not many did, even among more elevated families. But her work and her letters pleased Lieutenant Awn, and took the edge off her present distress.

The children on the plaza ran away home, laughing. The adolescent sighed, heavily, the way adolescents do, and dropped a pebble in the water and stared at the ripples.

Ancillary units that only ever woke for annexations often wore nothing but a force shield generated by an implant in each body, rank on rank of featureless soldiers that might have been poured from mercury. But I was always out of the holds, and I wore the same uniform human soldiers did, now the fighting was done. My bodies sweated under my uniform jackets, and, bored, I opened three of my mouths, all in close proximity to each other on the temple plaza, and sang with those three voices, "My heart is a fish, hiding in the water-grass…" One person walking by looked at me, startled, but everyone else ignored me—they were used to me by now.

3

The next morning the correctives had fallen off, and the bruising on Seivarden's face had faded. She seemed comfortable, but she still seemed high, so that was hardly surprising.

I unrolled the bundle of clothes I had bought for her—insulated underclothes, quilted shirt and trousers, undercoat and hooded overcoat, gloves—and laid them out. Then I took her chin and turned her head toward me. "Can you hear me?"

"Yes." Her dark brown eyes stared somewhere distant over my left shoulder.

"Get up." I tugged on her arm, and she blinked, lazily, and got as far as sitting up before the impulse deserted her. But I managed to dress her, in fits and starts, and then I stowed what few things were still out, shouldered my pack, took Seivarden by the arm, and left.

There was a flier rental at the edge of town, and predictably the proprietor wouldn't rent to me unless I put down twice the advertised deposit. I told her I intended to fly northwest, to visit a herding camp—an outright lie, which she likely knew. "You're an offworlder," she said. "You don't know what it's like away from the towns. Offworlders are always flying out to herding camps and getting lost. Sometimes we find them again, sometimes not." I said nothing. "You'll lose my flier and then where will I be? Out in the snow with my starving children, that's where." Beside me Seivarden stared vaguely off into the distance.

I was forced to put down the money. I had a strong suspicion I would never see it again. Then the proprietor demanded extra because I couldn't display a local pilot certification—something I knew wasn't required. If it had been, I would have forged one before I came.

In the end, though, she gave me the flier. I checked its engine, which seemed clean and in good repair, and made sure of the fuel. When I was satisfied, I put my pack in, seated Seivarden, and then climbed into the pilot's seat.

Two days after the storm, the snowmoss was beginning to show again, sweeps of pale green with darker threads here and there. After two more hours we flew over a line of hills, and the green darkened dramatically, lined and irregularly veined in a dozen shades, like malachite. In some places the moss was smeared and trampled by the creatures that grazed on it, herds of long-haired bov making their way southward as spring advanced. And along those paths, on the edges here and there, ice devils lay in carefully tunneled lairs, waiting for a bov to put a foot wrong so they could drag it down. I saw no trace of them, but even the herders who lived their lives following the bov couldn't always tell when one was near.

It was easy flying. Seivarden sat, half-lying and quiet beside me. How could she be alive? And how had she ended up here, now? It was beyond improbable. But improbable things happened. Nearly a thousand years before Lieutenant Awn was even born, Seivarden had captained a ship of her own, *Sword of Nathtas*, and had lost it. Most of the human crew, including Seivarden, had managed to get to an escape pod, but hers had never been found, that I had heard. Yet here she was. Someone must have found her relatively recently. She was lucky to be alive.

I was four billion miles away when Seivarden lost her ship. I was patrolling a city of glass and polished red stone, silent but for the sound of my own feet, and the conversation of my lieutenants, and, occasionally, me trying my voices against the echoing pentagonal plazas. Falls of flowers, red and yellow and blue, draped the walls surrounding houses with five-sided courtyards. The flowers were wilting; no one dared walk the streets except me and my officers, everyone knew the likely fate of any person placed under arrest. Instead they huddled in their houses, waiting for what would come next, wincing or shuddering at the sound of a lieutenant laughing, or my singing.

What trouble we'd run into, I and my lieutenants, had been sporadic. The Garseddai had put up only nominal resistance. Troop carriers had emptied, the Swords and Mercies were essentially on guard duty around the system. Representatives from the five zones of each of the five regions, twenty-five in all, speaking for the various moons, planets, and stations in the Garseddai system, had surrendered in the name of their constituents, and were separately on their way to *Sword of Amaat* to meet Anaander Mianaai, Lord of the Radch, and beg for the lives of their people. Hence that frightened, silent city.

In a narrow, diamond-shaped park, by a black granite monument inscribed with the Five Right Actions, and the name of the Garseddai patron who had wished to impress them on the local residents, one of my lieutenants passed another and complained that this annexation had been disappointingly dull. Three seconds later I received a message from Captain Seivarden's *Sword of Nathtas*.

The three Garseddai electors she was carrying had killed two of her lieutenants, and twelve of *Sword of Nathtas*'s ancillary segments. They had damaged the ship—cut conduits, breached the hull. Accompanying the report, a recording from *Sword of Nathtas*—the gun that an ancillary segment saw, irrefutably, but that according to *Sword of Nathtas*'s other sensors just didn't exist. A Garseddai elector, against all expectations surrounded by the gleaming silver of Radchaai-style armor that only the ancillary's eyes could see, firing the gun, the bullet piercing the ancillary's armor, killing the segment, and, with its eyes gone, the gun and armor flickering back into nonexistence.

All the electors had been searched before boarding, and *Sword of Nathtas* should have been able to detect any weapon or shield-generating device or implant. And while Radchaai-style armor had once been in common use in the regions surrounding the Radch itself, those regions had been absorbed a thousand years before. The Garseddai didn't use it, didn't know how to make it, let alone how to use it. And even if they had, that gun, and its bullet, were flatly impossible.

Three people armed with such a gun, and armored, could do a great deal of damage on a ship like *Sword of Nathtas*. Especially if even one Garseddai could reach the engine, and if such a gun could pierce the engine's heat shield. Radchaai warship engines burned star-hot, and a failed heat shield meant instant vaporization, an entire ship dissolved in a brief, bright flash.

But there was nothing I could do, nothing anyone could do. The message was nearly four hours old, a signal from the past, a ghost. The issue had been decided even before it had reached me.

A harsh tone sounded, and a blue light blinked on the panel in front of me, beside the fuel indicator. An instant before the indicator had read nearly full. Now it read empty. The engine would shut down in a matter of minutes. Beside me Seivarden sprawled, relaxed and quiet.

I landed.

The fuel tank had been rigged in a way I hadn't detected. It seemed three-quarters full, but it wasn't, and the alarm that ought to have sounded when I'd used half of what I'd started with had been disconnected.

I thought of the double deposit I certainly wouldn't see again. Of the proprietor, so concerned that she might lose her valuable flier. Of course there would be a transmitter, whether or not I triggered the emergency call. The proprietor wouldn't want to lose the flier, just strand me alone in the middle of this plain of moss-streaked snow. I could call for help—I had disabled my communication implants, but I did have a handheld I could use. But we were very, very far from anyone who might be moved to send assistance. And even if help came, and came before the proprietor who clearly meant me no good, I wouldn't get where I was going, a matter of great importance to me.

The air was minus eighteen degrees; the breeze from the south, at approximately eight kph, implied snow sometime in the near future. Nothing serious, if the morning's weather report could be trusted.

My landing had left a green-edged smear of white in the snowmoss, easily visible from the air. The terrain seemed gently hilly, though the hills we'd flown over were no longer visible.

Had this been an ordinary emergency, the best course would have been to stay inside the flier until help came. But this was not an ordinary emergency, and I did not expect rescue.

Either they would come as soon as their transmitter told them we were grounded, prepared to murder, or they would wait. The rental had several other vehicles, the proprietor would likely not be inconvenienced if she waited even several weeks to retrieve her flier. As she herself had said, no one would be surprised if a foreigner lost herself in the snow.

I had two choices. I could wait here and hope to ambush anyone who came to murder and rob me, and take their transport. This would, of course, be futile in the event that they decided to wait for cold and hunger to do their job for them. Or I could pull Seivarden out of the flier, shoulder my pack, and walk. My intended destination was some sixty kilometers to the southeast. I could walk that in a day if I had to, ground and weather—and ice devils—permitting, but I would be lucky if Seivarden could do it in twice that time. And that course would be futile if the proprietor decided not to wait, but to retrieve her flier more or less immediately. Our trail through the moss-striated snow would be clear, they would need only to follow us and dispose of us. I would have lost any advantage of surprise I might have gained by hiding near the downed flier.

And I would be lucky if I found anything, once I reached my destination. I had spent the past nineteen years following the most tenuous of threads, weeks and months of searching or waiting, punctuated by moments like this, when success or even life hung on the toss of a coin. I had been lucky to come this far. I could not reasonably expect to go farther.

A Radchaai would have tossed that coin. Or more accurately a handful of them, a dozen disks, each with its meaning and import, the pattern of their fall a map of the universe as Amaat willed it to be. Things happen the way they happen because the world is the way it is. Or, as a Radchaai would say, the universe is the shape of the gods. Amaat conceived of light, and conceiving of light also necessarily conceived of not-light, and light and darkness sprang forth. This was the first Emanation, EtrepaBo; Light/Darkness. The other three, implied and necessitated by that first, are EskVar (Beginning/Ending), IssaInu (Movement/Stillness), and VahnItr (Existence/Nonexistence). These four Emanations variously split and recombined to create the universe. Everything that is, emanates from Amaat.

The smallest, most seemingly insignificant event is part of an intricate whole and to understand why one particular mote of dust falls in one particular path, and lands in one particular location, is to understand the will of Amaat. There is no such thing as "just a coincidence." Nothing happens by chance, but only according to the mind of God.

Or so official Radchaai orthodoxy teaches. I myself have never understood religion very well. It was never required that I should. And though the Radchaai had made me, I was not Radchaai. I knew and cared nothing about the will of the gods. I only knew that I would land where I myself had been cast, wherever that would be.

I took my pack from the flier, opened it, and removed an extra magazine, which I stowed inside my coat near my gun. I shouldered the pack, went around to the other side of the flier, and opened the hatch there. "Seivarden," I said.

She didn't move, only breathed a quiet *hmmm*. I took her arm and pulled, and she half-slid, half-stepped out into the snow.

I had gotten this far by taking one step, and then another. I turned northeast, pulling Seivarden along, and walked.

Dr. Arilesperas Strigan, whose home I very much hoped I was walking toward, had been, at one time, a medic in private practice on Dras Annia Station, an aggregation of at least five different stations, one built onto another, at the intersection of two dozen different routes, well outside Radch territory. Nearly anything could end up there, given enough time, and in the course of her work she had met a wide variety of people, with a wide variety of antecedents. She had been paid in currency, in favors, in antiques, in nearly anything that might imaginably be said to have value.

I'd been there, seen the station and its convoluted, interpenetrating layers, seen where Strigan had worked and lived, seen the things she'd left behind when one day, for no reason anyone seemed to know, she'd bought passage on five different ships and then disappeared. A case full of stringed instruments, only three of which I could name. Five shelves of icons, a dizzying array of gods and saints worked in wood, in shell, in gold. A dozen guns, each one carefully labeled with its station permit number. These were collections that had begun as single items, received in payment, sparking her curiosity. Strigan's lease had been paid in full for 150 years, and as a result station authorities had left her apartment untouched.

A bribe had gotten me in, to see the collection I had come for—a few five-sided tiles in colors still flower-bright after a thousand years. A shallow bowl inscribed around its gilt edge in a language Strigan couldn't possibly have read. A flat plastic rectangle I knew was a voice recorder. At a touch it produced laughter, voices speaking that same dead language.

Small as it was, this had not been an easy collection to assemble. Garseddai artifacts were scarce, because once Anaander Mianaai had realized the Garseddai possessed the means to destroy Radchaai ships and penetrate Radchaai armor, she had ordered the utter destruction of Garsedd and its people. Those pentagonal plazas, the flowers, every living thing on every planet, moon, and station in the system, all gone. No one would ever live there again. No one would ever be permitted to forget what it meant to defy the Radch.

Had a patient given her, say, the bowl, and had that sent her looking for more information? And if one Garseddai object had fetched up there, what else might have? Something a patient might have given her as payment, maybe not knowing what it was—or knowing and wanting desperately to be rid of it. Something that had led Strigan to flee, to disappear, leaving nearly everything she owned behind, perhaps. Something dangerous, something she couldn't bring herself to destroy, to be rid of in the most efficient way possible.

Something I wanted very badly.

I wanted to get as far as we possibly could, as quickly as we possibly could, and so we walked for hours with only the briefest of stops when absolutely necessary. Though the day was clear, and bright as it ever gets on Nilt, I felt blind in a way that I had thought I had learned to ignore by now. I had once had twenty bodies, twenty pairs of eyes, and hundreds of others that I could access if I needed or desired it. Now I could only see in one direction, could only see the vast expanse behind me if I turned my head and blinded myself to what was in front of me. Usually I dealt with this by avoiding too-open spaces, by making sure of just what was at my back, but here that was impossible.

My face burned, despite the very gentle breeze, then numbed. My hands and feet ached at first—I hadn't bought my gloves or boots with the intention of walking sixty kilometers in the cold—and then grew heavy and numb. I was fortunate I hadn't come in winter, when temperatures could be a great deal lower.

Seivarden must have been just as cold, but she walked steadily as I pulled her along, step after apathetic step, feet dragging through the mossy snow, staring down, not complaining or even speaking at all. When the sun was nearly on the horizon she shifted her shoulders just slightly and raised her head. "I know that song," she said.

"What?"

"That song you're humming." Lazily she turned her head toward me, her face showing no anxiety or perplexity at all. I wondered if she had made any effort to conceal her accent. Likely not—on kef, as she was, she wouldn't care. Inside Radch territories that accent declared her a member of a wealthy and influential house, someone who, after taking the aptitudes at fifteen, would have ended up with a prestigious assignment. Outside those territories, it was an easy shorthand for a villain—rich, corrupt, and callous—in a thousand entertainments.

The faint sound of a flier reached us. I turned without stopping, searched the horizon, and saw it, small and distant. Flying low and slowly, following our trail, it seemed. It wasn't a rescue, I was sure. My toss had landed wrong, and now we were exposed and defenseless.

We kept walking as the sound of the flier grew nearer. We couldn't have outraced it even if Seivarden hadn't begun to half-stumble, catching herself, but clearly at the end of her endurance. If she was speaking unprompted, noticing anything around her, she was likely beginning to come down. I stopped, dropped her arm, and she came to a halt beside me.

The flier sailed over us, banked, and landed in our path, approximately thirty meters in front of us. Either they didn't have the means to shoot us from the air, or they didn't wish to. I shrugged off my pack and loosened the fastenings of my outer coat, the better to reach my gun.

Four people got out of the flier—the owner I had rented from, two people I didn't recognize, and the person from the bar, who had called me a "tough little girl," and whom I had wanted to kill but had refrained from killing. I slid my hand into my coat and grasped the gun. My options were limited.

"Don't you have any common sense?" called the proprietor, when they were fifteen meters away. All four stopped. "You stay with the flier when it goes down, so we can find you."

I looked at the person from the bar, saw her recognize me, and see that I recognized her. "In the bar, I said that anyone who tried to rob me would die," I reminded her. She smirked.

One of the people I didn't recognize produced a gun from somewhere on her person. "We aren't gonna just *try*," she said.

I drew my gun and fired, hitting her in the face. She crumpled to the snow. Before the others could react, I shot the person from the bar, who likewise fell, and then the person beside her, all three in quick succession, taking less than one second.

The proprietor swore, and turned to flee. I shot her in the back, and she took three steps and then fell.

"I'm cold," said Seivarden beside me, placid and heedless.

* * *

They had left the flier unguarded, all four approaching me. Foolish. The whole venture had been foolish, undertaken without any sort of serious planning, it seemed. I had only to load Seivarden and my pack into their flier and be off.

The residence of Arilesperas Strigan was barely visible from the air, only a circle slightly more than thirty-five meters in diameter, within which the snowmoss was perceptibly lighter and thinner. I brought the flier down outside the circle and waited a moment to assess the situation. From this angle it was obvious there were buildings, two of them, snow-covered mounds. It might have been an unoccupied herding camp, but if I could trust my information, it was not. There was no sign of a wall or fence, but I would make no assumptions about her security.

After consideration, I opened the hatch on the flier and got out, pulling Seivarden out behind me. We walked slowly to the line where the snow changed, Seivarden stopping when I stopped. She stood incuriously, staring straight ahead.

Beyond this I had not been able to plan. "Strigan!" I called, and waited, but no answer came. I left Seivarden standing where she was and walked the circumference of the circle. The entrances of the two snow-mounded buildings seemed oddly shadowed, and I stopped, and looked again.

Both hung open, dark beyond. Buildings like these would probably have double-doored entrances—like an airlock, to keep warm air inside—but I didn't think anyone would leave either door hanging ajar.

Either Strigan had security in place, or she did not. I stepped over the line, into the circle. Nothing happened.

The doors were open, both inner and outer, and there

were no lights. One of the buildings was just as cold inside as out. I presumed that when I found a light I would discover it was used for storage, filled with tools and sealed packages of food and fuel. The other was two degrees Celsius inside—I guessed that it had been heated until relatively recently. Living quarters, evidently. "Strigan!" I called into the darkness, but the way my voice echoed back told me the building was likely unoccupied.

Outside again, I found the marks where her flier had sat. She was gone, then, and the open doors and the darkness were a message for whoever would come. For me. I had no means to discover where she'd gone. I looked up at the empty sky, and down again at the imprint of the flier. I stood there a while, looking at that empty space.

When I returned to Seivarden, I found she'd lain down in the green-stained snow and gone to sleep.

In the back of the flier I found a lantern, a stove, a tent, and some bedding. I took the lantern into the building I presumed was living quarters and switched it on.

Wide, light-colored rugs covered the floor, and woven hangings the walls; these were blue and orange and an eye-hurting green. Low benches, backless, with cushions, lined the room. Beyond benches and the bright hangings, there was little else. A game board with counters, but the board had a pattern of holes I didn't recognize, and I didn't understand the distribution of the counters among the holes. I wondered whom Strigan played with. Perhaps the board was only decorative. It was finely carved, and the pieces brightly colored.

A wooden box sat on a table in a corner, a long oval with a carved, pierced lid and three strings stretched tight across. The wood was pale gold, with a waving, curling grain. The holes cut in the flat top were as uneven and intricate as the grain of the wood. It was a beautiful thing. I plucked a string and it rang softly.

Doors led to kitchen, bath, sleeping quarters, and what was obviously a small infirmary. I opened a cabinet door and found a neat stack of correctives. Each drawer I pulled out revealed instruments and medicines. She might have gone to a herding camp to tend to some emergency. But the lights and the heat being off, and those doors left open, argued otherwise.

Barring a miracle, it was the end of nineteen years of planning and effort.

The house controls were behind a panel in the kitchen. I found the power supply in place, hooked it back in, and switched on the heat and the lights. Then I went out and got Seivarden, and dragged her into the house.

I made a pallet of blankets I found in Strigan's bedroom, then stripped Seivarden and laid her on it, and covered her with more blankets. She didn't wake, and I used the time to search the house more thoroughly.

The cabinets held plenty of food. A cup sat on a counter, a thin layer of greenish liquid glazing the bottom. Next to it sat a plain white bowl holding the last bits of a hunk of hard bread disintegrating into ice-rimmed water. It looked as though Strigan had left without cleaning up after a meal, leaving nearly everything behind—food, medical supplies. I checked the bedroom, found warm clothes in good repair. She had left on short notice, not taking much.

She knew what she had. Of course she did—that was why she'd fled to begin with. If she was not stupid—and I was quite certain she was not—she had gone the moment she realized what I was, and would keep going until she was as far from me as she could get.

But where would that be? If I represented the power of the Radch, and had found her even here, so distant from both Radch space and her own home, where could she go that they would not ultimately find her? Surely she would realize that. But what other course would be open to her?

Surely she would not be foolish enough to return.

In the meantime, Seivarden would be sick soon, unless I found kef for her. I had no intention of doing that. And there was food here, and heat, and perhaps I could find something, some hint, some clue to what Strigan had been thinking, in the moment she had thought the Radch were coming for her, and fled. Something that would tell me where she'd gone.

4

At night, in Ors, I walked the streets, and looked out over the still, stinking water, dark beyond the few lights of Ors itself, and the blinking of the buoys surrounding the prohibited zones. I slept, also, and sat watch in the lower level of the house, in case anyone should need me, though that was rare in those days. I finished any of the day's work still uncompleted, and watched over Lieutenant Awn, who lay sleeping.

Mornings I brought water for Lieutenant Awn to bathe in, and dressed her, though the local costume was a good deal less effort than her uniform, and she had stopped wearing any sort of cosmetics two years before, as they were difficult to maintain in the heat.

Then Lieutenant Awn would turn to her icons—four-armed Amaat, an Emanation in each hand, sat on a box downstairs, but the others (Toren, who received devotions from every officer on *Justice of Toren*, and a few gods particular to Lieutenant Awn's family) sat near where Lieutenant Awn slept, in the upper part of the house, and it was to them that she made her morning devotions. "The flower of justice

42

is peace," the daily prayer began, that every Radchaai soldier said on waking, every day of her life in the military. "The flower of propriety is beauty in thought and action." The rest of my officers, still on *Justice of Toren*, were on a different schedule. Their mornings rarely coincided with Lieutenant Awn's, so it was almost always Lieutenant Awn's voice alone in prayer, and the others, when they spoke so far away, in chorus, without her. "The flower of benefit is Amaat whole and entire. I am the sword of justice..." The prayer is antiphonal, but only four verses long. I can sometimes hear it still when I wake, like a distant voice somewhere behind me.

Every morning, in every official temple throughout Radchaai space, a priest (who doubles as a registrar of births and deaths and contracts of all kinds) casts the day's omens. Households and individuals sometimes cast their own as well, and there's no obligation to attend the official casting— but it's as good an excuse as any to be seen, and speak to friends and neighbors, and hear gossip.

There was, as yet, no official temple in Ors—these are all primarily dedicated to Amaat, any other gods on the premises take lesser places, and the head priest of Ikkt had not seen her way clear to demoting her god in its own temple, or identifying Ikkt with Amaat closely enough to add Radchaai rites to her own. So for the moment Lieutenant Awn's house served. Each morning the makeshift temple's flower-bearers removed dead flowers from around the icon of Amaat and replaced them with fresh ones—usually a local species with small, bright-pink, triple-lobed petals that grew in the dirt that collected on the outside corners of buildings, or cracks in slabs, and was the nearest thing to a weed but greatly admired by the children. And lately small cupped blue-and-white lilies had been blooming in the lake, especially near the buoy-barricaded prohibited areas.

Then Lieutenant Awn would lay out the cloth for the omen-casting and the omens themselves, a handful of weighty metal disks. These, and the icons, were Lieutenant Awn's personal possessions, gifts from her parents when she had taken the aptitudes and received her assignment.

Occasionally only Lieutenant Awn and the day's attendants came to the morning ritual, but usually others were present. The town's medic, a few of the Radchaai who had been granted property here, other Orsian children who could not be persuaded to go to school, or care about being on time for it, and liked the glitter and ring of the disks as they fell. Sometimes even the head priest of Ikkt would come—that god, like Amaat, not demanding that its followers refuse to acknowledge other gods.

Once the omens fell, and came to rest on the cloth (or, to any spectators' dread, rolled off the cloth and away somewhere harder to interpret), the priest officiating was supposed to identify the pattern, match it with its associated passage of scripture, and recite that for those present. It wasn't something Lieutenant Awn was always able to do. So instead she tossed the omens, I observed their fall, and then I transmitted the appropriate words to her. *Justice of Toren* was, after all, nearly two thousand years old, and had seen nearly every possible configuration.

The ritual done, she would have breakfast—usually a round of bread from whatever local grain was available, and (real) tea—and then take her place on the mat and platform and wait for the day's requests and complaints.

"Jen Shinnan invites you to supper this evening," I told her, that next morning. I also ate breakfast, cleaned weapons, walked the streets, and greeted those who spoke to me.

Jen Shinnan lived in the upper city, and before the annexation she had been the wealthiest person in Ors, in influence second only to the head priest of Ikkt. Lieutenant Awn disliked her. "I suppose I don't have a good excuse to refuse."

"Not that I can see," I said. I also stood at the perimeter of the house, nearly on the street, and watched. An Orsian approached, saw me, slowed. Stopped about eight meters away, pretending to look above me, at something else.

"Anything else?" asked Lieutenant Awn.

"The district magistrate reiterates the official policy regarding fishing reserves in the Ors Marshes…"

Lieutenant Awn sighed. "Yes, of course she does."

"Can I help you, citizen?" I asked the person still hesitating in the street. The impending arrival of her first grandchild hadn't yet been announced to the neighbors, so I pretended I didn't know either, and used only the simple respectful address toward a male person.

"I wish," Lieutenant Awn continued, "the magistrate would come here herself and try living on stale bread and those disgusting pickled vegetables they send, and see how she likes being forbidden to fish where all the fish actually are."

The Orsian in the street started, looked for a moment as if she were going to turn around and walk away, and changed her mind. "Good morning, Radchaai," she said, quietly, coming closer. "And to the lieutenant as well." Orsians were blunt when it suited them, and at other times oddly, frustratingly reticent.

"I know there's a reason for it," said Lieutenant Awn to me. "And she's right, but still." She sighed again. "Anything else?"

"Denz Ay is outside and wishes to speak to you." As I spoke, I invited Denz Ay to step within the house.

"What about?"

"Something she seems unwilling to mention." Lieutenant Awn gestured acknowledgment and I brought Denz Ay around the screens. She bowed, and sat on the mat in front of Lieutenant Awn.

"Good morning, citizen," said Lieutenant Awn. I translated.

"Good morning, Lieutenant." And by slow, careful degrees, beginning with an observation on the heat and the cloudless sky, progressing through inquiries about Lieutenant Awn's health to mild local gossip, she finally came around to hinting at her reason for coming. "I...I have a friend, Lieutenant." She stopped.

"Yes?"

"Yesterday evening my friend was fishing." Denz Ay stopped again.

Lieutenant Awn waited three seconds, and when nothing further seemed forthcoming, she asked, "Did your friend catch much?" When the mood was on them, no amount of direct questioning, or begging an Orsian to come to the point, would avail.

"N-not much," said Denz Ay. And then, irritation flashing across her face, just for an instant: "The best fishing, you know, is near the breeding areas, and those are all prohibited."

"Yes," said Lieutenant Awn. "I'm sure your friend would never fish illegally."

"No, no, of course not," Denz Ay protested. "But...I don't want to get her in trouble...but maybe sometimes she digs tubers. *Near* the prohibited zones."

There weren't really any plants that produced edible tubers near the prohibited zones—they'd all been dug up months

46

ago, if not longer. Poachers were more careful about the ones inside—if the plants decreased too noticeably, or disappeared entirely, we'd be forced to find out who was taking them, and guard them much more closely. Lieutenant Awn knew this. Everyone in the lower city knew it.

Lieutenant Awn waited for the rest of the story, not for the first time annoyed at the Orsian tendency to approach topics by stealth, but managing mostly not to show it. "I've heard they're very good," she ventured.

"Oh, yes!" agreed Denz Ay. "They're best right out of the mud!" Lieutenant Awn suppressed a grimace. "But you can slice them and grill them too..." Denz Ay stopped, with a shrewd look. "Perhaps my friend can get some for you."

I saw Lieutenant Awn's dissatisfaction with her rations, the momentary desire to say, *Yes, please,* but instead she said, "Thank you, there's no need. You were saying?"

"Saying?"

"Your...friend." As she spoke Lieutenant Awn was asking me questions, with minute twitches of her fingers. "Was digging tubers *near* a prohibited zone. And?"

I showed Lieutenant Awn the spot this person was most likely to have been digging in—I patrolled all of Ors, saw the boats go in and out, saw where they were at night when they doused lights and maybe even thought they were running invisible to me.

"And," said Denz Ay, "they found something."

Anyone missing? Lieutenant Awn asked me, silently, alarmed. I replied in the negative. "What did they find?" Lieutenant Awn asked Denz Ay, aloud.

"Guns," said Denz Ay, so quietly Lieutenant Awn almost didn't hear. "A dozen, from before." From before the annexation, she meant. All the Shis'urnan militaries had been relieved of their weapons, no one on the planet should have had any guns we didn't already know about. The answer was so surprising that for a blinking two seconds Lieutenant Awn didn't react at all.

Then came puzzlement, alarm, and confusion. *Why is she telling me this?* Lieutenant Awn asked me silently.

"There's been some talk, Lieutenant," said Denz Ay. "Perhaps you've heard it."

"There's always talk," acknowledged Lieutenant Awn, the answer so formulaic I didn't need to translate it for her, she could say it in the local dialect. "How else are people to pass the time?" Denz Ay conceded this conventional point with a gesture. Lieutenant Awn's patience frayed, and she attacked directly. "They might have been put there before the annexation."

Denz Ay made a negative motion with her left hand. "They weren't there a month ago."

Did someone find a pre-annexation cache, and hide them there? Lieutenant Awn asked me, silently. Aloud she asked, "When people talk, do they say things that might account for the appearance of a dozen guns underwater in a prohibited zone?"

"Such guns are no good against *you*." Because of our armor, Denz Ay meant. Radchaai armor is an essentially impenetrable force shield. I could extend mine at a thought, the moment I desired to do so. The mechanism that generated it was implanted in each of my segments, and Lieutenant Awn had it as well—though hers was an externally worn unit. It didn't make us completely invulnerable, and in combat we sometimes wore actual pieces of armor under it, lightweight and articulated, covering head and limbs and torso, but even without that a handful of guns wouldn't do much damage to either of us.

"So who would those guns be meant for?" asked Lieutenant Awn.

Denz Ay considered, frowning, biting her lip, and then said, "The Tanmind are more like the Radchaai than we are."

"Citizen," said Lieutenant Awn, laying noticeable, deliberate stress on that word, which was only what *Radchaai* meant in the first place, "if we were going to shoot anyone here, we'd already have done it." Had already done it, in fact. "We wouldn't need secret stashes of weapons."

"This is why I came to you," said Denz Ay, emphatic, as though explaining something in very simple terms, for a child. "When you shoot a person, you say why and do it, without excuse. This is how the Radchaai are. But in the upper city, before you came, when they would shoot Orsians, they would always be careful to have an excuse. They wanted someone dead," she explained, to Lieutenant Awn's uncomprehending, appalled expression, "they did not say, *You are trouble we want you gone* and then shoot. They said, *We are only defending ourselves* and when the person was dead they would search the body or a house and discover weapons, or incriminating messages." Not, the implication was clear, genuine ones.

"Then how are we alike?"

"Your gods are the same." They weren't, not explicitly so, but the fiction was encouraged, in the upper city and elsewhere. "You live in space, you go all wrapped up in clothes. You are rich, the Tanmind are rich. If someone in the upper city"—and by this I suspected she meant a specific someone—"cries out that some Orsian threatens them, most Radchaai will believe her, and not some Orsian who is surely lying to protect her own."

And that was why she had come to Lieutenant Awn—so

that, whatever happened, it would be plain and clear to Radchaai authorities that she—and by extension anyone else in the lower city—had in fact had nothing to do with that cache of weapons, if the accusation should materialize.

"These things," said Lieutenant Awn. "Orsian, Tanmind, Moha, they mean nothing now. That's done. Everyone here is Radchaai."

"As you say, Lieutenant," answered Denz Ay, voice quiet and nearly expressionless.

Lieutenant Awn had been in Ors long enough to recognize the unstated refusal to agree. She tried another angle. "No one is going to shoot anybody."

"Of course not, Lieutenant," said Denz Ay, but in that same quiet voice. She was old enough to know firsthand that we had, indeed, shot people in the past. She could hardly be blamed for fearing we might do so in the future.

After Denz Ay left, Lieutenant Awn sat thinking. No one interrupted; the day was quiet. In the green-lit temple interior, the head priest turned to me and said, "Once there would have been two choirs, a hundred voices each. You would have liked it." I had seen recordings. Sometimes the children would bring me songs that were distant echoes of that music, five hundred years gone and more. "We're not what we used to be," said the head priest. "Everything passes, eventually." I agreed that it was so.

"Take a boat tonight," said Lieutenant Awn, stirring at last. "See if there's anything to indicate where the weapons came from. I'll decide what to do once I have a better idea of what's going on."

"Yes, Lieutenant," I said.

*   *   *

Jen Shinnan lived in the upper city, across the Fore-Temple lake. Few Orsians lived there who weren't servants. The houses there were built to a slightly different plan from those in the lower; hip-roofed, the central part of each floor walled in, though windows and doors were left open on mild nights. All of the upper city had been built over older ruins, and thus much more recently than the lower, within the last fifty or so years, and made much larger use of climate control. Many residents wore trousers and shirts, and even jackets. Radchaai immigrants who lived here tended to wear much more conventional clothes, and Lieutenant Awn, when she visited, wore her uniform without too much discomfort.

But Lieutenant Awn was never comfortable, visiting Jen Shinnan. She didn't like Jen Shinnan, and though of course it was never even hinted at, very likely Jen Shinnan didn't like Lieutenant Awn much either. This sort of invitation was only extended out of social necessity, Lieutenant Awn being a local representative of Radchaai authority. The table this evening was unusually small, just Jen Shinnan, a cousin of hers, and Lieutenant Awn and Lieutenant Skaaiat. Lieutenant Skaaiat commanded *Justice of Ente* Seven Issa, and administered the territory between Ors and Kould Ves—farmland, mostly, where Jen Shinnan and her cousin had their holdings. Lieutenant Skaaiat and her troops assisted us during pilgrimage season, so she was nearly as well-known in Ors as Lieutenant Awn was.

"They confiscated my entire harvest." This was the cousin of Jen Shinnan's, the owner of several tamarind orchards not far from the upper city. She tapped her plate emphatically with her utensil. "The *entire* harvest."

The center of the table was laden with trays and bowls filled with eggs, fish (not from the marshy lake, but from the sea beyond), spiced chicken, bread, braised vegetables, and half a dozen relishes of various types.

"Didn't they pay you, citizen?" asked Lieutenant Awn, speaking slowly and carefully, as she always did when she was anxious her accent might slip. Jen Shinnan and her cousin both spoke Radchaai, so there was no need to translate, nor any anxiety over gender or status or anything else that would have been essential in Tanmind or Orsian.

"Well, but I would certainly have gotten more if I could have taken it to Kould Ves and sold it myself!"

There had been a time when a property owner like her would have been shot early on, so someone's client could take over her plantation. Indeed, not a few Shis'urnans had died in the initial stages of the annexation simply because they were in the way, and *in the way* could mean any number of things.

"As I'm sure you understand, citizen," said Lieutenant Awn, "food distribution is a problem we're still solving, and we all need to endure some hardship while that's accomplished." Her sentences, when she was uncomfortable, became uncharacteristically formal, and sometimes dangerously convoluted.

Jen Shinnan gestured to a laden plate of fragile pale-pink glass. "Another stuffed egg, Lieutenant Awn?"

Lieutenant Awn held up one gloved hand. "They're delicious, but no thank you, citizen."

But the cousin had landed in a track she found it hard to deviate from, despite Jen Shinnan's diplomatic attempt to derail her. "It's not like fruit is a necessity. Tamarind, of all things! And it's not like anyone is starving."

"Indeed it isn't!" agreed Lieutenant Skaaiat, heartily. She

smiled brightly at Lieutenant Awn. Lieutenant Skaaiat—dark-skinned, amber-eyed, aristocratic as Lieutenant Awn was not. One of her Seven Issas stood near me, by the door of the dining room, as straight and still as I was.

Though Lieutenant Awn liked Lieutenant Skaaiat a good deal, and appreciated her sarcasm on this occasion, she could not bring herself to smile in response. "Not this year."

"Your business is doing better than mine, Cousin," said Jen Shinnan, voice placating. She too owned farmland not far from the upper city. But she had also owned those dredgers that sat, silent and still, in the marsh water. "Though I suppose I can't be too regretful, it was a great deal of trouble for very little return."

Lieutenant Awn opened her mouth to speak, and then closed it again. Lieutenant Skaaiat saw it, and said, vowels effortlessly broad and refined, "What is it, another three years for the fishing prohibitions, Lieutenant?"

"Yes," said Lieutenant Awn.

"Foolishness," said Jen Shinnan. "Well-intentioned, but foolishness. You saw what it was like when you arrived. As soon as you open them, they'll be fished out again. The Orsians may have been a great people once, but they're no longer what their ancestors were. They have no ambition, no sense of anything beyond their short-term advantage. If you show them who's boss, then they can be quite obedient, as I'm sure you've discovered, Lieutenant Awn, but in their natural state they are, with few exceptions, shiftless and superstitious. Though I suppose that's what comes of living in the Underworld." She smiled at her own joke. Her cousin laughed outright.

The space-dwelling nations of Shis'urna divided the universe into three parts. In the middle lay the natural environment of humans—space stations, ships, constructed habitats. Outside those was the Black—heaven, the home of God and everything holy. And within the gravity well of the planet Shis'urna itself—or for that matter any planet—lay the Underworld, the land of the dead from which humanity had had to escape in order to become fully free of its demonic influence.

You can see, perhaps, how the Radchaai conception of the universe as being God itself might seem the same as the Tanmind idea of the Black. You might also see why it seemed a bit odd, to Radchaai ears, to hear someone who believed gravity wells were the land of the dead call people superstitious for worshiping a lizard.

Lieutenant Awn managed a polite smile, and Lieutenant Skaaiat said, "And yet you live here too."

"I don't confuse abstract philosophical concepts with reality," said Jen Shinnan. Though that too sounded odd, to a Radchaai who knew what it meant for a Tanmind stationer to descend to the Underworld and return. "Seriously. I have a theory."

Lieutenant Awn, who had been exposed to several Tanmind theories about the Orsians, managed a neutral, even almost curious expression and said, blandly, "Oh?"

"Do share!" encouraged Lieutenant Skaaiat. The cousin, having scooped a quantity of spiced chicken into her mouth moments before, made a gesture of support with her utensil.

"It's the way they live, all out in the open like that, with nothing but a roof," Jen Shinnan said. "They can't have any privacy, no sense of themselves as real individuals, you understand, no sense of any sort of separate identity."

"Let alone private property," said Jen Taa, having swallowed her chicken. "They think they can just walk in and take whatever they want."

Actually, there were rules—if unstated ones—about entering a house uninvited, and theft was rarely a problem in the lower city. Occasionally during pilgrimage season, almost never otherwise.

Jen Shinnan gestured acknowledgment. "And no one *here* is ever really starving, Lieutenant. No one has to work, they just fish in the swamp. Or fleece visitors during pilgrimage season. They have no chance to develop any ambition, or any desire to improve themselves. And they don't—can't, really—develop any sort of sophistication, any kind of..." She trailed off, searching for the right word.

"Interiority?" suggested Lieutenant Skaaiat, who enjoyed this game much more than Lieutenant Awn did.

"That's it exactly!" agreed Jen Shinnan. "Interiority, yes."

"So your theory is," said Lieutenant Awn, her tone dangerously even, "that the Orsians aren't really *people*."

"Well, not *individuals*." Jen Shinnan seemed to sense, remotely, that she'd said something to make Lieutenant Awn angry, but didn't seem entirely certain of it. "Not as such."

"And of course," interjected Jen Taa, oblivious, "they see what we have, and don't understand that you have to *work* for that sort of life, and they're envious and resentful and blame *us* for not letting them have it, when if they'd only *work*..."

"They send what money they have to support that half-broken-down temple, and then complain they're poor," said Jen Shinnan. "And they fish out the marsh and then blame us. They'll do the same to you, Lieutenant, when you open the prohibited zones again."

"Your dredging up the mud by the ton to sell as fertilizer didn't have anything to do with the fish disappearing?" asked Lieutenant Awn, her voice edged. Actually, the fertilizer had been a by-product of the main business of selling the mud to space-dwelling Tanmind for religious purposes. "That was due to irresponsible fishing on the part of the Orsians?"

"Well of course it had *some* effect," said Jen Taa, "but if they'd only managed their resources properly..."

"Quite right," agreed Jen Shinnan. "You blame me for ruining the fishing. But I gave those people jobs. Opportunities to improve their lives."

Lieutenant Skaaiat must have sensed that Lieutenant Awn was at a dangerous point. "Security on a planet is very different from on a station," she said, her voice cheerful. "On a planet there's always going to be some...some slippage. Some things you don't see."

"Ah," said Jen Shinnan, "but you've got everyone tagged so you always know where we are."

"Yes," agreed Lieutenant Skaaiat. "But we're not always *watching*. I suppose you could grow an AI big enough to watch a whole planet, but I don't think anyone has ever tried it. A station, though..."

I watched Lieutenant Awn see Lieutenant Skaaiat spring the trap Jen Shinnan had walked into moments ago. "On a station," Lieutenant Awn said, "the AI sees everything."

"So much easier to manage," agreed Lieutenant Skaaiat happily. "Almost no need for security at all." That wasn't quite true, but this was no time to point that out.

Jen Taa set down her utensil. "Surely the AI doesn't see *everything*." Neither lieutenant said anything. "Even when you...?"

"Everything," answered Lieutenant Awn. "I assure you, citizen."

Silence, for nearly two seconds. Beside me, Lieutenant Skaaiat's Seven Issa guard's mouth twitched, something that might have been an itch or some unavoidable muscle spasm, but was, I suspected, the only outward manifestation of her amusement. Military ships possessed AIs just as stations did, and Radchaai soldiers lived utterly without privacy.

Lieutenant Skaaiat broke the silence. "Your niece, citizen, is taking the aptitudes this year?"

The cousin gestured yes. So long as her own farming provided income, she wouldn't need an assignment, and neither would her heir—however many heirs the land might support. The niece, however, had lost her parents during the annexation.

"These aptitudes," said Jen Shinnan. "You took them, Lieutenants?" Both indicated affirmatively. The aptitudes were the only way into the military, or any government post—though that didn't encompass all assignments available.

"No doubt," said Jen Shinnan, "the test works well for you, but I wonder if it's suited to us Shis'urnans."

"Why is that?" asked Lieutenant Skaaiat, with slightly frowning amusement.

"Has there been a problem?" asked Lieutenant Awn, still stiff, still annoyed with Jen Shinnan.

"Well." Jen Shinnan picked up a napkin, soft and bleached a snowy white, and wiped her mouth. "Word is, last month in Kould Ves all the candidates for civil service were ethnic Orsians."

Lieutenant Awn blinked in confusion. Lieutenant Skaaiat smiled. "You mean to say," she said, looking at Jen Shinnan but also directing her words to Lieutenant Awn, "that you think the testing is biased."

Jen Shinnan folded her napkin and set it down on the table beside her bowl. "Come now, Lieutenant. Let us be honest. There's a reason so few Orsians occupied such posts before you arrived. Every now and then you find an exception—the Divine is a very respectable person, I grant you. But she's an exception. So when I see twenty Orsians destined for civil service posts, and not a single Tanmind, I can't help but think either the test is flawed, or... well. I can't help but remember that it was the Orsians who first surrendered, when you arrived. I can't blame you for appreciating that, for wanting to... acknowledge that. But it's a mistake."

Lieutenant Awn said nothing. Lieutenant Skaaiat asked, "Assuming you're correct, why would that be a mistake?"

"It's as I said before. They just aren't suited to positions of authority. Some exceptions, yes, but..." She waved a gloved hand. "And with the bias of the assignments being so obvious, people won't have confidence in it."

Lieutenant Skaaiat's smile grew broader in proportion to Lieutenant Awn's silent, indignant anger. "Your niece is nervous?"

"A bit!" admitted the cousin.

"Understandably," drawled Lieutenant Skaaiat. "It's a momentous event in any citizen's life. But she needn't fear."

Jen Shinnan laughed, sardonic. "Needn't fear? The lower city resents us, always has, and now we can't make any legal contracts without either taking transport to Kould Ves or going through the lower city to your house, Lieutenant." Any legally binding contract had to be made in the temple of Amaat. Or, a recent (and extremely controversial) concession, on its steps, if one of the parties was an exclusive monotheist. "During that pilgrimage thing it's nearly impossible. We either lose an entire day traveling to Kould Ves, or endanger ourselves."

Jen Shinnan visited Kould Ves quite frequently, often merely to visit friends, or shop. All the Tanmind in the upper city did, and had done so before the annexation. "Has there

58

been some unreported difficulty?" asked Lieutenant Awn, stiff, angry. Utterly polite.

"Well," said Jen Taa. "In fact, Lieutenant, I've been wanting to mention. We've been here a few days, and my niece seems to have had a bit of trouble in the lower city. I told her it was better not to go, but you know how teenagers are when you tell them not to do something."

"What sort of trouble?" asked Lieutenant Awn.

"Oh," said Jen Shinnan, "you know the sort of thing. Rude words, threats—empty, no doubt, and of course nothing next to what things will be like in a week or two, but the child was quite shaken."

The child in question had spent the past two afternoons staring at the Fore-Temple water and sighing. I had spoken to her once and she had turned her head away without answering. After that I had left her alone. No one had troubled her. *No problems that I saw*, I messaged Lieutenant Awn.

"I'll keep an eye on her," said Lieutenant Awn, silently acknowledging my information with a twitch of her fingers.

"Thank you, Lieutenant," said Jen Shinnan. "I know we can count on you."

"You think it's funny." Lieutenant Awn tried to relax her too-tight jaw. I could tell from the increasing tension of her facial muscles that without intervention she would soon have a headache.

Lieutenant Skaaiat, walking beside her, laughed outright. "It's pure comedy. Forgive me, my dear, but the angrier you get the more painstakingly correct your speech becomes, and the more Jen Shinnan mistakes you."

"Surely not. Surely she's asked about me."

"You're still angry. Worse," said Lieutenant Skaaiat,

hooking her arm around Lieutenant Awn's, "you're angry with *me*. I'm sorry. And she *has* asked. Very obliquely, just *interested* in you, only natural, of course."

"And you answered," suggested Lieutenant Awn, "equally obliquely."

I walked behind them, alongside the Seven Issa who had stood with me in Jen Shinnan's dining room. Directly ahead, along the street and across the Fore-Temple water, I could see myself where I stood in the plaza.

Lieutenant Skaaiat said, "I said nothing untrue. I told her that lieutenants on ships with ancillaries tended to be from old, high-ranking families with lots of money and clients. Her connections in Kould Ves might have said a bit more, but not much. On the one hand, since you aren't such a person, they have cause to resent you. On the other hand, you *do* command ancillaries and not vulgar human troops, which the old-fashioned deplore just as much as they deplore the scions of obscure, nobody houses getting assigned as officers. They approve of your ancillaries and disapprove of your antecedents. Jen Shinnan gets a very ambivalent picture of you." Her voice was quiet, pitched so that only someone standing very near could hear it, though the houses we passed were closed up, and dark on the lower levels. It was very unlike the lower city, where even late into the night people sat nearly in the street, even small children.

"Besides," Lieutenant Skaaiat said, "she's right. Oh, not that foolishness about Orsians, no, but she's right to be suspicious about the aptitudes. You know yourself the tests are susceptible to manipulation." Lieutenant Awn felt a sick, betrayed indignation at Lieutenant Skaaiat's words, but said nothing, and Lieutenant Skaaiat continued. "For centuries only the wealthy and well-connected tested as suitable for certain jobs. Like, say, officers in the military. In the last, what, fifty, seventy-five years, that hasn't been true. Have the lesser houses suddenly begun to produce officer candidates where they didn't before?"

"I don't like where you're headed with this," snapped Lieutenant Awn, tugging slightly at their linked arms, trying to pull away. "I didn't expect it from you."

"No, no," protested Lieutenant Skaaiat, and didn't let go, drew her closer. "The question is the right one, and the answer the same. The answer is no, of course. But does that mean the tests were rigged before, or rigged now?"

"And your opinion?"

"Both. Before and now. And our friend Jen Shinnan doesn't fully understand that the question can even be asked—she just knows that if you're going to succeed you've got to have the right connections, and she knows the aptitudes are part of that. And she's utterly shameless—you heard her imply the Orsians were being rewarded for collaboration, and in nearly the same breath imply her people would be even better collaborators! And you notice neither she nor her cousin are sending their *own* children for testing, just this orphaned niece. Still, they're invested in her doing well. If we'd asked for a bribe to ensure it, she'd have handed it over, no question. I'm surprised she didn't offer one, actually."

"You wouldn't," protested Lieutenant Awn. "You won't. You can't deliver anyway."

"I won't need to. The child will test well, likely get herself sent to the territorial capital for training to take a nice civil service post. If you ask me, the Orsians *are* being rewarded for collaborating—but they're a minority in this system. And now the unavoidable unpleasantness of the annexation is over, we want people to start realizing that being Radchaai will benefit them. Punishing local houses for not being quick enough to surrender won't help."

They walked in silence for a bit, and stopped at the edge of the water, arms still linked.

"Walk you home?" asked Lieutenant Skaaiat. Lieutenant Awn didn't answer, but looked away over the water, still angry. The green skylights in the temple's slanted roof shone, and light poured out the open doors onto the plaza and reflected on the water—this was a season of nightly vigils. Lieutenant Skaaiat said, with an apologetic half-smile, "I've upset you, let me make it up to you."

"Sure," said Lieutenant Awn, with a small sigh. She never could resist Lieutenant Skaaiat, and indeed there was no real reason to do so. They turned and walked along the water's edge.

"What's the difference," Lieutenant Awn said, so quietly it didn't seem like a break in the silence, "between citizens and noncitizens?"

"One is civilized," said Lieutenant Skaaiat with a laugh, "and the other isn't." The joke only made sense in Radchaai— *citizen* and *civilized* are the same word. To be Radchaai is to be civilized.

"So in the moment the Lord of Mianaai bestowed citizenship on the Shis'urnans, in that very instant they became civilized." The sentence was a circular one—the question Lieutenant Awn was asking is a difficult one in that language. "I mean, one day your Issas are shooting people for failing to speak respectfully enough—don't tell me it didn't happen, because I know it did, and worse—and it doesn't matter because they're not Radchaai, not civilized." Lieutenant Awn had switched momentarily into the bit of the local Orsian language she knew, because the Radchaai words refused to let her mean what she wished to say. "And any measures are justified in the name of civilization."

"Well," said Lieutenant Skaaiat, "it was effective, you have to admit. Everyone speaks very respectfully to us these days." Lieutenant Awn was silent. Unamused. "What brought this on?" Lieutenant Awn told her about her conversation with the head priest the day before.

"Ah. Well. You didn't protest at the time."

"What good would it have done?"

"Absolutely none," answered Lieutenant Skaaiat. "But that's not why you didn't. Besides, even if ancillaries don't beat people, or take bribes, or rape, or shoot people out of pique—those people human troops shot…a hundred years ago they'd have been stored in suspension for future use as ancillary segments. Do you know how many we still have stockpiled? *Justice of Toren's* holds will be full of ancillaries for the next million years. If not longer. Those people are effectively dead. So what's the difference? And you don't like my saying that, but here's the truth: luxury always comes at someone else's expense. One of the many advantages of civilization is that one doesn't generally have to see that, if one doesn't wish. You're free to enjoy its benefits without troubling your conscience."

"It doesn't trouble yours?"

Lieutenant Skaaiat laughed, gaily, as though they were discussing something completely different, a game of counters or a good tea shop. "When you grow up knowing that you deserve to be on top, that the lesser houses exist to serve your house's glorious destiny, you take such things for granted. You're born assuming that someone else is paying the cost of your life. It's just the way things are. What happens during annexation—it's a difference of degree, not a difference of kind."

"It doesn't seem that way to me," answered Lieutenant Awn, short and bitter.

"No, of course it doesn't," answered Lieutenant Skaaiat, her voice kinder. I'm quite sure she genuinely liked Lieutenant Awn. I know that Lieutenant Awn liked her, even if Lieutenant Skaaiat sometimes said things that upset her, like this evening. "Your family has been paying some of that cost, however small. Maybe that makes it easier to sympathize with whoever might be paying for *you*. And I'm sure it's hard not to think of what your own ancestors went through when they were annexed."

"*Your* ancestors were never annexed." Lieutenant Awn's voice was biting.

"Well, some of them probably were," admitted Lieutenant Skaaiat. "But they're not in the official genealogy." She stopped, pulling Lieutenant Awn to a halt beside her. "Awn, my good friend. Don't trouble yourself over things you can't help. Things are as they are. You have nothing to reproach yourself with."

"You've just said we all do."

"That wasn't what I said." Lieutenant Skaaiat's voice was gentle. "But you'll take it that way all the same, won't you? Listen—life will be better here, because we're here. It already is, not just for the people here but for those who were transported. And even for Jen Shinnan, even though just now she's preoccupied with her own resentment at no longer being the highest authority in Ors. She'll come around in time. They all will."

"And the dead?"

"Are dead. No use fretting over them."

5

When Seivarden woke, she was fidgety and irritable. She asked me twice who I was, and complained three times that my answer—which was a lie in any event—conveyed no meaningful information to her. "I don't know anyone named Breq. I've never seen you before in my life. Where am I?"

Nowhere with a name. "You're on Nilt."

She drew a blanket around her bare shoulders, and then, sulkily, shoved it off again and folded her arms across her chest. "I've never even heard of Nilt. How did I end up here?"

"I have no idea." I set the food I was holding down on the floor in front of her.

She reached for the blanket again. "I don't want that."

I gestured my indifference. I had eaten and rested while she slept. "Does this happen to you often?"

"What?"

"Waking up and finding you don't know where you are, who you're with, or how you got there?"

She fidgeted the blanket on and off again, and rubbed her arms and wrists together. "A couple of times."

"I'm Breq, from the Gerentate." I had already told her, but I knew she would ask me again. "I found you two days ago in front of a tavern. I don't know how you got there. You would have died if I'd left you. I'm sorry if that's what you wanted."

For some reason that angered her. "How very charming you are, Breq from the Gerentate." She sneered slightly as she said it. It was mildly, irrationally surprising to hear that tone from her, naked and disheveled as she was, and not in uniform.

That tone made me angry. I knew very precisely why I was angry, and knew as well that if I dared to explain my anger to Seivarden she would respond with nothing but contempt, and that made me even angrier. I held my face in the neutral, slightly interested expression I had used with her from the moment she'd awakened, and made the same indifferent gesture I had made moments before.

I had been the first ship Seivarden ever served on. She'd arrived fresh out of training, seventeen years old, plunged straight into the tail end of an annexation. In a tunnel carved through red-brown stone under the surface of a small moon she had been ordered to guard a line of prisoners, nineteen of them, crouched naked and shivering along the chill passageway, waiting to be evaluated.

Actually I was doing the guarding, seven of me ranged along the corridor, weapons ready. Seivarden—so young then, still slight, dark hair, brown skin, and brown eyes unremarkable, unlike the aristocratic lines of her face, including a nose she hadn't quite grown into yet. Nervous, yes, left in charge here just days after arriving, but also proud of herself and her sudden, small authority. Proud of that dark-brown uniform jacket, trousers, and gloves, that lieutenant's insignia. And, I thought, a tiny bit too excited at holding an actual gun in what certainly wasn't a training exercise.

One of the people along the wall—broad-shouldered, muscled, cradling a broken arm against her torso—wept noisily, moaning each exhale, gasping every inhale. She knew, everyone in this line knew, that they would either be stored for future use as ancillaries—like the ancillaries of mine that stood before them even now, identities gone, bodies appendages to a Radchaai warship—or else they would be disposed of.

Seivarden, pacing importantly up and down the line, grew more irritated with this piteous captive's every convulsive breath, until finally she halted in front of her. "Aatr's tits! Stop that *noise!*" Small movements of Seivarden's arm muscles told me she was about to raise her weapon. No one would have cared if she'd taken the butt of her gun and beaten the prisoner senseless. No one would have cared if she'd shot the prisoner in the head, so long as no vital equipment was damaged in the process. Human bodies to make into ancillaries weren't exactly a scarce resource.

I stepped in front of her. "Lieutenant," I said, flat and toneless. "The tea you asked for is ready." Actually it had been ready five minutes before but I'd said nothing, held it in reserve.

In the readings coming from that terribly young Lieutenant Seivarden I saw startlement, frustration, anger. Irritation. "That was fifteen minutes ago," she snapped. I didn't answer. Behind me the prisoner still sobbed and moaned. "Can't you shut her up?"

"I'll do my best, Lieutenant," I said, though I knew there was only one way to really do that, only one thing that would silence that captive's grief. The newly minted Lieutenant Seivarden seemed unaware of that.

Twenty-one years after arriving on *Justice of Toren*—just over a thousand years before I found her in the snow—Seivarden was senior Esk lieutenant. Thirty-eight, still quite young by Radchaai standards. A citizen could live some two hundred years.

Her last day, she sat drinking tea on her bunk in her quarters, three meters by two meters by two, white-walled, severely neat. She was grown into that aristocratic nose by now, grown into herself. No longer awkward or unsure.

Beside her on the tightly made-up bunk sat the Esk decade's most junior lieutenant, arrived just weeks ago, a sort of cousin of Seivarden's, though from another house. Taller than Seivarden had been at that age, broader, a bit more graceful. Mostly. Nervous at being asked to confer in private here with the senior lieutenant, cousin or no, but concealing it. Seivarden said to her, "You want to be careful, Lieutenant, who you favor with your...attentions."

The very young lieutenant frowned, embarrassed, realizing suddenly what this was about.

"You know who I mean," continued Seivarden, and I knew too. One of the other Esk lieutenants had definitely noticed when the very young lieutenant had come on board, had been slowly, discreetly sounding out the possibility of the very young lieutenant perhaps noticing her back. But not so discreetly that Seivarden hadn't seen it. In fact, the entire decade room had seen it, and seen, as well, the very young lieutenant's intrigued response.

"I know who you mean," said the very young lieutenant. Indignant. "But I don't see why..."

"Ah!" said Seivarden, sharp and peremptory. "You think it's harmless fun. Well, it would probably be fun." Seivarden had slept with the lieutenant in question herself at one point and knew whereof she spoke. "But it wouldn't be harmless. She's a good enough officer, but her house is very provincial. If she weren't senior to you, there would be no problem."

The very young lieutenant's house was definitely *not* "very provincial." Naive as she was, she knew immediately what Seivarden meant. And was angry enough at it to address Seivarden in a way that was less formal than propriety demanded. "Aatr's tits, Cousin, no one's said anything about clientage. No one could, none of us can make contracts until we retire." Among the wealthy, clientage was a very hierarchical relationship—a patron promised certain sorts of assistance to her client, both financial and social, and a client provided support and services to her patron. These were promises that could last generations. In the oldest, most prestigious houses the servants were nearly all the descendants of clients, for instance, and many businesses owned by wealthy houses were staffed by client branches of lower ones.

"These provincial houses are ambitious," Seivarden explained, voice the slightest bit condescending. "And clever as well or they wouldn't have gotten as far as they have. She's senior to you, and you've both got years to serve yet. Grant her intimacy on those terms, let it continue, and depend on it, one of these days she'll be offering *you* clientage when it ought to be the other way around. I don't think your mother would thank you for exposing your house to that sort of insult."

The very young lieutenant's face heated with anger and chagrin, the shine of her first adult romance suddenly gone, the whole thing turned sordid and calculating.

Seivarden leaned forward, reached out for the tea flask and stopped, with a surge of irritation. Said silently to me, the fingers of her free hand twitching, "This cuff has been torn for three days."

I said, directly into her ear, "I'm sorry, Lieutenant." I ought to have offered to make the repair immediately, dispatched a segment of One Esk to take the offending shirt away. I ought, in fact, to have mended it three days before. Ought not to have dressed her in that shirt that day.

Silence in the cramped compartment, the very young lieutenant still preoccupied with her discomfiture. Then I said, directly into Seivarden's ear, "Lieutenant, the decade commander will see you at your earliest convenience."

I had known the promotion was coming. Had taken a petty satisfaction in the fact that even if she ordered me that moment to mend her sleeve, I would have no time to do it. As soon as she left her quarters I started packing her things, and three hours later she was on her way to her new command, freshly made captain of *Sword of Nathtas*. I hadn't been particularly sorry to see her go.

Such small things. It wasn't Seivarden's fault if she had reacted badly in a situation that few (if any) seventeen-year-olds could have handled with aplomb. It was hardly surprising that she was precisely as snobby as she had been brought up to be. Not her fault that over my (at the time) thousand years of existence I had come to have a higher opinion of ability than of breeding, and had seen more than one "very provincial" house rise far enough to lose that label, and turn out its own versions of Seivarden.

All the years between young Lieutenant Seivarden and Captain Seivarden, they were made up of tiny moments.

Minor things. I never hated Seivarden. I had just never particularly liked her. But I couldn't see her, now, without thinking of someone else.

The next week at Strigan's house was unpleasant. Seivarden needed constant looking after, and frequent cleaning up. She ate very little (which in some respects was fortunate), and I had to work to make sure she didn't get dehydrated. But by the end of the week she was keeping her food down, and sleeping at least intermittently. Even so she slept lightly, twitching and turning, often trembling, breathing hard, and waking suddenly. When she was awake, and not weeping, she complained that everything was too harsh, too rough, too loud, too bright.

Another few days after that, when she thought I was asleep, she went to the outer door and stared out over the snow, and then put on her clothes and a coat and trudged to the outbuilding, and then the flier. She tried to start it, but I had removed an essential part and kept it close. When she returned to the house she had at least the presence of mind to close both doors before she tracked snow into the main room, where I sat on a bench holding Strigan's stringed instrument. She stared, unable to conceal her surprise, still shrugging slightly, uncomfortable in the heavy coat, itchy.

"I want to leave," she said, in a voice oddly half cowed and half arrogant, commanding Radchaai.

"We'll leave when I'm ready," I said, and fingered a few notes on the instrument. Her feelings were too raw for her to be able to conceal them just now, and her anger and despair showed plainly on her face. "You are where you are," I said, in an even tone, "as a result of decisions you made yourself."

Her spine straightened, her shoulders went back. "You

don't know anything about me, or what decisions I have or haven't made."

It was enough to make me angry again. I knew something about making decisions, and not making them. "Ah, I forget. Everything happens as Amaat wills, nothing is *your* fault."

Her eyes went wide. She opened her mouth to speak, drew breath, but then blew it out, sharp and shaky. She turned her back, ostensibly to remove her outer coat and drop it on a nearby bench. "You don't understand," she said, contemptuous, but her voice trembled with suppressed tears. "You're not Radchaai."

Not civilized. "Did you start taking kef before or after you left the Radch?" It shouldn't have been available in Radchaai territory, but there was always some minor smuggling station authorities might turn a blind eye toward.

She slumped down onto the bench beside where she'd sloppily left her coat. "I want tea."

"There's no tea here." I set the instrument aside. "There's milk." More specifically, there was fermented bov milk, which the people here thinned with water and drank warm. The smell—and taste—was reminiscent of sweaty boots. And too much of it would likely make Seivarden slightly sick.

"What sort of place doesn't have *tea*?" she demanded, but leaned forward, elbows on her knees, and put her forehead on her wrists, her bare hands palm-up, fingers outstretched.

"This sort of place," I answered. "Why were you taking kef?"

"You wouldn't understand." Tears dropped into her lap.

"Try me." I picked up the instrument again, picked out a tune.

After six seconds of silent weeping, Seivarden said, "She said it would make everything clearer."

"The kef would?" No answer. "What would be clearer?"

"I know that song," she said, her face still resting on her wrists. I realized it was very likely the only way she would recognize me, and changed to a different tune. In one region of Valskaay, singing was a refined pastime, local choral associations the center of social activity. That annexation had brought me a great deal of the sort of music I had liked best, when I had had more than one voice. I chose one of those. Seivarden wouldn't know it. Valskaay had been both before and after her time.

"She said," Seivarden said finally, lifting her face from her hands, "that emotions clouded perception. That the clearest sight was pure reason, undistorted by feeling."

"That's not true." I'd had a week with this instrument and very little else to do. I managed two lines at once.

"It seemed true at first. It was *wonderful* at first. It all went away. But then it would wear off, and things would be the same. Only worse. And then after a while it was like not feeling felt bad. I don't know. I can't describe it. But if I took more that went away."

"And coming down got less and less endurable." I'd heard the story a few times, in the past twenty years.

"Oh, Amaat's grace," she moaned. "I want to die."

"Why don't you?" I changed to another song. *My heart is a fish, hiding in the water-grass. In the green, in the green...*

She looked at me as though I were a rock that had just spoken.

"You lost your ship," I said. "You were frozen for a thousand years. You wake up to find the Radch has changed—no more invasions, a humiliating treaty with the Presger, your house has lost financial and social status. No one knows you or remembers you, or cares whether you live or die. It's not what you were used to, not what you were expecting out of your life, is it?"

It took three puzzled seconds for the fact to dawn. "You know who I am."

"Of course I know who you are. You told me," I lied.

She blinked, tearily, trying, I supposed, to remember if she had or not. But her memories were, of course, incomplete.

"Go to sleep," I said, and laid my fingers across the strings, silencing them.

"I want to leave," she protested, not moving, still slumped on the bench, elbows on her knees. "Why can't I leave?"

"I have business here," I told her.

She curled her lip and scoffed. She was right, of course, waiting here was foolish. After so many years, so much planning and effort, I had failed.

Still. "Go back to bed." *Bed* was the pallet of cushions and blankets beside the bench, where she sat. She looked at me, half-sneering still, and contemptuous, and slid down to the floor and lay, pulled a blanket over herself. She wouldn't sleep at first, I was sure. She would be trying to think of some way to leave, to overpower me or convince me to do what she wanted. Any such planning would be useless until she knew *what* she wanted, of course, but I didn't say that.

Within the hour her muscles slackened and her breathing slowed. Had she still been my lieutenant I would have known for certain she slept, known what stage of sleep she was in, known whether or not she dreamed. Now I could only see externals.

Still wary, I sat on the floor, leaning against another bench, and pulled a blanket up over my legs. As I had done every time I'd slept here, I opened my inner coat and put my hand on my gun, leaned back, and closed my eyes.

* * *

Two hours later a faint sound woke me. I lay unmoving, my hand still on my gun. The faint sound repeated itself, slightly louder—the second door closing. I opened my eyes, just the slightest bit. Seivarden lay too quiet on her pallet—surely she had heard the sound as well.

Through my eyelashes I saw a person in outdoor clothes. Just under two meters tall, thin under the bulk of the double coat, skin iron-gray. When she pushed back her hood I saw her hair was the same. She was certainly not a Nilter.

She stood, watching me and Seivarden, for seven seconds, and then quietly stepped to where I lay, and bent to pull my pack toward her with one hand. In the other she held a gun, pointed steadily at me, though she seemed not to know I was awake.

The lock baffled her for a few moments, and then she pulled a tool out of her pocket, which she used to bypass the lock quite a bit more quickly than I had anticipated. Her gun still trained on me, and glancing occasionally at still-motionless Seivarden, she emptied the pack.

Spare clothes. Ammunition, but no gun, so she would know or suspect that I was armed. Three foil-wrapped packets of concentrated rations. Eating utensils, and a bottle for water. A gold disk five centimeters in diameter, one and a half centimeters thick that she puzzled over, frowning, and then set aside. A box, which she opened to find money—she let out an astonished breath when she realized how much, and looked over at me. I didn't move. I don't know what she had thought she would find, but she seemed not to have found it, whatever it was.

She picked up the disk that had puzzled her, and sat on a bench from which she had a clear view of both me and

Seivarden. Turning the disk over, she found the trigger. The sides fell away, opening like a flower, and the mechanism disgorged the icon, a person nearly naked except for short trousers and tiny jewel-and-enamel flowers. The image smiled, serene. She had four arms. One hand held a ball, the other arm was encased in a cylindrical armguard. Her other hands held a knife and a severed head, which dripped jeweled blood at her bare feet. The head smiled the same smile of saintly utter calm as she did.

Strigan—it had to be Strigan—frowned. The icon had been unexpected. It had piqued her curiosity yet further.

I opened my eyes. She tightened her grip on her gun—the gun I was now looking at as closely as I could, now my eyes were fully open, now I could turn my head toward it.

Strigan held the icon out, raised a steel-gray eyebrow. "Relative?" she asked, in Radchaai.

I kept my face pleasantly neutral. "Not exactly," I said, in her own language.

"I thought I knew what you were when you came," she said, after a long silence, thankfully following my language switch. "I thought I knew what you were doing here. Now I'm not so sure." She glanced at Seivarden, to all appearances completely undisturbed by our talking. "I *think* I know who *he* is. But who are *you*? *What* are you? Don't tell me *Breq from the Gerentate*. You're as Radchaai as that one." She gestured slightly toward Seivarden with her elbow.

"I came here to buy something," I said, determined to keep from staring at the gun she held. "He's incidental." Since we weren't speaking Radchaai I had to take gender into account—Strigan's language required it. The society she lived in professed at the same time to believe gender was insignificant. Males and females dressed, spoke, acted indistinguishably. And yet no one I'd met had ever hesitated, or guessed wrong. And they had invariably been offended when I *did* hesitate or guess wrong. I hadn't learned the trick of it. I'd been in Strigan's own apartment, seen her belongings, and still wasn't sure what forms to use with her now.

"Incidental?" asked Strigan, disbelieving. I couldn't blame her. I wouldn't have believed it myself, except I knew it to be true. Strigan said nothing else, likely realizing that to say much more would be extremely foolish, if I was what she feared I was.

"Coincidence," I said. Glad on at least one count that we weren't speaking Radchaai, where the word implied significance. "I found him unconscious. If I'd left him where he was he'd have died." Strigan didn't believe that either, from the look she gave me. "Why are you here?"

She laughed, short and bitter—whether because I'd chosen the wrong gender for the pronoun, or something else, I wasn't certain. "I think that's my question to ask."

She hadn't corrected my grammar, at least. "I came to talk to you. To buy something. Seivarden was ill. You weren't here. I'll pay you for what we've eaten, of course."

She seemed to find that amusing, for some reason. "Why are you here?" she asked.

"I'm alone," I said, answering her unspoken question. "Except for him." I nodded at Seivarden. My hand was still on my gun, and Strigan likely knew why I kept that hand so still, under my coat. Seivarden still feigned sleep.

Strigan shook her head slightly, disbelieving. "I'd have sworn you were a corpse soldier." An ancillary, she meant. "When you arrived I was certain of it." She'd been hiding nearby, then, waiting for us to leave, and the entire place had been under her surveillance. She must have trusted her hiding place quite extravagantly—if I had been what she feared, staying anywhere near would have been extremely foolish. I would certainly have found her. "But when you saw there was no one here you wept. And him..." She shrugged toward Seivarden, slack and motionless on the pallet.

"Sit up, citizen," I said to Seivarden, in Radchaai. "You're not fooling anyone."

"Fuck off," she answered, and pulled a blanket over her head. Then shoved it off again and rose, slightly shaky, and went into the sanitary facility and closed the door.

I turned back to Strigan. "That business with the flier rental. Was that you?"

She shrugged ruefully. "He told me a couple of Radchaai were coming out this way. Either he badly underestimated you, or you're even more dangerous than I thought."

Which would be considerably dangerous. "I'm used to being underestimated. And you didn't tell her...him why you thought I was coming."

Her gun hadn't wavered. "Why are you here?"

"You know why I'm here." A quick change in her expression, instantly suppressed. I continued. "Not to kill you. Killing you would defeat the purpose."

She raised an eyebrow, tilted her head slightly. "Would it."

The fencing, the feinting, frustrated me. "I want the gun."

"What gun?" Strigan would never be so foolish as to admit the thing existed, that she knew what gun I was talking about. But her pretended ignorance didn't convince. She knew. If she had what I thought she had, what I had gambled my life she had, further specificity would be unnecessary. She *knew*.

Whether she would give it to me was another question. "I'll pay you for it."

"I don't know what you're talking about."

"The Garseddai did everything in fives. Five right actions, five principal sins, five zones times five regions. Twenty-five representatives to surrender to the Lord of the Radch."

For three seconds Strigan was utterly still. Even her breathing seemed to have stopped. Then she spoke. "Garsedd, is it? What does that have to do with me?"

"I'd never have guessed if you'd stayed where you were."

"Garsedd was a thousand years ago, and very, very far away from here."

"Twenty-five representatives to surrender to the Lord of the Radch," I repeated. "And twenty-four guns recovered or otherwise accounted for."

She blinked, drew in a breath. "Who are you?"

"Someone ran. Someone fled the system before the Radchaai arrived. Maybe she was afraid the guns wouldn't work as advertised. Maybe she knew that even if they did it wouldn't help."

"On the contrary, no? Wasn't that the point? No one defies Anaander Mianaai." She spoke bitterly. "Not if they want to live."

I said nothing.

Strigan's hold on the gun didn't waver. Even so, she was in danger from me, if I decided to harm her, and I thought she suspected that. "I don't know why you think I have this gun you're talking about. Why would I have it?"

"You collected antiques, curiosities. You already had a small collection of Garseddai artifacts. They'd made their way to Dras Annia Station, somehow. Others might do so as well. And then one day you disappeared. You took care you wouldn't be followed."

"That's a very slight basis for such a large assumption."

"So why this?" I gestured carefully with my free hand, the other still under my coat, holding my gun. "You had a comfortable post on Dras Annia, patients, plenty of money, associations and reputation. Now you're in the icy middle of nowhere, giving first aid to bov herders."

"Personal crisis," she said, the words carefully, deliberately pronounced.

"Certainly," I agreed. "You couldn't bring yourself to destroy it, or pass it on to someone who might not be wise enough to realize what a danger it presented. You knew, as soon as you realized what you had, that if Radch authorities ever even dreamed of half-imagining it existed, they would track you down and kill you, and anyone else who might have seen it."

While the Radch wanted everyone to remember what had happened to the Garseddai, they wanted no one to know just how the Garseddai had managed to do what they'd done, what no one had managed to do for a thousand years before or another thousand years after—destroy a Radchaai ship. Almost no one alive remembered. I knew, and any still-extant ships that had been there. Anaander Mianaai certainly did. And Seivarden, who had seen for herself what the Lord of the Radch wanted no one to think was possible—that invisible armor and gun, those bullets that defeated Radchaai armor—and her ship's heat shield—so effortlessly.

"I want it," I told Strigan. "I'll pay you for it."

"*If* I had such a thing…if! It's entirely possible no amount of money in the world would be sufficient."

"Anything is possible," I agreed.

"You're Radchaai. And you're military."

"Was," I corrected. And when she scoffed, I added, "If I still were, I wouldn't be here. Or if I were, you would already have given me whatever information I wanted, and you'd be dead."

"Get out of here." Strigan's voice was quiet, but vehement. "Take your stray with you."

"I'm not leaving until I have what I came for." There would be little point in doing so. "You'll have to give it to me, or shoot me with it." As much as admitting I still had armor. Implying I was precisely what she feared, a Radchaai agent come to kill her and take the gun.

Frightened of me as she must be, she could not avoid her own curiosity. "Why do you want it so badly?"

"I want," I told her, "to kill Anaander Mianaai."

"What?" The gun in her hand trembled, moved slightly aside, then steadied again. She leaned forward three millimeters, and cocked her head as though she was certain she hadn't heard me correctly.

"I want to kill Anaander Mianaai," I repeated.

"Anaander Mianaai," she said, bitterly, "has thousands of bodies in hundreds of locations. You can't possibly kill him. Certainly not with one gun."

"I still want to try."

"You're insane. Or is that even possible? Aren't all Radchaai brainwashed?"

It was a common misconception. "Only criminals, or people who aren't functioning well, are reeducated. Nobody really cares what you think, as long as you do what you're supposed to."

She stared, dubious. "How do you define 'not functioning well'?"

I made an indefinite, *not my problem* gesture with my free hand. Though perhaps it *was* my problem. Perhaps that question did concern me now, insofar as it might very well concern Seivarden. "I'm going to take my hand out of my coat," I said. "And then I'm going to go to sleep."

Strigan said nothing, only twitched one gray eyebrow.

"If I found you, Anaander Mianaai certainly can," I said. We were speaking Strigan's language. What gender had she assigned to the Lord of the Radch? "He hasn't, yet, possibly because he is currently preoccupied with other matters, and for reasons that ought to be clear to you, he is likely hesitant to delegate in this affair."

"I'm safe, then." She sounded more convinced of that than she could possibly be.

Seivarden came noisily out of the bathroom and sank back onto her pallet, hands trembling, breathing quick and shallow.

"I'm taking my hand out of my coat now," I said, and then did that. Slowly. Empty.

Strigan sighed and lowered her gun. "I probably couldn't shoot you anyway." Because she was sure I was Radchaai military, and hence armored. Of course, if she could take me unawares, or fire before I could extend my armor, she could indeed shoot me.

And of course, she had that gun. Though she might not have it near to hand. "Can I have my icon back?"

She frowned, and then remembered she was still holding it. "*Your* icon."

"It belongs to me," I clarified.

"That's quite a resemblance," she said, looking at it again. "Where's it from?"

"Very far away." I held out my hand. She returned it, and one-handed I brushed the trigger and the image folded into itself, and the base closed into its gold disk.

Strigan looked over at Seivarden intently, and frowned. "Your stray is having some anxiety."

"Yes."

Strigan shook her head, frustrated or exasperated, and went into her infirmary. She returned, went to where Seivarden sat, leaned over, and reached for her.

Seivarden started, shoving herself up and back, grabbing Strigan's wrist in a move I knew was meant to break it. But Seivarden wasn't what she had once been. Dissipation and what I suspected was malnutrition had taken a toll. Strigan left her arm in Seivarden's grasp, and with her other hand plucked a small white tab out of her own fingers and stuck it to Seivarden's forehead. "I don't feel sorry for you," she said, in Radchaai. "It's just that I'm a doctor." Seivarden looked at her with an unaccountable expression of horror. "Let go of me."

"Let go, Seivarden, and lie down." I said, sharply. She stared two seconds more at Strigan, but then did as she was told.

"I'm not taking him as my patient," Strigan said to me, as Seivarden's breathing slowed and her muscles slackened. "It isn't more than first aid. And I don't want him panicking and breaking my things."

"I'm going to sleep now," I answered. "We can talk more in the morning."

"It *is* morning." But she didn't argue further.

She wouldn't be foolish enough to search my person while I slept. She would know how dangerous that would be.

She wouldn't shoot me in my sleep either, though it would be a simple and effective way to be rid of me. Asleep, I would be an easy target for a bullet, unless I extended my armor now and left it up.

But there was no need. Strigan wouldn't shoot me, at least not until she had the answers to her many questions. Even then she might not. I was too good a puzzle.

*   *   *

Strigan wasn't in the main room when I woke, but the door into the bedroom was closed, and I assumed she was either asleep or wanted privacy. Seivarden was awake, staring at me, fidgeting, rubbing her arms and shoulders. A week earlier I'd had to prevent her from scraping her skin raw. She'd improved a great deal.

The box of money lay where Strigan had left it. I checked it—it was undisturbed—put it away, latched my pack closed, thinking the while what my next step should be.

"Citizen," I said to Seivarden, brisk and authoritative. "Breakfast."

"What?" She was surprised enough to stop moving for a moment.

I lifted the corner of my lip, just slightly. "Shall I ask the doctor to check your hearing?" The stringed instrument lay beside me, where I had set it the night before. I picked it up, plucked a fifth. "Breakfast."

"I'm not your servant," she protested. Indignant.

I increased my sneer, just the smallest increment. "Then what are you?"

She froze, anger visible in her expression, and then very visibly debated with herself how best to answer me. But the question was, now, too difficult for her to answer easily. Her confidence in her superiority had apparently taken too severe a blow for her to deal with just now. She didn't seem to be able to find a response.

I bent to the instrument and began to pick out a line of music. I expected her to sit where she was, sullen, until at the very least hunger drove her to prepare her own meal. Or maybe, much delayed, find something to say to me. I found I half-hoped she'd take a swing at me, so I could retaliate, but perhaps she was still under the influence of whatever Strigan had given her last night, even if only slightly.

The door to Strigan's room opened, and she walked into the main living space, stopped, folded her arms, and cocked an eyebrow. Seivarden ignored her. None of us said anything, and after five seconds Strigan turned and strode to the kitchen and swung open a cabinet.

It was empty. Which I'd known the evening before. "You've cleaned me out, Breq from the Gerentate," Strigan said, without rancor. Almost as though she thought it was funny. We were in very little danger of starving—even in summer here, the outdoors effectively functioned as a huge freezer, and the unheated storage building held plenty of provisions. It was only a matter of fetching some, and thawing them.

"Seivarden." I spoke in the casually disdainful tone I had heard from Seivarden herself in the distant past. "Bring some food from the shed."

She froze, and then blinked, startled. "Who the *hell* do you think you are?"

"Language, citizen," I chided. "And I might ask you the same question."

"You...you ignorant *nobody*." The sudden intensity of her anger had brought her close to tears again. "You think you're better than me? You're barely even *human*." She didn't mean because I was an ancillary. I was fairly sure she hadn't yet realized that. She meant because I wasn't Radchaai, and perhaps because I might have implants that were common some places outside Radch space and that would, in Radchaai eyes, compromise my humanity. "I wasn't bred to be your servant."

I can move very, very quickly. I was standing, and my arm halfway through its swing, before I registered my intention to move. The barest fraction of a second passed during which

I could have possibly checked myself, and then it was gone, and my fist connected with Seivarden's face, too quickly for her to even look surprised.

She dropped, falling backward onto her pallet, blood pouring from her nose, and lay unmoving.

"Is he dead?" asked Strigan, still standing in the kitchen, her voice mildly curious.

I made an ambiguous gesture. "You're the doctor."

She walked over to where Seivarden lay, unconscious and bleeding. Gazed down at her. "Not dead," she pronounced. "Though I'd like to make sure the concussion doesn't turn into anything worse."

I gestured resignation. "It is as Amaat wills," I said, and put on my coat and went outside to bring in food.

6

On Shis'urna, in Ors, the *Justice of Ente* Seven Issa who had accompanied Lieutenant Skaaiat to Jen Shinnan's sat with me in the lower level of the house. She had a name beyond her designation—one I never used, though I knew it. Even Lieutenant Skaaiat sometimes addressed individual human soldiers under her command as merely "Seven Issa." Or by their segment numbers.

I brought out a board and counters, and we played a silent two games. "Can't you let me win a time or two?" she asked, when the second was concluded, and before I could answer a thump sounded from the upper floor and she grinned. "It looks like Lieutenant Stiff can unbend after all!" and she cast me a look intended to share the joke, her amusement at the contrast between Awn's usual careful formality and what was obviously going on upstairs between her and Lieutenant Skaaiat. But the instant after Seven Issa had spoken, her smile faded. "I'm sorry. I didn't mean anything by it, it's just what we..."

"I know," I said. "I took no offense."

Seven Issa frowned, and made a doubtful gesture with her left hand, awkwardly, her gloved fingers still curled around half a dozen counters. "Ships have feelings."

"Yes, of course." Without feelings insignificant decisions become excruciating attempts to compare endless arrays of inconsequential things. It's just easier to handle those with emotions. "But as I said, I took no offense."

Seven Issa looked down at the board, and dropped the counters she held into one of its depressions. She stared at them a moment, and then looked up. "You hear rumors. About ships and people they like. And I'd swear your face never changes, but..."

I engaged my facial muscles, smiled, an expression I'd seen many times.

Seven Issa flinched. "Don't *do* that!" she said, indignant, but still hushed lest the lieutenants hear us.

It wasn't that I'd gotten the smile wrong—I knew I hadn't. It was the sudden change, from my habitual lack of expression to something human, that some of the Seven Issas found disturbing. I dropped the smile.

"Aatr's tits," swore Seven Issa. "When you do that it's like you're possessed or something." She shook her head, and scooped up the counters and began to distribute them around the board. "All right, then, you don't want to talk about it. One more game."

The evening grew later. The neighbors' conversations turned slow and aimless and finally ceased as people picked up sleeping children and went to bed.

Denz Ay arrived four hours before dawn, and I joined her, stepping into her boat without speaking. She did not acknowledge my presence, and neither did her daughter, sitting in the stern. Slowly, nearly noiselessly, we slid away from the house.

The vigil at the temple continued, the priests' prayers audible on the plaza as an intermittent shushing murmur. The streets, upper and lower, were silent except for my own footsteps and the sound of the water, dark but for the stars brilliant overhead, the blinking of the prohibited zones' encircling buoys, and the light from the temple of Ikkt. The Seven Issa who had accompanied us back to Lieutenant Awn's house slept on a pallet on the ground floor.

Lieutenant Awn and Lieutenant Skaaiat lay together on the upper floor, still and on the edge of sleep.

No one else was out on the water with us. In the bottom of the boat I saw rope, nets, breathers, and a round, covered basket tied to an anchor. The daughter saw me look at it, and she kicked it under her seat, with studied nonchalance. I looked away, over the water, toward the blinking buoys, and said nothing. The fiction that they could hide or alter the information coming from their trackers was a useful one, even if no one actually believed it.

Just inside the buoys, Denz Ay's daughter put a breather in her mouth and slid over the edge, a rope in her hand. The lake wasn't terribly deep, especially at this time of year. Moments later she reemerged and climbed back aboard, and we pulled the crate up—a relatively easy job until it reached the surface, but the three of us managed to tip it into the boat without taking on too much water.

I wiped mud off the lid. It was of Radchaai manufacture, but that wasn't too alarming in itself. I found the latch and popped it open.

The guns within—long, sleek, and deadly—were the sort

that had been carried by Tanmind troops before the annexation. I knew each one would have an identifying mark, and the marks of any guns confiscated by us would have been listed and reported, so that I could consult the inventory and determine more or less immediately if these were confiscated weapons, or ones we had missed.

If they were confiscated weapons, this situation would suddenly become a great deal more complicated than it seemed at the moment—and it was already a complicated situation.

Lieutenant Awn was in stage one of NREM sleep. Lieutenant Skaaiat seemed to be as well. I could consult the inventory on my own initiative. Indeed, I *should*. But I didn't—partly because I had just been reminded, yesterday, of the corrupt authorities at Ime, the misuse of accesses, the most appalling abuse of power, something any citizen would have thought was impossible. That reminder itself was enough to make me cautious. But also, after Denz Ay's assertions about residents of the upper city planting evidence in the past, and the evening's dinner conversation with its clear reminder of resentment in that upper city, something didn't seem quite right. No one in the upper city would know I had requested information about confiscated weapons, but what if someone else was involved? Someone who could set alerts to notify her if certain questions were asked in certain places? Denz Ay and her daughter sat quietly in the boat, to all appearances unconcerned and not particularly eager to be anywhere, or to be doing anything else.

Within a few moments I had *Justice of Toren*'s attention. I had seen no few of those confiscated weapons—not I, One Esk, but I, *Justice of Toren*, whose thousands of ancillary troops had been on the planet during the annexation. If I could not consult an official inventory without alerting an authority to the fact that I had found this cache, I could consult my own memory to see if any of them had passed under my own eyes.

And they had.

I went in to where Lieutenant Awn was sleeping and put a hand on her bare shoulder. "Lieutenant," I said, softly. In the boat I closed the crate with a soft snap and said, "Back to the city."

Lieutenant Awn jerked awake. "I'm not asleep," she said blearily. In the boat, Denz Ay and her daughter silently picked up their oars and started back.

"The weapons were confiscated," I said to Lieutenant Awn, still quiet. Not wanting to wake Lieutenant Skaaiat, not wanting anyone else to hear what I was saying. "I recognized the serial numbers."

Lieutenant Awn looked at me dazedly for a few moments, uncomprehending. Then I saw her understand. "But..." And then she woke fully, and turned to Lieutenant Skaaiat. "Skaaiat, wake up. I've got a problem."

I brought the guns to the upper level of Lieutenant Awn's house. Seven Issa didn't even stir when I went past.

"You're sure?" asked Lieutenant Skaaiat, kneeling by the open crate, naked but for gloves, a bowl of tea in one hand.

"I confiscated these myself," I answered. "I remember them." We were all speaking very quietly, so that no one outside could hear.

"Then they would have been destroyed," argued Lieutenant Skaaiat.

"Obviously they weren't," said Lieutenant Awn. And then, after a brief silence, "Oh, *shit*. This is not good."

Silently I messaged her. *Language, Lieutenant.*

Lieutenant Skaaiat made a short, breathy sound, un-amused laughter. "To put it mildly." She frowned. "But why? Why would anyone go to the trouble?"

"And *how?*" asked Lieutenant Awn. She seemed to have forgotten her own tea, in a bowl on the floor beside her. "They put them there without us seeing them." I'd looked at the logs for the past thirty days and seen nothing I couldn't already account for. Indeed, no one had been to that spot at all besides Denz Ay and her daughter thirty days ago, and just the other night.

"*How* is the easy part, if you've got the right accesses," said Lieutenant Skaaiat. "Which might tell us something. It's not someone who's got high-level access to *Justice of Toren*, or they'd have made sure it didn't remember these guns. Or at least couldn't say it did."

"Or they didn't think of that particular detail," suggested Lieutenant Awn. She was puzzled. And only beginning to be frightened. "Or maybe that's part of the plan to begin with. But we're back to *why*, aren't we? It doesn't much matter how, not right this moment."

Lieutenant Skaaiat looked up at me. "Tell me about the trouble Jen Taa's niece had in the lower city."

Lieutenant Awn looked at her, frowning. "But..." Lieutenant Skaaiat shushed her with a gesture.

"There was no trouble," I said. "She sat by herself and threw rocks in the Fore-Temple water. She bought some tea in the shop behind the temple. Beyond that, no one spoke to her."

"You're certain?" asked Lieutenant Awn.

"She was in my view the entire time." And I would take care that she would be on any future visits, but that hardly needed saying.

The two lieutenants were silent a moment. Lieutenant Awn closed her eyes and took a deep breath. She was now truly frightened. "They're lying about that," she said, eyes still closed. "They want some excuse to accuse someone in the lower city of...something."

"Sedition," Lieutenant Skaaiat said. She remembered her tea, and took a sip. "And getting above themselves. That's easy enough to see."

"Yes, I can see that," said Lieutenant Awn. Her accent had slipped entirely, but she hadn't noticed. "But why the hell would anyone with this sort of access"—she gestured at the crate of guns—"want to help them?"

"That would seem to be the question," answered Lieutenant Skaaiat. They were silent for several seconds. "What are you going to do?"

The question upset Lieutenant Awn, who presumably had been wondering just that. She looked up at me. "I wonder if this is all."

"I can ask Denz Ay to take me out again," I said.

Lieutenant Awn gestured affirmatively. "I'll write the report, but I won't file it just yet. Pending our further investigation." Everything Lieutenant Awn did and said was observed and recorded—but as with the trackers everyone in Ors wore, there wasn't always someone paying attention.

Lieutenant Skaaiat made a low whistle. "Is someone setting you up, dear?" Lieutenant Awn looked incomprehension at her. "Like maybe," Lieutenant Skaaiat continued, "Jen Shinnan? I may have underestimated her. Or can you trust Denz Ay?"

"If someone wants me gone, they're in the upper city," said Lieutenant Awn, and privately I agreed but I didn't say it. "But that can't be it. If anyone who could do this," she gestured at the crate, "wanted me out of here, it would be easy enough—just give the order. And Jen Shinnan couldn't have done this." Unspoken, hanging behind every word, was the memory of news from Ime. Of the fact that the person who had revealed the corruption there was condemned to die, probably was already dead. "No one in Ors could have, not without..." Not without help, from a very high level, she would surely have said, but she let the sentence trail off.

"True," mused Lieutenant Skaaiat. Understanding her. "So it's someone high up. Who would benefit?"

"The niece," said Lieutenant Awn, distressed.

"Jen Taa's niece would benefit?" asked Lieutenant Skaaiat, puzzled.

"No, no. The niece is insulted or assaulted—allegedly. I won't do anything, *I* say nothing happened."

"Because nothing happened," said Lieutenant Skaaiat, looking as though something was beginning to come clear to her, but still puzzled.

"They can't get justice from me, so they come down to the lower city to get it for themselves. It's the sort of thing that happened before we came."

"And afterward," said Lieutenant Skaaiat, "they find all these guns. Or even during. Or..." She shook her head. "It's not all fitting together. Let's say you're right. Still. *Who benefits?* Not the Tanmind, not if they cause trouble. They can accuse all they like, but no matter what anyone finds in the lake, they're still for reeducation if they riot."

Lieutenant Awn gestured doubtfully. "Someone who could get those guns here without our seeing them might be able to keep the Tanmind out of trouble. Or believably say they could."

"Ah." Lieutenant Skaaiat understood immediately. "A

minor fine, mitigating circumstances. No doubt of it. It'll be someone high up. Very dangerous. But why?"

Lieutenant Awn looked at me. "Go to the head priest and ask her a favor. Tell her, from me, even though it's not the rainy season, to station someone near the storm alarm at all times." The alarm, an earsplitting siren, was on the top of the temple residence. Its sounding would trigger the storm shutters of most of the buildings in the lower city, and would certainly wake the inhabitants of any building not automated in that fashion. "Ask her to be ready to sound it if I ask."

"Excellent," said Lieutenant Skaaiat. "Any mob will at least have to work a bit harder to get past the shutters. And then?"

"It might not even happen," said Lieutenant Awn. "Whatever it is, we'll have to take it as it comes."

What came, the next morning, was news that Anaander Mianaai, Lord of the Radch, would be visiting us some time in the next few days.

For three thousand years Anaander Mianaai had ruled Radch space absolutely. She resided in each of the thirteen provincial palaces, and was present at every annexation. She was able to do this because she possessed thousands of bodies, all of them genetically identical, all of them linked to each other. She was still in Shis'urna's system, some of her on the flagship of this annexation, *Sword of Amaat*, and some of her on Shis'urna Station. It was she who made Radchaai law, and she who decided on any exceptions to that law. She was the ultimate commander of the military, the highest head priest of Amaat, the person to whom, ultimately, all Radchaai houses were clients.

And she was coming to Ors, at some unspecified date

within the next few days. It was, in fact, mildly surprising she hadn't visited Ors sooner—small as it was, far as Orsians had fallen from their former glory, still the yearly pilgrimage made Ors a moderately important place. Important enough that officers of higher families and more influence than Lieutenant Awn had wanted this post—and tried continually to pry her out of it, despite the determined resistance of the Divine of Ikkt.

So the visit itself wasn't unexpected. Though the timing seemed odd. It was two weeks before the start of the pilgrimage, when hundreds of thousands of Orsians and tourists would pass through the city. During pilgrimage Anaander Mianaai's presence would be highly visible, an opportunity to impress a high number of the worshippers of Ikkt. Instead she was coming just before. And of course it was impossible not to notice the sharp coincidence between her arrival and the discovery of the guns.

Whoever had placed those guns was acting either for or against the interests of the Lord of the Radch. She should have been the one logical person to tell, and to ask for further instructions. And her being in Ors in person was incredibly convenient—it presented an opportunity to tell her about the situation without anyone else intercepting the message and either spoiling whatever the plan was, or alerting wrongdoers that their plan had been discovered, making them harder to catch.

On that account alone, Lieutenant Awn was relieved to hear of her visit. Even though for the next few days, and while she was here, Lieutenant Awn would have to wear her full uniform.

In the meantime I listened more closely to conversations in the upper city—more difficult than in the lower, because the houses were all enclosed and of course any Tanmind involved would be closemouthed if they knew I was in earshot. And no one was foolish enough to have the sort of conversation I was listening for anywhere but in person, in private. I also watched Jen Taa's niece—or as well as I could. After the dinner party she never left Jen Shinnan's house, but I could see her tracker data.

For two nights I went out on the marsh with Denz Ay and her daughter, and we found two more crates of guns. Once again I had no way of determining who had left them, or when, though Denz Ay's oblique statements, careful not to implicate the fishermen I knew usually poached in those areas, implied that they must have arrived some time in the past month or two.

"I'll be glad when the Lord of Mianaai gets here," said Lieutenant Awn to me, quietly, late one night. "I don't think I should be handling something like this."

And in the meantime I noticed that no one but Denz Ay went out on the water at night, and in the lower city no one sat or lay where the shutters might come down—a routine precaution during the rainy season, even though there were safeties to stop them if someone was in their way, but one that was usually ignored in the dry season.

The Lord of the Radch arrived in the middle of the day, on foot, a single one of her walking down through the upper city, no trace of her in the tracker logs, and went straight to the temple of Ikkt. She was old, gray-haired, broad shoulders slightly stooping, the almost-black skin of her face lined— which accounted for the lack of guards. The loss of one body that was more or less near death anyway would not be a large one. The use of such older bodies allowed the Lord of the

Radch to walk unprotected, without any sort of entourage, when she wished, without much risk.

She wore not the jeweled coat and trousers of the Radchaai, nor the coverall or trousers and shirt a Shis'urnan Tanmind would wear, but instead the Orsian lungi, shirtless.

As soon as I saw her, I messaged Lieutenant Awn, who came as quickly as she could to the temple, and arrived while the head priest was prostrating herself in the plaza before the Lord of the Radch.

Lieutenant Awn hesitated. Most Radchaai were never in the personal presence of Anaander Mianaai in such circumstances. Of course she was always present during annexations, but the sheer number of troops compared to the number of bodies the Lord of the Radch sent made it unlikely one would run into her by chance. And any citizen can travel to one of the provincial palaces and ask for an audience—for a request, for an appeal in a legal case, for whatever reason—but in such a case, an ordinary citizen is briefed beforehand on how to conduct herself. Perhaps someone like Lieutenant Skaaiat would know how to draw Anaander Mianaai's attention to herself without breaching propriety, but Lieutenant Awn did not.

"My lord," Lieutenant Awn said, heart speeding with fear, and knelt.

Anaander Mianaai turned to her, eyebrow raised.

"I beg my lord's pardon," said Lieutenant Awn. She was slightly dizzy, either from the weight of her uniform in the heat, or from nerves. "I must speak with you."

The eyebrow rose farther. "Lieutenant Awn," she said, "yes?"

"Yes, my lord."

"This evening I attend the vigil in the temple of Ikkt. I'll speak to you in the morning."

It took Lieutenant Awn a few moments to digest this. "My lord, a moment only. I don't think that's a good idea."

The Lord of the Radch tilted her head inquisitively. "I understood you had this area under control."

"Yes, lord, it's just..." Lieutenant Awn stopped, panicked, at a loss for words for a second. "Relations between the upper and lower city just now..." She halted again.

"Concern yourself with your own job," said Anaander Mianaai. "And I will concern myself with mine." She turned away from Lieutenant Awn.

A public slight. An inexplicable one—there was no reason the Lord of the Radch could not have turned aside for a few urgent words with the officer who was chief of local security. And Lieutenant Awn had done nothing to deserve such a slight. At first I thought that was the only reason for the distress I read coming from Lieutenant Awn. The matter of the guns could be communicated in the morning just as well as now, and there seemed no other difficulty. But as the Lord of the Radch had walked through the upper city, word of Anaander Mianaai's presence had spread, as of course it would, and the residents of the upper city had come out of their houses and begun gathering on the northern edge of the Fore-Temple water to watch the Lord of the Radch, dressed like an Orsian, stand in front of the temple of Ikkt with the Divine. And listening to the mutterings of the watching Tanmind, I realized that at this particular instant the guns were only a secondary concern.

The Tanmind residents of the upper city were wealthy, well-fed, the owners of shops and farms and tamarind orchards. Even in the precarious months following the annexation, when supplies had been scarce and food expensive, they had managed to keep their families fed. When Jen

Shinnan had said, a few evenings earlier, that no one here had starved, she had likely believed that to be true. She had not, nor had anyone she knew well, nearly all of them wealthy Tanmind. As much as they complained, they had come out of the annexation relatively comfortably. And their children did well when they took the aptitudes, and would continue to do so, as Lieutenant Skaaiat had said.

And yet these same people, when they saw the Lord of the Radch walk straight through the upper city to the temple of Ikkt, concluded that this gesture of respect to the Orsians was a calculated insult to them. This was clear in their expressions, in their indignant exclamations. I had not foreseen it. Perhaps the Lord of the Radch had not foreseen it. But Lieutenant Awn had realized it would happen, when she saw the Divine on the ground in front of the Lord of the Radch.

I left the plaza, and some of the upper city streets, and went to where the Tanmind were standing, a half-dozen of me. I didn't draw any weapons, didn't make any threats. I said, merely, to anyone near me, "Go home, citizens."

Most turned away and left, and if their expressions weren't pleasant, they offered no actual protest. Others took longer to leave, testing my authority, perhaps, though not far—anyone with the stomach to do such a thing had been shot sometime in the last five years, or at least had learned to restrain such a near-suicidal impulse.

The Divine, rising to escort Anaander Mianaai into the temple, cast an unreadable look at Lieutenant Awn, where she still knelt on the plaza stones. The Lord of the Radch did not even glance at her.

7

"And then," Strigan said as we ate, latest in a long list of grievances against the Radchaai, "there's the treaty with the Presger."

Seivarden lay still, eyes closed, breathing even, blood caked on her lip and chin, spattered on the front of her coat. Across her nose and forehead lay a corrective.

"You resent the treaty?" I asked. "You'd prefer the Presger felt free to do as they always have done?" The Presger didn't care if a species was sentient or not, conscious or not, intelligent or not. The word they used—or the concept, at any rate, as I understood they didn't speak in words—was usually translated as *significance*. And only the Presger were *significant*. All other beings were their rightful prey, property, or playthings. Mostly they just didn't care about humans, but some of them liked to stop ships and pull them—and their contents—apart.

"I'd prefer the Radch not make binding promises on behalf of all humanity," Strigan answered. "Not dictate policy for every single human government and then tell us we're supposed to be grateful."

"The Presger don't recognize such divisions. It was all or none."

"It was the Radch extending control yet another way, one cheaper and easier than outright conquest."

"It might surprise you to learn that some high-ranking Radchaai dislike the treaty as much as you do."

Strigan raised an eyebrow, set down her cup of stinking fermented milk. "Somehow I doubt I'd find these high-ranking Radchaai sympathetic." Her tone was bitter, slightly sarcastic.

"No," I answered. "I don't think you'd like them much. They certainly wouldn't have much use for you."

She blinked and looked intently at my face, as though trying to read something from my expression. Then she shook her head and made a dismissing gesture. "Do tell."

"When one is the agent of order and civilization in the universe, one doesn't stoop to negotiate. Especially with nonhumans." Which included quite a number of people who considered themselves human, but that was a topic best left undiscussed just now. "Why make a treaty with such an implacable enemy? Destroy them and be done."

"Could you?" Strigan asked, incredulous. "Could you have destroyed the Presger?"

"No."

She folded her arms, leaned back in her chair. "So why any debate at all?"

"I would think it was obvious," I answered. "Some find it difficult to admit the Radch might be fallible, or that its power might have limits."

Strigan glanced across the room, toward Seivarden. "But this is meaningless. *Debate*. There's no real debate possible."

"Certainly," I agreed. "You're the expert."

"Oh ho!" she exclaimed, sitting straighter. "I've made you angry."

I was sure I hadn't changed my expression. "I don't think you've ever been to the Radch. I don't think you know many Radchaai, not personally. Not well. You look at it from the outside, and you see conformity and brainwashing." Rank on rank of identical silver-armored soldiers, with no wills of their own, no minds of their own. "And it's true the lowest Radchaai thinks herself immeasurably superior to any non-citizen. What people like Seivarden think of themselves is past bearing." Strigan made a brief, amused snort. "But they are people, and they do have different opinions about things."

"Opinions that don't matter. Anaander Mianaai declares what will be, and that's how it is."

That was a more complicated issue than she realized, I was certain. "Which only adds to their frustration. Imagine. Imagine your whole life aimed at conquest, at the spread of Radchaai space. *You* see murder and destruction on an unimaginable scale, but they see the spread of civilization, of Justice and Propriety, of Benefit for the universe. The death and destruction, these are unavoidable by-products of this one, supreme good."

"I don't think I can muster much sympathy for their perspective."

"I don't ask it. Only stand there a moment, and look. Not only your life, but the lives of all your house, and your ancestors for a thousand years or more before you, are invested in this idea, these actions. Amaat wills it. God wills it, the universe itself wills all this. And then one day someone tells you maybe you were mistaken. And your life won't be what you imagined it to be."

"Happens to people all the time," said Strigan, rising from her seat. "Except most of us don't delude ourselves that we ever had great destinies."

"The exception is not an insignificant one," I pointed out.

"And you?" She stood beside the chair, her cup and bowl in her hands. "You're certainly Radchaai. Your accent, when you speak Radchaai"—we were speaking her own native language—"sounds like you're from the Gerentate. But you have almost no accent right now. You might just be very good with languages—inhumanly good, I might even say—" She paused. "The gender thing is a giveaway, though. Only a Radchaai would misgender people the way you do."

I'd guessed wrong. "I can't see under your clothes. And even if I could, that's not always a reliable indicator."

She blinked, hesitated a moment as though what I'd said made no sense to her. "I used to wonder how Radchaai reproduced, if they were all the same gender."

"They're not. And they reproduce like anyone else." Strigan raised one skeptical eyebrow. "They go to the medic," I continued, "and have their contraceptive implants deactivated. Or they use a tank. Or they have surgery so they can carry a pregnancy. Or they hire someone to carry it."

None of it was very different from what any other kind of people did, but Strigan seemed slightly scandalized. "You're *certainly* Radchaai. And certainly *very* familiar with Captain Seivarden, but you're not *like* him. I wondered from the start if you were an ancillary, but I don't see much in the way of implants. Who are you?"

She would have to look a good deal closer than she already had to see evidence of what I was—to a casual observer I looked as though I had one or two communications and optical implants, the sort of thing millions of people got as a matter of course, Radchaai or not. And during the last twenty years I'd found ways of concealing the specifics of what I had.

I picked up my own dishes, rose. "I'm Breq, from the Gerentate." Strigan snorted, disbelieving. The Gerentate was far enough from where I'd been for the last nineteen years to conceal any small mistakes I might make.

"Just a tourist," Strigan observed, in a tone that made it clear she didn't believe me at all.

"Yes," I agreed.

"So what's the interest in..." She gestured again at Seivarden, still sleeping, breathing slow and even. "Just a stray animal that needed rescuing?"

I didn't answer. I didn't know the answer, truthfully.

"I've met people who collect strays. I don't think you're one of them. There's something...something cold about you. Something edged. You're far more self-possessed than any tourist I've ever seen." And of course I knew she had the gun, which no one but herself and Anaander Mianaai should have known existed. But she couldn't say that without admitting she had it. "There's no way in seventeen hells you're a Gerentate tourist. *What are you?*"

"If I told you it would spoil your fun," I said.

Strigan opened her mouth to say something—possibly something angry, to judge from her expression—when an alarm tone sounded. "Visitors," she said instead.

By the time we got our coats on, and got out the two doors, a crawler had made a ragged path up to the house, dragging a white trench across the moss-tinged snow, its half-spinning halt missing my flier by centimeters.

The door popped open and a Nilter slid out, shorter than many I had met, bundled in a scarlet coat embroidered in bright blue and a screaming shade of yellow, but overlaid with dark stains—snowmoss, and blood. The person halted a moment, and then saw us standing at the entrance to the house.

"Doctor!" she called. "Help!"

Before she was done speaking, Strigan was striding across the snow. I followed.

On closer inspection I saw the driver was only a child, barely fourteen. In the passenger seat lay sprawled an adult, unconscious, clothes torn nearly to shreds, in places all the way through every layer. Blood soaked the cloth, and the seat. Her right leg was missing below the knee, and her left foot.

Among the three of us we got the injured person into the house, into the infirmary. "What happened?" Strigan asked as she removed bloody fragments of coat.

"Ice devil," said the girl. "We didn't see it!" Tears welled in her eyes, but didn't fall. She swallowed hard.

Strigan appraised the makeshift tourniquets the girl had obviously applied. "You did everything you could," she told the girl. She nodded toward the door to the main room. "I'll take it from here."

We left the infirmary, the girl apparently not even aware of my presence, or Seivarden's, where she still lay on her pallet. She stood for a few seconds in the middle of the room, uncertain, seeming paralyzed, and then she sank down on a bench.

I brought her a cup of fermented milk and she started, as though I had suddenly appeared from nowhere. "Are you injured?" I asked her. No misgendering this time—I had already heard Strigan use the feminine pronoun.

"I..." She stopped, looking at the cup of milk as though it might bite her. "No, not...a little." She seemed on the verge of collapse. She might well be. By Radchaai standards she was still a child, but she had seen this adult injured—was she a parent, a cousin, a neighbor?—and had the presence of mind to render some small bits of first aid, get her into a crawler, and come here. Small wonder if she was about to fall to pieces now.

"What happened to the ice devil?" I asked.

"I don't know." She looked up at me, from the milk, still not taking it. "I kicked it. I stabbed it with my knife. It went away. I don't know."

It took a few minutes for me to get the information out of her, that she'd left messages for the others at her family's camp but that no one had been near enough to help, or was near enough to be here terribly soon. While we were talking she seemed to collect herself, at least slightly, at least enough to take the milk I offered and drink it.

Within a few minutes she was sweating, and she removed both her coats and laid them on the bench beside her, and then sat, quiet and awkward. I knew of nothing that might relieve her distress. "Do you know any songs?" I asked her.

She blinked, startled. "I'm not a singer," she said.

It might have been a language issue. I hadn't paid much attention to customs in this part of this world, but I was fairly sure there was no division between songs anyone might sing and songs that were, usually for religious reasons, only sung by specialists—not in the cities near the equator. Maybe it was different this far south. "Excuse me," I said, "I must have used the wrong word. What do you call it when you're working or playing, or trying to get a baby to sleep? Or just…"

"Oh!" Comprehension animated her, for just a moment. "You mean *songs*!"

I smiled encouragingly, but she lapsed into silence again. "Try not to worry too much," I said. "The doctor is very good at what she does. And sometimes you just have to leave things to the gods."

She curled her lower lip inward and bit it. "I don't believe in any god," she said, with a slight vehemence.

"Still. Things will happen as they happen." She gestured agreement, perfunctory. "Do you play counters?" I asked. Maybe she could show me the game Strigan's board was meant for, though I doubted it was from Nilt.

"No." And with that, I had exhausted what small means I might have had to amuse or distract her.

After ten minutes of silence she said, "I have a Tiktik set."

"What's Tiktik?"

Her eyes widened, round in her round, pale face. "How can you not know what Tiktik is? You must be from very far away!" I acknowledged that I was, and she answered, "It's a game. It's mostly a game for children." Her tone implied she wasn't a child, but I'd best not ask why she was carrying a child's game set. "You've really never played Tiktik?"

"Never. Where I come from we mostly play counters, and cards, and dice. But even those are different, in different places."

She pondered that a moment. "I can teach you," she said finally. "It's easy."

Two hours later, as I was tossing my handful of tiny bov-bone dice, the visitor alarm sounded. The girl looked up, startled. "Someone's here," I said. The door to the infirmary stayed shut, Strigan paying no attention.

"Mama," the girl suggested, hope and relief lending the tiniest tremble to her voice.

"I hope so. I hope it's not another patient." Immediately I realized I shouldn't have suggested it. "I'll go see."

It was Mama, unquestionably. She jumped out of the flier

she had arrived in, and made for the house with a speed I wouldn't have thought possible over the snow. She strode past me without acknowledging my existence in any way, tall for a Nilter and broad, as they all were, bundled in coats, the signs of her relationship to the girl inside clear in the lines of her face. I followed her in.

On seeing the girl, now standing by the abandoned Tiktik board, she said, "Well, then, what?"

A Radchaai parent would have put her arms around her daughter, kissed her, told her how relieved she was her daughter was well, maybe even would have wept. Some Radchaai would have thought this parent cold and affectionless. But I was sure that would have been a mistake. They sat down together on a bench, sides touching, as the girl gave her report, what she knew of the patient's condition, and what had happened out in the snow with the herd, and the ice devil. When she had finished, her mother patted her twice on the knee, briskly, and it was as though she were suddenly a different girl, taller, stronger, now she had, it seemed, not only her mother's strong, comforting presence, but her approval.

I brought them two cups of fermented milk, and Mama's attention snapped to me, but not, I thought, because I was of any interest in particular. "You're not the doctor," she said, bare statement. I could see her attention was still on her daughter; her interest in me stretched only as far as I might be a threat or a help.

"I'm a guest here," I told her. "But the doctor is busy, and I thought you might like something to drink."

Her eyes went to Seivarden, still sleeping, as she had for the last several hours, that black, trembling corrective spread across her forehead, the remains of bruising around her mouth and nose.

"She's from very far away," said the girl. "She didn't know how to play Tiktik!" Her mother's gaze flicked over the set on the floor, the dice, the board and flat, painted stone pieces halted in midcourse. She said nothing, but her expression changed, just slightly. She gave a small, almost imperceptible nod, and took the milk I offered.

Twenty minutes later Seivarden woke, brushed the black corrective off her head, and wiped fretfully at her upper lip, pausing at the flakes of dried blood that rubbed away. She looked at the two Nilters, sitting silent, side by side, on a nearby bench, studiously ignoring both her and me. Neither of them seemed to find it odd that I didn't go to Seivarden's side, or say anything to her. I didn't know if she remembered why I had hit her, or even that I had. Sometimes a blow to the head affects memories of the moments leading up to it. But she must have either remembered or suspected something, because she didn't look at me at all. After fidgeting a few minutes she rose and went to the kitchen and opened a cabinet. She stared for thirty seconds, and then got a bowl, and hard bread to put in it, and water to pour over it, and then stood, staring, waiting for it to soften, saying nothing, looking at no one.

8

At first the people I had sent away from the Fore-Temple water stood whispering in small groups on the street, and then dispersed when I approached, walking my regular rounds. But soon after, everyone disappeared into their houses, clustered together within. For the next few hours the upper city was quiet. Eerily so, and it didn't help that Lieutenant Awn continually asked me what was happening there.

Lieutenant Awn was sure increasing my presence in the upper city would only make the situation worse, so instead she ordered me to stay close to the plaza. If anything happened I would be there, between the upper and lower city. It was largely because of this that when things went to pieces, I was still able to function more or less effectively.

For hours nothing happened. The Lord of the Radch mouthed prayers along with the priests of Ikkt. In the lower city I passed the word that it might be a good idea to stay in tonight, and as a result there were no conversations in the streets, no knots of neighbors congregating on someone's ground floor to watch an entertainment. By dark nearly everyone had retired to an upper floor, and was talking quietly, or looking out over the railings, saying nothing.

Four hours before dawn, things went to pieces. Or, more accurately, *I* went to pieces. The tracker data I had been monitoring cut out, and suddenly all twenty of me were blind, deaf, immobile. Each segment could see only from a single pair of eyes, hear only through a single pair of ears, move only that single body. It took a few bewildered, panicked moments for my segments to realize that each was cut off from the others, each instance of me alone in a single body. Worst of all, in that same instant all data from Lieutenant Awn ceased.

From that moment I was twenty different people, with twenty different sets of observations and memories, and I can only remember what happened by piecing those separate experiences together.

At the moment the blow fell, all twenty segments immediately, without thought, extended my armor, those segments that were dressed not making even the least attempt to modify it to cover any part of my uniforms. In the house eight sleeping segments woke instantly, and once I had recovered my composure they rushed to where Lieutenant Awn lay trying to sleep. Two of those segments, Seventeen and Four, seeing Lieutenant Awn seemingly well, and several other segments around her, went to the house console to check communications status—the console wasn't working.

"Communications are out," my Seventeen segment called, voice distorted by the smooth, silver armor.

"Not possible," said Four, and Seventeen didn't answer, because no answer was necessary, given the actuality.

Some of my segments in the upper city actually turned toward the Fore-Temple water before realizing I'd best stay where I was. Every single segment in the plaza and the temple turned toward the house. One of me took off running to be sure of Lieutenant Awn, and two said, at once, "The upper city!" and another two, "The storm siren!" and for two confused seconds the pieces of me tried to decide what to do next. Segment Nine ran into the temple residence and woke the priest sleeping by the storm siren, who tripped it.

Just before the siren blew, Jen Shinnan ran out of her house in the upper city shouting, "Murder! Murder!" Lights came on in the houses around her, but further noise was drowned out by the shrieking of the siren. My nearest segment was four streets away.

All around the lower city, storm shutters rattled down. The priests in the temple ceased their prayers, and the head priest looked at me, but I had no information for her, and gestured my helplessness. "My communications are cut off, Divine," said that segment. The head priest blinked, uncomprehending. Speech was useless while the siren blew.

The Lord of the Radch hadn't reacted at the moment I had fragmented, though she was connected to the rest of herself in much the same way I ordinarily was. Her apparent lack of surprise was strange enough for my segment nearest her to notice it. But it might have been no more than self-possession; the siren elicited no more than an upward glance and a raised eyebrow. Then she stood and walked out onto the plaza.

It was the third worst thing that has ever happened to me. I had lost all sense of *Justice of Toren* overhead, all sense of myself. I had shattered into twenty fragments that could barely communicate with each other.

Just before the siren had blown, Lieutenant Awn had sent a segment to the temple, with orders to sound the alarm. Now that segment came running into the plaza, where it stood, hesitating, looking at the rest of itself, visible but *not there* as far as my sense of myself was concerned.

The siren stopped. The lower city was silent, the only sound was my footsteps, and my armor-filtered voices, trying to talk to myself, to get organized so I could function at least in some small way.

The Lord of the Radch raised one graying eyebrow. "Where is Lieutenant Awn?"

That was, of course, the question uppermost in the minds of all my segments that didn't already know, but now the one of me who had arrived with the order from Lieutenant Awn had something it knew it could do. "Lieutenant Awn is on her way, my lord," it said, and ten seconds later Lieutenant Awn and most of the rest of me that had been in the house arrived, rushing into the plaza.

"I thought you had this area under control." Anaander Mianaai didn't look at Lieutenant Awn as she spoke, but the direction of her words was clear.

"So did I." And then Lieutenant Awn remembered where she was, and to whom she was speaking. "My lord. Begging your pardon." Each of me had to restrain itself from turning entirely to watch Lieutenant Awn, to be sure she was really *there*, because I couldn't sense her otherwise. A few whispers sorted out which of my segments would keep close to her, and the rest would have to trust that.

My Ten segment came around the Fore-Temple water at a dead run. "Trouble in the upper city!" it called, and came to a halt in front of Lieutenant Awn, where I cleared the path for myself. "People are gathering at Jen Shinnan's house, they're angry, they're talking about murder, and getting justice."

"*Murder.* Oh, *fuck!*"

All the segments near Lieutenant Awn said, in unison, "Language, Lieutenant!" Anaander Mianaai turned a disbelieving look on me, but said nothing.

"Oh, *fuck!*" Lieutenant Awn repeated.

"Are you," asked Anaander Mianaai, calm and deliberate, "going to do anything except swear?"

Lieutenant Awn froze for half a second, then looked around, across the water, toward the lower city, at the temple. "Who's here? Count!" And when we had done so, "One through Seven, out here. The rest, with me." I followed her into the temple, leaving Anaander Mianaai standing in the plaza.

The priests stood near the dais, watching us approach. "Divine," said Lieutenant Awn.

"Lieutenant," said the head priest.

"There's a mob bent on violence headed here from the upper city. I'm guessing we have five minutes. They can't do much damage with the storm shutters down, I'd like to bring them in here, keep them from doing anything drastic."

"Bring them in here," the head priest repeated, doubtfully.

"Everything else is dark and shut. The big doors are open, it's the most obvious place to come, when most of them are in here we close the doors and One Esk surrounds them. We could just shut the temple doors and let them try their luck with the shutters on the houses, but I don't really want to find out how hard those are to breach. If," she added, seeing Anaander Mianaai come into the temple, walking slowly, as though nothing unusual were happening, "my lord permits."

The Lord of the Radch gestured a silent assent.

The head priest clearly didn't like the suggestion, but she agreed. By now my segments on the plaza were seeing hand lights sporadically visible in the nearest upper-city streets.

Within moments Lieutenant Awn had me behind the large temple doors, ready to close them on her signal, and a few of me dispatched to the streets around the plaza to help herd Tanmind toward the temple. The rest of me stood in the shadows around the perimeter inside the temple itself, and the priests returned to their prayers, their backs to the wide and inviting entrance.

More than a hundred Tanmind came down from the upper city. Most of them did precisely as we wished, and rushed in a swirling, shouting mass into the temple, except for twenty-three, a dozen of whom veered off down a dark, empty avenue. The other eleven, who had already been trailing the larger group, saw one segment of me standing quiet nearby, and thought better of their actions. They stopped, muttered among themselves for a moment, watching the mass of Tanmind run into the temple, the others rushing, shouting, down the street. They watched me close the temple doors, the segments posted there not uniformed, covered only with the silver of my own generated armor, and maybe it reminded them of the annexation. Several of them swore, and they turned and ran back to the upper city.

Eighty-three Tanmind had run into the temple; their angry voices echoed and reechoed, magnified. At the sound of the doors slamming closed, they turned and tried to rush back the way they had come, but I had surrounded them, my guns drawn and aimed at whoever was nearest each segment.

"Citizens!" shouted Lieutenant Awn, but she didn't have the trick of making herself heard.

"Citizens!" the various fragments of me shouted, my own voices echoing and then dying down. Along with the Tanmind's tumult: Jen Shinnan, and Jen Taa, and a few others I knew were friends or relations of theirs, shushed those near

116

them, urged them to calm themselves, to consider that the Lord of the Radch herself was here, and they could speak directly to her.

"Citizens!" Lieutenant Awn shouted again. "Have you lost your minds? What are you doing?"

"Murder!" shouted Jen Shinnan, who was at the front of the crowd, shouting over my head at Lieutenant Awn where she stood behind me, beside the Lord of the Radch and the Divine. The junior priests stood huddled together, seemingly frozen. The Tanmind voices grumbled, echoing, in support of Jen Shinnan. "We won't get justice from you so we'll take it ourselves!" Jen Shinnan cried. The grumbling from the crowd rolled around the stone walls of the temple.

"Explain yourself, citizen," said Anaander Mianaai, voice pitched to sound above the noise.

The Tanmind hushed each other for five seconds, and then, "My lord," said Jen Shinnan. Her respectful tone sounded almost sincere. "My young niece has been staying in my house for the past week. She was harassed and threatened by Orsians when she came to the lower city, which I reported to Lieutenant Awn, but nothing was done. This evening I found her room empty, the window broken, blood everywhere! What am I to conclude? The Orsians have always resented us! Now they mean to kill us all, is it any wonder we should defend ourselves?"

Anaander Mianaai turned to Lieutenant Awn. "Was this reported?"

"It was, my lord," said Lieutenant Awn. "I investigated and found that the young person in question had never left sight of *Justice of Toren* One Esk, who reported that she had spent all her time in the lower city alone. The only words that passed between her and anyone else were routine business transactions. She was not harassed or threatened at any time."

"You see!" cried Jen Shinnan. "You see why we are compelled to take justice into our own hands!"

"And what leads you to believe all your lives are threatened?" asked Anaander Mianaai.

"My lord," said Jen Shinnan, "Lieutenant Awn would have you believe everyone in the lower city is loyal and law-abiding, but we know from experience that the Orsians are anything but paragons of virtue. The fishermen go out on the water at night, unseen. Sources..." She hesitated, just a moment, whether because of the gun pointed directly at her, or Anaander Mianaai's continued impassivity, or something else, I couldn't tell. But it seemed to me something had amused her. Then she recovered her composure. "Sources I prefer not to name have seen the boatmen of the lower city depositing weapons in caches in the lake. What would those be for, except to finally take their revenge on us, who they believe have mistreated them? And how could those guns have come here without Lieutenant Awn's collusion?"

Anaander Mianaai turned her dark face toward Lieutenant Awn and raised one grayed eyebrow. "Do you have an answer for that, Lieutenant Awn?"

Something about the question, or the way it was asked, troubled all the segments that heard it. And Jen Shinnan actually smiled. She had *expected* the Lord of the Radch to turn on Lieutenant Awn, and was pleased by it.

"I do have an answer, my lord," said Lieutenant Awn. "Some nights ago, a local fisherman reported to me that she had found a cache of weapons under the lake. I removed them and took them to my house, and upon searching, discovered two more caches, which I also removed. I had intended to search further this evening, but events have, as you see, prevented me. My report is written but not yet sent, because I, too, wondered how the guns could have come here without my knowledge."

Perhaps it was only because of Jen Shinnan's smile, and the oddly accusatory questions from Anaander Mianaai—and the slight earlier, in the temple plaza—but in the charged air of the temple, the echoes of Lieutenant Awn's words themselves felt like an accusation.

"I have also wondered," Lieutenant Awn said, in the silence after those echoes died away, "why the young person in question would falsely accuse residents of the lower city of harassing her, when they assuredly did not. I am quite certain no one from the lower city has harmed her."

"Someone has!" shouted a voice in the crowd, and mutterings of assent started, and grew and echoed around the vast stone space.

"What time did you last see your cousin?" asked Lieutenant Awn.

"Three hours ago," said Jen Shinnan. "She told us good night, and went to her room."

Lieutenant Awn addressed the segment of me that was nearest her. "One Esk, did anyone cross from the lower city to the upper in the last three hours?"

The segment that answered—Thirteen—knew I should be careful about my answer, which by necessity everyone would hear. "No. No one crossed in either direction. Though I can't be certain about the last fifteen minutes."

"Someone might have come earlier," Jen Shinnan pointed out.

"In that case," answered Lieutenant Awn, "they're still in the upper city, and you ought to be looking for them there."

"The guns..." Jen Shinnan began.

"Are no danger to you. They're locked under the top floor of my house, and One Esk has disabled most of them by now."

Jen Shinnan cast an odd, appealing look to Anaander Mianaai, who had stood silent and impassive through this exchange. "But..."

"Lieutenant Awn," said the Lord of the Radch. "A word." She gestured aside, and Lieutenant Awn followed her to a spot fifteen meters off. One of my segments followed, which Mianaai ignored. "Lieutenant," she said in a quiet voice. "Tell me what you think is happening."

Lieutenant Awn swallowed, took a breath. "My lord. I'm certain no one from the lower city has harmed the young person in question. I am also certain the guns were not cached by anyone from the lower city. And the weapons were all ones which had been confiscated during the annexation. This can only originate from a very high level. That's why I haven't filed the report. I was hoping to speak directly to you about this when you arrived, but never had the opportunity."

"You were afraid if you reported it through regular channels, whoever did this would realize their plan had been detected, and cover their tracks."

"Yes, my lord. When I heard you were coming, my lord, I planned to speak to you about it immediately."

"*Justice of Toren.*" The Lord of the Radch addressed my segment without looking at me. "Is this true?"

"Entirely, my lord," I answered. The junior priests still huddled, the head priest standing apart from them, looking at Lieutenant Awn and the Lord of the Radch where they conferred, an expression on her face that I couldn't read.

"So," said Anaander Mianaai. "What's your assessment of this situation?"

Lieutenant Awn blinked in astonishment. "I...it looks

very much to me as though Jen Shinnan is involved with the weapons. How would she have known of their existence otherwise?"

"And this murdered young person?"

"If she *is* murdered, no one from the lower city did it. But can they have killed her themselves to have an excuse to..." Lieutenant Awn stopped, appalled.

"An excuse to come down to the lower city and murder innocent citizens in their beds. And then use the existence of the weapons caches to support their assertion that they were only acting in self-defense and you had refused to do your duty and protect them." She cast a glance at the Tanmind, ringed by my still-armed and -silver-armored segments. "Well. We can concern ourselves with details later. Right now we need to deal with these people."

"My lord," acknowledged Lieutenant Awn, with a slight bow.

"Shoot them."

To noncitizens, who only ever see Radchaai in melodramatic entertainments, who know nothing of the Radch besides ancillaries and annexations and what they think of as brainwashing, such an order might be appalling, but hardly surprising. But the idea of shooting citizens was, in fact, extremely shocking and upsetting. What, after all, was the point of civilization if not the well-being of citizens? And these people were citizens now.

Lieutenant Awn froze, for two seconds. "M...my lord?"

Anaander Mianaai's voice, which had been dispassionate, perhaps slightly stern, turned chill and severe. "Are you refusing an order, Lieutenant?"

"No, my lord, only...they're *citizens*. And we're in a temple. And we have them under control, and I've sent *Justice of Toren* One Esk to the next division to ask for reinforcements.

121

Justice of Ente Seven Issa should be here in an hour, perhaps two, and we can arrest the Tanmind and assign them to re-education very easily, since you're here."

"Are you," asked Anaander Mianaai, slowly and clearly, "refusing an order?"

Jen Shinnan's amusement, her willingness—even eagerness—to speak to the Lord of the Radch, it fell into a pattern for my listening segment. Someone very high up had made those guns available, had known how to cut off communications. No one was higher up than Anaander Mianaai. But it made no sense. Jen Shinnan's motivation was obvious, but how could the Lord of the Radch possibly profit by it?

Lieutenant Awn was likely having the same thoughts. I could read her distress in the tension of her jaw, the stiff set of her shoulders. Still, it seemed unreal, because the external signs were all I could see. "I won't refuse an order, my lord," she said after five seconds. "May I protest it?"

"I believe you already have," said Anaander Mianaai, coldly. "Now shoot them."

Lieutenant Awn turned. I thought she was the slightest bit shaky as she walked toward the surrounded Tanmind.

"*Justice of Toren*," Mianaai said, and the segment of me that had been about to follow Lieutenant Awn stopped. "When was the last time I visited you?"

I remembered the last time the Lord of the Radch had boarded *Justice of Toren* very clearly. It had been an unusual visit—unannounced, four older bodies with no entourage. She had mostly stayed in her quarters talking to me—*Justice of Toren*–me, not One Esk–me, but she had asked One Esk to sing for her. I had obliged with a Valskaayan piece. It had been ninety-four years, two months, two weeks, and six days before, shortly after the annexation of Valskaay. I opened my mouth to say so, but instead heard myself say, "Two hundred three years, four months, one week, and one day ago, my lord."

"Hmm," said Anaander Mianaai, but she said nothing else.

Lieutenant Awn approached me, where I ringed the Tanmind. She stood there, behind a segment, for three and a half seconds, saying nothing.

Her distress must have been obvious to more than just me. Jen Shinnan, seeing her stand there silent and unhappy, smiled. Almost triumphantly. "Well?"

"One Esk," Lieutenant Awn said, clearly dreading the finish of her sentence. Jen Shinnan's smile grew slightly larger. Expecting Lieutenant Awn to send the Tanmind home, no doubt. Expecting, in the fullness of time, Lieutenant Awn's dismissal and the decline of the lower city's influence. "I didn't want this," Lieutenant Awn said to her, quietly, "but I have a direct order." She raised her voice. "One Esk. Shoot them."

Jen Shinnan's smile disappeared, replaced by horror, and, I thought, betrayal, and she looked, plainly, directly, toward Anaander Mianaai. Who stood impassive. The other Tanmind clamored, crying out in fear and protest.

All my segments hesitated. The order made no sense. Whatever they had done, these were citizens, and I had them under control. But Lieutenant Awn said, loud and harsh, "Fire!" and I did. Within three seconds all the Tanmind were dead.

No one in the temple at that moment was young enough to be surprised at what had happened, though perhaps the several years since I'd executed anyone had lent the memories some distance, maybe even engendered some confidence that

123

citizenship meant an end to such things. The junior priests stood where they had since this had begun, not moving, saying nothing. The head priest wept openly, soundlessly.

"I think," said Anaander Mianaai into the vast silence that surrounded us, once the echoes of gunfire had died down, "there won't be any more trouble from the Tanmind here."

Lieutenant Awn's mouth and throat twitched slightly, as though she were about to speak, but she didn't. Instead she walked forward, around the bodies, tapping four of my segments on the shoulder as she passed and gesturing to them to follow. I realized she simply could not bring herself to speak. Or perhaps she feared what would come out of her mouth if she attempted it. Having only visual data from her was frustrating.

"Where are you going, Lieutenant?" asked the Lord of the Radch.

Her back to Mianaai, Lieutenant Awn opened her mouth, and then closed it again. Closed her eyes, took a breath. "With my lord's permission, I intend to discover whatever it is that's blocking communications." Anaander Mianaai didn't answer, and Lieutenant Awn turned to my nearest segment.

"Jen Shinnan's house," that segment said, since it was clear Lieutenant Awn was still in emotional distress. "I'll look for the young person as well."

Just before sunrise I found the device there. The instant I disabled it I was myself again—minus one missing segment. I saw the silent, barely twilit streets of the upper and lower city, the temple empty of anyone but myself and eighty-three silent, staring corpses. Lieutenant Awn's grief and distress and shame were suddenly clear and visible, to my combined relief and discomfort. And with a moment's willing it, the tracker signals of all the people in Ors flared into life in my vision, including the people who had died and still lay in the temple of Ikkt; my missing segment in an upper city street, neck broken; and Jen Shinnan's niece—in the mud at the bottom of the northern edge of the Fore-Temple water.

9

Strigan came out of the infirmary, undercoat bloody, and the girl and her mother, who had been talking quietly in a language I didn't understand, fell silent and looked expectantly to her.

"I've done what I can," Strigan said, with no preamble. "He's out of danger. You'll need to take him to Therrod to have the limbs regrown, but I've done some of the prep work, and they should grow back fairly easily."

"Two weeks," said the Nilter woman, impassive. As though it wasn't the first time something like this had happened.

"Can't be helped," said Strigan, answering something I hadn't heard or understood. "Maybe someone's got a few extra hands they can spare."

"I'll call some cousins."

"You do that," said Strigan. "You can see him now if you like, but he's asleep."

"When can we move him?" the woman asked.

"Now, if you like," answered Strigan. "The sooner the better, I suppose."

The woman made an affirmative gesture, and she and the girl rose and went into the infirmary without another word.

Not long after, we brought the injured person out to the girl's flier and saw them off, and trudged back into the house and shed our outer coats. Seivarden had by now returned to her pallet on the floor and sat, knees drawn up, arms tight around her legs as if she were holding them back and it took work.

Strigan looked at me, an odd expression on her face, one I couldn't read. "She's a good kid."

"Yes."

"She'll get a good name out of this. A good story to go with it."

I had learned the lingua franca that I thought would be most useful here, and done the sort of cursory research one needs to navigate unfamiliar places, but I knew almost nothing about the people who herded bov on this part of the planet. "Is it an adulthood thing?" I guessed.

"Sort of. Yes." She went to a cabinet, pulled out a cup and a bowl. Her movements were quick and steady, but I got somehow an impression of exhaustion. From the set of her shoulders perhaps. "I didn't think you'd be much interested in children. Aside from killing them, I mean."

I refused the bait. "She let me know she wasn't a child. Even if she did have a Tiktik set."

Strigan sat at her small table. "You played two hours straight."

"There wasn't much else to do."

Strigan laughed, short and bitter. Then she gestured toward Seivarden, who seemed to be ignoring us. She couldn't understand us anyway, we weren't speaking Radchaai. "I don't feel sorry for him. It's just that I'm a doctor."

"You said that."

"I don't think you feel sorry for him either."

"I don't."

"You don't make anything easy, do you?" Strigan's voice was half-angry. Exasperated.

"It depends."

She shook her head slightly, as though she hadn't heard quite clearly. "I've seen worse. But he needs medical attention."

"You don't intend to give it," I said. Not asking.

"I'm still figuring you out," Strigan said, as though her statement was related to mine, though I was sure it wasn't. "As a matter of fact, I'm considering giving him something more to keep him calm." I didn't answer. "You disapprove." It wasn't a question. "I don't feel sorry for him."

"You keep saying that."

"He lost his ship." Very likely her interest in her Garseddai artifacts had led her to learn what she could about the events that had led to the destruction of Garsedd. "Bad enough," Strigan continued, "but Radchaai ships aren't just ships, are they? And his crew. It was a thousand years ago for us, but for him—one moment everything is the way it should be, next moment *everything's* gone." With one hand she made a frustrated, ambivalent gesture. "He needs medical attention."

"If he hadn't fled the Radch, he'd have received it."

Strigan cocked one gray eyebrow, sat on a bench. "Translate for me. My Radchaai isn't good enough."

One moment an ancillary had shoved Seivarden into a suspension pod, next she'd found herself freezing and choking as the pod's fluids exited through her mouth and nose, drained away, and she found herself in the sick bay of a patrol ship. When Seivarden described it, I could see her agitation, her anger, barely masked. "Some dingy little Mercy, with a shabby, provincial captain."

"Your face is almost perfectly impassive," Strigan said to me. Not in Radchaai, so Seivarden didn't understand. "But I can see your temperature and heart rate." And probably a few other things, with the medical implants she likely had.

"The ship was human-crewed," I said to Seivarden.

That distressed her further—whether it was anger, or embarrassment, or something else, I couldn't tell. "I didn't realize. Not right away. The captain took me aside and explained."

I translated this for Strigan, and she looked at Seivarden in disbelief, and then at me with speculation. "Is that an easy mistake to make?"

"No," I answered, shortly.

"That was when she finally had to tell me how long it had been," Seivarden said, unaware of anything but her own story.

"And what had happened after," suggested Strigan.

I translated, but Seivarden ignored it, and continued as though neither of us had spoken. "Eventually we put in to this tiny border station. You know the sort of thing, a station administrator who's either in disgrace or a jumped-up nobody, an officious inspector supervisor playing tyrant on the docks, and half a dozen Security whose biggest challenge is chasing chickens out of the tea shop.

"I'd thought the Mercy captain had a terrible accent, but I couldn't understand anyone on the station at all. The station AI had to translate for me, but my implants didn't work. Too antiquated. So I could only talk to it using wall consoles." Which would have made it extremely difficult to hold any sort of conversation. "And even when Station explained, the things people were saying didn't make sense.

"They assigned me an apartment, a room with a cot, hardly large enough to stand up in. Yes, they knew who I said I was, but they had no record of my financial data, and it would be weeks before it could possibly arrive. Maybe longer. Meantime I got the food and shelter any Radchaai was guaranteed. Unless, of course, I wanted to retake the aptitudes so I could get a new assignment. Because they didn't have my aptitudes data and even if they did it was certainly out of date. *Out of date*," she repeated, her voice bitter.

"Did you see a doctor?" Strigan asked. Watching Seivarden's face, I guessed what had finally sent her from Radchaai space. She must have seen a doctor, who had opted to wait and watch. Physical injuries weren't an issue, the medic of whatever Mercy had picked her up would have taken care of those, but psychological or emotional ones—they might resolve on their own, and if they didn't, the doctor would need that aptitudes data to work effectively.

"They said I could send a message to my house lord asking for assistance. But they didn't know who that was." Obviously Seivarden had no intention of talking about the station doctor.

"House lord?" asked Strigan.

"Head of her extended family," I explained. "It sounds very elevated in translation, but it isn't, unless your house is very wealthy or prestigious."

"And hers?"

"Was both."

Strigan didn't miss that. "*Was*."

Seivarden continued as though we hadn't spoken. "But it turned out, Vendaai was gone. My whole house didn't even

exist anymore. Everything, assets and contracts, everything
absorbed by *Geir*!" It had surprised everyone at the time,
some five hundred years ago. The two houses, Geir and
Vendaai, had hated each other. Geir's house lord had taken
malicious advantage of Vendaai's gambling debts, and some
foolish contracts.

"Catch up with current events?" I asked Seivarden.

She ignored my question. "Everything was *gone*. And what
was left, it was like it was *almost* right. But the colors were
wrong, or everything was turned slightly to the left of where
it should be. People would say things and I couldn't understand them at all, or I knew they were real words but my
mind couldn't take them in. Nothing seemed real."

Maybe it had been an answer to my question after all.
"How did you feel about the human soldiers?"

Seivarden frowned, and looked directly at me for the first
time since she'd awoken. I regretted asking the question. It
hadn't really been the question I'd wanted to ask. *What did
you think when you heard about Ime?* But maybe she hadn't.
Or if she had it might have been incomprehensible to her. *Did
anyone come to you whispering about restoring the rightful order of things?* Probably not, considering. "How did you
leave the Radch without permits?" That couldn't have been
easy. It would at the very least have cost money she wouldn't
have had.

Seivarden looked away from me, down and to the left. She
wasn't going to say.

"Everything was wrong," she said after nine seconds of
silence.

"Bad dreams," said Strigan. "Anxiety. Shaking, sometimes."

"Unsteady," I said. Translated it had very little sting, but

131

in Radchaai, for an officer like Seivarden, it said more. Weak, fearful, inadequate to the demands of her position. Fragile. If Seivarden was unsteady, she had never really deserved her assignment, never really been suited to the military, let alone to captain a ship. But of course Seivarden had taken the aptitudes, and the aptitudes had said she was what her house had always assumed she would be: steady, fit to command and conquer. Not prone to doubts or irrational fears.

"You don't know what you're talking about," Seivarden half-sneered, half-snarled. Arms still locked around her knees. "No one in my house is unsteady."

Of course (I thought but did not say), the various cousins who had served a year or so during this annexation or that and retired to take ascetic vows or paint tea sets hadn't done so because they had been unsteady. And the cousins who hadn't tested as anticipated, but surprised their parents with assignments in the minor priesthoods, or the arts—this had not indicated any sort of unsteadiness inherent in the house, no, never. And Seivarden wasn't the least bit afraid or worried about what new assignment a retake of the aptitudes would get her, and what that might say about her steadiness. Of *course* not.

"Unsteady?" asked Strigan, understanding the word, but not its context.

"The unsteady," I explained, "lack a certain strength of character."

"Character!" Strigan's indignation was plain to read.

"Of course." I didn't alter my facial expression, but kept it bland and pleasant, as it had been for most of the past few days. "Lesser citizens break down in the face of enormous difficulties or stress and sometimes require medical attention for it. But some citizens are bred better. They never break down. Though they may take early retirement, or spend a few years pursuing artistic or spiritual interests—prolonged meditation retreats are quite popular. This is how one knows the difference between highly placed families and lesser ones."

"But you Radchaai are so good at brainwashing. Or so I hear."

"Reeducation," I corrected. "If she'd stayed, she'd have gotten help."

"But she couldn't face needing the help to begin with." I said nothing to agree or disagree, though I thought Strigan was right. "How much can...reeducation do?"

"A great deal," I said. "Though much of what you've probably heard is greatly exaggerated. It can't turn you into someone you're not. Not in any useful way."

"Erase memories."

"Suppress them, I think. Add new ones, maybe. You have to know what you're doing or you could damage someone badly."

"No doubt."

Seivarden stared frowning at us, watching us talk, unable to understand what we were saying.

Strigan half-smiled. "*You* aren't a product of reeducation."

"No," I acknowledged.

"It was surgery. Sever a few connections, make a few new ones. Install some implants." She paused a moment, waiting for me to answer, but I didn't. "You pass well enough. Mostly. Your expression, your tone of voice, it's always right but it's always...always studied. Always a performance."

"You think you've solved the puzzle," I guessed.

"*Solved* isn't the right word. But you're a corpse soldier, I'm certain of it. Do you remember anything?"

"Many things," I said, still bland.

"No, I mean from before."

It took me nearly five seconds to understand what she meant. "That person is dead."

Seivarden suddenly, convulsively stood and walked out the inner door and, by the sound of it, through the outer as well.

Strigan watched her go, gave a quick, breathy *hm*, and then turned back to me. "Your sense of who you are has a neurological basis. One small change and you don't believe you exist anymore. But you're still there. I think you're still there. Why the bizarre desire to kill Anaander Mianaai? Why else would you be so angry with *him*?" She tilted her head to indicate the exit, Seivarden outside in the cold with only one coat.

"He'll take the crawler," I warned. The girl and her mother had taken the flier, and left the crawler outside Strigan's house.

"No he won't. I disabled it." I gestured my approval, and Strigan continued, returning to her previous subject. "And the music. I don't suppose you were a singer, not with a voice like yours. But you must have been a musician, before, or loved music."

I considered making the bitter laugh Strigan's guess called for. "No," I said, instead. "Not actually."

"But you *are* a corpse soldier, I'm right about that." I didn't answer. "You escaped somehow or...are you from *his* ship? Captain Seivarden's?"

"*Sword of Nathtas* was destroyed." I had been there, been nearby. Relatively speaking. Seen it happen, nearly enough. "And that was a thousand years ago."

Strigan looked toward the door, back at me. Then she frowned. "No. No, I think you're Ghaonish, and they were only annexed a few centuries ago, weren't they? I shouldn't have forgotten that, it's why you're passing as someone from the Gerentate, isn't it? No, you escaped somehow. *I can bring you back.* I'm sure I can."

"You can kill me, you mean. You can destroy my sense of self and replace it with one you approve of."

Strigan didn't like hearing that, I could see. The outer door opened, and then Seivarden came shivering through the inner. "Put on your outer coat next time," I told her.

"Fuck off." She grabbed a blanket off her pallet and wrapped it around her shoulders, and stood, still shivering.

"Very unbecoming language, citizen," I said.

For a moment she looked as though she might lose her temper. Then she seemed to remember what might happen if she did. "Fuck." She sat on the nearest bench, heavily. "Off."

"Why didn't you leave him where you found him?" asked Strigan.

"I wish I knew." It was another puzzle for her, but not one I had made deliberately. I didn't know myself. Didn't know why I cared if Seivarden froze to death in the storm-swept snow, didn't know why I had brought her with me, didn't know why I cared if she took someone else's crawler and fled, or walked off into the green-stained frozen waste and died.

"And why are you so angry with him?"

That I knew. And truth to tell, it wasn't entirely fair to Seivarden that I was angry. Still, the facts remained what they were, and my anger as well.

"Why do you want to kill Anaander Mianaai?" Seivarden's head turned slightly, her attention hooked by the familiar name.

"It's personal."

"*Personal.*" Strigan's tone was incredulous.

"Yes."

"You're not a person anymore. You've said as much to me. You're equipment. An appendage to a ship's AI." I said nothing, and waited for her to consider her own words. "Is there a ship that's lost its mind? Recently, I mean."

Insane Radchaai ships were a staple of melodrama, inside and outside Radchaai space. Though Radchaai entertainments in that direction were usually historicals. When Anaander Mianaai had taken control of the core of Radch space some few ships had destroyed themselves upon the death or captivity of their captains, and rumor said some others still wandered space in the three thousand years since, half-mad, despairing. "None I know of."

She very likely followed news from the Radch—it was a matter of her own safety, considering what I was sure she was hiding, and what the consequences would be for her if Anaander Mianaai ever discovered that. She had, potentially, all the information she needed to identify me. But after half a minute she gestured doubtfully, disappointed. "You won't just tell me."

I smiled, calm and pleasant. "What fun would that be?"

She laughed, seeming truly amused at my answer. Which I thought a hopeful sign. "So when are you leaving?"

"When you give me the gun."

"I don't know what you're talking about."

A lie. Manifestly a lie. "Your apartment, on Dras Annia Station. It's untouched. Just as you left it, so far as I could tell."

Every one of Strigan's motions became deliberate, just slightly slowed—blinks, breaths. The hand carefully brushing dust from her coat sleeve. "That a fact."

"It cost me a great deal to get in."

"Where *did* a corpse soldier get all that money anyway?"

Strigan asked, still tense, still concealing it. But genuinely curious. Always that.

"Work," I said.

"Lucrative work."

"And dangerous." I had risked my life to get that money.

"The icon?"

"Not unrelated." But I didn't want to talk about that. "What do I need to do, to convince you? Is the money insufficient?" I had more, elsewhere, but saying so would be foolish.

"What did you see in my apartment?" Strigan asked, curiosity and anger in her voice.

"A puzzle. With pieces missing." I had deduced the existence and nature of those pieces correctly, I must have, because here I was, and here was Arilesperas Strigan.

Strigan laughed again. "Like you. Listen." She leaned forward, hands on her thighs. "You can't kill Anaander Mianaai. I wish to all that's good it were possible, but it's not. Even with...even if I had what you think I have you couldn't do it. You told me that twenty-five of these guns were insufficient..."

"Twenty-four," I corrected.

She waved that away. "Were insufficient to keep the Radchaai away from Garsedd. Why do you think *one* would be anything more than a minor irritant?"

She knew better, or she wouldn't have run. Wouldn't have asked the local toughs to take care of me before I got to her.

"And why are you so determined to do such a ridiculous thing? Everyone outside the Radch hates Anaander Mianaai. If by some miracle he died, the celebrations would last a hundred years. But it *won't happen*. It certainly won't happen because of one idiot with a gun. I'm sure you know that. You probably know it far better than I could."

"True."

"Then why?"

Information is power. Information is security. Plans made with imperfect information are fatally flawed, will fail or succeed on the toss of a coin. I had known, when I first knew I would have to find Strigan and obtain the gun from her, that this would be such a moment. If I answered Strigan's question—if I answered it fully, as she would certainly demand—I would be giving her something she could use against me, a weapon. She would almost certainly hurt herself in the process, but that wasn't always much of a deterrent, I knew.

"Sometimes," I began, and then corrected myself. "Quite frequently, someone will learn a little bit about Radchaai religion, and ask, *If everything that happens is the will of Amaat, if nothing can happen that is not already designed by God, why bother to do anything?*"

"Good question."

"Not particularly."

"No? Why bother, then?"

"I am," I said, "as Anaander Mianaai made me. Anaander Mianaai is as she was made. We will both of us do the things we are made to do. The things that are before us to do."

"I doubt very much that Anaander Mianaai made you so that you would kill him."

Any reply would reveal more than I wished, at the moment.

"And I," continued Strigan, after a second and a half of silence, "am made to demand answers. It's just God's will." She made a gesture with her left hand, *not my problem*.

"You admit you have the gun."

"I admit nothing."

I was left with blind chance, a step into unguessable dark,

waiting to live or die on the results of the toss, not knowing what the chances were of any result. My only other choice would be to give up, and how could I give up now? After so long, after so much? And I had risked as much, or more, before now, and gotten this far.

She had to have the gun. *Had to.* But how could I make her give it to me? What would make her choose to give it to me?

"*Tell me,*" Strigan said, watching me intently. No doubt seeing my frustration and doubt through her medical implants, fluctuations of my blood pressure and temperature and respiration. "Tell me why."

I closed my eyes, felt the disorientation of not being able to see through other eyes that I knew I had once had. Opened them again, took a breath to begin, and told her.

10

I had thought that perhaps the morning's temple attendants would (quite understandably) choose to stay home, but one small flower-bearer, awake before the adults in her household, arrived with a handful of pink-petaled weeds and stopped at the edge of the house, startled to see Anaander Mianaai kneeling in front of our small icon of Amaat.

Lieutenant Awn was dressing, on the upper floor. "I can't serve today," she said to me, her voice impassive as her emotions were not. The morning was already warm, and she was sweating.

"You didn't touch any of the bodies," I said as I adjusted her jacket collar, sure of the fact. It was the wrong thing to say.

Four of my segments, two on the northern edge of the Fore-Temple and two standing waist-deep in the lukewarm water and mud, lifted the body of Jen Taa's niece onto the ledge, and carried her to the medic's house.

On the ground floor of Lieutenant Awn's house, I said to the frightened, frozen flower-bearer, "It's all right." There was no sign of the water-bearer, and I was ineligible.

"You'll have to at least bring the water, Lieutenant," I said, above, to Lieutenant Awn. "The flower-bearer is here, but the water-bearer isn't."

For a few moments Lieutenant Awn said nothing, while I finished wiping her face. "Right," she said, and went downstairs and filled the bowl, and brought it to the flower-bearer, where she stood next to me, still frightened, clutching her handful of pink petals. Lieutenant Awn held the water out to her, and she set the flowers down and washed her hands. But before she could pick the flowers up again, Anaander Mianaai turned to look at her, and the child started back and grabbed my gloved hand with her bare one. "You'll have to wash your hands again, citizen," I whispered, and with a bit more encouragement she did so, and picked up the flowers again and performed her part of the morning's ritual correctly, if nervously. No one else came. I was not surprised.

The medic, speaking to herself and not to me, though I stood three meters away from her, said, "Throat cut, obviously, but she was also poisoned." And then, with disgust and contempt, "A child of their own house. These people aren't civilized."

Our one small attendant left, a gift from the Lord of the Radch clutched in one hand—a pin in the shape of a four-petaled flower, each petal holding an enameled image of one of the four Emanations. Anywhere else, a Radchaai who received one would treasure it, and wear it nearly constantly, a badge of having served in the temple with the Lord of the Radch herself. This child would probably toss it in a box and forget about it. When she was out of sight (of Lieutenant Awn and the Lord of the Radch, if not of me) Anaander Mianaai turned to Lieutenant Awn and said, "Aren't those weeds?"

A wave of embarrassment overcame Lieutenant Awn,

mixed a moment later with disappointment, and an intense anger I had never seen in her before. "Not to the children, my lord." She was unable to keep the edge out of her voice completely.

Anaander Mianaai's expression didn't change. "This icon, and this set of omens. They're your personal property, I think. Where are the ones that belong to the temple?"

"Begging my lord's pardon," Lieutenant Awn said, though I knew at this point she meant to do no such thing, and the fact was audible in her tone. "I used the funds for their purchase to supplement the term-end gifts for the temple attendants." She had also used her own money for the same purpose, but she didn't say that.

"I'm sending you back to *Justice of Toren*," said the Lord of the Radch. "Your replacement will be here tomorrow."

Shame. A fresh flare of anger. And despair. "Yes, my lord."

There wasn't much to pack. I could be ready to move in less than an hour. I spent the rest of the day delivering gifts to our temple attendants, who were all home. School had been canceled, and hardly anyone came out onto the streets. "Lieutenant Awn doesn't know," I told each one, "if the new lieutenant will make different appointments, or if she'll give the year-end gifts without your having served a whole year. You should come to the house anyway, her first morning." The adults in each house eyed me silently, not inviting me in, and each time I laid the gift—not the usual pair of gloves, which didn't yet matter much here, but a brightly colored and patterned skirt, and a small box of tamarind sweets. Fresh fruit was customary, but there was no time to obtain any. I left each small stack of gifts in the street, on the edge of the house, and no one moved to take them, or spoke any word to me.

The Divine spent an hour or two behind screens in the temple residence, and then emerged looking entirely unrested, and went into the temple, where she conferred with the junior priests. The bodies had been cleared away. I had offered to clean the blood, not knowing if my doing so would be permissible, but the priests had declined my assistance. "Some of us," said the Divine to me, still staring at the area of floor where the dead had lain, "had forgotten what you are. Now they are reminded."

"I don't think *you* forgot, Divine," I said.

"No." She was silent for two seconds. "Is the lieutenant going to see me before she leaves?"

"Possibly not, Divine," I said. I was at that moment doing what I could to encourage Lieutenant Awn to sleep, something she badly needed to do but was finding difficult.

"It's probably better if she doesn't," the head priest said, bitterly. She looked at me then. "It's unreasonable of me. I know it is. What else could she have done? It's easy for me to say—and I say it—that she could have chosen otherwise."

"She could have, Divine," I acknowledged.

"What is it you Radchaai say?" I wasn't Radchaai, but I didn't correct her, and she continued. "Justice, propriety, and benefit, isn't it? Let every act be just, and proper, and beneficial."

"Yes, Divine."

"Was that just?" Her voice trembled, for just an instant, and I could hear she was on the edge of tears. "Was it proper?"

"I don't know, Divine."

"More to the point, who benefited?"

"No one, Divine, so far as I can see."

"No one? Really? Come, One Esk, don't play the fool with

me." That look of betrayal on Jen Shinnan's face, plainly directed at Anaander Mianaai, had been obvious to everyone there.

Still, I couldn't see what the Lord of the Radch had stood to gain from those deaths. "They would have killed you, Divine," I said. "You, and anyone else they found undefended. Lieutenant Awn did what she could to prevent bloodshed last night. It wasn't her fault she failed."

"It was." Her back was still to me. "God forgive her for it. God forbid that I may ever be faced with such a choice." She made an invocatory gesture. "And you? What would you have done, if the lieutenant had refused, and the Lord of the Radch ordered you to shoot her? Could you have? I thought that armor of yours was impenetrable."

"The Lord of the Radch can force our armor down." But the code Anaander Mianaai would have had to transmit to force down Lieutenant Awn's armor—or mine, or any other Radchaai soldier's—would have to have been delivered over communications that had been blocked at the time. Still. "Speculating about such things does no good, Divine," I said. "It didn't happen."

The head priest turned, and looked intently at me. "You didn't answer the question."

It wasn't an easy question for me to answer. I had been in pieces, and at the time only one segment had even known that such a thing was possible, that for an instant Lieutenant Awn's life had hung, uncertain, on the outcome of that moment. I wasn't entirely sure that segment wouldn't have turned its gun on Anaander Mianaai instead.

It probably wouldn't have. "Divine, I am not a person." If I had shot the Lord of the Radch nothing would have changed, I was sure, except that not only would Lieutenant Awn still be dead, I would be destroyed, Two Esk would take my place, or a new One Esk would be built with segments from *Justice of Toren*'s holds. The ship's AI might find itself in some difficulty, though more likely my action would be blamed on my being cut off. "People often think they would have made the noblest choice, but when they find themselves actually in such a situation, they discover matters aren't quite so simple."

"As I said—God forbid. I will comfort myself with the delusion that you would have shot the Mianaai bastard first."

"Divine!" I cautioned. She could say nothing in my hearing that might not eventually reach the ears of the Lord of the Radch.

"Let her hear. Tell her yourself! *She* instigated what happened last night. Whether the target was us, or the Tanmind, or Lieutenant Awn, I don't know. I have my suspicions which. I'm not a fool."

"Divine," I said. "Whoever instigated last night's events, I don't think things happened the way they wished. I think they wanted open warfare between the upper and lower cities, though I don't understand why. And I think that was prevented when Denz Ay told Lieutenant Awn about the guns."

"I think as you do," said the head priest. "And I think Jen Shinnan knew more, and that was why she died."

"I'm sorry your temple was desecrated, Divine," I said. I wasn't particularly sorry Jen Shinnan was dead, but I didn't say so.

The Divine turned away from me again. "I'm sure you have a lot to do, getting ready to leave. Lieutenant Awn needn't trouble herself calling on me. You can give her my farewells yourself." She walked away from me, not waiting for any acknowledgment.

* * *

Lieutenant Skaaiat arrived for supper, with a bottle of arrack and two Seven Issas. "Your relief won't even reach Kould Ves until midday," she said, breaking the seal on the bottle. Meanwhile the Seven Issas stood stiff and uncomfortable on the ground floor. They had arrived just before I'd restored communications. They'd seen the dead in the temple of Ikkt, had guessed without being told what had happened. And they had only been out of the holds for the last two years. They hadn't seen the annexation itself.

All of Ors, upper and lower, was similarly quiet, similarly tense. When people left their houses they avoided looking at me or speaking to me. Mostly they only went out to visit the temple, where the priests led prayers for the dead. A few Tanmind even came down from the upper city, and stood quietly at the edges of the small crowd. I kept myself in the shadows, not wanting to distract or distress any further.

"Tell me you didn't almost refuse," said Lieutenant Skaaiat, in the house on the upper floor, with Lieutenant Awn, behind screens. They sat on fungal-smelling cushions, facing each other. "I know you, Awn, I swear when I heard what Seven Issa saw when they got to the temple I was afraid I'd hear next that you were dead. Tell me you didn't."

"I didn't," said Lieutenant Awn, miserable and guilty. Her voice bitter. "You can see I didn't."

"I can't see that. Not at all." Lieutenant Skaaiat poured a hefty slug of liquor into the cup I held out, and I handed it to Lieutenant Awn. "Neither can One Esk, or it wouldn't be so silent this evening." She looked at the nearest segment. "Did the Lord of the Radch forbid you to sing?"

"No, Lieutenant." I hadn't wanted to disturb Anaander

Mianaai, when she was here, or interrupt what sleep Lieutenant Awn could get. And anyway, I hadn't much felt like it.

Lieutenant Skaaiat made a frustrated sound and turned back to Lieutenant Awn. "If you'd refused, nothing would have changed, except you'd be dead too. You did what you had to do, and the idiots...Hyr's cock, those *idiots*. They should have known better."

Lieutenant Awn stared at the cup in her hand, not moving.

"I *know* you, Awn. If you're going to do something that crazy, save it for when it'll make a difference."

"Like *Mercy of Sarrse* One Amaat One?" She was talking about events at Ime, about the soldier who had refused her order, led that mutiny five years before.

"She made a difference, at least. Listen, Awn, you and I both know something was going on. You and I both know that what happened last night doesn't make sense unless..." She stopped.

Lieutenant Awn set her cup of arrack down, hard. Liquor sloshed over the lip of the cup. "Unless what? How does it make sense?"

"Here." Lieutenant Skaaiat picked up the cup and pressed it into Lieutenant Awn's hand. "Drink this. And I'll explain. At least as much as makes sense to me.

"You know how annexations work. I mean, yes, they work by sheer, undeniable force, but after. After the executions and the transportations and once all the last bits of idiots who think they can fight back are cleaned up. Once all that's done, we fit whoever's left into Radchaai society—they form up into houses, and take clientage, and in a generation or two they're as Radchaai as anybody. And mostly that happens because we go to the top of the local hierarchy—there pretty much always is one—and offer them all sorts of benefits in exchange for behaving like citizens, offer them clientage contracts, which allows them to offer contracts to whoever is below them, and before you know it the whole local setup is tied into Radchaai society, with minimal disruption."

Lieutenant Awn made an impatient gesture. She already knew this. "What does that have to do with—"

"You fucked that up."

"I…"

"What you did *worked*. And the local Tanmind were going to have to swallow that. Fair enough. If I'd done what you did—gone straight to the Orsian priest, set up house in the lower city instead of using the police station and jail already built in the upper city, set about making alliances with lower city authorities and ignoring—"

"I didn't *ignore* anyone!" Lieutenant Awn protested.

Lieutenant Skaaiat waved her protest away. "And ignoring what anyone else would have seen as the natural local hierarchy. Your house can't afford to offer clientage to anyone here. *Yet*. Neither you nor I can make any contracts with anyone. *For now*. We had to exempt ourselves from our houses' contracts and take clientage directly from Anaander Mianaai, while we serve. But we still have those family connections, and those families can use connections we make now, even if we can't. And we can certainly use them when we retire. Getting your feet on the ground during an annexation is the one sure way to increase your house's financial and social standing.

"Which is fine until the wrong person does it. We tell ourselves that everything is the way Amaat wants it to be, that everything that is, is because of God. So if we're wealthy and respected, that's how things *should* be. The aptitudes prove that it's all just, that everyone gets what they deserve, and when the right people test into the right careers, that just goes to show how right it all is."

"I'm not the right people." Lieutenant Awn set down her empty cup, and Lieutenant Skaaiat refilled it.

"You're only one of thousands, but you're a noticeable one, to someone. And this annexation is different, it's the last one. Last chance to grab property, to make connections on the sort of scale the upper houses have always been accustomed to. They don't like to see any of those last chances go to houses like yours. And to make it worse, your subverting the local hierarchy—"

"I *used* the local hierarchy!"

"Lieutenants," I cautioned. Lieutenant Awn's outburst had been loud enough to be heard in the street, if anyone had been on the street this evening.

"If the Tanmind were running things here, that was as things must be in Amaat's mind. Right?"

"But they..." Lieutenant Awn stopped. I wasn't sure what she had been about to say. Perhaps that they had imposed their authority over Ors relatively recently. Perhaps that they were, in Ors, a numerical minority and Lieutenant Awn's goal had been to reach the largest number of people she could.

"Careful," warned Lieutenant Skaaiat, though Lieutenant Awn hadn't needed the warning. Any Radchaai soldier knew not to speak without thinking. "If you hadn't found those weapons, someone would have had an excuse not only to toss you out of Ors, but to come down hard on the Orsians and favor the upper city. Restoring the universe to its proper order. And then, of course, anyone inclined could have used the incident as an example of how soft we've gotten. If we'd stuck to so-called impartial aptitudes testing, if we'd executed more people, if we still made ancillaries..."

"I *have* ancillaries," Lieutenant Awn pointed out.

Lieutenant Skaaiat shrugged. "Everything else would have fit, they could ignore that. They'll ignore anything that doesn't get them what they want. And what they want is anything they can grab." She seemed so calm. Even almost relaxed. I was used to not seeing data from Lieutenant Skaaiat, but this disjunction between her demeanor and the seriousness of the situation—Lieutenant Awn's still-extreme distress, and, to be honest, my own discomfort at events—made her seem oddly flat and unreal to me.

"I understand Jen Shinnan's part in this," Lieutenant Awn said. "I do, I get that. But I don't understand how...how anyone else would benefit." The question she couldn't ask directly was, of course, why Anaander Mianaai would be involved, or why she would want to return to some previous, proper order, given she herself had certainly approved any changes. And why, if she wanted such a thing, she didn't merely order the things she desired. If questioned, both lieutenants could, and likely would, say they weren't speaking of the Lord of the Radch, but about some unknown person who must be involved, but I was certain that wouldn't hold up under an interrogation with drugs. Fortunately, such an event was unlikely. "And I don't see why anyone with that sort of access couldn't just order me gone and put someone they preferred in my place, if that was all they wanted."

"Maybe that wasn't *all* they wanted," answered Lieutenant Skaaiat. "But clearly, someone did at the very least want those things, and thought they would benefit from doing it this particular way. And you did as much as you could to avoid people getting killed. Anything else wouldn't have made any difference." She emptied her own cup. "You're going to stay in touch with me," she said, not a question, not a request. And then, more gently, "I'll miss you."

For a moment I thought Lieutenant Awn might cry again. "Who's replacing me?"

Lieutenant Skaaiat named an officer, and a ship.

"Human troops then." Lieutenant Awn was momentarily disquieted, and then sighed, frustrated. I imagine she was remembering that Ors was no longer her problem.

"I know," said Lieutenant Skaaiat. "I'll talk to her. You watch yourself. Now annexations are a thing of the past, ancillary troop carriers are crowded with the useless daughters of prestigious houses, who can't be assigned to anything lower." Lieutenant Awn frowned, clearly wanting to argue, thinking, maybe, of her fellow Esk lieutenants. Or of herself. Lieutenant Skaaiat saw her expression and smiled ruefully. "Well. Dariet is all right. It's the rest I'm warning you to look out for. Very high opinions of themselves and very little to justify it." Skaaiat had met some of them during the annexation, had always been entirely, correctly polite to them.

"You don't need to tell me that," said Lieutenant Awn.

Lieutenant Skaaiat poured more arrack, and for the rest of the night their conversation was the sort that needs no reporting.

At length Lieutenant Awn slept again, and by the time she woke I had hired boats to take us to the mouth of the river, near Kould Ves, and loaded them with our scant luggage, and my dead segment. In Kould Ves the mechanism that controlled its armor, and a few other bits of tech, would be removed for another use.

If you're going to do something that crazy, save it for when it'll make a difference, Lieutenant Skaaiat had said, and I had agreed. I still agree.

The problem is knowing when what you are about to do will make a difference. I'm not only speaking of the small actions that, cumulatively, over time, or in great numbers, steer the course of events in ways too chaotic or subtle to trace. The single word that directs a person's fate and ultimately the fates of those she comes in contact with is of course a common subject of entertainments and moralizing stories, but if everyone were to consider all the possible consequences of all one's possible choices, no one would move a millimeter, or even dare to breathe for fear of the ultimate results.

I mean, on a larger and more obvious scale. In the way that Anaander Mianaai herself determined the fates of whole peoples. Or the way my own actions could mean life or death for thousands. Or merely eighty-three, huddled in the temple of Ikkt, surrounded. I ask myself—as surely Lieutenant Awn asked herself—what would have been the consequences of refusing the order to fire? Straightforwardly, obviously, her own death would have been an immediate consequence. And then, immediately afterward, those eighty-three people would have died, because I would have shot them at Anaander Mianaai's direct order.

No difference, except Lieutenant Awn would be dead. The omens had been cast, and their trajectories were straightforward, calculable, direct, and clear.

But neither Lieutenant Awn nor the Lord of the Radch knew that in that moment, had one disk shifted, just slightly, the whole pattern might have landed differently. Sometimes, when omens are cast, one flies or rolls off where you didn't expect and throws the whole pattern out of shape. Had Lieutenant Awn chosen differently, that one segment, cut off, disoriented, and yes, horrified at the thought of shooting Lieutenant Awn, might have turned its gun on Mianaai instead. What then?

Ultimately, such an action would only have delayed Lieutenant Awn's death, and ensured my own—One Esk's—destruction. Which, since I didn't exist as any sort of individual, was not distressing to me.

But the death of those eighty-three people would have been delayed. Lieutenant Skaaiat would have been forced to arrest Lieutenant Awn—I am convinced she would not have shot her, though she would have been legally justified in doing so—but she would not have shot the Tanmind, because Mianaai would not have been there to give the order. And Jen Shinnan would have had time and opportunity to say whatever it was that the Lord of the Radch had, as things actually happened, prevented her from saying. What difference would that have made?

Perhaps a great deal of difference. Perhaps none at all. There are too many unknowns. Too many apparently predictable people who are, in reality, balanced on a knife-edge, or whose trajectories might be easily changed, if only I knew.

If you're going to do something that crazy, save it for when it'll make a difference. But absent near-omniscience there's no way to know when that is. You can only make your best approximate calculation. You can only make your throw and try to puzzle out the results afterward.

11

The explanation, why I needed the gun, why I wanted to kill Anaander Mianaai, took a long time. The answer was not a simple one—or, more accurately, the simple answer would only raise further questions for Strigan, so I did not attempt to use it but instead began the whole story at the beginning and let her infer the simple answer from the longer, complex one. By the time I was done the night was far advanced. Seivarden was asleep, breathing slow, and Strigan herself was clearly exhausted.

For three minutes there was no sound but Seivarden's breath accelerating as she transitioned into some state closer to wakefulness, or perhaps was troubled by a dream.

"And now I know who you are," Strigan said finally, tiredly. "Or who you think you are." There was no need for me to say anything in reply to that; by now she would believe what she wished about me, despite what I had told her. "Doesn't it bother you," Strigan continued, "didn't it ever bother you, that you're slaves?"

"Who?"

"The ships. The warships. So powerful. Armed. The officers inside are at your mercy every moment. What stops you from killing them all and declaring yourselves free? I've never been able to understand how the Radchaai can keep the ships enslaved."

"If you think about it," I said, "you'll see you already know the answer to your question."

She was silent again, inward-looking. I sat motionless. Waiting on the results of my throw.

"You were at Garsedd," she said after a while.

"Yes."

"Did you know Seivarden? Personally, I mean?"

"Yes."

"Did you...did you participate?"

"In the destruction of the Garseddai?" She gestured acknowledgment. "I did. Everyone who was there did."

She grimaced, with disgust I thought. "No one refused."

"I didn't say that." In fact, my own captain had refused, and died. Her replacement had qualms—she couldn't have hidden that from her ship—but said nothing and did as she was told. "It's easy to say that if you were there you would have refused, that you would rather die than participate in the slaughter, but it all looks very different when it's real, when the moment comes to choose."

Her eyes narrowed, in disagreement I thought, but I had only spoken the truth. Then her expression changed; she was thinking, perhaps, of that small collection of artifacts in her rooms on Dras Annia Station. "You speak the language?"

"Two of them." There had been more than a dozen.

"And you know their songs, of course." Her voice was slightly mocking.

"I didn't have a chance to learn as many as I would have liked."

"And if you had been free to choose, would you have refused?"

"The question is pointless. The choice was not presented to me."

"I beg to differ," she said, quietly angry at my answer. "The choice has always been presented to you."

"Garsedd was a turning point." It wasn't a direct answer to her accusation, but I couldn't think of what *would* be a direct answer, that she would understand. "The first time so many Radchaai officers came away from an annexation without the certainty that they had done the right thing. Do you still think Mianaai controls the Radchaai through brainwashing or threats of execution? Those are there, they exist, yes, but most Radchaai, like people most places I have been, do what they're supposed to because they believe it's the right thing to do. No one *likes* killing people."

Strigan made a sardonic noise. "No one?"

"Not many," I amended. "Not enough to fill the Radch's warships. But at the end, after all the blood and grief, all those benighted souls who without us would have suffered in darkness are happy citizens. They'll agree if you ask! It was a fortunate day when Anaander Mianaai brought civilization to them."

"Would their parents agree? Or their grandparents?"

I gestured, halfway between *not my problem* and *not relevant*. "You were surprised to see me deal gently with a child. It should not have surprised you. Do you think the Radchaai don't have children, or don't love their children? Do you think they don't react to children the way nearly any human does?"

"So virtuous!"

"Virtue is not a solitary, uncomplicated thing." Good necessitates evil and the two sides of that disk are not always clearly marked. "Virtues may be made to serve whatever end profits you. Still, they exist and will influence your actions. Your choices."

Strigan snorted. "You make me nostalgic for the drunken philosophical conversations of my youth. But these are not abstract things we're talking about here, this is life and death."

My chances of getting what I had come for were slipping from my grasp. "For the first time, Radch forces dealt death on an unimaginable scale without renewal afterward. Cut off irrevocably any chance of good coming from what they had done. This affected everyone there."

"Even the ships?"

"Everyone." I waited for the next question, or the sardonic *I don't feel sorry for you*, but she just sat silent, looking at me. "The first attempts at diplomatic contact with the Presger began shortly afterward. As did, I am fairly certain, the beginnings of the move to replace ancillaries with human soldiers." Only fairly certain because much of the groundwork must have been laid in private, behind the scenes.

"Why would the Presger get involved with Garsedd?" Strigan asked.

She could certainly see my reaction to her question, nearly a direct admission that she had the gun; had to know—had to have known before she spoke—what that admission would tell me. She wouldn't have asked that question if she hadn't seen the gun, examined it closely. Those guns had come from the Presger, the Garseddai had dealt with the aliens, whoever had made the first overture. So much we got from the captured representatives. But I kept my face still. "Who knows why the Presger do anything? But Anaander Mianaai asked herself the same question, *Why did the Presger interfere?* It wasn't because they wanted anything the Garseddai had, they could have reached out and taken whatever they wanted." Though I knew the Presger had made the Garseddai pay, and heavily. "And what if the Presger decided to destroy the Radch? Truly to destroy it? And the Presger had such weapons?"

"You're saying," said Strigan, disbelieving, appalled, "that the Presger set the Garseddai up in order to compel Anaander Mianaai to negotiate."

"I am speaking of Mianaai's reaction, Mianaai's motives. I don't know or understand the Presger. But I imagine if the Presger meant to compel anything, it would be unmistakable. Unsubtle. I think it was meant merely as a *suggestion*. If indeed that had anything to do with their actions."

"All of that, a *suggestion*."

"They're aliens. Who can understand them?"

"Nothing you can do," she said, after five seconds of silence, "can possibly make any difference."

"That's probably true."

"*Probably.*"

"If everyone who had…" I searched for the right words. "If everyone who objected to the destruction of the Garseddai had refused, what would have happened?"

Strigan frowned. "How many refused?"

"Four."

"Four. Out of…?"

"Out of thousands." Each Justice alone, in those days, had hundreds of officers, along with its captain, and dozens of us had been there. Add the smaller-crewed Mercies and Swords. "Loyalty, the long habit of obedience, a desire for revenge— even, yes, those four deaths kept anyone else from such a drastic choice."

"There were enough of your sort to deal with even everyone refusing."

I said nothing, waited for the change of expression that would tell me she had thought twice about what she had just said. When it came, I said, "I think it might have turned out differently."

"You're not one of thousands!" Strigan leaned forward, unexpectedly vehement. Seivarden started out of her sleep, looked at Strigan, alarmed and bleary.

"There are no others on the edge of choosing," Strigan said. "No one to follow your lead. And even if there were, you by yourself wouldn't be enough. If you even get as far as facing Mianaai—facing one of Mianaai's bodies—you'll be alone and helpless. You'll die without achieving anything!" She made a breathy, impatient sound. "Take your money." She gestured toward my pack, leaning against the bench I sat on. "Buy land, buy rooms on a station, hell, buy a station! Live the life that was denied you. Don't sacrifice yourself for nothing."

"Which *me* are you talking to?" I asked. "Which life that was denied me do you intend I live? Should I send you monthly reports, so you can be sure my choices meet with your approval?"

That silenced her, for a full twenty seconds.

"Breq," said Seivarden, as though testing the sound of the name in her mouth, "I want to leave."

"Soon," I answered. "Be patient." To my utter surprise she didn't object, but leaned back against a bench and put her arms around her knees.

Strigan looked speculatively at her for a moment, then turned to me. "I need to think." I gestured acknowledgment and she rose and went into her room and shut the door.

"What's *her* problem?" asked Seivarden, apparently innocent of irony. Voice just slightly contemptuous. I didn't answer, only looked at her, not changing my expression. The blankets had marked a line across her cheek, fading now, and her clothes, the Nilter trousers and quilted shirt under the unfastened inner coat, were wrinkled and disheveled. In the past several days of regular food, and no kef, her skin had regained a slightly healthier-looking color, but she still looked thin and tired. "Why are you bothering with her?" she asked me, undisturbed by my scrutiny. As though something had shifted and she and I were suddenly comrades. Fellows.

Surely not equals. Not ever. "Business I need to attend to." More explanation would be useless, or foolish, or both. "Are you having trouble sleeping?"

Something subtle in her expression communicated withdrawal, closure. I wasn't on her side anymore. She sat silent for ten seconds, and I thought she wouldn't speak to me anymore that night, but instead she drew a long breath and let it out. "Yeah. I...I need to move around. I'm going to go outside."

Something had definitely changed, but I didn't know quite what it was, or what had caused it.

"It's night," I said. "And very cold. Take your outer coat and gloves and don't go too far."

She gestured acquiescence, and even more astonishingly, put on her outer coat and gloves before going out the two doors without a single bitter word, or even a resentful glance.

And what did I care? She would wander off and freeze, or she would not. I arranged my own blankets and lay down to sleep, without waiting to see if Seivarden came back safe or not.

When I woke, Seivarden was asleep on her own pile of blankets. She hadn't thrown her coat on the floor, but instead hung it beside the others, on a hook near the door. I rose and went to the cupboard to find she had also replenished the food stores—more bread, and a bowl on the table holding a block of slushy, slowly melting milk, another beside it holding a chunk of bov fat.

Behind me Strigan's door clicked open. I turned. "He wants something," she said to me, quietly. Seivarden didn't stir. "Or anyway there's some angle he's playing. I wouldn't trust him if I were you."

"I don't." I dropped a hunk of bread in a bowl of water and set it aside to soften. "But I do wonder what's come over her." Strigan looked amused. "Him," I amended.

"Probably the thought of all the money you're carrying," observed Strigan. "You could buy a lot of kef with that."

"If that's the case, it's not a problem. It's all for paying you." Except my fare back up the ribbon, and a bit more for emergencies. Which, in this case, would probably mean Seivarden's fare as well.

"What happens to addicts in the Radch?"

"There aren't any." She raised one eyebrow, and then another, disbelieving. "Not on the stations," I amended. "You can't get too far down that road with the station AI watching you all the time. On a planet, that's different, it's too big for that. Even then, once you get to the point where you're not functioning, you're reeducated and usually sent away somewhere else."

"So as not to embarrass."

"For a new start. New surroundings, new assignment." And if you arrived from somewhere very far away to take some job nearly anyone could have filled, everyone knew why that was, though no one would be so gauche as to say it within your hearing. "It bothers you, that the Radchaai don't have the freedom to destroy their lives, or other citizens' lives."

"I wouldn't have put it that way."

"No, of course not."

She leaned against the doorframe, folded her arms. "For someone who wants a favor—an incredibly, unspeakably huge and dangerous favor at that—you're unexpectedly adversarial."

One-handed, I gestured. *It is as it is.*

"But then, dealing with him makes you angry." She tilted her head in Seivarden's general direction. "Understandably, I think."

The words *I'm so glad you approve* rose to my lips, but I didn't say them. I wanted, after all, an incredibly, unspeakably huge and dangerous favor. "All the money in the box," I said, instead. "Enough for you to buy land, or rooms on a station, or hell, even a station."

"A very small one." Her lips quirked in amusement.

"And you wouldn't have it anymore. It's dangerous even to have seen it, but it's worse to actually have it."

"And you," she pointed out, straightening, dropping her arms, voice now unamused, "will bring it directly to the attention of the Lord of the Radch. Who will then be able to trace it back to me."

"That will always be a danger," I agreed. I would not even pretend that once I fell into Mianaai's control she would not be able to extract any information from me she wished, no matter what I wanted to reveal or conceal. "But it has been a danger since the moment you laid eyes on it, and will continue to be for as long as you live, whether you give it to me or not."

Strigan sighed. "That's true. Unfortunately enough. And truth to tell, I want very badly to go home."

Foolish beyond belief. But it wasn't my concern, my concern was getting that gun. I said nothing. Neither did Strigan. Instead, she put on her outer coat and gloves and went out the two doors, and I sat down to eat my breakfast, trying very hard not to guess where she had gone, or whether I had any reason at all to be hopeful.

She returned fifteen minutes later with a wide, flat black box. Strigan set the box on the table. It seemed like one solid block, but she lifted off a thick layer of black, revealing more black beneath.

Strigan stood, waiting, the lid in her hands, watching me. I reached out and touched a spot on the black, with one finger, gently. Brown spread from where I touched, pooling out into the shape of a gun, now exactly the color of my skin. I lifted my finger and black flooded back. Reached out, lifted off another layer of black, beneath which it finally began to look like a box, with actual things in it, if a disturbingly light-suckingly black box, filled with ammunition.

Strigan reached out and touched the upper surface of the layer of black I still held. Gray spread from her fingers into a thick strap curled alongside where the gun lay. "I wasn't sure what that was. Do you know?"

"It's armor." Officers and human troops used externally worn armor units, instead of the sort that was installed in one's body. Like mine. But a thousand years ago everyone's had been implanted.

"It's never tripped a single alarm, never shown up in any scan I've been through." *That* was what I wanted. The ability to walk onto any Radchaai station without alerting anyone to the fact I was armed. The ability to carry a weapon into the very presence of Anaander Mianaai without anyone

163

realizing it. Most Anaanders had no need for armor; being able to shoot through it was just an extra.

Strigan asked, "How does it do that? How does it hide itself?"

"I don't know." I replaced the layer I was holding, and then the very top.

"How many of the bastard do you think you can kill?"

I looked up, away from the box, from the gun, the unlikely goal of nearly twenty years' efforts, in front of me, real and solid. In my grasp. I wanted to say, *As many as I can reach, before they take me down.* But realistically I could only expect to meet one, a single body out of thousands. Then again, realistically I could never have expected to find this gun. "That depends," I said.

"If you're going to make a desperate, hopeless act of defiance you should make it a good one."

I gestured my agreement. "I plan to ask for an audience."

"Will you get one?"

"Probably. Any citizen can ask for one, and will almost certainly receive it. I wouldn't be going as a citizen..."

Strigan scoffed. "How are *you* going to pass as non-Radchaai?"

"I will walk onto the docks of a provincial palace with no gloves, or the wrong ones, announce my foreign origin, and speak with an accent. Nothing more will be required."

She blinked. Frowned. "Not really."

"I assure you. As a noncitizen my chances of obtaining an audience will depend on my reasons for asking." I hadn't thought that part all the way through yet. It would depend on what I found when I got there. "Some things can't be planned too far in advance."

"And what are you going to do about..." She waved an ungloved hand toward unconscious Seivarden.

I had avoided asking myself that question. Avoided, from the moment I found her, thinking more than one step ahead when it came to what I was going to do about Seivarden.

"*Watch him*," she said. "He might have reached the point where he's ready to give up the kef for good, but I don't think he has."

"Why not?"

"He hasn't asked me for help."

It was my turn to raise a skeptical eyebrow. "If he asked, would you help?"

"I'd do what I could. Though of course, he'd need to address the problems that led him to use in the first place, if it was going to work long-term. Which I don't see any sign of him doing." Privately I agreed, but I didn't say anything.

"He could have asked for help anytime," Strigan continued. "He's been wandering around for, what, at least five years? Any doctor could have helped him, if he'd wanted it. But that would mean admitting he had a problem, wouldn't it? And I don't see that happening anytime soon."

"It would be best if sh—if he went back to the Radch." Radch medics could solve all her problems. And would not trouble themselves with whether or not Seivarden had asked for their help, or wanted it in any way.

"He won't go back to the Radch unless he admits he has a problem."

I gestured, *not my concern*. "He can go where he likes."

"But you're feeding him, and no doubt you'll pay his fare up the ribbon, and to whatever system you take ship for next. He'll stay with you as long as it's to his advantage, as long as there's food and shelter. And he'll steal anything he thinks will get him another hit of kef."

Seivarden wasn't as strong as she had once been, or as clear, mentally. "Do you think he'll find that easy?"

"No," admitted Strigan, "but he'll be very determined."

"Yes."

Strigan shook her head, as though to clear it. "What am I doing? You won't listen to me."

"I'm listening."

But she clearly didn't believe me. "It's none of my concern, I know. Just…" She pointed to the black box. "Just kill as many of Mianaai as you can. And don't send him after *me*."

"You're leaving?" Of course she was, there was no need to answer such a foolish question, and she didn't bother. Instead she went back into her room, saying nothing else, and closed the door.

I opened my pack, took out the money and set it on the table, slid the black box into its place. Touched it in the pattern that would make it disappear, nothing but folded shirts, a few packets of dried food. Then I went over to where Seivarden lay, and prodded her with one booted foot. "Wake up." She started, sitting suddenly, and flung her back against the nearby bench, breathing hard. "Wake up," I said again. "We're leaving."

12

Except for those hours when communications had been cut off, I had never really lost the sense of being part of *Justice of Toren*. My kilometers of white-walled corridor, my captain, the decade commanders, each decade's lieutenants, each one's smallest gesture, each breath, was visible to me. I had never lost the knowledge of my ancillaries, twenty-bodied One Amaat, One Toren, One Etrepa, One Bo, and Two Esk, hands and feet for serving those officers, voices to speak to them. My thousands of ancillaries in frozen suspension. Never lost the view of Shis'urna itself, all blue and white, old boundaries and divisions erased by distance. From that perspective events in Ors were nothing, invisible, completely insignificant.

In the approaching shuttle I felt the distance decrease, felt more forcefully the sensation of *being* the ship. One Esk became even more what it had always been—one small part of myself. My attention was no longer commanded by things apart from the rest of the ship.

Two Esk had taken One Esk's place while One Esk was on

the planet. Two Esk prepared tea in the Esk decade room for its lieutenants—my lieutenants. It scrubbed the white-walled corridor outside Esk's baths, mended uniforms torn on leave. Two of my lieutenants sat over a game board in the decade room, placing counters around, swift and quiet, three others watching. The lieutenants of the Amaat, Toren, Etrepa, and Bo decades, the decade commanders, Hundred Captain Rubran, administrative officers, and medics, talked, slept, bathed, according to their schedules and inclinations.

Each decade held twenty lieutenants and its decade commander, but Esk was now my lowest occupied deck. Below Esk, from Var down—half of my decade decks—was cold and empty, though the holds were still full. The emptiness and silence of those spaces where officers had once lived had disturbed me at first, but I was used to it by now.

On the shuttle, in front of One Esk, Lieutenant Awn sat silent, jaw clenched. She was in some respects more physically comfortable than she had ever been in Ors—the temperature, twenty degrees C, was more suitable for her uniform jacket and trousers. And the stink of swamp water had been replaced by the more familiar and more easily tolerable smell of recycled air. But the tiny spaces—which when she had first come to *Justice of Toren* had excited pride in her assignment and anticipation of what the future might hold—now seemed to trap and confine her. She was tense and unhappy.

Esk Decade Commander Tiaund sat in her tiny office. It held only two chairs and a desk close against one wall, barely more than a shelf, and space for perhaps two more people to stand. "Lieutenant Awn has returned," I said to her, and to Hundred Captain Rubran on the command deck. The shuttle docked with a *thunk*.

Captain Rubran frowned. She had been surprised and dismayed at the news of Lieutenant Awn's sudden return. The order had come directly from Anaander Mianaai, who was not to be questioned. Along with it had come orders not to ask what had happened.

In her office on the Esk deck, Commander Tiaund sighed, closed her eyes, and said, "Tea." She sat silent till Two Esk brought her a cup and a flask, poured, and set both at the commander's elbow. "She'll see me at her earliest convenience."

One Esk's attention was mostly on Lieutenant Awn, threading her way through the lift and the narrow white corridors that would take her to the Esk decade, to her own quarters. I read relief when she found those corridors empty except for Two Esk.

"Commander Tiaund will see you at your earliest convenience," I said to Lieutenant Awn, transmitting directly to her. She acknowledged with a brief twitch of her fingers as she entered the Esk corridors.

Two Esk vacated the deck, filing down the corridor to the hold and its waiting suspension pods, and One Esk took up whatever tasks Two Esk had been doing, and also followed Lieutenant Awn. Above, on Medical, a tech medic began to lay out what she needed to replace One Esk's missing segment.

At the door of her own small quarters—the same that more than a thousand years before had belonged to Lieutenant Seivarden—Lieutenant Awn turned to say something to the segment that followed her, and then stopped. "What?" she asked after an instant. "Something's wrong, what is it?"

"Please excuse me, Lieutenant," I said. "In the next few minutes the tech medic will connect a new segment. I might be unresponsive for a short while."

"Unresponsive," she said, feeling momentarily overwhelmed

for some reason I couldn't quite understand. And then guilty, and angry. She stood before the unopened door of her quarters, took two breaths, and then turned and went back down the corridor toward the lift.

A new segment's nervous system has to be more or less functional for the hookup. They'd tried it in the past with dead bodies, and failed. The same with fully sedated bodies— the connection was never made properly. Sometimes the new segment is given a tranquilizer, but sometimes the tech medic prefers to thaw the new body out and tie it down quickly, without any sedation at all. This eliminates the chancy step of sedating just the right amount, but it always makes for an uncomfortable hookup.

This particular tech medic didn't care much about my comfort. She wasn't obliged to care, of course.

Lieutenant Awn entered the lift that would bring her to Medical just as the tech medic triggered the release on the suspension pod that held the body. The lid swung up, and for a hundredth of a second the body lay still and icy within its pool of fluid.

The tech medic rolled the body out of the pod onto a neighboring table, the fluid sliding and sheeting off it, and in the same moment it awoke, convulsive, choking and gagging. The preserving medium slides out of throat and lungs easily on its own, but the first few times the experience is a discomfiting one. Lieutenant Awn exited the lift, strode down the corridor toward Medical with One Esk Eighteen close behind her.

The tech medic went swiftly to work, and suddenly I was on the table (I was walking behind Lieutenant Awn, I was taking up the mending Two Esk had set down on its way to the holds, I was laying myself down on my small, close bunks,

I was wiping a counter in the decade room) and I could see and hear but I had no control of the new body and its terror raised the heart rates of all One Esk's segments. The new segment's mouth opened and it screamed and in the background it heard laughter. I flailed, the binding came loose and I rolled off the table, fell a meter and a half to the floor with a painful *thud. Don't don't don't*, I thought at the body, but it wasn't listening. It was sick, it was terrified, it was dying. It pushed itself up and crawled, dizzy, where it didn't care so long as it got away.

Then hands under my arms (elsewhere One Esk was motionless) urging me up, and Lieutenant Awn. "Help," I croaked, not in Radchaai. Damn medic pulled out a body without a decent voice. "Help me."

"It's all right." Lieutenant Awn shifted her grip, put her arms around the new segment, pulled me in closer. It was shivering, still cold from suspension, and from terror. "It's all right. It'll be all right." The segment gasped and sobbed for what seemed forever and I thought maybe it was going to throw up until...the connection clicked home and I had control of it. I stopped the sobbing.

"There," said Lieutenant Awn. Horrified. Sick to her stomach. "Much better." I saw that she was newly angry, or perhaps this was another edge of the distress I'd seen since the temple. "Don't injure my unit," Lieutenant Awn said curtly, and I realized that though she was still looking at me, she was talking to the tech medic.

"I didn't, Lieutenant," answered the tech medic, with a trace of scorn in her voice. They'd had this conversation at greater and more acrimonious length, during the annexation. The medic had said, *It's not like it's human. It's been in the hold a thousand years, it's nothing but a part of the ship.*

Lieutenant Awn had complained to Commander Tiaund, who hadn't understood Lieutenant Awn's anger, and said so, but thereafter I hadn't dealt with that particular medic. "If you're so squeamish," the medic continued, "maybe you're in the wrong place."

Lieutenant Awn turned, angry, and left the room without saying anything further. I turned and walked back to the table with some trepidation. The segment was already resisting, and I knew that this tech medic wouldn't care if it hurt when she put in my armor, and the rest of my implants.

Things were always a bit clumsy while I got used to a new segment—it would occasionally drop things, or fire off disorienting impulses, random jolts of fear or nausea. Things always seemed off-kilter for a bit. But after a week or two it would usually settle down. Most of the time, anyway. Sometimes a segment simply would not function properly, and then it would have to be removed and replaced. They screen the bodies, of course, but it's not perfect.

The voice wasn't the sort I preferred, and it didn't know any interesting songs. Not ones I didn't already know, anyway. I still can't shake the slight, and definitely irrational, suspicion that the tech medic chose that particular body just to annoy me.

After a quick bath, in which I assisted, and a change into a clean uniform, Lieutenant Awn presented herself to Commander Tiaund.

"Awn." The decade commander waved Lieutenant Awn to the opposite chair. "I'm glad to have you back, of course."

"Thank you, sir," said Lieutenant Awn, sitting.

"I didn't expect to see you so soon. I was sure you'd be downside for a while longer." Lieutenant Awn didn't answer.

Commander Tiaund waited for five seconds in silence, and then said, "I would ask what happened, but I'm ordered not to."

Lieutenant Awn opened her mouth, took a breath to speak, stopped. Surprised. I had said nothing to her about the orders not to ask what had happened. Corresponding orders to Lieutenant Awn not to tell anyone had not come. A test, I suspected, which I was quite confident Lieutenant Awn would pass.

"Bad?" asked Commander Tiaund. Wanting very much to know more, pushing her luck asking even that much.

"Yes, sir." Lieutenant Awn looked down at her gloved hands, resting in her lap. "Very."

"Your fault?"

"Everything on my watch is my responsibility, isn't it, sir?"

"Yes," Commander Tiaund acknowledged. "But I'm having trouble imagining you doing anything…improper." The word was weighted in Radchaai, part of a triad of justice, propriety, and benefit. Using it, Commander Tiaund implied more than just that she expected Lieutenant Awn to follow regulations or etiquette. Implied she suspected some injustice was behind events. Though she could certainly not say so plainly—she possessed none of the facts of the matter and surely did not wish to give anyone the impression she did. And if Lieutenant Awn were to be punished for some breach, she wouldn't want to have publicly taken Lieutenant Awn's part no matter what her private opinion.

Commander Tiaund sighed, perhaps out of frustrated curiosity. "Well," she continued, with feigned cheerfulness. "Now you've got plenty of time to catch up on gym time. And you're way behind on renewing your marksmanship certification."

Lieutenant Awn forced a humorless smile. There had been no gym in Ors, nor anyplace remotely resembling a firing range. "Yes, sir."

"And Lieutenant, please don't go up to Medical unless you really need to."

I could see Lieutenant Awn wanted to protest, to complain. But that, too, would have been a repeat of an earlier conversation. "Yes, sir."

"Dismissed."

By the time Lieutenant Awn finally entered her quarters, it was nearly time for supper—a formal meal, eaten in the decade room in the company of the other Esk lieutenants. Lieutenant Awn pled exhaustion—no lie, as it happened: she had barely slept six hours since she'd left Ors nearly three days before.

She sat on her bunk, slumped and staring, until I entered, eased off her boots, and took her coat. "All right," she said then, closed her eyes and swiveled her legs up onto the bunk. "I get the hint." She was asleep five seconds after she laid her head down.

The next morning eighteen of my twenty Esk lieutenants stood in the decade room, drinking tea and waiting for breakfast. By custom they couldn't sit without the seniormost lieutenant.

The Esk decade room's walls were white, with a blue-and-yellow border painted just under the ceiling. On one wall, opposite a long counter, were secured various trophies of past annexations—scraps of two flags, red and black and green; a pink clay roof tile with a raised design of leaves molded into it; an ancient sidearm (unloaded) and its elegantly styled holster; a jeweled Ghaonish mask. An entire window from a Valskaayan temple, colored glass arranged to form a picture of a woman holding a broom in one hand, three small animals at her feet. I remembered taking it out of the wall myself and carrying it back here. Every decade room on the ship had a window from that same building. The temple's vestments and equipment had been thrown into the street, or found their way to other decade rooms on other ships. It was normal practice to absorb any religion the Radch ran across, to fit its gods into an already blindingly complex genealogy, or to say merely that the supreme, creator deity was Amaat under another name and let the rest sort themselves out. Some quirk of Valskaayan religion made this difficult for them, and the result had been destructive. Among the recent changes in Radch policy, Anaander Mianaai had legalized the practice of Valskaay's insistently separate religion, and the governor of Valskaay had given the building back. There had been talk of returning the windows, since we had still at that time been in orbit around Valskaay itself, but ultimately they were replaced with copies. Not long after, the decades below Esk were emptied and closed, but the windows still hung on the walls of the empty, dark decade rooms.

Lieutenant Issaaia entered, walked straight to the icon of Toren in its corner niche, and lit the incense waiting in the red bowl at the icon's feet. Six officers frowned, and two made a very quiet, surprised murmur. Only Lieutenant Dariet spoke. "Is Awn not coming to breakfast?"

Lieutenant Issaaia turned toward Lieutenant Dariet, showed an expression of surprise that did not, so far as I could tell, mirror her actual feelings, and said, "Amaat's grace! I completely forgot Awn was back."

At the back of the group, safely shielded from Lieutenant

Issaaia's view, one very junior lieutenant cast a look at another very junior lieutenant.

"It's been so very quiet," Lieutenant Issaaia continued. "It's difficult to believe she *is* back."

"Silence and cold ashes," quoted the junior lieutenant who had received the other's meaningful glance, more daring than her companion. The poem quoted was an elegy for someone whose funeral offerings had been deliberately neglected. I saw Lieutenant Issaaia react with an instant of ambivalence—the next line spoke of food offerings not made for the dead, and the junior lieutenant conceivably might have been criticizing Lieutenant Awn for not coming to supper the night before, or breakfast on time this morning.

"It really is One Esk," said another lieutenant, concealing her smirk at the very junior lieutenant's cleverness, looking closely at the segments that were at the moment laying out plates of fish and fruit on the counter. "Maybe Awn broke it of its bad habits. I hope so."

"Why so quiet, One?" asked Lieutenant Dariet.

"Oh, don't get it started," groaned another lieutenant. "It's too early for all that noise."

"If it was Awn, good for her," said Lieutenant Issaaia. "A little late though."

"Like now," said a lieutenant at Lieutenant Issaaia's elbow. "Give me food while yet I live." Another quote, another reference to funeral offerings and a rebuttal in case the junior lieutenant had intended insult in the wrong direction. "Is she coming or not? If she isn't coming she should say so."

At that moment Lieutenant Awn was in the bath, and I was attending her. I could have told the lieutenants that Lieutenant Awn would be there soon, but I said nothing, only noted the level and temperature of the tea in the black glass bowls various lieutenants held, and continued to lay out breakfast plates.

Near my own weapons storage, I cleaned my twenty guns, so I could stow them, along with their ammunition. In each of my lieutenants' quarters I stripped the linen from their beds. The officers of Amaat, Toren, Etrepa, and Bo were all well into breakfast, chattering, lively. The captain ate with the decade commanders, a quieter, more sober conversation. One of my shuttles approached me, four Bo lieutenants returning from leave, strapped into their seats, unconscious. They would be unhappy when they woke.

"Ship," said Lieutenant Dariet, "will Lieutenant Awn be joining us for breakfast?"

"Yes, Lieutenant," I said, with One Esk Six's voice. In the bath I poured water over Lieutenant Awn, who stood, eyes closed, on the grating over the drain. Her breathing was even, but her heart rate was slightly elevated, and she showed other signs of stress. I was fairly sure her tardiness was deliberate, designed to give her the bath to herself. Not because she couldn't handle Lieutenant Issaaia—she certainly could. But because she was still distressed from the past days' events.

"When?" asked Lieutenant Issaaia, frowning just slightly.

"About five minutes, Lieutenant."

A chorus of groans went up. "Now, Lieutenants," Lieutenant Issaaia admonished. "She *is* our senior. And we should all have patience with her right now. Such a sudden return, when we all thought the Divine would *never* agree to her leaving Ors."

"Found out she wasn't such a good choice, eh?" sneered the lieutenant at Lieutenant Issaaia's elbow. She was close to Lieutenant Issaaia in more than one sense. None of them knew what had happened, and couldn't ask. And I, of course, had said nothing.

"Not likely," said Lieutenant Dariet, her voice a shade louder than usual. She was angry. "Not after five years." I took the tea flask, turned from the counter, went over to where Lieutenant Dariet stood, and poured eleven milliliters of tea into the nearly full bowl she held.

"You like Lieutenant Awn, of course," said Lieutenant Issaaia. "We all do. But she doesn't have *breeding*. She wasn't born for this. She works so very hard at what comes naturally to us. I would hardly be surprised if five years was all she could take without cracking." She looked at the empty bowl in her gloved hand. "I need more tea."

"You think you'd have done a better job, in Awn's place," observed Lieutenant Dariet.

"I don't trouble myself with hypotheticals," answered Lieutenant Issaaia. "The facts are what they are. There's a reason Awn was senior Esk lieutenant long before any of us got here. Obviously Awn has some ability or she'd never have done as well as she has, but she's reached her limit." A quiet murmur of agreement. "Her parents are *cooks*," Lieutenant Issaaia continued. "I'm sure they're excellent at what they do. I'm sure she would manage a kitchen admirably."

Three lieutenants snickered. Lieutenant Dariet said, her voice tight and edged, "Really?" Finally dressed, uniform as perfect as I could make it, Lieutenant Awn stepped out of the dressing room, into the corridor, five steps away from the decade room.

Lieutenant Issaaia noticed Lieutenant Dariet's mood with a familiar ambivalence. Lieutenant Issaaia was senior, but Lieutenant Dariet's house was older, wealthier than Lieutenant Issaaia's, and Lieutenant Dariet's branch of that house were direct clients to a prominent branch of Mianaai itself. Theoretically that didn't matter here. Theoretically.

All the data I had received from Lieutenant Issaaia that morning had had an underlying taste of resentment, which grew momentarily stronger. "Managing a kitchen is a perfectly respectable job," said Lieutenant Issaaia. "But I can only imagine how difficult it must be, to be bred to be a servant and instead of taking an assignment that truly suits, to be thrust into a position of such authority. Not everyone is cut out to be an officer." The door opened, and Lieutenant Awn stepped in just as the last sentence left Lieutenant Issaaia's mouth.

Silence engulfed the decade room. Lieutenant Issaaia looked calm and unconcerned, but felt abashed. She had clearly not intended—would never have dared—to say such things openly to Lieutenant Awn.

Only Lieutenant Dariet spoke. "Good morning, Lieutenant."

Lieutenant Awn didn't answer, didn't even look at her, but went to the corner of the room where the decade shrine sat, with its small figure of Toren and bowl of burning incense. Lieutenant Awn made her obeisance to the figure and then looked at the bowl with a slight frown. As before, her muscles were tense, her heart rate elevated, and I knew she guessed at the content or at least the drift of the conversation before she had entered, knew who it was who wasn't cut out to be an officer.

She turned. "Good morning, Lieutenants. I apologize for having kept you waiting." And launched without any other preamble into the morning prayer. "The flower of justice is peace…" The others joined, and when they were finished Lieutenant Awn went to her place at the head of the table, sat.

Before the others had time to settle themselves, I had tea and breakfast in front of her.

I served the others, and Lieutenant Awn took a sip of her tea and began to eat.

Lieutenant Dariet picked up her utensil. "It's good to have you back." Her voice was just slightly edged, only barely managing to conceal her anger.

"Thank you," said Lieutenant Awn, and took another bite of fish.

"I still need tea," said Lieutenant Issaaia. The rest of the table was tense and hushed, watching. "The quiet is nice, but perhaps there's been a decline in efficiency."

Lieutenant Awn chewed, swallowed, took another drink of tea. "Pardon?"

"You've managed to silence One Esk," explained Lieutenant Issaaia, "but..." She raised her empty bowl.

At that moment I was behind her with the flask, and poured, filling the bowl.

Lieutenant Awn raised one gloved hand, gesturing toward the mootness of Lieutenant Issaaia's point. "I haven't silenced One Esk." She looked at the segment with the flask and frowned. "Not intentionally, anyway. Go ahead and sing if you want, One Esk." A dozen lieutenants groaned. Lieutenant Issaaia smiled insincerely.

Lieutenant Dariet stopped, a bite of fish halfway to her mouth. "I like the singing. It's nice. And it's a distinction."

"It's embarrassing is what it is," said the lieutenant close to Lieutenant Issaaia.

"I don't find it embarrassing," said Lieutenant Awn, a bit stiffly.

"Of course not," said Lieutenant Issaaia, malice concealed in the ambiguity of her words. "Why so quiet, then, One?"

"I've been busy, Lieutenant," I answered. "And I haven't wanted to disturb Lieutenant Awn."

"Your singing doesn't disturb me, One," said Lieutenant Awn. "I'm sorry you thought it did. Please, sing if you want."

Lieutenant Issaaia raised an eyebrow. "An apology? And a *please*? That's a bit much."

"Courtesy," said Lieutenant Dariet, her voice uncharacteristically prim, "is always proper, and always beneficial."

Lieutenant Issaaia smirked. "Thank you, Mother."

Lieutenant Awn said nothing.

Four and a half hours after breakfast, the shuttle bearing those four Second Bo lieutenants home from their leave docked.

They'd been drinking for three days, and had continued right up to the moment they left Shis'urna Station. The first of them through the lock staggered slightly, and then closed her eyes. "Medic," she breathed.

"They expect you," I said through the segment of One Bo I'd placed there. "Do you need help onto the lift?"

The lieutenant made a feeble attempt to wave my offer away, and moved off slowly down the corridor, one shoulder against the wall for support.

I boarded the shuttle, kicking off past the boundary of my artificially generated gravity—the shuttle was too small to have its own. Two of the officers, still drunk themselves, were trying to wake the fourth, passed out cold in her seat. The pilot— the most junior of the Bo officers—sat stiff and apprehensive. I thought at first her discomfort was due to the reek of spilled arrack and vomit—thankfully the former had apparently been spilled onto the lieutenants themselves, on Shis'urna Station, and nearly all of the latter had gone into the appropriate

181

receptacles—but then I looked (One Bo looked) toward the stern and saw three Anaander Mianaais sitting silent and impassive in the rear seats. Not *there*, to me. She would have boarded at Shis'urna Station, quietly. Told the pilot to say nothing to me. The others had, I suspected, been too intoxicated to notice her. I thought of her asking me, on the planet, when she had last visited me. Of my inexplicable and reflexive lie. The real last time had been a good deal like this.

"My lord," I said when all the Bo lieutenants were out of earshot. "I'll notify the hundred captain."

"No," said one Anaander. "Your Var deck is empty."

"Yes, my lord," I acknowledged.

"I'll stay there while I'm on board." Nothing further, no why or how long. Or when I could tell the captain what I was doing. I was obliged to obey Anaander Mianaai, even over my own captain, but I rarely had an order from one without the knowledge of the other. It was uncomfortable.

I sent segments of One Esk to retrieve One Var from the hold, started one section of Var deck warming. The three Anaander Mianaais declined my offer of assistance with their luggage, carried their things down to Var.

This had happened before, at Valskaay. My lower decks had been mostly empty, because many of my troops had been out of the hold and working. She had stayed on the Esk deck that time. What had she wanted then, what had she done?

To my dismay I found my thoughts slipping around the answer, which remained vague, invisible. That wasn't right. It wasn't right at all.

Between the Esk and Var decks was direct access to my brain. What had she done, at Valskaay, that I couldn't remember, and what was she preparing to do now?

13

Further south the snow and ice became impermanent, though it was still cold by non-Nilt standards. Nilters regard the equatorial region as a sort of tropical paradise, where grain can actually grow, where the temperature can easily exceed eight or nine degrees C. Most of Nilt's large cities are on or near the equatorial ring.

The same is true of the planet's one claim to any sort of fame—the glass bridges.

These are approximately five-meter-wide ribbons of black hanging in gentle catenaries across trenches nearly as wide as they are deep—dimensions measured in kilometers. No cables, no piers, no trusses. Just the arc of black attached to each cliff face. Fantastic arrangements of colored glass coils and rods hang from the bottoms of the bridges, sometimes projecting sideways.

The bridges themselves are, according to all observations, also made of glass, though glass could never possibly withstand the sort of stress these bridges do—even their own weight should be too much for them, suspended as they are with nothing for support. There are no rails or handholds, just the drop, and at the bottom, kilometers down, a cluster of thick-walled tubes, each one just a meter and a half wide, empty and smooth-walled. These are made of the same material as the bridges. No one knows what the bridges and the tubes beneath them were for, or who built them. They were here when humans first colonized Nilt.

Theories abound, each one less likely than the one before. Inter-dimensional beings feature prominently in many of them—these either created or shaped humanity for its own purposes, or left a message for humans to decipher for obscure reasons of their own. Or they were evil, bent on destruction of all life. The bridges were, somehow, part of their plan.

Another whole subfield claims the bridges were built by humans—some ancient, long-lost, fantastically advanced civilization that either died out (slowly, pathetically; or spectacularly as the result of some catastrophic mistake) or moved on to a higher level of existence. Advocates of this sort of theory often make the additional claim that Nilt is, in reality, the birthplace of humans. Nearly everywhere I've been, popular wisdom has it that the location of humanity's original planet is unknown, mysterious. In fact it isn't, as anyone who troubles to read on the subject will discover, but it *is* very, very, *very* far away from nearly anywhere, and not a tremendously interesting place. Or at the very least, not nearly as interesting as the enchanting idea that your people are not newcomers to their homes but in fact only recolonized the place they had belonged from the beginning of time. One meets this claim anywhere one finds a remotely human-habitable planet.

The bridge outside Therrod wasn't much of a tourist attraction. Most of the jewel-bright arabesques of glass had shattered over thousands of years, leaving it nearly plain. And Therrod is still too far north for non-Nilters to endure comfortably. Offworld visitors generally confine themselves to the better-preserved bridges on the equator, buy a bov-hair blanket guaranteed hand-spun and handwoven by masters of the craft in the unbearably cold reaches of the world (though these are almost certainly turned out on machines, by the dozen, a few kilometers from the gift shop), choke down a few fetid swallows of fermented milk, and return home to regale their friends and associates with tales of their adventure.

All this I learned within a few minutes of knowing I would need to visit Nilt to achieve my aim.

Therrod sat on a broad river, chunks of green-and-white ice bobbing and crashing in its current, the first boats of the season already moored at the docks. On the opposite side of the city, the dark slash of the bridge's huge trough made a definitive stop to the straggling edge of houses. The southern edge of the city was flier-parks, then a wide complex of blue-and-yellow-painted buildings that was, by the look of it, a medical facility, one that must have been the largest of its kind in the area. It was surrounded by squares of lodgings and food shops, and swaths of houses, bright pink, orange, yellow, red, in stripes and zigzags and crosshatches.

We had flown half the day. I might have flown all night, I was capable of it, though it would have been unpleasant. But I saw no need for haste. I set down in the first empty space I found, told Seivarden curtly to get out, and did so myself. I shouldered my pack, paid the parking fee, disabled the flier as I had at Strigan's, and set off toward the city, not looking to see if Seivarden followed.

I had set down near the medical facility. The lodgings

surrounding it were some of them luxurious, but many were smaller and less comfortable than the one I'd rented in the village where I'd found Seivarden, though a bit more expensive. Bright-coated southerners came and went, speaking a language I didn't understand. Others spoke the one I knew, and fortunately this was the same language the signs used.

I chose lodging—roomier, at least, than the suspension-pod-size holes that were the cheapest available—and took Seivarden off to the first clean-looking and moderately priced food shop I could find.

When we entered, Seivarden eyed the shelves of bottles on the far wall. "They have arrack."

"It'll be incredibly expensive," I said, "and probably not very good. They don't make it here. Have a beer instead."

She had been showing some signs of stress, and wincing slightly at the profusion of bright colors, so I expected some sort of irritable outburst, but instead she merely gestured acquiescence. Then she wrinkled her nose, slight disgust. "What do they make beer out of here?"

"Grain. It grows nearer the equator. It's not as cold there." We found seats on the benches that lined three rows of long tables, and a waiter brought us beer, and bowls of something she told us was the house specialty, *Extra beautiful eating, yes*, she said, in a badly mangled approximation of Radchaai, and it was in fact quite good, and turned out to have actual vegetables in it, a good proportion of thinly sliced cabbage among whatever the rest of it was. The smaller lumps appeared to be meat—probably bov. Seivarden cut one of the larger lumps in two with her spoon, revealing plain white. "Probably cheese," I said.

She grimaced. "Why can't these people eat *real* food? Don't they know better?"

"Cheese is real food. So is cabbage."

"But this sauce..."

"Tastes good." I took another spoonful.

"This whole place smells funny," she complained.

"Just eat." She looked dubiously at her bowl, scooped a spoonful, sniffed it. "It can't possibly smell worse than that fermented milk drink," I said.

She actually half-smiled. "No."

I took another spoonful, pondering the implications of this better behavior. I wasn't sure what it meant, about her state of mind, about her intentions, about who or what she thought I was. Maybe Strigan had been right, and Seivarden had decided the most profitable course, for now, was to not alienate the person who was feeding her, and that would change as soon as her options changed.

A high voice called out from another table. "Hello!"

I turned—the girl with the Tiktik set waved to me from where she sat with her mother. For an instant I was surprised, but we were near the medical center, where I knew they had brought their injured relative, and they had come from the same direction we had, and so they had likely parked on the same side of town. I smiled and nodded, and she got up and came to where we were sitting. "Your friend is better!" she said, brightly. "That's good. What are you eating?"

"I don't know," I admitted. "The waiter said it was the house specialty."

"Oh, that's very good, I had it yesterday. When did you get here? It's so hot it's like summer already, I can't imagine what it's like further north." Clearly she'd had time to recover her more usual spirits since the accident that had brought her to Strigan's house. Seivarden, spoon in hand, watched her, bemused.

187

"We've been here an hour," I said. "We're only stopping for the night, on our way to the ribbon."

"We're here until Uncle's legs are better. Which will probably be another week." She frowned, counting days. "A little longer. We're sleeping in our flier, which is terribly uncomfortable, but Mama says the price for lodging here is outright theft." She sat down on the end of the bench, next to me. "I've never been in space, what's it like?"

"It's very cold—even *you* would find it cold." She thought that was funny, gave a little laugh. "And of course there's no air and hardly any gravity so everything just floats."

She frowned at me, mock rebuke. "You know what I mean."

I glanced over to where her mother sat, stolid, eating. Unconcerned. "It's really not very exciting."

The girl made a gesture of indifference. "Oh! You like music. There's a singer at a place down the street tonight." She used the word I had used mistakenly, not the one she had corrected me with, in Strigan's house. "We didn't go to hear her last night because they charge. And besides she's my cousin. Or she's in the next lineage over from mine, and she's my mother's cousin's daughter's aunt, that's close enough anyway. I heard her at the last ingather, she's very good."

"I'll be sure to go. Where is it?"

She gave me the name of the place, and then said she had to finish her supper. I watched her go back to her mother, who only looked up, briefly, and gave a curt nod, which I returned.

The place the girl had named was only a few doors down, a long, low-ceilinged building, its back wall all shutters, open just now on a walled yard, where Nilters sat uncoated in the one-degree air, drinking beer, listening silently to a woman playing a bowed, stringed instrument I'd never seen before.

I quietly ordered beer for myself and Seivarden, and we took seats on the inner side of the shutters—slightly warmer than the yard for the lack of a breeze, and with a wall to put our backs against. A few people turned to look at us, stared a moment, then turned away more or less politely.

Seivarden leaned three centimeters in my direction and whispered, "Why are we here?"

"To hear the music."

She raised an eyebrow. "This is *music*?"

I turned to look at her directly. She flinched, just slightly. "Sorry. It's just..." She gestured helplessly. Radchaai do have stringed instruments, quite a variety of them, in fact, accrued through several annexations, but playing them in public is considered a slightly risqué act, because one has to play either bare-handed, or in gloves so thin as to be nearly pointless. And this music—the long, slow, uneven phrases that made its rhythms difficult for the Radchaai ear to hear, the harsh, edged tone of the instrument—was not what Seivarden had been brought up to appreciate. "It's so..."

A woman at a nearby table turned and made a reproving, shushing noise. I gestured conciliation, and turned a cautioning look on Seivarden. For a moment her anger showed in her face and I was sure I would have to take her outside, but she took a breath, and looked at her beer, and drank, and afterward looked steadily ahead in silence.

The piece ended, and the audience rapped fists gently on their tables. The string player somehow looked both impassive and gratified, and launched into another, this one noticeably faster and loud enough for Seivarden to safely whisper to me again. "How long are we going to be here?"

"A while," I said.

"I'm tired. I want to go back to the room."

"Do you know where it is?"

She gestured assent. The woman at the other table eyed us disapprovingly. "Go," I whispered, as quietly as I could and still, I hoped, be heard by Seivarden.

Seivarden left. Not my concern anymore, I told myself, whether she found her way back to our lodgings (and I congratulated myself on having had the foresight to lock my pack in the facility's safe for the night—even without Strigan's warning I didn't trust Seivarden with my belongings or my money) or wandered aimlessly through the city, or walked into the river and drowned—whatever she did, it was no concern of mine and nothing I needed to worry about. I had, instead, a jar of sufficiently decent beer and an evening of music, with the promise of a good singer, and songs I'd never heard before. I was nearer to my goal than I'd ever dared hope to be, and I could, for just this one night, relax.

The singer was excellent, though I didn't understand any of the words she sang. She came on late, and by then the place was crowded and noisy, though the audience occasionally fell silent over their beer, listening to the music, and the knocking between pieces grew loud and boisterous. I ordered enough beer to justify my continued presence, but did not drink most of it. I'm not human, but my body is, and too much would have dulled my reactions unacceptably.

I stayed quite late, and then walked back to our lodgings along the darkened street, here and there a pair or threesome walking, conversing, ignoring me.

In the tiny room I found Seivarden asleep—motionless, breathing calm, face and limbs slack. Something indefinably still about her suggested that this was the first I'd seen her in real, restful sleep. For the briefest instant I found myself wondering if she'd taken kef, but I knew she had no money, didn't know anyone here, and didn't speak any of the languages I had heard so far.

I lay down beside her and slept.

I woke six hours later, and incredibly, Seivarden still lay beside me, still asleep. I didn't think she had waked while I slept.

She might as well get as much rest as she could. I was, after all, in no hurry. I rose and went out.

Further toward the medical center the street became noisy and crowded. I bought a bowl of hot, milky porridge from a vendor along the side of the walkway, and continued along where the road curved around the hospital and off toward the center of the town. Buses stopped, let passengers off, picked others up, continued on.

In the stream of people, I saw someone I recognized. The girl from Strigan's, and her mother. They saw me. The girl's eyes widened, and she frowned slightly. Her mother's expression didn't change, but they both swerved to approach me. They had, it seemed, been watching for me.

"Breq," said the girl, when they had stopped in front of me. Subdued. Uncharacteristically, it seemed.

"Is your uncle all right?" I asked.

"Yes, Uncle is fine." But clearly something troubled her.

"Your friend," said her mother, impassive as always. And stopped.

"Yes?"

"Our flier is parked near yours," the girl said, clearly dreading the communication of bad news. "We saw it when we got back from supper last night."

"Tell me." I didn't enjoy suspense.

Her mother actually frowned. "It's not there now."

I said nothing, waiting for the rest.

"You must have disabled it," she continued. "Your friend took money, and the people who paid him towed the flier away."

The lot staff must not have questioned it, they had seen Seivarden with me.

"She doesn't speak any languages," I protested.

"They made lots of motions!" explained the girl, gesturing widely. "Lots of pointing and speaking very slow."

I had badly underestimated Seivarden. Of course—she had survived, going from place to place with no language but Radchaai, and likely no money, but still had managed to nearly overdose on kef. More than once, likely. She could manage herself, even if she managed badly. She was entirely capable of getting what she wanted without help. And she had wanted kef, and she had obtained it. At my expense, but that was of no importance to her.

"We knew it couldn't be right," said the girl, "because you said you were only stopping the night on the way to space, but no one would have listened to us, we're just bov herders." And no doubt the sort of person who would buy a flier with no documentation, no proof of ownership—a flier, moreover, that had obviously been deliberately disabled to prevent its being moved by anyone but the owner—it might very well be a good idea to avoid confronting such a person.

"I would not presume to say," said the girl's mother, oblique condemnation, "what sort of friend your friend is."

Not my friend. Never my friend, now or at any other time. "Thank you for telling me."

I walked to the lot, and the flier was indeed gone. When I returned to the room, I found Seivarden still sleeping, or at any rate still unconscious. I wondered just how much kef the flier had bought her. I only wondered long enough to retrieve my pack from the lodging's safe, pay for the night—after this Seivarden would have to fend for herself, which apparently posed very little problem for her—and went looking for transport out of town.

There was a bus, but the first had left fifteen minutes before I asked after it, and the next would not leave for three hours. A train ran alongside the river, northward once a day, and like the bus it had already left.

I didn't want to wait. I wanted to be gone from here. More specifically, I didn't want to chance seeing Seivarden again, even briefly. The temperature here was mostly above freezing and I was entirely capable of walking long distances. The next town worth the name was, according to maps I'd seen, only a day away, if I cut across the glass bridge and then straight across the countryside instead of following the road, which curved to avoid the river and the bridge's wide chasm.

The bridge was several kilometers out of town. The walk would do me good; I had not had enough exercise lately. The bridge itself might be mildly interesting. I set off toward it.

When I had walked a little over half a kilometer, past the lodgings and food shops that surrounded the medical center, into what looked like a residential neighborhood—smaller buildings, groceries, clothes shops, complexes of low, square houses joined by covered passageways—Seivarden came up behind me. "Breq!" she gasped, out of breath. "Where are you going?"

I didn't answer, only walked faster. "Breq, damn it!"

I stopped, but did not turn around. Considered speaking. Nothing I thought of saying was remotely temperate, nor would anything I said do any sort of good. Seivarden caught up with me.

"Why didn't you wake me up?" she asked. Answers occurred to me. I refrained from speaking any of them aloud, and instead began walking again.

I didn't look back. I didn't care if she followed me or not, hoped, in fact, she wouldn't. I could certainly have no continued sense of responsibility, no fears that without me she would be helpless. She could take care of herself.

"Breq, damn it!" Seivarden called again. And then swore, and I heard her footsteps behind me, and her labored breath again as she caught up. This time I didn't stop, but quickened my pace slightly.

After another five kilometers, during which she had intermittently fallen behind and then raced, gasping, to catch up, she said, "Aatr's tits, you hold a grudge, don't you."

Still I said nothing, and didn't stop.

Another hour passed, the town well behind us, and the bridge came in sight, flat black arcing across the drop, spikes and curls of glass below, brilliant red, intense yellow, ultramarine, and jagged stubs of others. The chasm walls were striated, black, green-gray, and blue, frosted here and there with ice. Below, the bottom of the chasm was lost in cloud. A sign in five languages proclaimed it to be a protected monument, access permitted only to a certain class of license holders—what license, to what purpose, was mysterious to me, as I did not recognize all the words on the sign. A low barrier blocked the entrance, nothing I could not easily step over, and there was no one here but me and Seivarden. The bridge itself was five meters wide, like all the others, and while the wind blew strong, it wasn't strong enough to endanger me. I strode forward and stepped over the barrier and out onto the bridge.

Had heights troubled me, I might have found it dizzying.

Fortunately they did not, and my only discomfort was the feeling of open spaces behind and under me that I could not see unless I turned my attention away from other places. My boots thunked on the black glass, and the whole structure swayed slightly, and shuddered in the wind.

A new pattern of vibrations told me Seivarden had followed me.

What happened next was largely my own fault.

We were halfway across when Seivarden spoke. "All right, all right. I get it. You're angry."

I stopped, but did not turn. "How much did it get you?" I asked, finally, only one of the things I had considered saying.

"What?" Though I hadn't turned, I could see the motion as she leaned over, hands on her knees, could hear her still breathing hard, straining to be heard against the wind.

"How much kef?"

"I only wanted a little," she said, not quite answering my question. "Enough to take the edge off. I *need* it. And it's not like you paid for that flier to begin with." For an instant I thought she had remembered how I had acquired the flier, unlikely as that seemed. But she continued, "You've got enough in that pack to buy ten fliers, and none of it's yours, it belongs to the Lord of the Radch, docsn't it? Making me walk like this is just you being pissy."

I stood, still facing forward, my coat flattened against me in the wind. Stood trying to understand what her words meant, about who or what she thought I was. Why she thought I had troubled myself about her.

"I know what you are," she said, as I stood silent. "No doubt you wish you could leave me behind, but you can't, can you? You've got orders to bring me back."

"What am I?" I asked, still without turning. Loud, against the wind.

"*Nobody*, that's who." Seivarden's voice was scornful. She was standing upright now, just behind my left shoulder. "You tested into military, in the aptitudes, and like a million other nobodies these days, you think that makes you *somebody*. And you practiced the accent and how to hold your utensils, and knelt your way to Special Missions and now *I'm* your special mission, you've got to bring me home in one piece even though you'd rather not, wouldn't you? You've got a problem with me, at a guess your problem is that try all you like, whoever you kneel to, you'll never be what I was born to be, and people like you *hate* that."

I turned toward her. I'm certain my face was without expression, but when my eyes met hers she flinched—no edge taken off, none at all—and took three quick, reflexive steps backward.

Over the edge of the bridge.

I stepped to the edge, looked down. Seivarden hung six meters below, hands clenched around a complicated swirl of red glass, her eyes wide, mouth open slightly. She looked up at me and said, "You were going to hit me!"

The calculations came easily to me. All my clothes knotted would only reach 5.7 meters. The red glass was connected somewhere under the bridge I couldn't see, no sign of anything she could climb. The colored glass wasn't as strong as the bridge itself—I guessed the red spiral would shatter under Seivarden's weight sometime in the next three to seven seconds. Though that was only a guess. Still, any help I might call would certainly arrive too late. Clouds still veiled the bottom reaches of the chasm. Those tubes were just a few centimeters narrower than my outstretched arms, and were themselves very deep.

"Breq?" Seivarden's voice was breathy and strained. "Can you do something?" Not, at least, *You have to do something.*

"Do you trust me?" I asked.

Her eyes widened further, her gasps became a bit more ragged. She didn't trust me, I knew. She was only still with me because she thought I was official, hence inescapable, and she was important enough for the Radch to send someone after her—underestimating her own importance was never one of Seivarden's failings—and perhaps because she was tired of running, from the world, from herself. Ready to give up. But I still didn't understand why *I* was with *her.* Of all the officers I've served with, she was never one of my favorites.

"I trust you," she lied.

"When I grab you, raise your armor and put your arms around me." Fresh alarm flashed across her face, but there was no more time. I extended my armor under my clothes and stepped off the bridge.

The instant my hands touched her shoulders, the red glass shattered, sharp-edged fragments flying out and away, glittering briefly. Seivarden closed her eyes, ducked her head, face into my neck, held me tight enough that if I hadn't been armored my breathing would have been impeded. Because of the armor I couldn't feel her panicked breath on my skin, couldn't feel the air rushing past, though I could hear it. But she didn't extend her own armor.

If I had been more than just myself, if I had had the numbers I needed, I could have calculated our terminal velocity, and just how long it would take to reach it. Gravity was easy, but the drag of my pack and our heavy coats, whipping up around us, affecting our speed, was beyond me. It would have been much easier to calculate in a vacuum, but we weren't falling in a vacuum.

But the difference between fifty meters a second and 150 was, at that moment, only large in the abstract. I couldn't see the bottom yet, the target I was hoping to hit was small, and I didn't know how much time we'd have to adjust our attitude, if we even could. For the next twenty to forty seconds we had nothing to do but wait, and fall.

"Armor!" I shouted into Seivarden's ear.

"Sold it," she answered. Her voice shook slightly, straining against the rushing air. Her face was still pressed hard against my neck.

Suddenly gray. Moisture formed on exposed portions of my armor and blew streaming upward. One point three five seconds later I saw the ground, dark circles packed tight. Bigger, and therefore closer, than I liked. A surge of adrenaline surprised me; I must have gotten too used to falling. I turned my head, trying to look straight down past Seivarden's shoulder to what lay directly below us.

My armor was made to spread out the force of a bullet's impact, bleed some of it away as heat. It was theoretically impenetrable, but I could still be injured or even killed with the application of sufficient force. I'd suffered broken bones, lost bodies under an unrelenting hail of bullets. I wasn't sure what the friction of decelerating would do to my armor, or to me; I had some skeletal and muscular augmentation, but whether it would be sufficient for this, I had no idea. I was unable to calculate just exactly how fast we were going, just exactly how much energy needed to be bled away to slow to a survivable speed, how hot it would get inside and outside my armor. And unarmored, Seivarden wouldn't be able to assist.

Of course, if I had still been what I once was, it wouldn't matter. This wouldn't have been my only body. I couldn't help thinking I should have let Seivarden fall. Shouldn't have jumped. Falling, I still didn't know why I had done it. But at the moment of choice I had found I couldn't walk away.

By then I knew our distance in centimeters. "Five seconds," I said, shouted, above the wind. By then it was four. If we were very, very lucky we'd fall straight into the tube below us and I'd push my hands and feet against the walls. If we were very, very lucky the heat from the friction wouldn't burn unarmored Seivarden too badly. If I was even luckier I'd only break my wrists and ankles. All of it struck me as unlikely, but the omens would fall as Amaat intended.

Falling didn't bother me. I could fall forever and not be hurt. It's stopping that's the problem. "Three seconds," I said.

"Breq," Seivarden said, a gasping sob. "Please."

Some answers I would never have. I abandoned what calculations I was still making. I didn't know why I had jumped but at that moment it no longer mattered, at that moment there was nothing else. "Whatever you do"—one second—"don't let go."

Darkness. No impact. I thrust out my arms, which were immediately forced upward, wrists and one ankle breaking on impact despite my armor's reinforcement, tendons and muscles tearing, and we began a tumble sideways. Despite the pain I pulled my arms and legs in and reached and kicked out again, quickly, steadying us the instant after. Something in my right leg broke as I did, but I couldn't afford to worry about it. Centimeter by centimeter we slowed.

I could no longer control my hands or feet, could only push against the walls and hope we wouldn't be pushed off balance again, and fall helpless, headfirst, to our deaths. The pain was sharp, blinding, blocking out everything except numbers—a distance (estimated) decreasing by centimeters (also estimated); speed (estimated) decreasing; external armor temperature (increasing at my extremities, possible danger of exceeding acceptable parameters, possible resulting injury), but the numbers were near-meaningless to me, the pain was louder, more immediate, than anything else.

But the numbers were important. A comparison of distance and our rate of deceleration suggested disaster ahead. I tried to take a deep breath, found I was incapable of it, and tried to push harder against the walls.

I have no memory of the rest of the descent.

I woke, on my back, in pain. My hands and arms, my shoulders. Feet and legs. In front of me—directly above—a circle of gray light. "Seivarden," I tried to say, but it came out as a convulsive sigh that echoed just slightly against the walls. "Seivarden." The name came out this time, but barely audible, and distorted by my armor. I dropped the armor and tried speaking again, managing this time to engage my voice. "Seivarden."

I raised my head, just slightly. In the dim light from above I saw that I lay on the ground, knees bent and turned to one side, the right leg at a disturbing angle, my arms straight beside my body. I tried to move a finger, failed. A hand. Failed—of course. I tried shifting my right leg, which responded with more pain.

There was no one here but me. Nothing here but me—I didn't see my pack.

At one time, if there had been a Radchaai ship in orbit, I could have contacted it, easy as thought. But if I had been anywhere a Radchaai ship was likely to be, this would never have happened.

If I had left Seivarden in the snow, this would never have happened.

I had been so close. After twenty years of planning and working, of maneuvering, two steps forward here, a step backward there, slowly, patiently, against all likelihood I had gotten this far. So many times I had made a throw like this, not only my success at hazard, but my life, and each time I had won, or at least not lost in any way that prevented me from trying again.

Until now. And for such a stupid reason. Above me clouds hid the unreachable sky, the future I no longer had, the goal I was now incapable of accomplishing. Failed.

I closed my eyes against tears not brought on by physical pain. If I failed, it would not be because I had ever, at any time, given up. Seivarden had left somehow. I would find her. I would rest a moment, recollect myself, find the strength to pull out the handheld I kept in my coat and call for help, or discover some other way to leave here, and if it meant I dragged myself out on the bloody, useless remains of my limbs, I would do that, pain or no pain, or I would die trying.

14

One of the three Mianaais did not even arrive at the Var deck, but transmitted the code for my central access deck. *Invalid access*, I thought, receiving it, but stopped the lift on that level and opened the door anyway. That Mianaai made her way to my main console, gestured up records, scanned quickly through a century of log headings. Stopped, frowned, at a point in the list that would have been made in the five years surrounding that last visit, that I had concealed from her.

The other two of her stowed their bags in quarters, and went to the newly lit and slowly warming Var decade room. Both of her sat at the table, the silent colored-glass Valskaayan saint smiling mildly down. Without speaking aloud she requested information from me—a random sample of memories from that five-year span that had so attracted her attention, above on the central access deck. Silent, expressionless—unreal, in a sense, since I could only see her exteriors—she watched as my memories played out before her visions, in her ears. I began to doubt the truth of my memory of that other visit. There seemed to be no trace of it in the information Anaander Mianaai was accessing, nothing during that time but routine operations.

But something had attracted her attention to that stretch of time. And there was that *Invalid access* to account for—none of Anaander Mianaai's accesses were ever invalid, never could be. And why had I opened to an invalid access? And when one Anaander, in the Var decade room, frowned and said, "No, nothing," and the Lord of the Radch turned her attention to more recent memories, I found myself tremendously relieved.

In the meantime my captain and all my other officers went about the routine business of the day—training, exercising, eating, talking—completely unaware that the Lord of the Radch was aboard. The whole thing was wrong.

The Lord of the Radch watched my Esk lieutenants fencing over breakfast. Three times. With no visible change of expression. One Var set tea at the elbow of each of the two identical black-clad bodies in the Var decade room.

"Lieutenant Awn," said one Anaander. "Has she been out of your presence at all since the incident?" She hadn't specified which incident she meant, but she could only have meant the business in the temple of Ikkt.

"She has not, my lord," I said, using One Var's mouth.

On my central access deck, the Lord of the Radch keyed accesses and overrides that would allow her to change nearly anything about my mind she wished. *Invalid, invalid, invalid.* One after another. But each time I flashed acknowledgment, confirmed access she didn't actually have. I felt something like nausea, beginning to realize what must have happened, but having no accessible memory of it to confirm my suspicions, to make the matter clear and unambiguous to me.

"Has she at any time discussed this incident with anyone?"

This much was clear—Anaander Mianaai was acting against *herself*. Secretly. She was divided in two—at least two. I could only see traces of the other Anaander, the one who had changed the accesses, the accesses she thought she was only now changing to favor herself.

"Has she at any time discussed this incident with anyone?"

"Briefly, my lord," I said. Truly frightened for the first time in my long life. "With Lieutenant Skaaiat of *Justice of Ente*." How could my voice—One Var—speak so calmly? How could I even know what words to say, what answer to make, when the whole basis for all my actions—even my reason for existence—was thrown into doubt?

One Mianaai frowned—not the one that had been speaking. "Skaaiat," she said, with slight distaste. Seeming unaware of my sudden fear. "I've had my suspicions about Awer for some time." Awer was Lieutenant Skaaiat's house name, but what that had to do with events in the temple of Ikkt, I had no idea. "I never could find any proof." This, also, was mysterious to me. "Play me the conversation."

When Lieutenant Skaaiat said, *If you're going to do something that crazy, save it for when it'll make a difference*, one body leaned forward sharply and gave a breathy *ha*, an angry sound. Moments later, at the mention of Ime, eyebrows twitched. I feared momentarily that my dismay at the incautious, frankly dangerous tenor of that conversation would be detectable to the Lord of the Radch, but she made no mention of it. Had not seen it, perhaps, as she had not seen my profound disturbance at realizing she was no longer one person but two, in conflict with each other.

"Not proof. Not enough," Mianaai said, oblivious. "But dangerous. Awer *ought* to tip my way." Why she thought this, I didn't immediately understand. Awer had come from the Radch itself, from the start had had wealth and influence enough to allow it to criticize, and criticize it did, though generally with shrewdness enough to keep itself out of real trouble.

I had known Awer House for a long time, had carried its young lieutenants, known them as captains of other ships. Granted, no Awer suited for military service exhibited her house's tendencies to their utmost extent. An overly keen sense of injustice or a tendency to mysticism didn't mesh well with annexations. Nor with wealth and rank—any Awer's moral outrage inevitably smelled slightly of hypocrisy, considering the comforts and privileges such an ancient house enjoyed, and while some injustices were unignorably obvious to them, some others they never saw.

In any event, Lieutenant Skaaiat's sardonic practicality wasn't foreign to her house. It was only a milder, more livable version of Awer's tendency to moral outrage.

Doubtless each Anaander thought her cause was the more just. (The more proper, the more beneficial. Certainly.) Assuming Awer's penchant for just causes, the citizens of that house ought to support the proper side. Given they knew anything like sides were involved at all.

This assumed, of course, that any part at all of Anaander Mianaai thought any Awer was guided by a passion for justice and not by self-interest covered over with self-righteousness. And any given Awer could, at various times, be guided by either.

Still. It was possible some part of Anaander Mianaai thought that Awer (or any particular Awer) needed only to be convinced of the justice of her cause to champion it. And surely she knew that if Awer—any Awer—could not be convinced, it would be her implacable enemy.

"Suleir, now…" Anaander Mianaai turned to One Var, standing silent at the table. "Dariet Suleir seems to be an ally of Lieutenant Awn. Why?"

The question troubled me for reasons I couldn't quite identify. "I can't be entirely certain, my lord, but I believe Lieutenant Dariet considers Lieutenant Awn to be an able officer, and of course she defers to Lieutenant Awn as decade senior." And, perhaps, was secure enough in her own standing not to resent Lieutenant Awn's having authority over her. Unlike Lieutenant Issaaia. But I didn't say that.

"Nothing to do with political sympathies, then?"

"I am at a loss to understand what you mean, my lord," I said, quite sincerely but with growing alarm.

Another Mianaai body spoke up. "Are you playing stupid with me, Ship?"

"Begging my lord's pardon," I answered, still speaking through One Var, "if I knew what my lord was looking for I would be better able to supply relevant data."

In answer, Mianaai said, "*Justice of Toren*, when did I last visit you?"

If those accesses and overrides had been valid, I would have been utterly unable to conceal anything from the Lord of the Radch. "Two hundred three years, four months, one week, and five days ago, my lord," I lied, now sure of the significance of the question.

"Give me your memories of the incident in the temple," Mianaai commanded, and I complied.

And lied again. Because while nearly every instant of each of those individual streams of memory and data was unaltered, that moment of horror and doubt when one segment feared it might have to shoot Lieutenant Awn was, impossibly, missing.

* * *

It seems very straightforward when I say "I." At the time, "I" meant *Justice of Toren*, the whole ship and all its ancillaries. A unit might be very focused on what it was doing at that particular moment, but it was no more apart from "me" than my hand is while it's engaged in a task that doesn't require my full attention.

Nearly twenty years later "I" would be a single body, a single brain. That division, I–*Justice of Toren* and I–One Esk, was not, I have come to think, a sudden split, not an instant before which "I" was one and after which "I" was "we." It was something that had always been possible, always potential. Guarded against. But how did it go from potential to real, incontrovertible, irrevocable?

On one level the answer is simple—it happened when all of *Justice of Toren* but me was destroyed. But when I look closer I seem to see cracks everywhere. Did the singing contribute, the thing that made One Esk different from all other units on the ship, indeed in the fleets? Perhaps. Or is *anyone's* identity a matter of fragments held together by convenient or useful narrative, that in ordinary circumstances never reveals itself as a fiction? Or is it really a fiction?

I don't know the answer. But I do know that, though I can see hints of the potential split going back a thousand years or more, that's only hindsight. The first I noticed even the bare possibility that I–*Justice of Toren* might not also be I–One Esk, was that moment that *Justice of Toren* edited One Esk's memory of the slaughter in the temple of Ikkt. The moment I—"I"—was *surprised* by it.

It makes the history hard to convey. Because still, "I" was me, unitary, one thing, and yet I acted against myself, contrary to my interests and desires, sometimes secretly, deceiving myself as to what I knew and did. And it's difficult for me even now to know who performed what actions, or knew which information. Because *I* was *Justice of Toren.* Even when I wasn't. Even if I'm not anymore.

Above, on Esk, Lieutenant Dariet asked for admittance to Lieutenant Awn's quarters, found Lieutenant Awn lying on her bunk, staring sightlessly up, gloved hands behind her head. "Awn," she began, stopped, made a rueful smile. "I'm here to pry."

"I can't talk about it," answered Lieutenant Awn, still staring up, dismayed and angry but not letting it reach her voice.

In the Var decade room, Mianaai asked, "What are Dariet Suleir's political sympathies?"

"I believe she has none to speak of," I answered, with One Var's mouth.

Lieutenant Dariet stepped into Lieutenant Awn's quarters, sat on the edge of the bed, next to Lieutenant Awn's unbooted feet. "Not about that. Have you heard from Skaaiat?"

Lieutenant Awn closed her eyes. Still dismayed. Still angry. But with a slightly different feel. "Why should I have?"

Lieutenant Dariet was silent for three seconds. "I like Skaaiat," she said, finally. "I know she likes you."

"I was *there*. I was there and convenient. You know, we all know we'll be moving some time soon, and once we do Skaaiat has no reason to care whether or not I exist anymore. And even if…" Lieutenant Awn stopped. Swallowed. Breathed. "Even if she did," she continued, her voice just barely less steady than before, "it wouldn't matter. I'm not anyone she wants to be connected with, not anymore. If I ever was."

Below, Anaander Mianaai said, "Lieutenant Dariet seems pro-reform."

That puzzled me. But One Var had no opinion, of course, being only One Var, and it had no physical response to my puzzlement. I saw suddenly, clearly, that I was using One Var as a mask, though I didn't understand why or how I would do such a thing. Or why the idea would occur to me now. "Begging my lord's pardon, I don't see that as a political stance."

"Don't you?"

"No, my lord. You ordered the reforms. Loyal citizens will support them."

That Mianaai smiled. The other stood, left the decade room, to walk the Var corridors, inspecting. Not speaking to or acknowledging in any way the segments of One Var it passed.

Lieutenant Awn said, to Lieutenant Dariet's skeptical silence, "It's easy for you. Nobody thinks you're kneeling for advantage when you go to bed with someone. Or getting above yourself. Nobody wonders what your partner could be thinking, or how you ever got here."

"I've told you before, you're too sensitive about that."

"Am I?" Lieutenant Awn opened her eyes, levered herself up on her elbows. "How do you know? Have you experienced it much? I have. All the time."

"That," said Mianaai, in the decade room, "is a more complicated issue than many realize. Lieutenant Awn is pro-reform, of course." I wished I had physical data from Mianaai, so I could interpret the edge in her voice when she named Lieutenant Awn. "And Dariet, perhaps, though how strongly is a question. And the rest of the officers? Who here are pro-reform, and who anti-?"

In Lieutenant Awn's quarters, Lieutenant Dariet sighed. "I just think you worry too much about it. Who cares what people like that say?"

"It's easy not to care when you're rich, and the social equal of *people like that*."

"That sort of thing shouldn't matter," Lieutenant Dariet insisted.

"It shouldn't. But it does."

Lieutenant Dariet frowned. Angry, and frustrated. This conversation had happened before, had gone the same way each time. "Well. Regardless. You should send Skaaiat a message. What is there to lose? If she doesn't answer, she doesn't answer. But maybe…" Lieutenant Dariet lifted one shoulder, and her arm just slightly. A gesture that said, *Take a chance and see what fate deals you.*

If I hesitated in answering Anaander Mianaai's question for even the smallest instant, she would know the overrides weren't working. One Var was very, very impassive. I named a few officers who had definite opinions one way or the other. "The rest," I finished, "are content to follow orders and perform their duties without worrying too much about policy. As far as I can tell."

"They might be swayed one way or the other," Mianaai observed.

"I couldn't say, my lord." My sense of dread increased, but in a detached way. Perhaps the absolute unresponsiveness of my ancillaries made the feeling seem distant and unreal. Ships I knew who had exchanged their ancillary crews for human ones had said their experience of emotion had changed, though this didn't seem quite like the data they had shown me.

The sound of One Esk singing came faintly to Lieutenant Awn and Lieutenant Dariet, a simple song with two parts.

> *I was walking, I was walking*
> *When I met my love*

I was in the street walking
When I saw my true love
I said, "She is more beautiful than jewels, lovelier than
jade or lapis, silver or gold."

"I'm glad One Esk is itself again," said Lieutenant Dariet. "That first day was eerie."

"Two Esk didn't sing," Lieutenant Awn pointed out.

"Right, but..." Lieutenant Dariet gestured doubt. "It wasn't right." She looked speculatively at Lieutenant Awn.

"I can't talk about it," said Lieutenant Awn, and lay back down, crossing her arms over her eyes.

On the command deck Hundred Captain Rubran met with the decade commanders, drank tea, talked about schedules and leave times.

"You haven't mentioned Hundred Captain Rubran," said Mianaai, in the Var decade room.

I hadn't. I knew Captain Rubran extremely well, knew her every breath, every twitch of every muscle. She had been my captain for fifty-six years. "I have never heard her express an opinion on the matter," I said, quite truthfully.

"Never? Then it's certain she has one and is concealing it."

This struck me as something of a double bind. Speak and your possession of an opinion was plain, clear to anyone. Refrain from speaking and still this was proof of an opinion. If Captain Rubran were to say, *Truly, I have no opinion on the matter*, would that merely be another proof she had one?

"Surely she's been present when others have discussed it," Mianaai continued. "What have her feelings been in such cases?"

"Exasperation," I answered, through One Var. "Impatience. Sometimes boredom."

"Exasperation," mused Mianaai. "At what, I wonder?" I did not know the answer, so I said nothing. "Her family connections are such that I can't be certain where her sympathies are most likely to lie. And some of them I don't want to alienate before I can move openly. I have to tread carefully with Captain Rubran. But so will *she*."

She meaning, of course, herself.

There had been no attempt to discover *my* sympathies. Perhaps—no, certainly—they were irrelevant. And I was already well along the path the other Mianaai had set me on. These few Mianaais, and the four segments of One Var thawed for her service, only made the Var deck seem emptier, and all the decks between here and my engines. Hundreds of thousands of ancillaries slept in my holds, and they would likely be removed within the next few years, either stored or destroyed, never waking again. And I would be placed in orbit somewhere, permanently. My engines almost certainly disabled. Or I would be destroyed outright—though none of us had been so far, and I was fairly sure I would more likely serve as a habitat, or the core of a small station.

Not the life I had been built for.

"No, I can't be hasty with Rubran Osck. But your Lieutenant Awn is another matter. And perhaps she can be of use in discovering where Awer stands."

"My lord," I said, through one of One Var's mouths. "I am at a loss to understand what's happening. I would feel a great deal more comfortable if the hundred captain knew you were here."

"You dislike concealing things from your captain?" Anaander asked, with a tone that was equal parts bitter and amused.

"Yes, my lord. I will, of course, proceed precisely as you order me." A sudden sense of déjà vu overcame me.

"Of course. I should explain some things." The sense of déjà vu grew stronger. I had had this conversation before, in almost exactly these circumstances, with the Lord of the Radch. *You know that each of your ancillary segments is entirely capable of having its own identity*, she would say next. "You know that each of your ancillary segments is entirely capable of having its own identity."

"Yes." Every word, familiar. I could feel it, as though we were reciting lines we had memorized. Next she would say, *Imagine you became undecided about something.*

"Imagine some enemy separated part of you from yourself."

Not what I had been expecting. *What is it people say, when that happens? They're divided. They're of two minds.*

"Imagine that enemy managed to forge or force its way past all the necessary accesses. And that part of you came back to you—but wasn't really part of you anymore. But you didn't realize it. Not right away."

You and I, we really can be of two minds, can't we.

"That's a very alarming thought, my lord."

"It is," agreed Anaander Mianaai, all the time sitting in the Var decade room, inspecting the corridors and rooms of the Var deck. Watching Lieutenant Awn, alone again, and miserable. Gesturing through my mind, on the central access deck. Or so she thought. "I don't know precisely who has done it. I suspect the involvement of the Presger. They have been meddling in our affairs since before the Treaty. And after—five hundred years ago, the best surgicals and correctives were made in Radch space. Now we buy from the Presger. At first only at border stations, but now they're everywhere. Eight hundred years ago the Translators Office was a collection of minor officials who assisted in the interpretation of extra-Radch intelligence, and who smoothed linguistic problems during annexations. Now they dictate policy. Chief among them the Emissary to the Presger." The last sentence was spoken with audible distaste. "Before the Treaty, the Presger destroyed a few ships. Now they destroy all of Radch civilization.

"Expansion, annexation, is very expensive. Necessary—it has been from the beginning. From the first, to surround the Radch itself with a buffer zone, protecting it from any sort of attack or interference. Later, to protect *those* citizens. And to expand the reach of civilization. And…" Mianaai stopped, gave a short, exasperated sigh. "To pay for the previous annexations. To provide wealth for Radchaai in general."

"My lord, what do you suspect the Presger of having done?" But I knew. Even with my memory obscured and incomplete, I knew.

"Divided me. Corrupted part of me. And the corruption has spread, the other me has been recruiting—not only more parts of me but also my own citizens. My own soldiers." *My own ships.* "My own ships. I can only guess what her goal is. But it can't be anything good."

"Do I understand correctly," I asked, already knowing the answer, "that this other Anaander Mianaai is the force behind the ending of annexations?"

"She will destroy everything I've built!" I had never seen the Lord of the Radch so frustrated and angry. Had not thought her capable of it. "Do you realize—there's no reason you should ever have thought of it—that it's the appropriation of resources during annexations that drives our economy?"

"I am afraid, my lord, that I am only a troop carrier and have never concerned myself with such things. But what you say makes sense."

"And you. I doubt you're looking forward to losing your ancillaries."

Outside me my distant companions, the Justices parked around the system, sat silent, waiting. How many of them had received this visit—or both these visits? "I am not, my lord."

"I can't promise that I can prevent it. I'm not prepared for open warfare. All my moves are in secret, pushing here, pulling there, making sure of my resources and support. But in the end, she is me, and there is little I can do she will not already have thought of. She has outmaneuvered me several times already. It's why I have been so cautious in approaching you. I wanted to be sure she had not already suborned you."

I felt it was safer not to comment on that, and instead said, through One Var, "My lord, the guns in the lake, in Ors." *Was that your enemy?* I almost asked, but if we were faced with two Anaanders, each opposing the other, how did anyone know which was which?

"Events in Ors didn't come out precisely the way I wished," answered Anaander Mianaai. "I never expected anyone would find those guns, but if some Orsian fisherman had found them and said nothing, or even taken them, my purpose would still have been served." Instead, Denz Ay had reported her find to Lieutenant Awn. The Lord of the Radch hadn't expected that, I saw, hadn't thought the Orsians trusted Lieutenant Awn that much. "I didn't get what I wanted there, but perhaps the results will still serve my purpose. Hundred Captain Rubran is about to receive orders to depart this system for Valskaay. It was past time for you to leave, and you would have a year ago, if not for the Divine of Ikkt's insistence that Lieutenant Awn stay, and my own opposition. Whether knowingly or not, Lieutenant Awn is the instrument of my enemy, I'm certain of it."

I did not trust even One Var's impassivity to answer that,

and therefore did not speak. Above, on the central access deck, the Lord of the Radch continued to make changes, give orders, alter my thoughts. Still believing she could in fact do that.

No one was surprised at the order to depart. Four other Justices already had in the last year, to destinations meant to be final. But neither I nor any of my officers had expected Valskaay, six gates away.

Valskaay, that I had been sorry to leave. One hundred years ago, in the city of Vestris Cor, on Valskaay itself, One Esk had discovered volume upon volume of elaborate, multi-voiced choral music, all intended for the rites of Valskaay's troublesome religion, some of it dating from before humans had ever reached space. Downloaded everything it found so that it hardly regretted being sent away from such a treasure out to the countryside, hard work prying rebels from a reserve, forest and caverns and springs, that we couldn't just blast because it was a watershed for half the continent. A region of small rivers and bluffs, and farms. Grazing sheep and peach orchards. And music—even the rebels, trapped at last, had sung, either in defiance against us or as consolation for themselves, their voices reaching my appreciative ears as I stood at the mouth of the cave where they hid.

> *Death will overtake us*
> *In whatever manner already fated*
> *Everyone falls to it*
> *And so long as I'm ready*
> *I don't fear it*
> *No matter what form it takes.*

When I thought of Valskaay, I thought of sunshine and the sweet, bright taste of peaches. Thought of music. But I was sure I wouldn't be sent down to the planet this time—there would be no orchards for One Esk, no visits (unofficial, as unobtrusive as possible) to choral society meetings.

Traveling to Valskaay I would not, it turned out, take the gates, but generate my own, moving more directly. The gates most travelers used had been generated millennia ago, were held constantly open, stable, surrounded by beacons broadcasting warnings, notifications, information about local regulations and navigation hazards. Not only ships, but messages and information streamed constantly through them.

In the two thousand years I had been alive, I had used them once. Like all Radchaai warships, I was capable of making my own shortcut. It was more dangerous than using the established gates—an error in my calculations could send me anywhere, or nowhere, never to be heard from again. And since I left no structures behind to hold my gate open, I traveled in a bubble of normal space, isolated from everyone and everywhere until I exited at my destination. I didn't make such errors, and in the course of arranging an annexation the isolation could be an advantage. Now, though, the prospect of months alone, with Anaander Mianaai secretly occupying my Var deck, made me nervous.

Before I gated out, a message came from Lieutenant Skaaiat for Lieutenant Awn. Brief. *I said keep in touch. I meant it.*

Lieutenant Dariet said, "See, I told you." But Lieutenant Awn didn't answer.

15

At some point I opened my eyes again, thinking I had heard voices. All around me, blue. I tried to blink, found I could only close my eyes and leave them closed.

Sometime later I opened my eyes again, turned my head to the right, and saw Seivarden and the girl squatting on either side of a Tiktik board. So I was dreaming, or hallucinating. At least I no longer hurt, which on consideration was a bad sign, but I couldn't bring myself to care much. I closed my eyes again.

I woke, finally, actual wakefulness, and found myself in a small blue-walled room. I lay in a bed, and on a bench beside it Seivarden sat, leaning against the wall, looking as though she hadn't slept recently. Or, that is to say, even more as though she hadn't slept recently than she usually did.

I lifted my head. My arms and legs were immobilized by correctives.

"You're awake," said Seivarden.

I set my head back down. "Where's my pack?"

"Right here." She bent, lifted it into my line of sight.

"We're at the medical center in Therrod," I guessed, and closed my eyes.

"Yes. Do you think you can talk to the doctor? Because I can't understand anything she says."

I remembered my dream. "You learned to play Tiktik."

"That's different." So, not a dream.

"You sold the flier." No answer. "You bought kef."

"No, I didn't," she protested. "I was *going* to. But when I woke up and you were gone..." I heard her shift uncomfortably on the bench. "I was going to find a dealer, but it bothered me that you were gone and I didn't know where you were. I started to think maybe you'd left me behind."

"You wouldn't have cared once you took the kef."

"But I didn't have the kef," she said, voice surprisingly reasonable. "And then I went to the front and found you'd checked out."

"And you decided to find me, and not the kef," I said. "I don't believe you."

"I don't blame you." She was silent for five seconds. "I've been sitting here, thinking. I accused you of hating me because I was better than you."

"That's not why I hate you."

She ignored that. "Amaat's grace, that fall... it was my own stupid fault, I was sure I was dead, and if it had been the other way around I'd never have jumped to save anyone's life. You never knelt to get anywhere. You are where you are because you're fucking capable, and willing to risk everything to do right, and I'll never be half what you are even if I tried my whole life, and I was walking around thinking I was better than you, even half dead and no use to anyone, because my family is old, because I was *born better*."

"That," I said, "is why I hate you."

She laughed, as though I'd said something moderately witty. "If that's what you're willing to do for someone you hate, what would you do for someone you loved?"

I found I was incapable of answering. Fortunately the doctor came in, broad, round-faced, pale. Frowning slightly, slightly more when she saw me. "It seems," she said, in an even tone that seemed impartial but implied disapproval, "that I don't understand your friend when he tries to explain what happened."

I looked at Seivarden, who made a helpless gesture and said, "I don't understand any of it. I tried my best and the whole day she's been giving me that look, like I'm biological waste she stepped in."

"It's probably just her normal expression." I turned my head back to the doctor. "We fell off the bridge," I explained.

The doctor's expression didn't change. "Both of you?"

"Yes."

A moment of impassive silence, and then, "It does not pay to be dishonest with your doctor." And then when I didn't answer, "You would not be the first tourist to enter a restricted area and be injured. You are, however, the first to claim they'd fallen off the bridge and lived. I don't know whether to admire the brazenness, or be angry you take me for such a fool."

Still I said nothing. No story I could invent would account for my injuries in the way the truth did.

"Members of military forces must register on arrival in the system," the doctor continued.

"I remember hearing so."

"Did you register?"

"No, because I am not a member of any military force."

Not quite a lie. I was not a member, I was a piece of equipment. A lone, useless fragment of equipment at that.

"This facility is not equipped," the doctor said, just a shade more sternly than the moment before, "to deal with the sort of implants and augmentations you apparently have. I can't predict the results of the repairs I've programmed. You should see a doctor when you return home. To the Gerentate." That last sounded just slightly skeptical, the barest indication of the doctor's disbelief.

"I intend to go straight home once I leave here," I said, but I wondered if the doctor had reported us as possible spies. I thought not—if she had, likely she would have avoided expressing any sort of suspicion, merely waited for authorities to deal with us. She had not, then. Why not?

A possible answer stuck her head into the room and called cheerily, "Breq! You're awake! Uncle's on the level just above. What happened? Your friend seemed like he was saying you jumped off the bridge but that's impossible. Do you feel better?" The girl came fully into the room. "Hello, Doctor, is Breq going to be all right?"

"Breq will be fine. The correctives should drop off by tomorrow. Unless something goes wrong." And with that cheerful observation she turned and left the room.

The girl sat on the edge of my bed. "Your friend is a terrible Tiktik player, I'm glad I didn't teach him the gambling part or he wouldn't have had any money to pay the doctor with. And it's *your* money, isn't it? From the flier."

Seivarden frowned. "What? What is she saying?"

I resolved to check the contents of my pack as soon as I could. "He'd have won it back playing counters."

From the look on her face, the girl didn't believe that at all. "You really shouldn't go under the bridge, you know. I know someone who had a friend whose cousin went under the bridge and someone dropped a piece of bread off, and it was going so fast it hit them in the head and broke their skull open and went into their brain and *killed* them."

"I enjoyed your cousin's singing very much." I didn't want to reopen the discussion about what had happened.

"Isn't she wonderful? Oh!" She turned her head, as though she'd heard something. "I have to go. I'll visit you again!"

"I'd appreciate that," I said, and she was out the door and away. I looked at Seivarden. "How much did this cost?"

"About what I got for the flier," she said, ducking her head slightly, maybe out of embarrassment. Maybe something else.

"Did you take anything out of my pack?"

That brought her head up again. "No! I swear I didn't." I didn't answer. "You don't believe me. I don't blame you. You can check, as soon as your hands are free."

"I intend to. But then what?"

She frowned, not comprehending. And of course she didn't understand—she had gotten as far as (mistakenly) evaluating me as a human being who might be worthy of respect. She had not, it seemed, come to the point of considering she might not actually be important enough for the Radch to send a Special Missions officer after.

"I was never assigned to find you," I said. "I found you completely by accident. As far as I know, no one is looking for you." I wished I could gesture, wave her away.

"Why are you here, then? It's not groundwork for an annexation, there aren't any more. That's what they told me."

"No more annexations," I agreed. "But that's not the point. The point is, you can come or go as you like, I have no orders to bring you back."

Seivarden considered that for six seconds, and then said,

"I tried to quit before. I *did* quit. This station I was on had a program, you'd quit, they'd give you a job. One of their workers hauled me in and cleaned me up and told me the deal. The job was crap, the deal was bullshit, but I'd had enough. I thought I'd had enough."

"How long did you last?"

"Not quite six months."

"You see," I said, after a two-second pause, "why I don't exactly have confidence in you this time."

"Believe me, I do. But this is *different*." She leaned forward, earnest. "Nothing quite clarifies your thoughts like thinking you're about to die."

"The effect is often temporary."

"They said, back on that station, that they could give me something to make kef never work on me. But first I had to fix whatever had made me take it to begin with, because otherwise I'd just find something else. Bullshit, like I said, but if I'd really wanted to, really meant to, I'd have done it then."

Back at Strigan's she'd spoken as though her reason for starting was simple, clear-cut. "Did you tell them why you started?" She didn't answer. "Did you tell them who you were?"

"Of course not."

The two questions were the same in her mind, I guessed. "You faced death back at Garsedd."

She flinched, just slightly. "And everything changed. I woke up and all I had was past. Not a very good past, either, no one liked telling me what had happened, everyone was so polite and cheerful and it was all *fake*. And I couldn't see any kind of future. Listen." She leaned forward, earnest, breathing slightly harder. "You're out here on your own, all by yourself, and obviously it's because you're suited to it or you wouldn't have been assigned." She paused a moment, maybe considering that issue of just who was suited to what, who was assigned where, and dismissing it. "But in the end, you can go back to the Radch and find people who know you, people who remember you, personally, a place where you *fit* even if you're not always there. No matter where you go, you're still part of that pattern, even if you never go back you always know it's *there*. But when they opened that suspension pod, anyone who ever had any personal interest in me was already seven hundred years dead. Probably longer. Not even…" Her voice trembled, and she stopped, staring ahead at some fixed point beyond me. "Even the ships."

Even the ships. "Ships? More than just *Sword of Nathtas*?"

"My…the first ship I ever served on. *Justice of Toren*. I thought maybe if I could find where it was stationed I could send a message and…" She made a negating gesture, wiping out the rest of that sentence. "It disappeared. About ten…wait…I've lost track of time. About fifteen years ago." Closer to twenty. "Nobody could tell me what happened. Nobody knows."

"Were any of the ships you served on particularly fond of you?" I asked, voice carefully even. Neutral.

She blinked. Straightened. "That's an odd question. Do you have any experience with ships?"

"Yes," I said. "Actually."

"Ships are always attached to their captains."

"Not like they used to be." Not like when some ships had gone mad on the deaths of their captains. That had been long, long ago. "And even so, they have favorites." Though a favorite wouldn't necessarily know it. "But it doesn't matter, does it? Ships aren't people, and they're made to serve you, to be attached, as you put it."

Seivarden frowned. "Now you're angry. You're very good at hiding it, but you're angry."

"Do you grieve for your ships," I asked, "because they're dead? Or because their loss means they aren't here to make you feel connected and cared about?" Silence. "Or do you think those are the same thing?" Still no answer. "I will answer my own question: you were never a favorite of any of the ships you served on. You don't believe it's possible for a ship to have favorites."

Seivarden's eyes widened—maybe surprise, maybe something else. "You know me too well for me to believe you aren't here because of me. I've thought so from the moment I actually started thinking about it."

"Not too long ago, then," I said.

She ignored what I had just said. "You're the first person, since that pod opened, to feel *familiar*. Like I recognize you. Like you recognize me. I don't know why that is."

I knew, of course. But this was not the moment to say so, to explain, immobilized and vulnerable as I was. "I assure you I'm not here because of you. I'm here on my own personal business."

"You jumped off that bridge for me."

"And I'm not going to be your reason for quitting kef. I take no responsibility for you. You're going to have to do that yourself. If you really are going to do that."

"You jumped off that *bridge* for me. That had to be a three-kilometer drop. Higher. That's...that's..." She stopped, shaking her head. "I'm staying with you."

I closed my eyes. "The moment I even *think* you're going to steal from me again, I will break both your legs and leave you there, and it will be utter coincidence if you ever see me again." Except that to Radchaai, there were no coincidences.

"I guess I can't really argue with that."

"I don't recommend it."

She gave a short laugh, and then was silent for fifteen seconds. "Tell me, then, Breq," she said after that. "If you're here on personal business, and nothing at all to do with me, why do you have one of the Garseddai guns in your pack?"

The correctives held my arms and legs completely immobile. I couldn't even get my shoulders off the bed. The doctor came heavily into the room, pale face flushed. "Lie still!" she admonished, and then turned to Seivarden. "What did you do?"

This was, apparently, comprehensible to Seivarden. She spread her hands in a helpless gesture. "Not!" she replied, vehemently, in the same language.

The doctor frowned, pointed at Seivarden, one finger out. Seivarden straightened, indignant at the gesture, which was much ruder to a Radchaai than it was here. "You bother," the doctor said, sternly, "you go!" Then she turned to me. "*You* will lie still and heal properly."

"Yes, Doctor." I subsided from the very small amount of movement I had managed. Took a breath, attempting to calm myself.

This seemed to mollify her. She watched me a moment, doubtless seeing my heart rate, my breathing. "If you can't settle, I can give you medication." An offer, a question, a threat. "I can make him"—with a glance at Seivarden—"leave."

"I don't need it. Either one."

The doctor gave a skeptical *hmph*, and turned and left the room.

"I'm sorry," said Seivarden when the doctor was gone. "That was stupid. I should have thought before I spoke." I didn't answer. "When we got to the bottom," she continued, as though it was logically connected to what she had said before, "you were unconscious. And obviously badly injured, and I was afraid to move you much, because I couldn't see if maybe bones were broken. I didn't have any way to call for help, but I thought maybe you had something I could use to help climb out, or maybe some first-aid correctives I could use, but of course that was foolish, your armor was still up, which was how I knew you were still alive. I did take your handheld out of your coat, but there was no signal, I had to climb up to the top before I could reach anyone. When I got back your armor was down and I was afraid you were dead. Everything's still in there."

"If the gun is gone," I said, voice calm and neutral, "I won't just break your legs."

"It's there," she insisted. "But this can't possibly be personal business, can it?"

"It's personal." It was just that with me *personal* affected a great many others. But how could I explain that, without revealing more than I wanted to just now?

"Tell me."

This was not a good time. Not a good moment. But there was a great deal to explain, especially since Seivarden's knowledge of the past thousand years of history was sure to be patchy and superficial. Years of previous events leading up to this, which she would almost certainly be ignorant of, which would take time to explain, before I ever got to who I was and what I intended.

And that history would make a difference. Without understanding it, how could Seivarden understand anything? Without that context, how could she understand why anyone had acted as they did? If Anaander Mianaai had not reacted with such fury to the Garseddai, would she have done the things she'd done in the thousand years since then? If Lieutenant Awn had never heard of the events at Ime five years before, twenty-five years ago now, would she have acted as she did?

When I imagined it, the moment that *Mercy of Sarrse* soldier had chosen to defy her orders, I saw her as a segment of an ancillary unit. She had been number One of *Mercy of Sarrse*'s Amaat unit, its senior member. Even though she had been human, had had a name beyond her place on her ship, beyond *Mercy of Sarrse* One Amaat One. But I had never seen a recording, had never seen her face.

She had been human. She had endured events at Ime— perhaps even enforced the corrupt dictates of the governor herself, when ordered. But something about that particular moment had changed things. Something had been too much for her.

What had it been? The sight, perhaps, of a Rrrrrr, dead or dying? I'd seen pictures of the Rrrrrr, snake-long, furred, multi-limbed, speaking in growls and barks; and the humans associated with them, who could speak that language and understand it. Had it been the Rrrrrr who had knocked *Mercy of Sarrse* One Amaat One off her expected path? Did she care so much for the threat of breaking the treaty with the Presger? Or had it been the thought of killing so many helpless human beings? If I had known more about her, perhaps I could have seen why in that moment she had decided that she would rather die.

I knew almost nothing about her. Probably by design. But even the little I had known, the little Lieutenant Awn had known, had made a difference. "Did anyone tell you about what happened at Ime Station?"

Seivarden frowned. "No. Tell me."

I told her. About the governor's corruption, her preventing Ime Station or any of the ships from reporting what she was doing, so far from anywhere else in Radch space. About the ship that had arrived one day—they'd assumed it was human, no one knew of any aliens anywhere nearby, and it obviously wasn't Radchaai and so it was fair game. I told Seivarden as much as I knew about the soldiers from *Mercy of Sarrse* who boarded the unknown ship with orders to take it and kill anyone aboard who resisted, or who obviously couldn't be made into ancillaries. I didn't know much—only that once the One Amaat unit had boarded the alien ship, its One had refused to continue to follow orders. She had convinced the rest of One Amaat to follow her, and they had defected to the Rrrrr and taken the ship out of reach.

Seivarden's frown only deepened, and when I was done she said, "So, you're telling me the governor of Ime was completely corrupt. And somehow had the accesses to prevent Ime Station from reporting her? How does that happen?" I didn't answer. Either the obvious conclusion would occur to her, or she would be unable to see it. "And how could the aptitudes have put her in such a position, if she was capable of that? It isn't possible.

"Of course," Seivarden continued, "everything else follows from that, doesn't it? A corrupt governor appoints corrupt officials, never mind the aptitudes. But the captains stationed there...no, it isn't possible."

She wouldn't be able to see it. I shouldn't have said anything at all. "When that soldier refused to kill the Rrrrr who had come into the system, when she convinced the rest of her unit to do likewise, she created a situation that could not be concealed for long. The Rrrrr could generate their own gate, so the governor couldn't prevent them from leaving. They had only to make a single jump to the next inhabited system and tell their story. Which was exactly what they did."

"Why did anyone care about the Rrrrr?" Seivarden couldn't quite get her throat around the sound. "Seriously? They're called that?"

"It's what they call themselves," I explained, in my most patient voice. When a Rrrrr said it, or one of their human translators, it sounded like a sustained growl, not much different from any other Rrrrr speech. "It's kind of hard to say. Most people I've heard just say a long *r* sound."

"Rrrrr," Seivarden said, experimentally. "Still sounds funny. So why did anyone care about the Rrrrr?"

"Because the Presger had made a treaty with us on the basis of their having decided humans were Significant. Killing the Insignificant is nothing, to the Presger, and violence between members of the same species means nothing to them, but indiscriminate violence toward other Significant species is unacceptable." Not to say no violence is allowed, but it's subject to certain conditions, none of which make obvious sense to most humans so it's safest just to avoid it altogether.

Seivarden made a breathy *huh*, pieces falling into place.

"So then," I continued, "the entire One Amaat unit of *Mercy of Sarrse* had defected to the Rrrrr. They were out of reach, safe with the aliens, but to the Radchaai they were guilty of treason. It might have been better just to leave them where they were, but instead the Radch demanded them back, so they could be executed. And of course the Rrrrr didn't want to do that. The One Amaat unit had saved their lives. Things were very tense for several years, but eventually they compromised. The Rrrrr handed over the unit leader, the one who'd started the mutiny, in exchange for immunity for the others."

"But..." Seivarden stopped.

After seven seconds of silence, I said, "You're thinking that of course she had to die, no disobedience can be tolerated, for very good reasons. But at the same time, her treason exposed the governor of Ime's corruption, which otherwise would have continued unabated, so ultimately she did the Radch a service. You're thinking that any fool knows better than to speak up and criticize a government official for any reason. And you're thinking that if anyone who speaks up to criticize something obviously evil is punished merely for speaking, civilization will be in a bad way. No one will speak who isn't willing to die for her speech, and..." I hesitated. Swallowed. "There aren't many willing to do that. You're probably thinking that the Lord of the Radch was in a difficult spot, deciding how to handle the situation. But also that these particular circumstances were extraordinary, and Anaander Mianaai is, in the end, the ultimate authority and might have pardoned her if she wished."

"I'm thinking," said Seivarden, "that the Lord of the Radch could have just let them stay with the Rrrrr and been free of the whole mess."

"She could have," I agreed.

"I'm also thinking that if I were the Lord of the Radch, I would never have let that news get much farther than Ime."

"You'd use accesses to prevent ships and stations from talking about it, maybe. You'd forbid any citizens who knew to say anything."

"Yes. I would."

"But it would still spread by rumor." Though that rumor would of necessity be vague and slow-moving. "And you'd lose the very instructive example you could make, letting everyone watch you line up nearly all of Ime's Administration on the station concourse and shoot them in the head, one after the other." And, of course, Seivarden was a single person, who was thinking of Anaander Mianaai as a single person who could be undecided about such things, but then choose a single course of action, without dividing herself over her decision. And there was a great deal more behind Anaander Mianaai's dilemma than Seivarden had grasped.

Seivarden was silent for four seconds, and then said, "Now I'm going to make you angry again."

"Really?" I asked, drily. "Aren't you getting tired of that?"

"Yes." Simply. Seriously.

"The governor of Ime was wellborn and well-bred," I said, and named her house.

"Never heard of them," said Seivarden. "There've been so many changes. And now things like this happening. You honestly don't think there's a connection?"

I turned my head away, without lifting it. Not angry, just very, very tired. "You mean to say, none of this would have happened if jumped-up provincials hadn't been jumped up. If the governor of Ime had been from a family of *real* proven quality."

Seivarden had wit enough not to answer.

"You've honestly never known anyone *born better* to be assigned or promoted past their ability? To crack under pressure? Behave badly?"

"Not like that."

Fair enough. But she'd conveniently forgotten that *Mercy of Sarrse* One Amaat One—human, not an ancillary—would also have been "jumped up" by her definition, was part of the very change Seivarden had mentioned. "Jumped-up provincials and the sort of thing that happened at Ime are both results of the same events. One did not cause the other."

She asked the obvious question. "What caused it, then?"

The answer was too complicated. How far back to begin?

It started at Garsedd. It started when the Lord of the Radch multiplied herself and set out to conquer all of human space. It started when the Radch was built. And further back. "I'm tired," I said.

"Of course," said Seivarden, more equably than I had expected. "We can talk about it later."

16

I spent a week moving in the non-space between Shis'urna and Valskaay—isolated, self-contained—before the Lord of the Radch made her move. No one else suspected anything, I had given no hint, no trace, not the faintest indication that anyone at all was on Var deck, that anything at all might be wrong.

Or so I had thought. "Ship," Lieutenant Awn said to me, a week in, "is something wrong?"

"Why do you ask, Lieutenant?" I replied. One Esk replied. One Esk attended Lieutenant Awn constantly.

"We were in Ors together a long time," Lieutenant Awn said, frowning slightly at the segment she was talking to. She had been in a constant state of misery since Ors, sometimes more intense, sometimes less, depending, I supposed, on what thoughts occurred to her at a given moment. "You just seem like something's troubling you. And you're quieter." She made a sound, breathy half-amusement. "You were always humming or singing in the house. It's too quiet now."

234

"There are walls here, Lieutenant," I pointed out. "There were none in the house in Ors."

Her eyebrow twitched just slightly. I could see she knew my words for an evasion, but she didn't pursue the question.

At the same time, in the Var decade room, Anaander Mianaai said to me, "You understand the stakes. What this means for the Radch." I acknowledged this. "I know this must be disturbing to you." It was the first acknowledgment of this possibility since she had come aboard. "I made you to serve my ends, for the good of the Radch. It's part of your design, to want to serve me. And now you must not only serve me, but also oppose me."

She was, I thought, making it remarkably easy for me to oppose her. One side or the other of her had done that, and I wasn't sure which. But I said, through One Var, "Yes, my lord."

"If she succeeds, ultimately the Radch will fragment. Not the center, not the Radch itself." When most people spoke of the Radch they meant all of Radchaai territory, but in truth the Radch was a single location, a Dyson sphere, enclosed, self-contained. Nothing ritually impure was allowed within, no one uncivilized or nonhuman could enter its confines. Very, very few of Mianaai's clients had ever set foot there, and only a few houses still existed who even had ancestors who had once lived there. It was an open question if anyone within knew or cared about the actions of Anaander Mianaai, or the extent or even existence of Radch territory. "The Radch itself, as the Radch, will survive longer. But my territory, that I built to protect it, to keep it pure, will shatter. I made myself into what I am, built all this"—she gestured sweepingly, the walls of the decade room encompassing, for her purposes, the entirety of Radch space—"all this, to keep that center safe. Uncontaminated. I couldn't trust it to anyone else. Now, it seems, I can't trust it to myself."

"Surely not, my lord," I said, at a loss for what else to say, not sure exactly what I was protesting.

"Billions of citizens will die in the process," she continued, as though I had not spoken. "Through war, or lack of resources. And I..."

She hesitated. Unity, I thought, implies the possibility of disunity. Beginnings imply and require endings. But I did not say so. The most powerful person in the universe didn't need me to lecture her on religion or philosophy.

"But I am already broken," she finished. "I can only fight to prevent my breaking further. Remove what is no longer myself."

I wasn't sure what I should, or could, say. I had no conscious memory of having this conversation previously, though I was certain now I must have, must have listened to Anaander Mianaai explain and justify her actions, after she used the overrides and changed...something. It must have been quite similar, perhaps even the same words. It had, after all, been the same person.

"And," Anaander Mianaai continued, "I must remove my enemy's weapons wherever I find them. Send Lieutenant Awn to me."

Lieutenant Awn approached the Var decade room with trepidation, not knowing why I had sent her there. I had refused to answer her questions, which had only fed a growing feeling on her part that something was very wrong. Her boots on the white floor echoed emptily, despite One Var's presence.

As she reached it the decade room door slid open, nearly noiseless.

The sight of Anaander Mianaai within hit Lieutenant Awn like a blow, a vicious spike of fear, surprise, dread, shock, doubt, and bewilderment. Lieutenant Awn took three breaths, shallower, I could see, than she liked, and then hitched her shoulders just the slightest bit, stepped in, and prostrated herself.

"Lieutenant," said Anaander Mianaai. Her accent, and tone, were the prototype of Lieutenant Skaaiat's elegant vowels, of Lieutenant Issaaia's thoughtless, slightly sneering arrogance. Lieutenant Awn lay facedown, waiting. Frightened.

As before I received no data from Mianaai that she did not deliberately send me. I had no information about her internal state. She seemed calm. Impassive, emotionless. I was sure that surface impression was a lie, though I didn't understand why I thought that, except that she had yet to speak favorably of Lieutenant Awn, when in my opinion she should have. "Tell me, Lieutenant," said Mianaai, after a long silence, "where those guns came from, and what you think happened in the temple of Ikkt."

A combination of relief and fear washed through Lieutenant Awn. She had, in the moments available to process Anaander Mianaai's presence here, formed an expectation that this question would be asked. "My lord, the guns could only have come from someone with sufficient authority to divert them and prevent their destruction."

"You, for instance."

A sharp stab of startlement and terror. "No, my lord, I assure you. I did disarm noncitizens local to my assignment, and some of them were Tanmind military." The police station in the upper city had been quite well-armed, in fact. "But

I had those disabled on the spot, before I sent them on. And according to their inventory numbers, these had been collected in Kould Ves."

"By *Justice of Toren* troops?"

"So I understand, my lord."

"Ship?"

I answered with one of One Var's mouths. "My lord, the guns in question were collected by Sixteen and Seventeen Inu." I named their lieutenant at the time, who had since been reassigned.

Anaander Mianaai made the barest hint of a frown. "So as far back as five years ago, someone with access—perhaps this Inu lieutenant, perhaps someone else, prevented these weapons from being destroyed, and hid them. For five years. And then, what, planted them in the Orsian swamp? To what end?"

Face still to the floor, blinking in confusion, Lieutenant Awn took one second to frame a reply. "I don't know, my lord."

"You're lying," said Mianaai, still sitting, leaning back in her chair as though quite relaxed and unconcerned, but her eyes had not left Lieutenant Awn. "I can see plainly that you are. And I've heard every conversation you've had, since the incident. Who did you mean when you spoke of someone else who would benefit from the situation?"

"If I'd known what name to put there, my lord, I would have used it. I only meant by it that there must be a specific person who acted, who caused it..." She stopped, took a breath, abandoned that sentence. "Someone conspired with the Tanmind, someone who had access to those guns. Whoever it was, they wanted trouble between the upper city and the lower. It was my job to prevent that. I did my best to prevent that." Certainly an evasion. From the moment Anaander Mianaai had ordered the hasty execution of those Tanmind citizens in the temple, the first, most obvious suspect had been the Lord of the Radch herself.

"Why would anyone want trouble between the upper city and the lower?" Anaander Mianaai asked. "Who would exert themselves over it?"

"Jen Shinnan, my lord, and her associates," answered Lieutenant Awn, on firmer ground, for the moment at least. "She felt the ethnic Orsians were unduly favored."

"By you."

"Yes, my lord."

"So you're saying that in the first months of the annexation, Jen Shinnan found some Radchaai official willing to divert crates full of weapons so that five years later she could start trouble between the upper and lower city. To get you in trouble."

"My lord!" Lieutenant Awn lifted her forehead one centimeter off the floor, then halted. "I don't know how, I don't know why. I don't know wh..." She swallowed that last, which I knew would have been a lie. "What I know is, it was my job to keep the peace in Ors. That peace was threatened and I acted to..." She stopped, realizing perhaps that the sentence would be an awkward one to finish. "It was my job to protect the citizens in Ors."

"Which is why you so vehemently protested the execution of the people who *endangered* the citizens in Ors." Anaander Mianaai's tone was dry, and sardonic.

"They were my responsibility, lord. And as I said at the time, they were under control, we could have held them until reinforcements arrived, very easily. You are the ultimate authority, and of course your orders must be obeyed, but I didn't understand why those people had to die. I still don't understand why they had to die right then." A half-second pause. "I don't need to understand why. I'm here to follow your orders. But I…" She paused again. Swallowed. "My lord, if you suspect anything of me, any wrongdoing or disloyalty, I beg you, have me interrogated when we reach Valskaay."

The same drugs used for aptitudes testing and reeducation could be used for interrogation. A skilled interrogator could pry the most secret thoughts from a person's mind. An unskilled one could throw up irrelevancies and confabulations, could damage her subject nearly as badly as an unskilled reeducator.

What Lieutenant Awn had asked for was something surrounded by legal obligations—not least among them the requirement that two witnesses be present, and Lieutenant Awn would have the right to name one of them.

I saw nausea and terror in her when Anaander Mianaai didn't answer. "My lord, may I speak plainly?"

"By all means, speak plainly," said Anaander Mianaai, dry and bitter.

Lieutenant Awn spoke, terrified, face still to the floor. "It was *you*. You diverted the guns, you planned that mob, with Jen Shinnan. But I don't understand why. It can't have been about me, I'm *nobody*."

"But you do not intend to *remain* nobody, I think," replied Anaander Mianaai. "Your pursuit of Skaaiat Awer tells me as much."

"My…" Lieutenant Awn swallowed. "I never pursued her. We were *friends*. She oversaw the next district."

"Friends, you call that."

Lieutenant Awn's face heated. And she remembered her

accent, and her diction. "I am not presumptuous enough to call it more." Miserable. Frightened.

Mianaai was silent for three seconds, and then said, "Perhaps not. Skaaiat Awer is handsome and charming, and no doubt good in bed. Someone like you would be easily susceptible to her manipulation. I have suspected Awer's disloyalty for some time."

Lieutenant Awn wanted to speak, I could see the muscles in her throat tense, but no sound came out.

"I am, yes, speaking of sedition. You say you're loyal. And yet you associate with Skaaiat Awer." Anaander Mianaai gestured and Skaaiat's voice sounded in the decade room.

"I know you, Awn. If you're going to do something that crazy, save it for when it'll make a difference."

And Lieutenant Awn's reply: "*Like* Mercy of Sarrse *One Amaat One?*"

"What difference," asked Anaander Mianaai, "would you wish to make?"

"The sort of difference," Lieutenant Awn replied, mouth gone dry, "that *Mercy of Sarrse* soldier made. If she hadn't done what she did, all the business at Ime would still be going on." As she spoke I'm sure she realized what it was she was saying. That this was dangerous territory. Her next words made it plain she *did* know. "She died for it, yes. But she revealed all that corruption to you."

I had had a week to think about the things Anaander Mianaai had said to me. By now I had worked out how the governor of Ime might have had the accesses that prevented Ime Station from reporting her activities. She could only have gotten those accesses from Anaander Mianaai herself. The only question was, which Anaander Mianaai had enabled it?

"It was on all the public news channels," Anaander

Mianaai observed. "I would have preferred it wasn't. Oh, yes," she said, in answer to Lieutenant Awn's surprise. "That wasn't by my desire. The entire incident has sown doubt where before there was none. Discontent and fear where there had been only confidence in my ability to provide justice and benefit.

"Rumors I could have dealt with, but reports through approved channels! Broadcast where every Radchaai could see and hear! And without the publicity I might have let the Rrrrrr take the traitors away quietly. Instead I had to negotiate for their return, or else let them stand as an invitation to further mutiny. It caused me a great deal of trouble. It's *still* causing trouble."

"I didn't realize," said Lieutenant Awn, panic in her voice. "It was on all the public channels." Then realization struck her. "I haven't...I haven't said anything about Ors. To anyone."

"Except Skaaiat Awer," the Lord of the Radch pointed out. Which was hardly just—Lieutenant Skaaiat had been nearby, close enough to see with her own eyes the evidence that something had happened. "No," Mianaai continued, in answer to Lieutenant Awn's inarticulate query, "it hasn't turned up on public channels. Yet. And I can see that the idea that Skaaiat Awer might be a traitor is distressing to you. I think you're having trouble believing it."

Once again, Lieutenant Awn struggled to speak. "That is correct, my lord," she finally managed.

"I can offer you," said Mianaai in reply, "the opportunity to prove her innocence. And to better your situation. I can manipulate your assignment so that you can be close to her again. You need only take clientship when Skaaiat offers—oh, she'll offer," the Lord of the Radch said, seeing,

I'm sure, Lieutenant Awn's despair and doubt at her words. "Awer has been collecting people like you. Upstarts from previously unremarkable houses who suddenly find themselves in positions advantageous for business. Take clientship, and observe." *And report* was left unsaid.

The Lord of the Radch was trying to turn her enemy's instrument into her own. What would happen if she couldn't do that?

But what would happen if she did? No matter what choice Lieutenant Awn made now, she would be acting against Anaander Mianaai, the Lord of the Radch.

I had already seen her choice once, when faced with death. She would choose the path that kept her alive. And she—and I—could puzzle out the implications of that path later, would see what the options were when matters were less immediately urgent.

In the Esk decade room Lieutenant Dariet asked, alarmed, "Ship, what's wrong with One Esk?"

"My lord," said Lieutenant Awn, her voice shaking with fear, face, as ever, to the floor. "Do you order me?"

"Stand by, Lieutenant," I said, directly into Lieutenant Dariet's ear, because I could not make One Esk speak.

Anaander Mianaai laughed, short and sharp. Lieutenant Awn's answer had been as bald a refusal as a plain *Never* would have been. Ordering such a thing would be useless.

"Interrogate me when we reach Valskaay," Lieutenant Awn said. "I demand it. I am loyal. So is Skaaiat Awer, I swear it, but if you doubt her, interrogate her as well."

But of course Anaander Mianaai couldn't do that. Any interrogation would have witnesses. Any skilled interrogator—and there would be no point in using an unskilled one—would hardly fail to understand the drift of the questions put to either Lieutenant Awn or Lieutenant Skaaiat. It would be too open a move, spread information this Mianaai didn't want spread.

Anaander Mianaai sat silent for four seconds. Impassive.

"One Var," she said, when those four seconds had passed, "shoot Lieutenant Awn."

I was not, now, a single fragmentary segment, alone and unsure what I might do if I received that order. I was all of myself. Taken as separate from me, One Esk was fonder of Lieutenant Awn than I was. But One Esk was not separate from me. It was, at the moment, very much part of me.

Still, One Esk was only one small part of me. And I had shot officers before. I had even, under orders, shot my own captain. But those executions, distressing and unpleasant as they had been, had clearly been just. The penalty for disobedience is death.

Lieutenant Awn had never disobeyed. Far from it. And worse, her death was meant to hide the actions of Anaander Mianaai's enemy. The entire purpose of my existence was to oppose Anaander Mianaai's enemies.

But neither Mianaai was ready to move openly. I must conceal from this Mianaai the fact that she herself had already bound me to the opposing cause, until all was in readiness. I must, for the moment, obey as though I had no other choice, as though I desired nothing else. And in the end, in the great scheme of things, what was Lieutenant Awn, after all? Her parents would grieve, and her sister, and they would likely be ashamed that Lieutenant Awn had disgraced them by disobedience. But they wouldn't question. And if they questioned, it would do no good. Anaander Mianaai's secret would be safe.

All this I thought in the 1.3 seconds it took for Lieutenant Awn, shocked and terrified, to reflexively raise her head. And in that same time, the segment of One Var said, "I am unarmed, my lord. It will take me approximately two minutes to acquire a sidearm."

It was betrayal, to Lieutenant Awn, I saw it plainly. But she must have known I had no other choice. "This is unjust," she said, head still up. Voice unsteady. "It's improper. No benefit will accrue."

"Who are your fellow conspirators?" asked Mianaai, coldly. "Name them and I may spare your life."

Half lifted up, hands under her shoulders, Lieutenant Awn blinked in complete confusion, bewilderment that was surely as visible to Mianaai as it was to me. "Conspirators? I have never conspired with anyone. I have always served you."

Above, on the command deck, I said in Captain Rubran's ear, "Captain, we have a problem."

"Serving me," said Anaander Mianaai, "is no longer sufficient. No longer sufficiently unambiguous. Which *me* do you serve?"

"Wh—" began Lieutenant Awn, and "Th—" And then, "I don't understand."

"What problem?" asked Captain Rubran, bowl of tea halfway to her mouth, only mildly alarmed.

"I am at war with myself," said Mianaai, in the Var decade room. "I have been for nearly a thousand years."

To Captain Rubran I said, "I need One Esk to be sedated."

"At war," Anaander Mianaai continued on Var deck, "over the future of the Radch."

Something must have come suddenly clear for Lieutenant Awn. I saw a sharp, pure rage in her. "Annexations and ancillaries, and people like *me* being assigned to the military."

"I don't understand you, Ship," said Captain Rubran, her voice even but definitely worried now. She set down her tea on the table beside her.

"Over the treaty with the Presger," said Mianaai, angrily. "The rest followed from that. Whether you know it or not, you are the instrument of my enemy."

"And *Mercy of Sarrse* One Amaat One exposed whatever it was you were doing at Ime," said Lieutenant Awn, her anger still clear and steady. "That was *you*. The system governor was making ancillaries—you needed them for your war with yourself, didn't you. And I'm sure that's not all she was doing for you. Is that why that soldier had to die even if it meant extra trouble getting her back from the Rrrrr? And I..."

"I'm still standing by, Ship," said Lieutenant Dariet, in the Esk decade room. "But I don't like this."

"*Mercy of Sarrse* One Amaat One knew almost nothing, but in the hands of the Rrrrr, she was a piece that my enemy might use against me. As an officer on a troop carrier, *you* are nothing, but in a position of even minor planetary authority, with the potential backing of Skaaiat Awer to help you increase your influence, you are a potential danger to me. I could have just maneuvered you out of Ors, out of Awer's way. But I wanted more. I wanted a graphic argument against recent decisions and policies. Had that fisherman not found the guns, or not reported them to you, had events that night gone as I wished, I would have made sure the story was on all the public channels. In one gesture I would have secured the loyalty of the Tanmind and removed someone troublesome to me, both minor aims, but I also would have been able to impress on everyone the danger of lowering our guard, of disarming in even a small way. And the danger of placing authority in less-than-competent hands." She made a short, bitter *ha*. "I admit, I underestimated you. Underestimated your relationship with the Orsians in the lower city."

One Var could delay no longer, and walked into the Var

decade room, gun in hand. Lieutenant Awn heard it come in, turned her head slightly to watch it. "It was my job, to protect the citizens of Ors. I took it seriously. I did it to the best of my ability. I failed, that once. But not because of you." She turned her head, looked straight at Anaander Mianaai, and said, "I should have died rather than obey you, in the temple of Ikkt. Even if it wouldn't have done any good."

"You can fix that now, can't you," said Anaander Mianaai, and gave me the order to fire.

I fired.

Twenty years later, I would say to Arilesperas Strigan that Radchaai authorities didn't care what a citizen thought, so long as she did as she ought to do. It was quite true. But since that moment, since I saw Lieutenant Awn dead on the floor of my Var decade room, shot by One Var (or, to speak with less self-deception, by me) I have wondered what the difference is between the two.

I was compelled to obey this Mianaai, in order to lead her to believe that she did indeed compel me. But in that case, she *did* compel me. Acting for one Mianaai or the other was indistinguishable. And of course, in the end, whatever their differences, they were both the same.

Thoughts are ephemeral, they evaporate in the moment they occur, unless they are given action and material form. Wishes and intentions, the same. Meaningless, unless they impel you to one choice or another, some deed or course of action, however insignificant. Thoughts that lead to action can be dangerous. Thoughts that do not, mean less than nothing.

Lieutenant Awn lay on the floor of the Var decade room, facedown again, dead. The floor under her would need repair, and cleaning. The urgent issue, the important thing, at that moment, was to get One Esk moving because in approximately half a second no amount of filtering I could do would hide the strength of its reaction and I really needed to tell the captain what had happened and I couldn't remember Mianaai's enemy—Mianaai herself—laying down the orders I knew she had laid on me and why couldn't One Esk see how important it was, we weren't ready to move openly yet and I'd lost officers before and who was One Esk anyway except me, myself, and Lieutenant Awn was dead and she had said, *I should have died rather than obey you.*

And then One Var swung the gun up and shot Anaander Mianaai point-blank in the face.

In a room down the corridor, Anaander Mianaai leaped with a cry of rage off the bed she'd been lying on. "Aatr's tits, *she was here before me*!" In the same moment she transmitted the code that would force One Var's armor down, until she reauthorized its use. It was a command that didn't rely on my obedience, an override neither Anaander would have wanted to do away with.

"Captain," I said, "now we *really* have a problem."

In another room down the same corridor, the third Mianaai—the second, now, I suppose—opened one of the cases she had brought with her and pulled out a sidearm, and stepped quickly into the corridor and shot the nearest One Var in the back of the head. The one who had spoken opened her own case, pulled out a sidearm and also a box I recognized from Jen Shinnan's house, in the upper city, on Shis'urna. Using it would disadvantage her as well as me, but it would disadvantage me badly. In the seconds she took to arm the device I formed intentions, transmitted orders to constituent parts.

"What problem?" asked Captain Rubran, now standing. Afraid.

And then I fell to pieces.

A familiar sensation. For the smallest fragment of a second I smelled humid air and lake water, thought, *Where's Lieutenant Awn?* and then I recovered myself, and the memory of what I had to do. Tea bowls rang and shattered as I dropped what I was holding and ran from the Esk decade room, down the corridor. Other segments, separated from me again as they had been in Ors, muttering, whispering, the only way I could think between all my bodies, opened lockers, handed guns, and the first to be armed forced the lift doors open and began to climb down the shaft. Lieutenants protested, ordered me to stop, to explain. Tried fruitlessly to block my way.

I—that is, almost the entirety of One Esk—would secure the central access deck, prevent Anaander Mianaai from damaging my—*Justice of Toren*'s—brain. So long as *Justice of Toren* lived, unconverted to her cause, it—I—was a danger to her.

I—One Esk Nineteen—had separate orders. Instead of climbing down the shaft to central access I ran the other way, toward the Esk hold and the airlock on its far side.

I wasn't, apparently, responding to any of my lieutenants, or even Commander Tiaund, but when Lieutenant Dariet cried, "Ship! Have you lost your mind?" I answered.

"The Lord of the Radch shot Lieutenant Awn!" cried a segment somewhere in the corridor behind me. "She's been on Var deck all this time."

That silenced my officers—including Lieutenant Dariet—for only a second.

"If that's even true...but if it is, the Lord of the Radch wouldn't have shot her for no reason."

Behind me the segments of myself that hadn't yet begun their climb down the lift shaft hissed and gasped in frustration and anger. "Useless!" I heard myself say to Lieutenant Dariet as at the end of the corridor I manually opened the hold door. "You're as bad as Lieutenant Issaaia! At least Lieutenant Awn *knew* she held her in contempt!"

An indignant cry, surely Lieutenant Issaaia, and Dariet said, "You don't know what you're talking about. You're not functioning right, Ship!"

The door slid open, and I could not stop to hear the rest, but plunged into the hold. A deep, steady thunking shook the deck I ran on, a sound just hours ago I thought I would never hear again. Mianaai was opening the Var holds. Any ancillary she thawed would have no memory of recent events, nothing to tell it not to obey this Mianaai. And its armor wouldn't have been disabled.

She would take Two Var and Three and Four and as many as she had time to awaken, and try to take either the central access deck or the engines. More likely both. She had, after all, Var and every hold below it. Though the segments would be clumsy and confused. They would have no memory of functioning apart, the way I had, no practice. But numbers were on her side. I had only the segments that had been awake at the moment I fragmented.

Above, my officers had access to the upper half of the holds. And they would have no reason not to obey Anaander Mianaai, no reason not to think I had lost my mind. I was, at this moment, explaining matters to Hundred Captain Rubran, but I had no confidence she would believe me, or think me even remotely sane.

Around me, the same thunking began that was sounding below my feet. My officers were pulling up Esk segments to thaw. I reached the airlock, threw open the locker beside it, pulled out the pieces of the vacuum suit that would fit this segment.

I didn't know how long I could hold central access, or the engines. I didn't know how desperate Anaander Mianaai might be, what damage she might think I could do to her. The engines' heat shield was, by design, extremely difficult to breach, but I knew how to do it. And the Lord of the Radch certainly did as well.

And whatever happened between here and there, it was a near-certainty I would die shortly after I reached Valskaay, if not before. But I would not die without explaining myself.

I would have to reach and board a shuttle, and then manually undock, and depart *Justice of Toren*—myself—at exactly the right time, at exactly the right speed, on exactly the right heading, fly through the wall of my surrounding bubble of normal space at exactly the right moment.

If I did all that, I would find myself in a system with a gate, four jumps from Irei Palace, one of Anaander Mianaai's provincial headquarters. I could tell her what had happened.

The shuttles were docked on this side of the ship. The hatches and the undocking ought to work smoothly, it was all equipment I had tested and maintained myself. Still, I found myself worrying that something would go wrong. At least it was better than thinking about fighting my own officers. Or the heat shield's failing.

I fastened my helmet. My breath hissed loud in my ears. Faster than it should have. I forced myself to slow my breathing, deepen it. Hyperventilating wouldn't help. I had to move quickly, but not so hastily that I made some fatally foolish mistake.

Waiting for the airlock to cycle, I felt my aloneness like

an impenetrable wall pressing around me. Usually one body's off-kilter emotion was a minor, easily dismissable thing. Now it was *only* this one body, nothing beyond to temper my distress. The rest of me was here, all around, but inaccessible. Soon, if things went right, I wouldn't even be near my self, or have any idea when I might rejoin it. And at this moment I could do nothing but wait. And remember the feel of the gun in One Var's hand—my hand. I was One Esk, but what was the difference? The recoil as One Var shot Lieutenant Awn. The guilt and helpless anger that had overwhelmed me had receded at that moment, overcome by more urgent necessity, but now I had time to remember. My next three breaths were ragged and sobbing. For a moment I was perversely glad I was hidden from myself.

I had to calm myself. Had to clear my mind. I thought of songs I knew. *My heart is a fish*, I thought, but when I opened my mouth to sing it, my throat closed. I swallowed. Breathed. Thought of another one.

> *Oh, have you gone to the battlefield*
> *Armored and well armed?*
> *And shall dreadful events*
> *Force you to drop your weapons?*

The outer door opened. If Mianaai had not used her device, officers on duty would have seen that the lock had opened, would have notified Captain Rubran, drawing Mianaai's attention. But she had used it, and she had no way of knowing what I did. I reached around the doorway for a handhold and pulled myself out.

Looking at the inside of a gateway often made humans queasy. It had never bothered me before, but now I was nothing but a single human body I found it did the same to me. Black, but a black that seemed simultaneously an unthinkable depth into which I might fall, *was* falling, and a suffocating closeness ready to press me into nonexistence.

I forced myself to look away. Here, outside, there was no floor, no gravity generator to keep me in place and give me an up and down. I moved from one handhold to the next. What was happening behind me, inside the ship that was no longer my body?

It took seventeen minutes to reach a shuttle, operate its emergency hatch, and perform a manual undock. At first I fought the desire to halt, to look behind me, to listen for the sounds of someone coming to stop me, never mind I couldn't have heard anything outside my own helmet. *Just maintenance*, I told myself. *Just maintenance outside the hull. You've done it hundreds of times.*

If anyone came I could do nothing. Esk would have failed— *I* would have failed. And my time was limited. I might not be stopped, and still fail. I could not think of any of that.

When the moment came, I was ready and away. My view was limited to fore and aft, the only two hardwired cameras on the shuttle. As *Justice of Toren* receded in the aft view, the rising sense of panic that I had mostly held in check till now overtook me. What was I doing? Where was I going? What could I possibly accomplish alone and single-bodied, deaf and blind and cut off? What could be the point of defying Anaander Mianaai, who had made me, who owned me, who was unutterably more powerful than I would ever be?

I breathed. I would return to the Radch. I would eventually return to *Justice of Toren*, even if only for the last moments of my life. My blindness and deafness were irrelevant. There was only the task before me. There was nothing to do but sit in the pilot's chair and watch *Justice of Toren* get smaller, and farther away. Think of another song.

According to the chronometer, if I had done everything exactly as I should, *Justice of Toren* would disappear from my screen in four minutes and thirty-two seconds. I watched, counting, trying not to think of anything else.

The aft view flashed bright, blue-white, and my breath stopped. When the screen cleared I saw nothing but black— and stars. I had exited my self-made gate.

I had exited more than four minutes too soon. And what had that flash been? I ought only to have seen the ship disappear, the stars suddenly spring into existence.

Mianaai had not attempted to take central access, or join forces with the officers on the upper decks. The moment she realized I had already fallen to her enemy, she must have resolved immediately to take the most desperate course available to her. She and what Var ancillaries she had serving her had taken my engines, and breached the heat shield. How I had escaped and not vaporized along with the rest of the ship, I couldn't account for, but there had been that flash, and here I still was.

Justice of Toren was gone, and all aboard it. I was not where I was supposed to be, might be unreachably distant from Radch space, or any human worlds at all. All possibility of being reunited with myself was gone. The captain was dead. All my officers were dead. Civil war loomed.

I had shot Lieutenant Awn.

Nothing would ever be right again.

17

Luckily for me, I had come out of gate-space on the fringes of a backwater, non-Radchaai system, a collection of habitats and mining stations inhabited by heavily modified people—not human, by Radchaai standards, people with six or eight limbs (and no guarantee any of them would be legs), vacuum-adapted skin and lungs, brains so meshed and crosshatched with implants and wiring it was an open question whether they were anything but conscious machines with a biological interface.

It was a mystery to them that anyone would choose the sort of primitive form most humans I knew were born with. But they prized their isolation, and it was a dearly held tenet of their society that, with a few exceptions (most of which they would not actually admit to), one did not ask for anything a person did not volunteer. They viewed me with a combi-nation of puzzlement and mild contempt, and treated me as though I were a child who had wandered into their midst and they might keep half an eye on me until my parents found me, but really I wasn't their responsibility. If any of them guessed my origin—and surely they did, the shuttle alone was enough—they didn't say so, and no one pressed me for answers, something they would have found appallingly rude. They were silent, clannish, self-contained, but they were also brusquely generous at unpredictable intervals. I would still be there, or dead, if not for that.

I spent six months trying to understand how to do anything—not just how to get my message to the Lord of the Radch, but how to walk and breathe and sleep and eat as myself. As a *myself* that was only a fragment of what I had been, with no conceivable future beyond eternally wishing for what was gone. Then one day a human ship arrived, and the captain was happy to take me on board in exchange for what little money I had left from scrapping the shuttle, which had been running up docking charges I couldn't pay otherwise. I found out later that a four-meter, tentacled eel of a person had paid the balance of my fare without telling me, because, she had told the captain, I didn't belong there and would be healthier elsewhere. Odd people, as I said, and I owe them a great deal, though they would be offended and distressed to think anyone owed them anything.

In the nineteen years since then, I had learned eleven languages and 713 songs. I had found ways to conceal what I was—even, I was fairly sure, from the Lord of the Radch herself. I had worked as a cook, a janitor, a pilot. I had settled on a plan of action. I had joined a religious order, and made a great deal of money. In all that time I only killed a dozen people.

By the time I woke the next morning, the impulse to tell Seivarden anything had passed, and she seemed to have forgotten her questions. Except one. "So where next?" She asked it casually, sitting on the bench by my bed, leaning against the wall, as though she were only idly curious about the answer.

When she heard, maybe she'd decide she liked it better on her own. "Omaugh Palace."

She frowned, just slightly. "That a new one?"

"Not particularly." It had been built seven hundred years ago. "But after Garsedd, yes." My right ankle began to tingle and itch, a sure sign the corrective was finished. "You left Radchaai space unauthorized. And you sold your armor to do it."

"Extraordinary circumstances," she said, still leaning back. "I'll appeal."

"That'll get you a delay, at any rate." Any citizen who wanted to see the Lord of the Radch could apply to do so, though the farther one was from a provincial palace, the more complicated, expensive, and time-consuming the journey would be. Sometimes applications were turned down, when the distance was great and the cause was judged hopeless or frivolous—and the petitioner was unable to pay her own way. But Anaander Mianaai was the final appeal for nearly any matter, and this case was certainly not routine. And she would be right there on the station. "You'll wait months for an audience."

Seivarden gestured her lack of concern. "What are you going to do there?"

Try to kill Anaander Mianaai. But I couldn't say that. "See the sights. Buy some souvenirs. Maybe try to meet the Lord of the Radch."

She lifted an eyebrow. Then she looked at my pack. She knew about the gun, and of course she understood how dangerous it was. She still thought I was an agent of the Radch. "Undercover the whole way? And when you hand that"—she shrugged toward my pack—"over to the Lord of the Radch, then what?"

"I don't know." I closed my eyes. I could see no further than arriving at Omaugh Palace, had not even the remotest shadow of an idea of what to do after that, how I might get close enough to Anaander Mianaai to use the gun.

No. That wasn't true. The beginning of a plan had this moment suggested itself to me, but it was horribly impractical, relying as it did on Seivarden's discretion and support.

She had constructed her own idea of what I was doing and why I would return to the Radch playing a foreign tourist. Why I would report directly to Anaander Mianaai instead of a Special Missions officer. I could use that.

"I'm coming with you," Seivarden said, and as though she had guessed my thoughts she added, "You can come to my appeal and speak on my behalf."

I didn't trust myself to answer. Pins and needles traveled up my right leg, started in my hands, arms, and shoulders, and my left leg. A slight ache began in my right hip. Something hadn't healed quite right.

"It's not as if I don't already know what's going on," Seivarden said.

"So when you steal from me, breaking your legs won't be enough. I'll have to kill you." My eyes still closed, I couldn't see her reaction to that. She might well take it as a joke.

"I won't," she answered. "You'll see."

I spent several more days in Therrod recovering sufficiently that the doctor would approve my leaving. All that time, and afterward all the way up the ribbon, Seivarden was polite and deferential.

It worried me. I had stashed money and belongings at the

top of the Nilt ribbon, and would have to retrieve them before we left. Everything was packaged, so I could do that without Seivarden seeing much more than a couple of boxes, but I had no illusions she wouldn't try to open them first chance she got.

At least I had money again. And maybe that was the solution to the problem.

I took a room on the ribbon station, left Seivarden there with instructions to wait, and went to recover my possessions. When I returned she was sitting on the single bed—no linens or blankets, that was conventionally extra here—fidgeting. One knee bouncing, rubbing her upper arms with her bare hands—I had sold our heavy outer coats, and the gloves, at the foot of the ribbon. She stilled when I came in, and looked expectantly at me, but said nothing.

I tossed into her lap a bag that made a tumbling clicking sound as it landed.

Seivarden gave it one frowning look, and then turned her gaze to me, not moving to touch the bag or claim it in any way. "What's this?"

"Ten thousand shen," I said. It was the most commonly negotiable currency in this region, in easily transportable (and spent) chits. Ten thousand would buy a lot, here. It would buy passage to another system with enough left over to binge for several weeks.

"Is that a lot?"

"Yes."

Her eyes widened, just slightly, and for half a second I saw calculation in her expression.

Time for me to be direct. "The room is paid up for the next ten days. After that—" I gestured at the bag on her lap. "That should last you a while. Longer if you're truly serious about staying off kef." But that look, when she'd realized she had access to money, made me fairly certain she wasn't. Not really.

For six seconds Seivarden looked down at the bag in her lap. "No." She picked the bag up gingerly, between her thumb and forefinger, as though it were a dead rat, and dropped it on the floor. "I'm coming with you."

I didn't answer, only looked at her. Silence stretched out.

Finally she looked away, crossed her arms. "Isn't there any tea?"

"Not the sort you're used to."

"I don't care."

Well. I didn't want to leave her here alone with my money and possessions. "Come on, then."

We left the room, found a shop on the main corridor that sold things for flavoring hot water. Seivarden sniffed one of the blends on offer. Wrinkled her nose. "This is *tea*?"

The shop's proprietor watched us from the corner of her vision, not wanting to seem to watch us. "I told you it wasn't the sort you were used to. You said you didn't care."

She thought about that a moment. To my utter surprise, instead of arguing, or complaining further about the unsatisfactory nature of the tea in question, she said, calmly, "What do you recommend?"

I gestured my uncertainty. "I'm not in the habit of drinking tea."

"Not in the..." She stared at me. "Oh. Don't they drink tea in the Gerentate?"

"Not the way you people do." And of course tea was for officers. For humans. Ancillaries drank water. Tea was an extra, unnecessary expense. A luxury. So I had never developed the habit. I turned to the proprietor, a Nilter, short and pale and fat, in shirtsleeves though the temperature here was a constant four C and Seivarden and I both still wore our inner coats. "Which of these has caffeine in it?"

She answered, pleasantly enough, and became pleasanter when I bought not only 250 grams each of two kinds of tea but also a flask with two cups, and two bottles, along with water to fill them.

Seivarden carried the whole lot back to our lodging, walking alongside me saying nothing. In the room she laid our purchases on the bed, sat down beside them, and picked up the flask, puzzling over the unfamiliar design.

I could have showed her how it worked, but decided not to. Instead I opened my newly claimed luggage and dug out a thick golden disk three centimeters larger in diameter than the one I had carried with me, and a small, shallow bowl of hammered gold, eight centimeters in diameter. I closed the trunk, set the bowl on it, and triggered the image in the disk.

Seivarden looked up to watch it unfold into a wide, flat flower in mother-of-pearl, a woman standing in its center. She wore a knee-length robe of the same iridescent white, inlaid with gold and silver. In one hand she held a human skull, itself inlaid with jewels, red and blue and yellow, and in the other hand a knife.

"That's like the other one," Seivarden said, sounding mildly interested. "But it doesn't look so much like you."

"True," I answered, and sat cross-legged before the trunk.

"Is that a Gerentate god?"

"It's one I met, traveling."

Seivarden made a breathy, noncommittal noise. "What's its name?"

I spoke the long string of syllables, which left Seivarden nonplussed. "It means *She Who Sprang from the Lily*. She is the creator of the universe." This would make her Amaat, in Radchaai terms.

"Ah," said Seivarden, in a tone I knew meant she'd made that equation, made the strange god familiar and brought it safely within her mental framework. "And the other one?"

"A saint."

"What a remarkable thing, that she should resemble you so much."

"Yes. Although she's not the saint. The head she's holding is."

Seivarden blinked, frowned. It was very un-Radchaai. "Still."

Nothing was just a coincidence, not for Radchaai. Such odd chances could—and did—send Radchaai on pilgrimages, motivate them to worship particular gods, change entrenched habits. They were direct messages from Amaat. "I'm going to pray now," I said.

With one hand Seivarden made a gesture of acknowledgment. I unfolded a small knife, pricked my thumb, and bled into the gold bowl. I didn't look to see Seivarden's reaction—no Radchaai god took blood, and I hadn't troubled to wash my hands first. It was guaranteed to lift Radchaai eyebrows, to register as foreign and even primitive.

But Seivarden didn't say anything. She sat silent for thirty-one seconds as I intoned the first of the 322 names of the Hundred of White Lily, and then she turned her attention to the flask, and making tea.

Seivarden had said she'd lasted six months at her last attempt to quit kef. It took seven months to reach a station with a Radchaai consulate. Approaching the first leg of the journey, I had told the purser in Seivarden's hearing that I wanted passage for myself and my servant. She hadn't reacted, that I could see. Perhaps she hadn't understood. But I had expected a more or less angry recrimination in private when she discovered her status, and she never mentioned it. And from then on I woke to find tea already made and waiting for me.

She also ruined two shirts attempting to launder them, leaving me with one for an entire month until we docked at the next station. The ship's captain—she was Ki, tall and covered in ritual scars—let fall in an oblique, circuitous way that she and all her crew thought I'd taken Seivarden on as a charity case. Which wasn't far from the truth. I didn't contest it. But Seivarden improved, and three months later, on the next ship, a fellow passenger tried to hire her away from me.

Which wasn't to say she had suddenly become a different person, or entirely deferential. Some days she spoke irritably to me, for no reason I could see, or spent hours curled in her bunk, her face to the wall, rising only for her self-imposed duties. The first few times I spoke to her when she was in that mood I only received silence in reply, so after that I left her alone.

The Radchaai consulate was staffed by the Translators Office, and the consular agent's spotless white uniform—including pristine white gloves—argued she either had a servant or spent a good deal of her free time attempting to appear as though she did. The tasteful—and expensive-looking—jeweled strands wound in her hair, and the names on the memorial pins that glittered everywhere on the white jacket, as well as the faint disdain in her voice when she spoke to me, argued *servant*. Though likely only one—this was an out-of-the-way posting.

"As a visiting noncitizen your legal rights are restricted."

It was clearly a rote speech. "You must deposit at minimum the equivalent of—" Fingers twitched as she checked the exchange rate. "Five hundred shen per week of your visit, per person. If your lodging, food, and any extra purchases, fines, or damages exceed the amount on deposit and you cannot pay the balance, you will be legally obligated to take an assignment until your debt is paid. As a noncitizen your right to appeal any judgment or assignment is limited. Do you still wish to enter Radch space?"

"I do," I said, and laid two million-shen chits on the slim desk between us.

Her disdain vanished. She sat slightly straighter and offered me tea, gesturing slightly, fingers twitching again as she communicated with someone else—her servant, it turned out, who, with a slightly harried air, brought tea in an elaborately enameled flask, and bowls to match.

While the servant poured, I brought out my forged Gerentate credentials and placed those on the desk as well.

"You must also provide identification for your servant, honored," said the consular agent, now all politeness.

"My servant is a Radchaai citizen," I answered, smiling slightly. Meaning to take the edge off what was going to be an awkward moment. "But she's lost her identification and her travel permits."

The consular agent froze, attempting to process that.

"The honored Breq," said Seivarden, standing behind me, in antique, effortlessly elegant Radchaai, "has been generous enough to employ me and pay my passage home."

This didn't resolve the consular agent's astonished paralysis quite as effectively as Seivarden perhaps had wished. That accent didn't belong on anyone's servant, let alone a noncitizen's. And she hadn't offered Seivarden a seat, or tea, thinking her too insignificant for such courtesies.

"Surely you can take genetic information," I suggested.

"Yes, of course," answered the consular agent, with a sunny smile. "Though your visa application will almost certainly come through before Citizen..."

"Seivarden," I supplied.

"...before Citizen Seivarden's travel permits are reissued. Depending on where she departed from and where her records are."

"Of course," I answered, and sipped my tea. "That's only to be expected."

As we left, Seivarden said to me, in an undertone, "What a snob. Was that real tea?"

"It was." I waited for her to complain about not having had any, but she said nothing more. "It was very good. What are you going to do if an arrest order comes through instead of travel permits?"

She made a gesture of denial. "Why should they? I'm already asking to come back, they can arrest me when I get there. And I'll appeal. Do you think the consul has that tea shipped from home, or might someone here sell it?"

"Find out, if you like," I said. "I'm going back to the room to meditate."

The consular agent's servant outright gave Seivarden half a kilo of tea, likely grateful for the opportunity to make up for her employer's unintentional slight earlier. And when my visa came through, so did travel permits for Seivarden, and no arrest order, or any additional comment or information at all.

That worried me, if only slightly. But likely Seivarden was right—why do anything else? When she stepped off the ship there would be time and opportunity enough to address her legal troubles.

Still. It was possible Radch authorities had realized I wasn't actually a citizen of the Gerentate. It was unlikely—the Gerentate was a long, long way from where I was going, and besides, despite fairly friendly—or at least, not openly antagonistic—relations between the Gerentate and the Radch, as a matter of policy the Gerentate didn't supply any information at all about its residents—not to the Radch. If the Radch asked—and they wouldn't—the Gerentate would neither confirm nor deny that I was one of its citizens. Had I been departing from the Gerentate for Radchaai space I would have been warned repeatedly that I traveled at my own risk and would receive no assistance if I found myself in difficulties. But the Radchaai officials who dealt with foreign travelers knew this already, and would be prepared to take my identification more or less at face value.

Anaander Mianaai's thirteen palaces were the capitals of their provinces. Metropolis-size stations, each one half ordinary large Radchaai station—with accompanying station AI—and half palace proper. Each palace proper was the residence of Anaander Mianaai, and the seat of provincial administration. Omaugh Palace wouldn't be any sort of quiet backwater. A dozen gates led to its system, and hundreds of ships came and went each day. Seivarden would be one of thousands of citizens seeking audience, or making an appeal in some legal case. A noticeable one, certainly—none of those other citizens were returned from a thousand years in suspension.

I spent the months of travel considering just what I wanted to do about that. How to use it. How to counter its disadvantages, or turn them to my favor. And considering just what it was I hoped to accomplish.

It's hard for me to know how much of myself I remember. How much I might have known, that I had hidden from myself all my life. Take, for instance, that last order, the instruction I–*Justice of Toren* had given to me–One Esk Nineteen. *Get to Irei Palace, find Anaander Mianaai, and tell her what's happened.* What did I mean by that? Over and above the obvious, the bare fact I'd wanted to get the message to the Lord of the Radch?

Why had it been so important? Because it had been. It hadn't been an afterthought, it had been an urgent necessity. At the time it had seemed clear. Of *course* I needed to get the message out, of course I needed to warn the right Anaander.

I would follow my orders. But in the time I'd spent recovering from my own death, the time working my way toward Radch space, I had decided I would do something else as well. I would defy the Lord of the Radch. And perhaps my defiance would amount to nothing, a feeble gesture she would barely notice.

The truth was, Strigan was right. My desire to kill Anaander Mianaai was unreasonable. Any actual attempt to do such a thing was not sane. Even given a gun that I could carry into the very presence of the Lord of the Radch herself without her knowing until I chose to reveal it—even given that, all I could hope to accomplish was a pitiful cry of defiance, gone as soon as made, easily disregarded. Nothing that could possibly make any difference.

But. All that secret maneuvering against herself. Designed, certainly, to avoid open conflict, to avoid damaging the Radch too badly. To avoid, perhaps, too badly fracturing Anaander Mianaai's conviction that she was unitary, one person. Once the dilemma had been clearly stated, could she pretend things were otherwise?

And if there were now two Anaander Mianaais, might there not also be more? A part, perhaps, that didn't know about the feuding sides of herself? Or told herself she didn't? What would happen if I said straight out the thing the Lord of the Radch had been concealing from herself? Something dire, surely, or she would not have gone to such lengths to hide herself from herself. Once the thing was open and acknowledged, how could she help tearing herself apart?

But how could I say anything straight out to Anaander Mianaai? Granted I could reach Omaugh Palace, granted I could leave the ship, step onto the station—if I could do that much then I could stand in the middle of the main concourse and shout my story aloud for everyone to hear.

I might begin to do that, but I would never finish. Security would come for me, maybe even soldiers, and that day's news would say a traveler had lost her mind on the concourse, but Security had dealt with the situation. Citizens would shake their heads, and mutter about uncivilized foreigners, and then forget all about me. And whichever part of the Lord of the Radch noticed me first could no doubt easily dismiss me as damaged and insane—or at least, convince the various other parts of herself that I was.

No, I needed the full attention of Anaander Mianaai, when I said what I had to say. How to get it was a problem I had worried at for nearly twenty years. I knew that it would be harder to ignore someone whose erasure would be noticed. I could visit the station and try to be seen, to become familiar, so that any part of Anaander couldn't just dispose of me without comment. But I didn't think that would be enough to force the Lord of the Radch—all of the Lord of the Radch—to listen to me.

But Seivarden. Captain Seivarden Vendaai, lost a thousand years, found by chance, lost again. Appearing now at Omaugh Palace. Any Radchaai would be curious about that, with a curiosity that carried a religious charge. And Anaander Mianaai was Radchaai. Perhaps the most Radchaai of Radchaai. She couldn't help but notice that I had returned in company with Seivarden. Like any other citizen she would wonder, even if only at the back of her mind, what, if anything, that might mean. And she being who she was, the back of her mind was a substantial thing.

Seivarden would ask for an audience. Would be, eventually, granted one. And that audience would have all of Anaander's attention; no part of her would ignore such an event.

And surely Seivarden would have the attention of the Lord of the Radch from the moment we stepped off the ship. So, arriving in Seivarden's company, would I. Tremendously risky. I might not have concealed my nature well enough, might be recognized for what I was. But I was determined to try.

I sat on the bunk waiting for permission to leave the ship at Omaugh Palace, my pack at my feet, Seivarden leaning negligently against the wall across from me, bored.

"Something's bothering you," Seivarden observed, casually. I didn't answer, and she said, "You always hum that tune when you're preoccupied."

My heart is a fish, hiding in the water-grass. I had been thinking of all the ways things could go wrong, starting now, starting the moment I stepped off the ship and confronted the dock inspectors. Or Station Security. Or worse. Thinking of how everything I had done would be for nothing if I was arrested before I could even leave the docks.

And I had been thinking about Lieutenant Awn. "I'm so transparent?" I made myself smile, as though I were mildly amused.

"Not transparent. Not exactly. Just..." She hesitated. Frowned slightly, as though she'd suddenly regretted speaking. "You have a few habits I've noticed, that's all." She sighed. "Are the dock inspectors having tea? Or just waiting till we've aged sufficiently?" We couldn't leave the ship without the permission of the Inspector's Office. The inspector would have received our credentials when the ship requested permission to dock, and had plenty of time to look over them and decide what to do when we arrived.

Still leaning against the bulkhead, Seivarden closed her eyes and began to hum. Wobbling, pitch sinking or rising by turns as she mis-sang intervals. But still recognizable. *My heart is a fish.* "Aatr's tits," she swore after a verse and a half, eyes still closed. "Now you've got me doing it."

The door chime sounded. "Enter," I said. Seivarden opened her eyes, sat straight. Suddenly tense. The boredom had been a pose, I suspected.

The door slid open to reveal a person in the dark-blue jacket, gloves, and trousers of a dock inspector. She was slight, and young, maybe twenty-three or -four. She looked familiar, though I couldn't think who it was she reminded me of. The sparser-than-usual scatter of jewelry and memorial pins might tell me, if I stared closely enough to read names. Which would be rude. Across from me, Seivarden tucked her bare hands behind her back.

"Honored Breq," the inspector adjunct said, with a slight

bow. She seemed unfazed by my own bare hands. Used to dealing with foreigners, I supposed. "Citizen Seivarden. Would you please accompany me to the inspector supervisor's office?"

And there should have been no need for us to visit the inspector supervisor herself. This adjunct could pass us onto the station on her own authority. Or order our arrest.

We followed her past the lock into the loading bay, past another lock into a corridor busy with people—dock inspectors in dark blue, Station Security in light brown, here and there the darker brown of soldiers, and spots of brighter color—a scatter of non-uniformed citizens. This corridor opened into a wide room, a dozen gods along the walls to watch over travelers and traders, on one end the entrance to the station proper, and opposite, the doorway into the inspector's office.

The adjunct escorted us through the outermost office, where nine blue-uniformed minor adjuncts dealt with complaining ship captains, and beyond them were offices for likely a dozen major adjuncts and their crews. Past those and into an inner office, with four chairs and a small table, and a door at the back, closed.

"I am sorry, cit…honored, and citizen," said the adjunct who had led us here, fingers twitching as she communicated with someone—likely the station AI, or the inspector supervisor herself. "The inspector supervisor *was* available, but something's come up. I'm sure it won't be more than a few minutes. Please have a seat. Will you have tea?"

A reasonably long wait, then. And the courtesy of tea implied this wasn't an arrest. That no one had discovered my credentials were forged. Everyone here—including Station—would assume I was what I said I was, a foreign traveler.

And possibly I would have a chance to discover just who this young inspector adjunct reminded me of. Now she'd spoken at a bit more length, I noticed a slight accent. Where was she from? "Yes, thank you," I said.

Seivarden didn't respond to the offer of tea right away. Her arms were folded, her bare hands tucked under her elbows. She likely wanted the tea but was embarrassed about her ungloved hands, couldn't hide them holding a bowl. Or so I thought until she said, "I can't understand a word she's saying."

Seivarden's accent and way of speaking would be familiar to most educated Radchaai, from old entertainments and the way Anaander Mianaai's speech was widely emulated by prestigious—or hopefully prestigious—families. I hadn't thought changes in pronunciation and vocabulary had been so extreme. But I'd lived through them, and Seivarden's ear for language had never been the sharpest. "She's offering tea."

"Oh." Seivarden looked briefly at her crossed arms. "No."

I took the tea the adjunct poured from a flask on the table, thanked her, and took a seat. The office had been painted a pale green, the floor tiled with something that had probably been intended to look like wood and might have succeeded if the designer had ever seen anything but imitations of imitations. A niche in the wall behind the young adjunct held an icon of Amaat and a small bowl of bright-orange, ruffle-petaled flowers. And beside that, a tiny brass copy of the cliffside in the temple of Ikkt. You could buy them, I knew, from vendors in the plaza in front of the Fore-Temple water, during pilgrimage season.

I looked at the adjunct again. Who was she? Someone I knew? A relative of someone I'd met?

"You're humming again," Seivarden said in an undertone.

"Excuse me." I took a sip of tea. "It's a habit I have. I apologize."

"No need," said the adjunct, and took her own seat by the table. This was, fairly clearly, her own office and so she was direct assistant to the inspector supervisor—an unusual place for someone so young. "I haven't heard that song since I was a child."

Seivarden blinked, not understanding. If she had, she likely would have smiled. A Radchaai could live nearly two hundred years. This inspector adjunct, probably a legal adult for a decade, was still impossibly young.

"I used to know someone else who sang all the time," the adjunct continued.

I knew her. Had probably bought songs from her. She would have been maybe four, maybe five, when I'd left Ors. Maybe slightly older, if she remembered me with any clarity.

The inspector supervisor behind that door would be someone who had spent time on Shis'urna—in Ors itself, most likely. What did I know about the lieutenant who had replaced Lieutenant Awn as administrator there? How likely was it she'd resigned her military assignment and taken one as a dock inspector? It wasn't unheard of.

Whoever the inspector supervisor was, she had money and influence enough to bring this adjunct here from Ors. I wanted to ask the young woman the name of her patron, but that would be unthinkably rude. "I'm told," I said, meaning to sound idly curious, and playing up my Gerentate accent just the smallest bit, "that the jewelry you Radchaai wear has some sort of significance."

Seivarden cast me a puzzled look. The adjunct only smiled. "Some of it." Her Orsian accent, now I had identified it, was clear, obvious. "This one for instance." She slid one gloved finger under a gold-colored dangle pinned near her left shoulder. "It's a memorial."

"May I look closer?" I asked, and receiving permission moved my chair near, and bent to read the name engraved in Radchaai on the plain metal, one I didn't recognize. It wasn't likely a memorial for an Orsian—I couldn't imagine anyone in the lower city adopting Radchaai funeral practices, or at least not anyone old enough to have died since I'd seen them last.

Near the memorial, on her collar, sat a small flower pin, each petal enameled with the symbol of an Emanation. A date engraved in the flower's center. This assured young woman had been the tiny, frightened flower-bearer when Anaander Mianaai had acted as priest in Lieutenant Awn's house twenty years ago.

No coincidences, not for Radchaai. I was quite sure now that when we were admitted to the inspector supervisor's presence, I would meet Lieutenant Awn's replacement in Ors. This inspector adjunct was, perhaps, a client of hers.

"They make them for funerals," the adjunct was saying, still talking about memorial pins. "Family and close friends wear them." And you could tell by the style and expense of the piece just where in Radchaai society the dead person stood, and by implication where the wearer stood. But the adjunct— her name, I knew, was Daos Ceit—didn't mention that.

I wondered then what Seivarden would make—had made—of changes in fashion since Garsedd, the way such signals had changed—or not. People still wore inherited tokens and memorials, testimony to the social connections and values of their ancestors generations back. And mostly that was the same, except "generations back" was Garsedd. Some tokens that had been insignificant then were prized now, and some that had been priceless were now meaningless. And the color and gemstone significances in vogue for the last hundred or so years wouldn't read at all, for Seivarden.

Inspector Adjunct Ceit had three close friends, all three of whom had incomes and positions similar to hers, to judge from the gifts they'd exchanged with her. Two lovers intimate enough to exchange tokens with but not sufficiently so to be considered very serious. No strands of jewels, no bracelets—though of course if she did any work actually inspecting cargo or ship systems such things might have been in her way—and no rings over her gloves.

And there, on the other shoulder, where now I could see it plainly and look straight at it without being excessively impolite, was the token I had been looking for. I had mistaken it for something less impressive, had, on first glance, taken the platinum for silver, and its dependent pearl for glass, the sign of a gift from a sibling—current fashions misleading me. This was nothing cheap, nothing casual. But it wasn't a token of clientage, though the metal and the pearl suggested a particular house association. An association with a house old enough that Seivarden could have recognized it immediately. Possibly had.

Inspector Adjunct Ceit stood. "The inspector supervisor is available now," she said. "I do apologize for your wait." She opened the inner door and gestured us through.

In the innermost office, standing to meet us, twenty years older and a bit heavier than when I'd last seen her, was the giver of that pin—Lieutenant—no, Inspector Supervisor Skaaiat Awer.

18

It was impossible that Lieutenant Skaaiat would recognize me. She bowed, oblivious to the fact that I knew her. It was strange to see her in dark blue, and so much more sober, more grave than when I'd known her in Ors.

An inspector supervisor in a station as busy as this likely never set foot on the ships her subordinates inspected, but Inspector Supervisor Skaaiat wore almost as little jewelry as her assistant. A long strand of green-and-blue jewels coiled from shoulder to opposite hip, and a red stone dangled from one ear, but otherwise a similar (though clearly more expensive) scattering of friends, lovers, dead relatives decorated her uniform jacket. One plain gold token hung on the cuff of her right sleeve, just next to the edge of the glove, the placement that of something she intended to be reminded of, as much for herself to see as anyone else. It looked cheap, machine-made. Not the sort of thing she would wear.

She bowed. "Citizen Seivarden. Honored Breq. Please sit. Will you have tea?" Still effortlessly elegant, even after twenty years.

"Your assistant already offered us tea, thank you, Inspector Supervisor," I said. Inspector Supervisor Skaaiat looked momentarily at me and then at Seivarden, slightly surprised, I thought. She had been addressing Seivarden primarily, thinking of Seivarden as the principal person between the two of us. I sat. Seivarden hesitated a moment and then sat in the seat beside me, arms still crossed to hide her bare hands.

"I wanted to meet you myself, citizen," Inspector Supervisor Skaaiat said, when she'd taken her own seat. "Privilege of office. It isn't every day you meet someone a thousand years old."

Seivarden smiled, small and tight. "Indeed not," she agreed.

"And I felt it would be improper for Security to arrest you on the dock. Though..." Inspector Supervisor Skaaiat gestured, placatory, the pin on her cuff flashing once as she did. "You are in some legal difficulty, citizen."

Seivarden relaxed, just slightly, shoulders lowering, jaw loosening. Barely detectable, unless you knew her. Skaaiat's accent and mildly deferential tone were having an effect. "I am," Seivarden acknowledged. "I intend to appeal."

"There's some question about the matter, then." Stilted. Formal. A query that wasn't a query. But no answer came. "I can take you to the palace offices myself and avoid any entanglement with Security." Of course she could. She'd worked this out with Security's chief already.

"I'd be grateful." Seivarden sounded more like her old self than I'd heard her in the last year. "Would it be worth asking you to assist me contacting Geir's lord?" Geir might conceivably have some responsibility for this last member of the house it had taken over. Hated Geir, which had absorbed its enemy—Vendaai, Seivarden's house. Vendaai's relations with

Awer hadn't been any better than with Geir, but I supposed the request was a measure of just how desperate and alone Seivarden was.

"Ah." Inspector Supervisor Skaaiat winced, just slightly. "Awer and Geir aren't as close as they used to be, citizen. About two hundred years ago there was an exchange of heirs. The Geir cousin killed herself." The verb Inspector Supervisor Skaaiat used implied that it hadn't been an approved, Medical-mediated suicide but something illicit and messy. "And the Awer cousin went mad and ran off to join some cult somewhere."

Seivarden made a breathy, amused noise. "Typical."

Inspector Supervisor Skaaiat raised an eyebrow, but only said, temperately, "It left some bad feeling on both sides. So my connections with Geir aren't what they could be, and I might or might not be able to be helpful to you. And their responsibilities toward you might be...difficult to determine, though you might find that useful in an appeal."

Seivarden gestured abortively, arms still tightly crossed, one elbow lifting slightly. "It doesn't sound like it's worth the trouble."

Inspector Supervisor Skaaiat gestured ambivalence. "You'll be fed and sheltered here in any event, citizen." She turned to me. "And you, honored. You're here as a tourist?"

"Yes." I smiled, looking, I hoped, very much like a tourist from the Gerentate.

"You're a very long way from home." Inspector Supervisor Skaaiat smiled, politely, as though the observation were an idle one.

"I've been traveling a long time." Of course she—and by implication others—were curious about me. I had arrived in company with Seivarden. Most of the people here wouldn't know her name, but those who did would be attracted by the staggering unlikelihood of her having been found after a thousand years, and the connection to an event as notorious as Garsedd.

Still smiling pleasantly, Inspector Supervisor Skaaiat asked, "Looking for something? Avoiding something? Just like to travel?"

I made a gesture of ambiguity. "I suppose I like to travel."

Inspector Supervisor Skaaiat's eyes narrowed slightly at my tone of voice, muscles tensing just perceptibly around her mouth. She thought, it seemed, that I was hiding something, and she was interested now, and more curious than before.

For an instant I wondered why I'd answered the way I had. And realized that Inspector Supervisor Skaaiat's being here was incredibly dangerous to me—not because she might recognize me, but because *I* recognized *her*. Because she was alive and Lieutenant Awn was not. Because everyone of her standing had failed Lieutenant Awn (*I* had failed Lieutenant Awn), and no doubt if then–Lieutenant Skaaiat had been put to the test, she would have failed as well. Lieutenant Awn herself had known this.

I was in danger of my emotions affecting my behavior. They already had, they always did. But I had never been confronted with Skaaiat Awer until now.

"My response is ambiguous, I know," I said, making that placatory gesture Inspector Supervisor Skaaiat had already used. "I've never questioned my desire to travel. When I was a baby, my grandmother said she could tell from the way I took my first steps that I was born to go places. She kept on saying it. I suppose I've just always believed it."

Inspector Supervisor Skaaiat gestured acknowledgment. "It would be a shame to disappoint your grandmother, in any event. Your Radchaai is very good."

"My grandmother always said I'd better study languages."

Inspector Supervisor Skaaiat laughed. Almost as I remembered her from Ors, but still that trace of gravity. "Forgive me, honored, but do you have gloves?"

"I meant to buy some before we boarded, but I decided to wait and buy the right sort. I hoped I'd be forgiven my bare hands on arrival since I'm an uncivilized foreigner."

"An argument could be made for either approach," Inspector Supervisor Skaaiat said, still smiling. A shade more relaxed than moments before. "Though." A serious turn. "You speak very well, but I don't know how much you understand other things."

I raised an eyebrow. "Which things?"

"I don't wish to be indelicate, honored. But Citizen Seivarden doesn't appear to have any money in her possession." Beside me, Seivarden grew tense again, tightened her jaw, swallowed something she had been about to say. "Parents," continued Inspector Supervisor Skaaiat, "buy clothes for their children. The temple gives gloves to attendants—flower-bearers and water-bearers and such. That's all right, because everyone owes loyalty to God. And I know from your entrance application that you've employed Citizen Seivarden as your servant, but…"

"Ah." I understood her. "If I buy gloves for Citizen Seivarden—which she clearly needs—it will look as though I've offered her clientage."

"Just so," agreed Inspector Supervisor Skaaiat. "Which would be fine if that's what you intended. But I don't think things work that way in the Gerentate. And honestly…" She hesitated, clearly on delicate ground again.

"And honestly," I finished for her, "she's got a difficult legal situation that might not be helped by her association with a foreigner." My normal habit was expressionlessness. I could keep my anger out of my voice easily. I could speak to Inspector Supervisor Skaaiat as though she were not in any way connected with Lieutenant Awn, as though Lieutenant Awn had had no anxieties or hopes or fears about future patronage from her. "Even a rich one."

"I'm not sure I'd say it quite that way," began Inspector Supervisor Skaaiat.

"I'll just give her some money now," I said. "That should take care of it."

"No." Seivarden's tone was sharp. Angry. "I don't need money. Every citizen is due basic necessities, and clothes are a basic necessity. I'll have what I need." At Inspector Supervisor Skaaiat's surprised, inquiring look Seivarden said further, "Breq has good reasons for not having given me money."

Inspector Supervisor Skaaiat had to know what that likely meant. "Citizen, I don't mean to lecture," she said. "But if that's the case, why not just let Security send you to Medical? I understand you're reluctant to do that." Reeducation wasn't the sort of thing that was easy to mention politely. "But really, it might make things better for you. It often does."

A year ago I'd have expected Seivarden to lose her temper at this suggestion. But something had changed for her in that time. She only said, slightly irritably, "No."

Inspector Supervisor Skaaiat looked at me. I raised one eyebrow and a shoulder, as if to say, *That's how she is.*

"Breq has been very patient with me," said Seivarden, astonishing me utterly. "And very generous." She looked at me. "I don't need money."

"Whatever you like," I said.

Inspector Supervisor Skaaiat had watched the whole exchange intently, frowning just slightly. Curious, I thought, not only about who and what I was, but what I was to Seivarden. "Well," she said now, "let me take you to the palace. Honored Breq Ghaiad, I'll have your things delivered to your lodgings." She rose.

I stood as well, and Seivarden beside me. We followed Inspector Supervisor Skaaiat to the outer office—empty, Daos Ceit (Inspector Adjunct Ceit, I would have to remember) likely gone for the day, given the hour. Instead of taking us through the front of the offices, Inspector Supervisor Skaaiat led us through a back corridor, through a door that opened at no perceptible cue from her—Station, that would be, the AI that ran this place, *was* this place, paying close attention to the inspector supervisor of its docks.

"Are you all right, Breq?" asked Seivarden, looking at me with puzzlement and concern.

"Fine," I lied. "Just a little tired. It's been a long day." I was sure my expression hadn't changed, but Seivarden had noticed something.

Through the door was more corridor, and a bank of lifts, one of which opened for us, then closed and moved with no signal. Station knew where Inspector Supervisor Skaaiat wanted to go. Which turned out to be the main concourse.

The lift doors slid open onto a broad and dazzling view— an avenue paved in black stone veined with white, seven hundred meters long and twenty-five wide, the roof sixty meters above. Directly ahead stood the temple. The steps were not really steps, but an area marked out on the paving with red and green and blue stones; actions on the steps of the temple potentially had legal significance. The entrance was itself forty meters high and eight wide, framed with representations of hundreds of gods, many human-shaped, some not, a riot of colors. Just inside the entrance lay a basin for worshippers to wash their hands in, and beyond that containers of cut flowers, a swath of yellow and orange and red, and baskets of incense, for purchase as offerings. Away down either side of the concourse, shops, offices, balconies with flowered vines snaking down. Benches, and plants, and even at an hour when most Radchaai would be at supper hundreds of citizens walked or stood talking, uniformed (white for the Translators Office, light brown for Station Security, dark brown for military, green for Horticulture, light blue for Administration) or not, all glittering with jewelry, all thoroughly Civilized. I saw an ancillary follow its captain into a crowded tea shop, and wondered which ship it was. What ships were here. But I couldn't ask, it wasn't the sort of thing Breq from the Gerentate would care about.

I saw them all, suddenly, for just a moment, through non-Radchaai eyes, an eddying crowd of unnervingly ambiguously gendered people. I saw all the features that would mark gender for non-Radchaai—never, to my annoyance and inconvenience, the same way in each place. Short hair or long, worn unbound (trailing down a back, or in a thick, curled nimbus) or bound (braided, pinned, tied). Thick-bodied or thin-, faces delicate-featured or coarse-, with cosmetics or none. A profusion of colors that would have been gender-marked in other places. All of this matched randomly with bodies curving at breast and hip or not, bodies that one moment moved in ways various non-Radchaai would call feminine, the next moment masculine. Twenty years of habit overtook me, and for an instant I despaired of choosing the right pronouns, the right terms of address. But I didn't need to do that here. I could drop that worry, a small but annoying weight I had carried all this time. I was home.

This was home that had never been home, for me. I had

spent my life at annexations, and stations in the process of becoming this sort of place, leaving before they did, to begin the whole process again somewhere else. This was the sort of place my officers came from, and departed to. The sort of place I had never been, and yet it was completely familiar to me. Places like this were, from one point of view, the whole reason for my existence.

"It's a bit longer walk, this way," Inspector Supervisor Skaaiat said, "but a dramatic entrance."

"It is," I agreed.

"Why all the jackets?" asked Seivarden. "That bothered me last time. Though the last place, anyone in a coat was wearing it knee-length. Here it looks like it's either jackets or coats down to the floor. And the collars are just *wrong*."

"Fashion didn't trouble you the other places we've been," I said.

"The other places were *foreign*," Seivarden answered, irritably. "They weren't supposed to be *home*."

Inspector Supervisor Skaaiat smiled. "I imagine you'll get used to it eventually. The palace proper is this way."

We followed her across the concourse, my and Seivarden's uncivilized clothes and bare hands attracting some curious and disgusted looks, and came to the entrance, marked simply with a bar of black over the doorway.

"I'll be fine," said Seivarden, as though I'd spoken. "I'll catch up with you when I'm done."

"I'll wait."

Inspector Supervisor Skaaiat watched Seivarden go into the palace proper and then said, "Honored Breq, a word, please."

I acknowledged her with a gesture, and she said, "You're very concerned about Citizen Seivarden. I understand that, and it speaks well of you. But there's no reason to worry for her safety. The Radch takes care of its citizens."

"Tell me, Inspector Supervisor, if Seivarden were some nobody from a nothing house who had left the Radch without permits—and whatever else it was she did, to be honest I don't know if there was anything else—if she were someone you had never heard of, with a house name you didn't recognize and know the history of, would she have been met courteously at the dock and given tea and then escorted to the palace proper to make her appeal?"

Her right hand lifted, the barest millimeter, and that small, incongruous gold tag flashed. "She's not in that position anymore. She's effectively houseless, and broke." I said nothing, only looked at her. "No, there's something in what you say. If I didn't know who she was I wouldn't have thought to do anything for her. But surely even in the Gerentate things work that way?"

I made myself smile slightly, hoping for a more pleasant impression than I had likely been making. "They do."

Inspector Supervisor Skaaiat was silent a moment, watching me, thinking about something, but I couldn't guess what. Until she said, "Do you intend to offer her clientage?"

That would have been an unspeakably rude question, if I had been Radchaai. But when I had known her Skaaiat Awer had often said things most others left unsaid. "How could I? I'm not Radchaai. And we don't make that sort of contract in the Gerentate."

"No, you don't," Inspector Supervisor Skaaiat said. Blunt. "I can't imagine what it would be like to suddenly wake up a thousand years from now having lost my ship in a notorious incident, all my friends dead, my house gone. I might run away too. Seivarden needs to find a way she can belong somewhere. To Radchaai eyes, you look like you're offering that to her."

"You're concerned I'm giving Seivarden false expectations." I thought of Daos Ceit in the outer office, that beautiful, very expensive pearl-and-platinum pin that wasn't a token of clientage.

"I don't know what expectations Citizen Seivarden has. It's just...you're acting as though you're responsible for her. It looks wrong to me."

"If I were Radchaai, would it still look wrong to you?"

"If you were Radchaai you would behave differently." The tightness of her jaw argued she was angry but trying to conceal it.

"Whose name is on that pin?" The question, unintended, came out more brusquely than was politic.

"What?" She frowned, puzzled.

"That pin on your right sleeve. It's different from everything else you're wearing." *Whose name is on it?* I wanted to ask again, and, *What have you done for Lieutenant Awn's sister?*

Inspector Supervisor Skaaiat blinked, and shifted slightly backward, almost as though I had struck her. "It's a memorial for a friend who died."

"And you're thinking about her now. You keep shifting your wrist, turning it toward yourself. You've been doing it for the past few minutes."

"I think of her frequently." She took a breath, let it out. Took another. "I think maybe I'm not being fair to you, Breq Ghaiad."

I knew. I knew what name was on that pin, even though I hadn't seen it. *Knew* it. Wasn't sure if, knowing, I felt better about Inspector Supervisor Skaaiat, or much, much worse.

But I was in danger, at this moment, in a way I had never anticipated, never predicted, never dreamed might happen. I had already said things I should never, ever have said. Was about to say more. Here was the one single person I had met in twenty long years who would know who I was. The temptation to cry out, *Lieutenant, look, it's me, I'm* Justice of Toren *One Esk* was overwhelming.

Instead, very carefully, I said, "I agree with you that Seivarden needs to find herself a home here. I just don't trust the Radch the way you do. The way she does."

Inspector Supervisor Skaaiat opened her mouth to answer me, but Seivarden's voice cut across whatever Inspector Supervisor Skaaiat would have said. "That didn't take long!" Seivarden came up beside me, looked at me, and frowned. "Your leg is bothering you again. You need to sit down."

"Leg?" asked Inspector Supervisor Skaaiat.

"An old injury that didn't heal quite right," I said, glad of it for the moment, that Seivarden would attribute any distress she saw to that. That Station would, if it was watching.

"And you've had a long day, and I've kept you standing here. I've been quite rude, please forgive me, honored," Inspector Supervisor Skaaiat said.

"Of course." I bit back words that wanted to come out of my mouth behind that, and turned to Seivarden. "So where do things stand now?"

"I've requested my appeal, and should have a date sometime in the next few days," she said. "I put your name in too." At Inspector Supervisor Skaaiat's raised eyebrow Seivarden added, "Breq saved my life. More than once."

Inspector Supervisor Skaaiat only said, "Your audience probably won't be for a few months."

"Meantime," continued Seivarden with a small, still-cross-armed acknowledging gesture, "I've been assigned lodgings and I'm on the ration list and I've got fifteen minutes to report to the nearest supplies office and get some clothes."

Lodgings. Well, if her staying with me had looked wrong to Inspector Supervisor Skaaiat, doubtless it would, for the same reasons, look wrong to Seivarden herself. And even if she was no longer my servant, she had requested I accompany her to her audience. That was, I reminded myself, the important issue. "Do you want me to come with you?" I didn't want to. I wanted to be alone, to recover my equilibrium.

"I'll be fine. You need to get off that leg. I'll catch up with you tomorrow. Inspector Supervisor, it was good to meet you." Seivarden bowed, perfectly calculated courtesy toward a social equal, received an identical bow from Inspector Supervisor Skaaiat, and then was off down the concourse.

I turned to Inspector Supervisor Skaaiat. "Where do you recommend I stay?"

Half an hour later I was as I had wished to be, alone in my room. It was an expensive one, just off the main concourse, an incredibly luxurious five meters square, a floor of what might almost have been real wood, dark-blue walls. A table and chairs, and an image projector in the floor. Many—though not all—Radchaai had optical and auditory implants that allowed them to view entertainments or listen to music or messages directly. But people still liked to watch things together, and the very wealthy sometimes made a point of turning their implants off.

The blanket on the bed felt as if it might be actual wool, not anything synthetic. On one wall a fold-down cot for a servant, which of course I no longer had. And, incredible lux-

ury for the Radch, the room had its own tiny bath—a necessity for me, given the gun and ammunition strapped to my
body under my shirt. Station's scans hadn't picked it up, and
wouldn't, but human eyes could see it. If I left it in the room,
a searcher might find it. I certainly couldn't leave it in the
dressing room of a public bath.

A console on the wall near the door would give me access
to communications. And Station. And it would allow Station
to observe me, though I was certain it wasn't the only way
Station could see into the room. I was back in the Radch,
never alone, never private.

My luggage had arrived within five minutes of my taking
the room, and with it a tray of supper from a nearby shop,
fish and greens, still steaming and smelling of spices.

There was always the chance that no one was paying attention. But my luggage, when I opened it, had clearly been
searched. Maybe because I was foreign. Maybe not.

I took out my tea flask and cups, and the icon of She Who
Sprang from the Lily, set them on the low table beside the
bed. Used a liter of my water allowance to fill the flask, and
then sat down to eat.

The fish was as delicious as it smelled, and improved my
mood slightly. I was, at least, better able to confront my situation once I'd eaten it, and had a cup of tea.

Station could certainly see a large percentage of its residents with the same intimate view I'd had of my officers. The
rest—including me, now—it saw in less detail. Temperature.
Heart rate. Respiration. Less impressive than the flood of
data from more closely monitored residents, but still a great
deal of information. Add to that a close knowledge of the
person observed, her history, her social context, and likely
Station could very nearly read minds.

Nearly. It couldn't *actually* read thoughts. And Station didn't know my history, had no prior experience with me. It would be able to see the traces of my emotions, but wouldn't have many grounds for guessing accurately why I felt as I did.

My hip had in fact been hurting. And Inspector Supervisor Skaaiat's words to me had been, in Radchaai terms, incredibly rude. If I had reacted with anger, visible to Station if it was looking (visible to Anaander Mianaai if she had been looking), that was entirely natural. Neither one could do more than guess what had angered me. I could play the part now of the exhausted traveler, pained by an old injury, in need of nothing more than food and rest.

The room was so quiet. Even when Seivarden had been in one of her sulking moods it hadn't seemed this oppressively silent. I hadn't grown as used to solitude as I had thought. And thinking of Seivarden, I saw suddenly what I had not seen, there on the concourse and blind-angry with Skaaiat Awer. I had thought then that Inspector Supervisor Skaaiat had been the only person I had met who might know me, but that wasn't true. Seivarden would have.

But Lieutenant Awn had never expected anything from Seivarden, had never stood to be hurt or disappointed by her. If they had ever met, Seivarden would surely have made her disdain clear. Lieutenant Awn would have been stiffly polite, with an underlying anger that I would have been able to see, but she would never have had that sinking dismay and hurt she felt when then–Lieutenant Skaaiat said, unthinkingly, something dismissive.

But perhaps I was wrong to think my reactions to the two, Skaaiat Awer and Seivarden Vendaai, were very different. I had already put myself in danger once, out of anger with Seivarden.

I couldn't untangle it. And I had a part to play, for whoever might be watching, an image I had carefully built on the way here. I set my empty cup beside the tea flask, and knelt on the floor before the icon, hip protesting slightly, and began to pray.

19

Next morning I bought clothes. The proprietor of the shop Inspector Supervisor Skaaiat had recommended was on the verge of throwing me out when my bank balance flashed onto her console, unbidden I suspected, Station sparing her embarrassment—and simultaneously telling me how closely it was watching me.

I needed gloves, certainly, and if I was going to play the part of the spendthrift wealthy tourist I would need to buy more than that. But before I could speak up to say so, the proprietor brought out bolts of brocade, sateen, and velvet in a dozen colors. Purple and orange-brown, three shades of green, gold, pale yellow and icy blue, ash gray, deep red.

"You can't wear those clothes," she told me, authoritative, as a subordinate handed me tea, managing to mostly conceal her disgust at my bare hands. Station had scanned me and provided my measurements, so I needed do nothing. A half-liter of tea, two excruciatingly sweet pastries, and a dozen insults later, I left in an orange-brown jacket and trousers, an icy white, stiff shirt underneath, and dark-gray gloves so thin

and soft I might almost have still been barehanded. Fortunately current fashion favored jackets and trousers cut gener-
ously enough to hide my weapon. The rest—two more jackets
and pairs of trousers, two pairs of gloves, half a dozen shirts,
and three pairs of shoes—would be delivered to my lodgings
by the time, the proprietor told me, I was done visiting the
temple.

I exited the shop, turned a corner onto the main concourse,
crowded at this hour with a throng of Radchaai going in and
out of the temple or the palace proper, visiting the (no doubt
expensive and fashionable) tea shops, or merely being seen in
the right company. When I had walked through before, on
my way to the clothes shop, people had stared and whispered,
or just raised their eyebrows. Now, it seemed, I was mostly
invisible, except for the occasional similarly well-dressed
Radchaai who dropped her gaze to my jacket front looking
for signs of my family affiliation, eyes widening in surprise to
see none. Or the child, one small gloved hand clutching the
sleeve of an accompanying adult, who turned to frankly stare
at me until she was drawn past and out of sight.

Inside the temple, citizens crowded the flowers and incense,
junior priests young enough to look like children to my eyes
bringing baskets and boxes of replacements. As an ancillary
I wasn't supposed to touch temple offerings, or make them
myself. But no one here knew that. I washed my hands in the
basin and bought a handful of bright yellow-orange flowers,
and a piece of the sort of incense I knew Lieutenant Awn had
favored.

There would be a place within the temple set aside for
prayers for the dead, and days that were auspicious for making such offerings, though this wasn't such a day, and as a foreigner I shouldn't have Radchaai dead to remember. Instead I

walked into the echoing main hall, where Amaat stood, a jeweled Emanation in each hand, already knee-deep in flowers, a hill of red and orange and yellow as high as my head, growing incrementally as worshippers tossed more blooms on the pile. When I reached the front of the crowd I added my own, made the gestures and mouthed the prayer, dropped the incense into the box that, when it filled, would be emptied by more junior priests. It was only a token—it would return to the entrance, to be purchased again. If all the incense offered had been burned, the air in the temple would have been too thick with smoke to breathe. And this wasn't even a festival day.

As I bowed to the god, a brown-uniformed ship's captain came up beside me. She made to throw her handful of flowers, and then stopped, staring at me. The fingers of her empty left hand twitched, just slightly. Her features reminded me of Hundred Captain Rubran Osck, though where Captain Rubran had been lanky, and worn her hair long and straight, this captain was shorter and thick-bodied, hair clipped close. A glance at her jewelry confirmed this captain was a cousin of hers, a member of the same branch of the same house. I remembered that Anaander Mianaai hadn't been able to predict Captain Rubran's allegiance, and didn't want to tug too hard on the web of clientage and contacts the hundred captain belonged to. I wondered if that was still true, or if Osck had come down on one side or the other.

It didn't matter. The captain still stared, presumably receiving by now answers to her queries. Station or her ship would tell her I was a foreigner and the captain would, I presumed, lose interest. Or not, if she learned about Seivarden. I didn't wait to see which was the case, but finished my prayer and turned to work my way through the people waiting to make offerings.

Off the sides of the temple were smaller shrines. In one,

three adults and two children stood around an infant they had laid at the breast of Aatr—the image being constructed to allow this, its arm crooked under the god's often-sworn-by breasts—hoping for an auspicious destiny, or at least some sign of what the future might hold for the child.

All the shrines were beautiful, glittering with gold and silver, glass and polished stone. The whole place rumbled and roared with the echoes of hundreds of quiet conversations and prayers. No music. I thought of the nearly empty temple of Ikkt, the Divine of Ikkt telling me of hundreds of singers long gone.

I was nearly two hours in the temple admiring the shrines of subsidiary gods. The entire place must have taken up whatever part of this side of the station was not occupied by the palace proper. The two were certainly connected, since Anaander Mianaai acted as priest here at regular intervals, though the accesses wouldn't be obvious.

I left the mortuary shrine for last. Partly because it was the part of the temple most likely to be crowded with tourists, and partly because I knew it would make me unhappy. It was larger than the other subsidiary shrines, nearly half the size of the vast main hall, filled with shelves and cases crowded with offerings for the dead. All food or flowers. All glass. Glass teacups holding glass tea, glass steam rising above. Mounds of delicate glass roses and leaves. Two dozen different kinds of fruit, fish and greens that nearly gave off a phantom aroma of my supper the night before. You could buy mass-produced versions of these in shops well away from the main concourse, and put them in your home shrine, for gods or for the dead, but these were different, each one a carefully detailed work of art, each one conspicuously labeled with the names of the living donor and the dead recipient, so every visitor could see the pious mourning—and wealth and status—on display.

I probably had enough money to commission such an offering. But if I did so, and labeled it with the appropriate names, it would be the last thing I ever did. And doubtless the priests would refuse it. I had already considered sending money to Lieutenant Awn's sister, but that, too, would attract unwelcome curiosity. Maybe I could arrange it so that whatever was left would go to her, once I had done what I'd come here to do, but I suspected that would be impossible. Still, thinking it, and thinking of my luxurious room and expensive, beautiful clothes, gave me a twinge of guilt.

At the temple entrance, just as I was about to step out onto the concourse, a soldier stepped into my path. Human, not an ancillary. She bowed. "Excuse me. I have a message from the citizen Vel Osck, captain of *Mercy of Kalr*."

The captain who had stared at me as I made my offering to Amaat. The fact she'd sent a soldier to accost me said she thought me worth more trouble than a message through Station's systems, but not enough to send a lieutenant, or approach me herself. Though that might also have been due to a certain social awkwardness she preferred to push off onto this soldier. It was hard not to notice the slight clumsiness of a sentence designed to avoid a courtesy title. "Your pardon, citizen," I said. "I don't know the citizen Vel Osck."

The soldier gestured, slight, deferential apology. "This morning's cast indicated the captain would have a fortuitous encounter today. When she noticed you making your offering she was sure you were who was meant."

Noticing a stranger in the temple, in a place as big as this, was hardly a fortuitous encounter. I was slightly offended that the captain hadn't even tried to put more effort into it. Mere seconds of thought would have produced something better. "What is the message, citizen?"

"The captain customarily takes tea in the afternoons," said the soldier, bland and polite, and named a shop just off the concourse. "She would be honored if you would join her."

The time and place suggested the sort of "social" meeting that was, in reality, a display of influence and associations, and where ostensibly unofficial business would be done.

Captain Vel had no business with me. And she would gain no advantage in being seen with me. "If the captain wants to meet citizen Seivarden..." I began.

"It wasn't Captain Seivarden the captain encountered in the temple," the solder answered, again slightly apologetic. Surely she knew how transparent her errand was. "But of course if you wanted to bring Captain Seivarden, Captain Vel would be honored to meet her."

Of course. And even houseless and broke, Seivarden would get a personal invitation from someone she knew, not a message through station systems, or a this-edge-of-insulting invite from Captain Vel's errand-runner. But it was exactly what I had wanted. "I can't speak for Citizen Seivarden, of course," I said. "Do please thank Captain Vel for the invitation." The soldier bowed, and left.

Off the concourse I found a shop selling cartons of what was advertised merely as "lunch," which turned out to be fish again, stewed with fruit. I took it back to my room and sat at the table, eating, considering that console on the wall, a visible link with Station.

Station was as smart as I had ever been, when I had still been a ship. Younger, yes. Less than half my age. But not to be dismissed, not at all. If I was discovered, it would almost certainly be because of Station.

Station hadn't detected my ancillary implants, all of which I had disabled and hidden as best I could. If it had, I would have already been under arrest. But Station could see at least the basics of my emotional state. Could, with enough information about me, tell when I was lying. Was, certainly, watching me closely.

But emotional states, from Station's view, from mine when I was *Justice of Toren*, were just assemblages of medical data, data that were meaningless without context. If, in my present dismal mood, I had just stepped off a ship, Station would possibly see it, but not understand why I felt the way I did, and would not be able to draw any conclusions from it. But the longer I was here, the more of me Station saw, the more data Station would have. It would be able to assemble its own context, its own picture of what I was. And would be able to compare that to what it thought I ought to be.

The danger would be if those two didn't match. I swallowed a mouthful of fish, looked at the console. "Hello," I said. "The AI who's watching me."

"Honored Ghaiad Breq," said Station from the console, a placid voice. "Hello. I am usually addressed as *Station*."

"Station, then." Another bite of fish and fruit. "So you *are* watching me." I was, genuinely, worried about Station's surveillance. I wouldn't be able to hide that from Station.

"I watch everyone, honored. Is your leg still troubling you?" It was, and doubtless Station could see me favor it, see the effects of it in the way I sat now. "Our medical facilities are excellent. I'm sure one of our doctors could find a solution to your problem."

An alarming prospect. But I could make that look entirely understandable. "No, thank you. I've been warned about Radchaai medical facilities. I'd rather endure a little inconvenience and still be who I am."

Silence, for a moment. Then Station asked, "Do you mean

the aptitudes? Or reeducation? Neither would change who you are. And you aren't eligible for either one, I assure you."

"All the same." I set my utensil down. "We have a saying, where I come from: Power requires neither permission nor forgiveness."

"I have never met anyone from the Gerentate before," said Station. I had, of course, been depending on that. "I suppose your misapprehension is understandable. Foreigners often don't understand what the Radchaai are really like."

"Do you realize what you've just said? Literally that the uncivilized don't understand civilization? Do you realize that quite a lot of people outside Radch space consider themselves to be civilized?" The sentence was nearly impossible in Radchaai, a self-contradiction.

I waited for *That wasn't what I meant*, but it didn't come. Instead, Station said, "Would you have come here if not for Citizen Seivarden?"

"Possibly," I answered, knowing I could not lie outright to Station, not with it watching me so closely. Knowing that now any anger or resentment—or any apprehension about Radchaai officials—that I felt would be attributed to my being resentful and fearful of the Radch. "Is there any music in this very civilized place?"

"Yes," answered Station. "Though I don't think I have any music from the Gerentate."

"If I only ever wanted to hear music from the Gerentate," I said, acid, "I would never have left there."

This did not seem to faze Station. "Would you prefer to go out or stay in?"

I preferred to stay in. Station called up an entertainment for me, new this year but a comfortably familiar sort of thing—a young woman of humble family with hopes of clientage to a more prestigious house. A jealous rival who undermines her, deceiving the putative patron as to her true, noble nature. The eventual recognition of the heroine's superior virtue, her loyalty through the most terrible trials, even uncontracted as she is, and the downfall of her rival, culminating in the long-awaited clientage contract and ten minutes of triumphant singing and dancing, the last of eleven such interludes over four separate episodes. It was a very small-scale work—some of these ran for dozens of episodes that added up to days or even weeks. It was mindless, but the songs were nice and improved my mood considerably.

I had nothing urgent to do until word came of Seivarden's appeal, and if Seivarden's request for an audience, and for me to accompany her, was granted, that would mean another, even longer wait. I rose, brushed my new trousers straight, put on shoes and jacket. "Station," I said. "Do you know where I can find the citizen Seivarden Vendaai?"

"The citizen Seivarden Vendaai," answered Station from the console, in its always even voice, "is in the Security office on sublevel nine."

"Excuse me?"

"There was a fight," said Station. "Normally Security would have contacted her family, but she has none here."

I wasn't her family, of course. And she could have called for me if she'd wanted me. Still. "Can you direct me to the Security office on sublevel nine, please?"

"Of course, honored."

The office on sublevel nine was tiny: nothing more, really, than a console, a few chairs, a table with mismatched tea things, and some storage lockers. Seivarden sat on a bench at the back wall. She wore gray gloves and an ill-fitting jacket and trousers of some stiff, coarse fabric, the sort of thing extruded on demand, not sewn, and probably produced in a preset range of sizes. My own uniforms, when I had been a ship, had been made that way, but had looked better. Of course I'd sized each one properly, it had been a simple thing for me to do at the time.

The front of Seivarden's gray jacket was spattered with blood, and one glove was soaked with it. Blood was crusted on her upper lip, and the small clear shell of a corrective sat across the bridge of her nose. Another corrective lay across a bruise forming on one cheek. She stared dully ahead, not looking up at me, or at the Security officer who had admitted me. "Here's your friend, citizen," said Security.

Seivarden frowned. Looked up, around the small space. Then she looked more closely at me. "Breq? Aatr's tits, that's you. You look…" She blinked. Opened her mouth to finish the sentence, stopped again. Took another, somewhat ragged breath. "Different," she concluded. "Really, really different."

"I only bought clothes. What happened to you?"

"There was a fight," said Seivarden.

"Just happened on its own, did it?" I asked.

"No," she admitted. "I was assigned a place to sleep, but there was already someone living there. I tried to talk to her but I could hardly understand her."

"Where did you sleep last night?" I asked.

She looked down at the floor. "I managed." Looked up again, at me, at the Security officer beside me. "But I wasn't going to be able to *keep* managing."

"You should have come to us, citizen," said Security. "Now you've got a warning on your record. Not something you want."

"And her opponent?" I asked.

Security made a negating gesture. It wasn't something I was supposed to ask.

"I'm not managing very well on my own, am I," said Seivarden, miserably.

Heedless of Skaaiat Awer's disapproval, I bought Seivarden new gloves and jacket, dark green, still the sort of thing that was extruded on demand, but at least it fit better, and the higher quality was obvious. The gray ones were past laundering, and I knew the supply office wouldn't issue more clothes so soon. When Seivarden had put them on, and sent the old ones for recycling, I said, "Have you eaten? I was planning to offer you supper when Station told me where you were." She'd washed her face, and now looked more or less reputable, give or take the bruising under the corrective on her cheek.

"I'm not hungry," she said. A flicker of something—regret? Annoyance? I couldn't quite tell—flashed across her face. She crossed her arms and quickly uncrossed them again, a gesture I hadn't seen in months.

"Can I offer you tea, then, while I eat?"

"I would *love* tea," she said with emphatic sincerity. I remembered that she had no money, had refused to let me give her any. All that tea we had carried with us was in my luggage, she had taken none of it with her when we'd parted the night before. And tea, of course, was an extra. A luxury. Which wasn't really a luxury. Not by Seivarden's standards, anyway. Likely not by any Radchaai's standards.

We found a tea shop, and I bought something rolled in a sheet of algae, and some fruit and tea, and we took a table in a corner. "Are you sure you don't want anything?" I asked. "Fruit?"

She feigned lack of interest in the fruit, and then took a piece. "I hope you had a better day than I did."

"Probably." I waited a moment, to see if she wanted to talk about what had happened, but she said nothing, just waited for me to continue. "I went to the temple this morning. And ran into some ship's captain who stared quite rudely and then sent one of her soldiers after me to invite me to tea."

"One of her *soldiers*." Seivarden realized her arms were crossed, uncrossed them, picked up her tea cup, set it down again. "Ancillary?"

"Human. I'm pretty sure."

Seivarden lifted an eyebrow briefly. "You shouldn't go. She should have invited you herself. You didn't say yes, did you?"

"I didn't say no." Three Radchaai entered the tea shop, laughing. All wore the dark blue of dock authority. One of them was Daos Ceit, Inspector Supervisor Skaaiat's assistant. She didn't seem to notice me. "I don't think the invitation was on my account. I think she wants me to introduce her to *you*."

"But..." She frowned. Looked at the bowl of tea in one green-gloved hand. Brushed the front of the new jacket with the other. "What's her name?"

"Vel Osck."

"Osck. Never heard of them." She took another drink of tea. Daos Ceit and her friends bought tea and pastries, sat at a table on the other side of the room, talking animatedly. "Why would she want to meet me?"

I raised an eyebrow, incredulous. "*You're* the one who believes any unlikely event is a message from God," I pointed out. "You're lost for a thousand years, found by accident, disappear again, and then turn up at a palace with a rich foreigner. And you're surprised when that gets attention." She made an ambiguous gesture. "Absent Vendaai as a functioning house, you need to establish yourself somehow."

She looked so dismayed, just for the shortest instant, that I thought my words had offended her in some way. But then she seemed to recover herself. "If Captain Vel wanted my good will, or cared at all about my opinion, she made a bad start by insulting you." Her old arrogance lurked behind those words, a startling difference from her barely suppressed dejection up to now.

"What about that inspector supervisor?" I asked. "Skaaiat, right? She seemed polite enough. And you seemed to know who she was."

"All the Awers *seem* polite enough," Seivarden said, disgustedly. Over her shoulder I watched Daos Ceit laugh at something one of her companions had said. "They *seem* totally normal at first," Seivarden went on, "but then they go having visions, or deciding something's wrong with the universe and they have to fix it. Or both at once. They're all insane." She was silent a moment, and then turned to see what I was looking at. Turned back. "Oh, *her*. Isn't she kind of...provincial-looking?"

I turned my full attention on Seivarden. Looked at her.

She looked down at the table. "I'm sorry. That was...that was just wrong. I don't have any..."

"I doubt," I interrupted, "that her pay allows her to wear clothes that make her look...'different.'"

"That's not what I meant." Seivarden looked up, distress and embarrassment obvious in her expression. "But what I meant was bad enough. I just...I was just surprised. All this time, I guess I've just assumed you were an ascetic. It just surprised me."

An ascetic. I could see why she would have assumed that,

but not why it would have mattered that she was wrong. Unless... "You're not *jealous*?" I asked, incredulous. Well-dressed or not, I was just as provincial-looking as Daos Ceit. Just from a different province.

"No!" And then the next moment, "Well, yes. But not like *that*."

I realized, then, that it wasn't just other Radchaai who might get the wrong impression from that gift of clothes I'd just made. Even though Seivarden surely knew I couldn't offer clientage. Even though I knew that if she thought about it for longer than thirty seconds, she would never want from me what that gift implied. Surely she couldn't think that I'd meant that. "Yesterday the inspector supervisor told me I was in danger of giving you false expectations. Or of giving others the wrong impression."

Seivarden made a scornful noise. "That would be worth considering if I had the remotest interest in what Awer thinks." I raised an eyebrow, and she continued, in a more contrite tone, "I thought I'd be able to handle things by myself, but all last night, and all today, I've just been wishing I'd stayed with you. I guess it's true, all citizens are taken care of. I didn't see anyone starving. Or naked." Her face momentarily showed disgust. "But those clothes. And the skel. Just skel, all the time, very carefully measured out. I didn't think I'd mind. I mean, I don't mind skel, but I could hardly choke it down." I could guess the mood she'd been in, when she'd gotten into that fight. "I think it was knowing I wasn't going to get anything else for weeks and weeks. And," she said, with a rueful smile, "knowing I'd have had better if I'd asked to stay with you."

"So you want your old job back, then?" I asked.

"*Fuck* yes," she said, emphatic and relieved. Loud enough

for the party across the room to hear and turn disapproving glances our way.

"Language, citizen." I took another bite of my algae roll. Relieved, I discovered, on several counts. "Are you sure you wouldn't rather take your chances with Captain Vel?"

"You can have tea with whoever you want," said Seivarden. "But she should have invited you herself."

"Your manners are a thousand years old," I pointed out.

"Manners are manners," she said, indignant. "But like I said, you can have tea with whoever you want."

Inspector Supervisor Skaaiat entered the shop, saw Daos Ceit and nodded to her, but came over to where Seivarden and I sat. Hesitated, just an instant, noticing the correctives on Seivarden's face, but then pretended she hadn't seen them. "Citizen. Honored."

"Inspector Supervisor," I replied. Seivarden merely nodded.

"I'm hosting a small get-together tomorrow evening." She named a place. "Just tea, nothing formal. I'd be honored if you both came."

Seivarden laughed outright. "Manners," she said again, "are manners."

Skaaiat frowned, nonplussed.

"Yours is the second such invitation today," I explained. "Citizen Seivarden tells me the first was less than entirely courteous."

"I hope mine met her exacting standards," Skaaiat said. "Who failed them?"

"Captain Vel," I answered. "Of *Mercy of Kalr*."

To someone who didn't know her well, Skaaiat probably looked as though she had no real opinions about Captain Vel. "Well. I admit I intended to introduce you, citizen, to friends of mine who might be useful to you. But you might find Captain Vel's acquaintance more congenial."

"You must have a low opinion of me," Seivarden said.

"It's possible," said Skaaiat, and oh how strange it was to hear her speak with such gravity, as I had known her twenty years ago but different, "that Captain Vel's approach was less than entirely respectful toward the honored Breq. But in other respects I suspect you'd find her sympathetic." Before Seivarden could answer, Skaaiat continued, "I have to go. I hope to see you both tomorrow evening." She looked over at the table where her assistant sat, and all three of the adjunct inspectors there stood, and left the shop behind her.

Seivarden was silent a moment, watching the door they had exited from.

"Well," I said. Seivarden looked back to me. "I guess if you're coming back I'd better pay you so you can buy some more decent clothes."

An expression I couldn't quite read flashed across Seivarden's face. "Where did you get yours?"

"I don't think I'll pay you *that* much," I said.

Seivarden laughed. Took a drink of her tea, another piece of fruit.

I wasn't at all certain she'd really eaten. "Are you sure you don't want anything else?" I asked.

"I'm sure. What *is* that thing?" She looked toward the last bit of my algae-covered supper.

"No idea." I hadn't ever seen anything quite like it in the Radch, it must have been recently invented, or an idea imported from some other place. "It's good, though, do you want one? We can take it back to the room if you like."

Seivarden made a face. "No, thanks. You're more adventurous than I am."

"I suppose I am," I agreed, pleasantly. I finished the last of my supper, drained my tea. "But you wouldn't know it to look at me, today. I spent the morning in the temple, like a good tourist, and the afternoon watching an entertainment in my room."

"Let me guess!" Seivarden raised an eyebrow, sardonic. "The one everyone is talking about. The heroine is virtuous and loyal, and her potential patron's lover hates her. She wins through because of her unswerving loyalty and devotion."

"You've seen it."

"More than once. But not for a very long time."

I smiled. "Some things never change?"

Seivarden laughed in response. "Apparently not. Songs any good?"

"Pretty good. You can watch back at the room, if you like."

But back in the room she folded down the servant's cot, saying, "I'm just going to sit down a moment," and was asleep two minutes and three seconds later.

20

It would almost certainly be weeks before Seivarden even had an audience date. In the meantime we were living here, and I would have a chance to see how things stood, who might side with which Mianaai if things came to an open breach. Maybe even whether one Mianaai or another was in ascendance here. Any information might prove crucial when the moment arrived. And it would arrive, I was increasingly sure. Anaander Mianaai might or might not realize what I was any time soon—but at this point there was no hiding me from the rest of herself. I was here, openly, noticeably, along with Seivarden.

Thinking of Seivarden, and Captain Vel Osck's eagerness to meet her, I thought also of Hundred Captain Rubran Osck. Of Anaander Mianaai complaining she couldn't guess her opinion, could rely on neither her opposition nor her support, nor could she pressure her in order to discover or compel it. Captain Rubran had been fortunate enough in her family connections to be able to take such a neutral stance, and keep it. Did that say something about the state of Mianaai's struggle with herself at the time?

Did the captain of *Mercy of Kalr* also take that neutral stance? Or had something changed in that balance during the time I had been gone? And what did it mean that Inspector Supervisor Skaaiat disliked her? I was certain dislike was the expression I had seen on her face when I had mentioned the name. Military ships weren't subject to dock authorities—except of course in the matter of arrivals and departures—and the relationship between the two usually involved some contempt on one side and mild resentment on the other, all covered over with guarded courtesy. But Skaaiat Awer had never been given to resentment, and besides she knew both sides of the game. Had Captain Vel offended her personally? Did she merely dislike her, as happened sometimes?

Or did her sympathies place her on the other side of some political dividing line? And after all, where was Skaaiat Awer likely to fall, in a divided Radch? Unless something had happened to change her personality and opinions drastically, I thought I knew where Skaaiat Awer would land in that toss. Captain Vel—and for that matter *Mercy of Kalr*—I didn't know well enough to say.

As for Seivarden, I was under no illusions as to where *her* sympathies would lie, given a choice between citizens who kept their proper places along with an expanding, conquering Radch, or no more annexations and the elevation of citizens with the wrong accents and antecedents. I was under no illusions as to what Seivarden's opinion of Lieutenant Awn would have been, had they ever met.

The place where Captain Vel customarily took tea was not prominently marked. It didn't need to be. It was probably not at the very top of fashion and society—not unless Osck's fortunes had soared in the last twenty years. But it was still the sort of place that if you didn't already know it was there you were almost certainly not welcome. The place was dark and the sound muffled—rugs and hangings absorbed echoes or unwanted noises. Stepping in from the noisy corridor it was as though I had suddenly put my hands over my ears. Groups of low chairs surrounded small tables. Captain Vel sat in one corner, flasks and bowls of tea and a half-empty tray of pastries on the table in front of her. The chairs were full, and an outer circle had been pulled around.

They had been here for at least an hour. Seivarden had said to me before we left the room, blandly, still irritated, that of course I wouldn't want to rush out to tea. If she'd been in a better mood she would have told me straight out that I should arrive late. It had been my own inclination even before she spoke, so I said nothing and let her have the satisfaction of thinking she'd influenced me, if she wished to have it.

Captain Vel saw me and rose, bowing. "Ah, Breq Ghaiad. Or is it Ghaiad Breq?"

I made my own bow in return, taking care that it was precisely as shallow as hers had been. "In the Gerentate we put our house names first." The Gerentate didn't have houses the way Radchaai did, but it was the only term Radchaai had for a name that indicated family relationship. "But I am not in the Gerentate at the moment. Ghaiad is my house name."

"You've already put it in the right order for us then!" Captain Vel said, falsely jovial. "Very thoughtful." I couldn't see Seivarden, who stood behind me. I wondered briefly what expression was on her face, and also why Captain Vel had invited me here if her every interaction with me was going to be mildly insulting.

Station was certainly watching me. It would see at least traces of my annoyance. Captain Vel would not. And likely would not care if she could have.

"And Captain Seivarden Vendaai," Captain Vel continued, and made another bow, noticeably deeper than the one before. "An honor, sir. A distinct honor. Do sit." She gestured to chairs near her own, and two elegantly attired and bejeweled Radchaai rose to make way for us, no complaint or expression of resentment apparent.

"Your pardon, Captain," said Seivarden. Bland. The correctives from the day before had come off, and she looked very nearly what she had been a thousand years ago, the wealthy and arrogant daughter of a highly placed house. In a moment she would sneer and say something sarcastic, I was sure, but she didn't. "I no longer deserve the rank. I am the honored Breq's servant." Slight stress on *honored*, as though Captain Vel might be ignorant of the appropriate courtesy title and Seivarden meant merely to politely and discreetly inform her. "And I thank you for the invitation she was good enough to convey to me." There it was, a hint of disdain, though it was possible only someone who knew her well would hear it. "But I have duties to attend to."

"I've given you the afternoon off, citizen," I said before Captain Vel could answer. "Spend it however you like." No reaction from Seivarden, and still I couldn't see her face. I took one of the seats cleared for us. A lieutenant had sat there previously, doubtless one of Captain Vel's officers. Though I saw more brown uniforms here than a small ship like *Mercy of Kalr* could account for.

The person next to me was a civilian in rose and azure, delicate satin gloves that suggested she never handled anything rougher or heavier than a bowl of tea, and an ostentatiously large brooch of woven and hammered gold wire set with sapphires—not, I was sure, glass. Likely the design advertised whatever wealthy house she belonged to, but I didn't recognize it. She leaned toward me and said, loudly, as Seivarden took the seat opposite me, "How fortunate you must have thought yourself, to find Seivarden Vendaai!"

"Fortunate," I repeated, carefully, as though the word were unfamiliar to me, leaning just slightly more heavily on my Gerentate accent. Almost wishing the Radchaai language concerned itself with gender so I could use it wrongly and sound even more foreign. Almost. "Is that the word for it?" I had guessed correctly why Captain Vel had approached me the way she had. Inspector Supervisor Skaaiat had done something similar, addressing Seivarden even though she knew Seivarden had come as my servant. Of course, the inspector supervisor had seen her mistake almost immediately.

Across from me, Seivarden was explaining to Captain Vel about the situation with her aptitudes. I was astonished at her icy calm, given I knew she'd been angry ever since I told her I'd intended to come. But this was, in some ways, her natural habitat. If the ship that had found her suspension pod had brought her somewhere like this, instead of a small, provincial station, things would have gone very differently for her.

"Ridiculous!" exclaimed Rose-and-Azure beside me, while Captain Vel poured a bowl of tea and offered it to Seivarden. "As though you were a child. As though no one knew what you were suited for. It used to be you could depend on officials to handle things properly." *Justly*, rang the silent companion of that last word. *Beneficially*.

"I did, citizen, lose my ship," Seivarden said.

"Not your fault, Captain," protested another civilian somewhere behind me. "Surely not."

"Everything that happens on my watch is my fault, citizen," answered Seivarden.

Captain Vel gestured agreement. "Still, there shouldn't have been any question of you taking the tests *again*."

Seivarden looked at her tea, looked over at me sitting empty-handed across from her, and set her bowl down on the table in front of her without drinking. Captain Vel poured a bowl and offered it to me, as though she hadn't noticed Seivarden's gesture.

"How do you find the Radch after a thousand years, Captain?" asked someone behind me as I accepted the tea. "Much changed?"

Seivarden didn't retrieve her own bowl. "Changed some. The same some."

"For the better, or for the worse?"

"I could hardly say," replied Seivarden, coolly.

"How beautifully you speak, Captain Seivarden," said someone else. "So many young people these days are careless about their speech. It's lovely to hear someone speak with real refinement."

Seivarden's lips quirked in what might be taken for appreciation of a compliment, but almost certainly wasn't.

"These lower houses and provincials, with their accents and their slang," agreed Captain Vel. "Really, my own ship, fine soldiers but to hear them talk you'd think they'd never gone to school."

"Pure laziness," opined a lieutenant behind Seivarden.

"You don't have that with ancillaries," said someone, possibly another captain behind me.

"A lot of things you don't have with ancillaries," said someone else, a comment that might be taken two ways, but I was fairly sure I knew which way was meant. "But that's not a safe topic."

"Not safe?" I asked, all innocence. "Surely it isn't illegal here to complain about young people these days? How cruel. I had thought it a basic part of human nature, one of the few universally practiced human customs."

"And surely," added Seivarden with a slight sneer, her mask finally cracking, "it's *always* safe to complain about lower houses and provincials."

"You'd *think*," said Rose-and-Azure beside me, mistaking Seivarden's intent. "But we are sadly changed, Captain, from your day. It used to be you could depend on the aptitudes to send the *right* citizen to the *right* assignment. I can't fathom some of the decisions they make these days. And atheists given privileges." She meant Valskaayans, who were, as a rule, not atheists but exclusive monotheists. The difference was invisible to many Radchaai. "And human soldiers! People nowadays are squeamish about ancillaries, but you don't see ancillaries drunk and puking on the concourse."

Seivarden made a sympathetic noise. "I've *never* known officers to be puking drunk."

"In your day, maybe not," answered someone behind me. "Things have changed."

Rose-and-Azure tipped her head toward Captain Vel, who to judge by her expression had finally understood Seivarden's words as Rose-and-Azure had not. "Not to say, Captain, that you don't keep *your* ship in order. But you wouldn't have to *keep* ancillaries in order, would you?"

Captain Vel waved the point away with an empty hand, her bowl of tea in the other. "That's command, citizen, it's just my job. But there are more serious issues. You can't fill troop carriers with humans. The human-crewed Justices are all half-empty."

"And of course," interjected Rose-and-Azure, "those all have to be *paid*."

Captain Vel gestured assent. "They say we don't need them anymore." *They* being, of course, Anaander Mianaai. No one would name her while being critical of her. "That our borders are proper as they are. I don't pretend to understand policy, or politics. But it seems to me it's less wasteful to store ancillaries than it is to train and pay humans and rotate them in and out of storage."

"They say," said Rose-and-Azure beside me, taking a pastry from the table in front of her, "that if it hadn't been for *Justice of Toren*'s disappearance they'd have scrapped one of the other carriers by now." My surprise at hearing my own name couldn't have been visible to anyone here, but surely Station could see it. And that surprise, that startlement, wasn't something that would fit into the identity I'd constructed. Station would be reevaluating me, I was sure. So would Anaander Mianaai.

"Ah," said a civilian behind me. "But our visitor here is doubtless glad to hear our borders are fixed."

I barely turned my head to answer. "The Gerentate would be a very large mouthful." I kept my voice even. No one here could see my continuing consternation at that startlement moments ago.

Except, of course, Station and Anaander Mianaai. And Anaander Mianaai—or part of her, at least—would have very good reasons for noticing talk about *Justice of Toren*, and reactions to it.

"I don't know, Captain Seivarden," Captain Vel was saying, "if you've heard about the mutiny at Ime. An entire unit refused their orders and defected to an alien power."

"Certainly wouldn't have happened on an ancillary-crewed ship," said someone behind Seivarden.

"Not too big a mouthful for the Radch, I imagine," said the person behind me.

"I daresay"—again I leaned just slightly on my Gerentate accent—"sharing a border with us this long, you've learned better table manners." I refused to turn all the way around to see whether the answering silence was amused, indignant, or merely distracted by Seivarden and Captain Vel. Tried not to think too hard about what conclusions Anaander Mianaai would draw from my reaction to hearing my name.

"I think I heard something about it," said Seivarden, frowning thoughtfully. "Ime. That was where the provincial governor and the captains of the ships in the system mur-dered and stole, and sabotaged the ships and station so they couldn't report to higher authorities. Yes?" No point worry-ing what Station—or the Lord of the Radch—would make of my reaction to *that*. It would fall where it fell. I needed to stay calm.

"That's beside the point," answered Rose-and-Azure. "The point is, it was mutiny. Mutiny winked at, but one can't make a plain statement of fact about the dangers of promot-ing the ill-bred and vulgar to positions of authority, or poli-cies that encourage the most vile sort of behavior, and even undermine everything civilization has always stood for, with-out losing business contacts or promotions."

"You must be very brave, then, to speak so," I observed. But I was sure Rose-and-Azure wasn't particularly brave. She spoke as she did because she could do so without danger to herself.

Calm. I could control my breathing, keep it smooth and regular. My skin was too dark to show a flush, but Station would see the temperature change. Station might just think I was angry about something. I had good reason to be angry.

"Honored," Seivarden said abruptly. From the set of her jaw and shoulders, she was suppressing an urge to cross her arms. Would be, quite soon, in one of those silently-facing-the-wall moods. "We'll be late to our next engagement." She rose, more abruptly than was strictly polite.

"Indeed," I acknowledged, and set down my untasted tea. Hoped her action was on her own account, and not because she'd seen any sign of my agitation. "Captain Vel, thank you for your very kind invitation. It was an honor to meet you all."

Out on the main concourse, Seivarden, walking behind me, muttered, "Fucking snobs." People passed, mostly not paying any attention to us. That was good. That was normal. I could feel my adrenaline levels dropping.

Better. I stopped and turned to look at Seivarden, raised an eyebrow.

"Well, but they *are* snobs," she said. "What do they think the aptitudes are *for*? The whole *point* is that anyone can test into anything."

I remembered twenty-years-younger Lieutenant Skaaiat asking, in the humid darkness of the upper city, if the aptitudes had lacked impartiality before, or lacked them now, and answering, for herself, *both*. And Lieutenant Awn's hurt and distress.

Seivarden crossed her arms, then uncrossed them, balled her gloved hands into fists. "And of *course* someone from a lower house is going to be ill-bred and have a vulgar accent. They can hardly help it.

"And what *were* they thinking," Seivarden continued, "to have a conversation like that. In a tea shop. On a *palace station*. I mean, not just *when we were young* and *provincials are vulgar* but the aptitudes are corrupt? The military is badly mismanaged?" I didn't speak, but she answered as though I had. "Oh, of course, everyone complains things are mismanaged. But not like *that*. What's going on?"

"Don't ask me." Though of course I knew—or thought I did. And wondered again what it meant that Rose-and-Azure, and others there, had felt so freely able to speak as they had. Which Anaander Mianaai might hold an advantage here? Though such free speaking might only mean the Lord of the Radch preferred to let her enemies identify themselves clearly and unambiguously. "And have you always been in favor of the ill-bred testing into high positions?" I asked, knowing she hadn't.

Realizing, suddenly, that if Station had never met anyone from the Gerentate, Anaander Mianaai very possibly had. Why had that not occurred to me before? Something programmed into my ship-mind, invisible to me until now, or just the limitations of this one small brain remaining to me?

I might have deceived Station, and everyone else here, but I had not for a moment deceived the Lord of the Radch. She had certainly known from the instant I set foot on the palace docks that I was not what I said I was.

It would fall where it fell, I told myself.

"I thought about what you told me, about Ime," Seivarden said, as though it answered my question. Oblivious to my renewed distress. "I don't know if that unit leader did the right thing. But I don't know what the right thing to do would have been. And I don't know if I'd have had the courage to die for that right thing if I knew what it was. I mean..." She paused. "I mean, I'd like to think I would. There was a time I'd have been sure I would. But I can't even…" She trailed off, her voice shaking slightly. She seemed on the verge of breaking into tears, like the Seivarden of a year ago, nearly any feelings at all too raw for her to handle. That sustained politeness, back in the tea shop, must have been the result of considerable effort.

I hadn't paid much attention to the people passing us as we walked. But now something struck me as wrong. I was suddenly aware of the location and direction of the people around us. Something indefinite troubled me, something about the way certain people moved.

At least four people were watching us, surreptitiously. Had no doubt been following us, and I had not noticed until now. This had to be new, surely. I would have noticed if I had been followed from the moment I'd stepped onto the docks. I was sure I would have.

Station had certainly seen my startlement back in the tea shop, when Rose-and-Azure had said, *"Justice of Toren."* Station would certainly have wondered why I had reacted the way I had. Would certainly have begun to watch me even more closely than it had been. Still, Station didn't need to have me followed to watch me. This was not merely observation.

This was not Station.

I had never been given to panic. I would not panic now. This throw was mine, and if I had miscalculated slightly the trajectory of one piece, I had not miscalculated the others. Keeping my voice very, very even I said to Seivarden, "We'll be early for the inspector supervisor."

"Do we have to go to that Awer's?" Seivarden asked.

"I think we should." Having said it, immediately wishing

I hadn't. I didn't want to see Skaaiat Awer, not now, not in this state.

"Maybe we shouldn't," said Seivarden. "Maybe we should go back to the room. You can meditate or pray or whatever it is, and then we can have supper and listen to some music. I think that would be better."

She was worried about *me*. Clearly she was. And she was right, back to the room would be better. I would have a chance to calm down, to take stock.

And Anaander Mianaai would have a chance to make me disappear with no one watching, no one the wiser. "The inspector supervisor's," I said.

"Yes, honored," Seivarden replied, subdued.

Skaaiat Awer's quarters were their own small maze of corridors and rooms. She lived there with a collection of dock inspectors and clients and even clients of clients. She was certainly not Awer's only presence here, and the house would have had its own quarters elsewhere on the station, but Skaaiat evidently preferred this arrangement. Eccentric, but that was expected of any Awer. Though as with so many Awers, there was a practical edge to her eccentricity—we were very near the docks here.

A servant admitted us, escorted us to a sitting room floored with blue-and-white stone, walled floor to ceiling with plants of all kinds, dark or light green, narrow-leaved or broad-, trailing or upright, some flowering, spots and swaths here and there of white, red, purple, yellow. Likely they were the entire occupation of at least one member of this household.

Daos Ceit waited for us there. Bowed low, seeming genuinely pleased to see us. "Honored Breq, Citizen Seivarden. Inspector Supervisor will be so pleased you've come. Do please sit." She gestured to the chairs spread around. "Will you have tea? Or are you full up? I know you had another engagement today."

"Tea would be nice, thank you," I said. Neither I nor Seivarden had actually drunk any at Captain Vel's gathering. But I didn't want to sit. All the chairs looked as though they'd impede my freedom of movement if I was attacked and had to defend myself.

"Breq?" Seivarden, voice very quiet. Concerned. She could see something was wrong, but she couldn't discreetly ask what it was.

Daos Ceit handed me a bowl of tea, smiling, to all appearances sincerely. Oblivious, it seemed, to the state of tension I was in, which was so obvious to Seivarden. How had I not recognized her the moment I'd seen her? Not immediately identified her Orsian accent?

How had I not realized I couldn't possibly deceive Anaander Mianaai for more than the smallest instant?

I couldn't stand through this, not courteously. I would have to choose a seat. None of the available chairs was tenable. But I was more dangerous than nearly anyone here realized, even sitting. I still had the gun, a reassuring pressure against my ribs, under my jacket. I still had the attention of Station, of *all* of Anaander Mianaai, yes, and that was what I had *wanted*. This was still my game. It was. Choose a seat. The omens will fall where they fall.

Before I could make myself sit, Skaaiat Awer came into the room. As modestly jeweled as when she was working, but I'd seen the pale-yellow fabric of her elegantly cut jacket on a bolt at that expensive clothier's shop. On her right sleeve cuff that cheap, machine-stamped gold tag flashed.

She bowed. "Honored Breq. Citizen Seivarden. How

good to see you both. I see Adjunct Ceit has given you tea."
Seivarden and I acknowledged this with polite gestures. "Let
me say, before anyone else arrives, that I'm hoping you'll both
stay to supper."

"You tried to warn us yesterday, didn't you?" asked
Seivarden.

"Seivarden," I began.

Inspector Supervisor Skaaiat raised one elegantly yellow-
gloved hand. "It's all right, honored. I knew Captain Vel
prided herself on being old-fashioned. On knowing how
much better things were when children respected their elders
and good taste and refined manners were the rule. All familiar enough, I'm sure you heard such talk a thousand years
ago, citizen." Seivarden gave a small, acknowledging *ha*. "I'm
sure you heard all about how Radchaai have a duty to bring
civilization to humanity. And that ancillaries are far more
efficient for that purpose than human soldiers."

"Well, as to that," said Seivarden, "I'd say they are."

"Of course you would." Skaaiat showed a small flash
of anger. Seivarden probably couldn't see it, didn't know
her well enough. "You probably don't know, citizen, that I
commanded human troops during an annexation myself."
Seivarden hadn't known that. Her surprise was obvious. I
had known, of course. My lack of surprise would be obvious
to Station. To Anaander Mianaai.

There was no point in worrying about it. "It's true,"
Skaaiat continued, "that you don't have to pay ancillaries,
and they never have personal problems. They do whatever
you ask them to, without any sort of complaint or comment,
and they do it well and completely. And that wasn't true of
my human troops. And most of my soldiers were good people, but it's so easy, isn't it, to decide the people you're fighting

aren't really human. Or maybe you have to do it, to be able to kill them. People like Captain Vel love pointing out the atrocities that human troops have committed, that ancillaries never would. As though making those ancillaries was not an atrocity in itself.

"They're more efficient, as I said." In Ors, Skaaiat would have been sarcastic on this topic, but she spoke seriously. Carefully and precisely. "And if we were still expanding we would have to still use them. Because we couldn't do it with human soldiers, not for long. And we're built to expand, we've been expanding for more than two thousand years and to stop will mean completely changing what we are. Right now most people don't see that, don't care. They won't, until it affects their lives directly, and for most people it doesn't yet. It's an abstract question, except to people like Captain Vel."

"But Captain Vel's opinion is meaningless," said Seivarden. "So is anyone else's. The Lord of the Radch has decided, for whatever reason. And it's foolish to go around saying anything against it."

"She might decide otherwise, if persuaded," answered Skaaiat. All of us still standing. I was too tense to sit, Seivarden too agitated, Skaaiat, I thought, angry. Daos Ceit standing frozen, trying to pretend she wasn't hearing any of this. "Or the decision might be a sign that the Lord of the Radch has been corrupted in some way. Captain Vel's sort certainly doesn't approve of all the talking with aliens we've been doing. The Radch has always stood for civilization, and civilization has always meant pure, uncorrupted humanity. Actually dealing with nonhumans instead of just killing them can't be good for us."

"Is that what that business at Ime was about?" asked Seivarden, who had clearly spent our walk here thinking about this. "Someone decided to set up a base and stockpile ancillaries and...and what? Force the issue? You're talking about rebellion. Treason. Why would anyone be talking about something like that now? Unless, when they got the people responsible for Ime, they didn't get everyone. And now they're letting a few people put their heads up and make some noise, and once they think everyone involved has identified themselves..." She was openly angry now. It was a fairly good guess, it might well be more or less right. Depending on which Anaander had the upper hand here. "Why didn't you warn us?"

"I tried, citizen, but I ought to have spoken more directly. Even so, I wasn't sure Captain Vel had gone so far. All I knew was that she idealized the past in a way I can't agree with. The noblest, most well-intentioned people in the world can't make annexations a good thing. Arguing that ancillaries are efficient and convenient is not, to me, a point in favor of using ancillaries. It doesn't make it better, it only makes it look a little cleaner."

And that only if you ignored what ancillaries were to begin with. "Tell me"—I almost said *Tell me, Lieutenant,* but caught myself in time—"Tell me, Inspector Supervisor, what happens to the people waiting to be made into ancillaries?"

"Some are still in storage, or on troop carriers," Skaaiat said. "But most have been destroyed."

"Well, that makes it all better then," I said, seriously. Evenly.

"Awer was against it from the start," said Skaaiat. She meant the continual expansion, not any expansion at all. And the Radch had used ancillaries long before Anaander Mianaai had made herself into what she was. There just hadn't been quite so many of them. "Awer's lords have said so to the Lord of the Radch, repeatedly."

"But the lords of Awer have not refused to profit from it." I kept my voice even. Pleasant.

"It's so easy to go along with things, isn't it?" Skaaiat said. "Especially when, as you say, it profits you." She frowned then, and cocked her head slightly, listened a few seconds to something only she could hear. Looked questioningly at me, at Seivarden. "Station Security is at the door. Asking for Citizen Seivarden." *Asking* was certainly more polite than the reality. "Excuse me a moment." She stepped into the corridor, followed by Daos Ceit.

Seivarden looked at me, oddly calm. "I'm beginning to wish I were still frozen in my escape pod." I smiled, but apparently it didn't convince her. "Are you all right? You haven't been all right since we left that Vel Osck person. Damn Skaaiat Awer for not speaking more directly! Usually you can't get an Awer to *stop* saying unpleasant things. She picks now to be discreet!"

"I'm fine," I lied.

As I spoke, Skaaiat returned with a citizen in the light brown of Station Security, who bowed and said to Seivarden, "Citizen, will you and this person come with me?" The courtesy was, of course, merely a form. One didn't refuse Station Security's invitations. Even if we tried there were reinforcements outside, placed there to make sure we didn't refuse. They wouldn't be Station Security, those people who had followed us from Captain Vel's meeting. They would be Special Missions, or even Anaander Mianaai's own guard. The Lord of the Radch had put all the pieces together and decided to remove me before I could do any serious damage. But it was almost certainly too late for that. All of her was paying attention. The fact that she'd sent Station Security to arrest me, and not some Special Missions officer to kill me quickly and quietly, told me that.

"Of course," Seivarden answered, all calm courtesy. Of course. She knew she was innocent of any wrongdoing, she was sure I was Special Missions and working for Anaander herself, why should she worry? But I knew that finally the moment had come. The omens that had been in the air for twenty years were about to come down and show me—show Anaander Mianaai—what pattern they made.

This Security officer didn't even twitch an eyebrow as she answered. "The Lord of the Radch wishes to speak with you privately, citizen." Not a glance at me. She likely didn't know why she'd been sent to escort us to the Lord of the Radch, didn't realize I was dangerous, that she needed the backup that awaited us out in the station's corridors. If she even knew it was there.

The gun still sat under my jacket, and extra magazines tucked here and there, wherever the bulge wouldn't show. Anaander Mianaai almost certainly didn't know what I intended.

"Is this my audience I requested, then?" asked Seivarden.

The Security officer gestured ambiguity. "I couldn't say, citizen."

Anaander Mianaai couldn't have known my object in coming, knew only that I had disappeared some twenty years ago. Part of her might know that she'd been aboard my last voyage, but none of her could know what had happened after I'd gated out of Shis'urna's system.

"I did ask," said Inspector Supervisor Skaaiat, "if you might have tea and supper first." The fact she'd asked said something about her relationship with Security. The fact she'd been refused said something about the urgency behind this arrest—it was an arrest, I was sure.

Security, oblivious, made an apologetic gesture. "My orders, Inspector Supervisor. Citizen."

"Of course," said Skaaiat, smooth and unruffled, but I knew her, heard worry hidden in her voice. "Citizen Seivarden. Honored Breq. If there's any assistance I can provide please don't hesitate to call on me."

"Thank you, Inspector Supervisor," I said, and bowed. My fear and uncertainty, my near panic, drained away. The omen Stillness had flipped, become Movement. And Justice was about to land before me, clear and unambiguous.

The Security officer escorted us not to the main entrance of the palace proper, but into the temple, quiet at this hour when many people were visiting, or sitting home with family and a bowl of tea. A young priest sat behind the now-half-empty baskets of flowers, bored and sullen. She gave us a resentful glance as we entered, but didn't even turn her head as we passed.

We went through the main hall, four-armed Amaat looming, the air still smelling of incense and the heap of flowers at the god's feet and knees, back to a tiny chapel tucked into a corner, dedicated to an old and now-obscure provincial god, one of those personifications of abstract concepts so many pantheons hold, in this case a deification of legitimate political authority. No doubt when the palace had been built there had been no question of this god's placement next to Amaat, but she seemed to have fallen out of favor, the demographic of the station, or perhaps just fashion, having changed. Or perhaps something more ominous had caused it.

In the wall behind the image of the god a panel slid open. Behind it an armed and armored guard, her weapon holstered but not far from her hand, silver-smooth armor covering her face. Ancillary, I thought, but there was no way to be sure. I wondered, as I had occasionally over the past twenty years, how that worked. Surely the palace proper wasn't guarded by Station. Were Anaander Mianaai's guards just another part of herself?

Seivarden looked at me, irritated, and, I thought, a bit afraid. "I didn't think I rated the secret entrance." Though it probably wasn't all that secret, just slightly less public than the one outside on the concourse.

The Security officer made that ambiguous gesture again, but said nothing.

"Well," I said, and Seivarden gave me an expectant look. Clearly she thought this was due to whatever special status she had decided I had. I stepped through the door, past the unmoving guard, who didn't acknowledge me at all, nor Seivarden coming behind me. The panel slid shut behind us.

21

Beyond the short stretch of blank corridor, another door opened onto a room four meters by eight, its ceiling three meters above. Leafy vines snaked across the walls, trailing from supports rising from the floor. Pale blue walls suggested vast distances beyond the greenery, making the room feel larger than it was, the last vestige of a fashion for false vistas, more than five hundred years out of date. At the far end a dais, and behind it images of the four Emanations hung in the vines.

On the dais stood Anaander Mianaai—two of her. The Lord of the Radch was so curious about us she wanted more than one part of herself here to question us, I guessed. Though likely she had rationalized it to herself some other way.

We walked to within three meters of the Lord of the Radch, and Seivarden knelt, and then prostrated herself. I was, supposedly, not Radchaai, not subject to Anaander Mianaai. But Anaander Mianaai knew, she had to know, who I really was. She had not summoned us this way without knowing. Still, I didn't kneel, or even bow. Neither Mianaai betrayed any surprise or indignation at this.

"Citizen Seivarden Vendaai," said the Mianaai on the right. "What exactly do you think you're playing at?"

Seivarden's shoulders twitched, as though, facedown on the floor, she had momentarily wanted to cross her arms.

The Mianaai on the left said, *"Justice of Toren*'s behavior has been alarming and perplexing enough, just on its own. Entering the temple and defiling the offerings! Whatever could you have meant by it? What am I to say to the priests?"

The gun still lay against my side, under my jacket, unremarked. I was an ancillary. Ancillaries were notorious for their expressionless faces. I could easily keep from smiling.

"If my lord pleases," said Seivarden into the pause that followed Anaander Mianaai's words. Her voice was slightly breathy, and I thought maybe she was hyperventilating slightly. "Wh...I don't..."

The Mianaai on the right let out a sardonic *ha*. "Citizen Seivarden is surprised, and doesn't understand me," that Mianaai continued. "And you, *Justice of Toren*. You intended to deceive me. Why?"

"When I first suspected who you were," said the Mianaai on the left before I could answer, "I almost didn't believe it. Another long-lost omen fetching up at my feet. I watched you, to see what you would do, to try to understand what you were intending by your rather extraordinary behavior."

If I had been human, I would have laughed. Two Mianaais before me. Neither trusted the other to hold this interview unsupervised, unobstructed. Neither knew the details of the destruction of *Justice of Toren*, each no doubt suspected the other's involvement. I might be an instrument of either, neither trusting the other. Which was which?

The Mianaai on the right said, "You've done a fairly decent job concealing your origin. It was Inspector Adjunct Ceit who first made me suspect." *I haven't heard that song since I was a child*, she'd said. That song, that had obviously come from Shis'urna. "I admit it took me an entire day to piece everything together, and even then I could hardly believe it. You hid your implants reasonably well. Station was completely deceived. But the humming would likely have given you away eventually, I imagine. Are you aware you do it almost constantly? I suspect you're making an effort not to do it now. Which I do appreciate."

Still facedown on the floor, Seivarden said, in a small voice, "Breq?"

"Not Breq," said the Mianaai on the left. "*Justice of Toren*."

"*Justice of Toren* One Esk," I corrected, dropping all pretense of a Gerentate accent, or human expression. I was done pretending. It was terrifying, because I knew I couldn't live long past this, but also, oddly, a relief. A weight gone.

The right-hand Mianaai gestured the obviousness of my statement. "*Justice of Toren* is destroyed," I said. Both Mianaais seemed to stop breathing. Stared at me. Again I might have laughed, if I were capable of it.

"Begging my lord's indulgence," said Seivarden from the floor, voice tentative. "Surely there's some mistake. Breq is human. She can't possibly be *Justice of Toren* One Esk. I served in *Justice of Toren*'s Esk decade. No *Justice of Toren* medic would give One Esk a body with a voice like Breq's. Not unless she wanted to seriously annoy the Esk lieutenants."

Silence, thick and heavy, for three seconds.

"She thinks I'm Special Missions," I said, breaking that silence. "I never told her I was. I never told her I was anything, except Breq from the Gerentate, and she never believed that. I wanted to leave her where I found her, but I couldn't and I don't know why. She was never one of my favorites." I knew that sounded insane. A particular sort of insane, an AI insanity. I didn't care. "She doesn't have anything to do with this."

The right-hand Mianaai lifted an eyebrow. "Then why is she here?"

"No one could ignore her arrival here. Since I arrived with her, no one could ignore or conceal mine. And you already know why I couldn't just come straight to you."

The slight twitch of a frown on the right-hand Mianaai.

"Citizen Seivarden Vendaai," said the Mianaai on the left, "it is now clear to me that *Justice of Toren* deceived you. You didn't know what it was. It would be best, I think, if you left now. Without, of course, speaking of this to anyone else."

"No?" breathed Seivarden into the floor, as though she were asking a question. Or as though she was surprised to hear the word come out of her mouth. "No," she said again, more certainly. "There's a mistake somewhere. Breq jumped off a *bridge* for me."

My hip hurt, thinking of it. "No sane human being would have done that."

"I never said you were *sane*," Seivarden said, quietly, sounding slightly choked.

"Seivarden Vendaai," said the left-hand Mianaai, "this ancillary—and it *is* an ancillary—isn't human. The fact you thought it was explains a good deal of your behavior that was unclear to me before. I'm sorry for its deception and your disappointment, but you need to leave. *Now.*"

333

"Begging my lord's indulgence." Seivarden still lay face-down, speaking into the floor. "Whether you give it or not. I'm not leaving Breq."

"Go away, Seivarden," I said, expressionless.

"Sorry," she said, sounding almost blithe except her voice still shook slightly. "You're stuck with me."

I looked down at her. She turned her head to look up at me, her expression a mix of fear and determination. "You don't know what you're doing," I told her. "You don't understand what's happening here."

"I don't need to."

"Fair enough," said the Mianaai on the right, seeming almost amused. The left-hand one seemed less so. I wondered why that was. "Explain yourself, *Justice of Toren*."

Here it was, the moment I had worked toward for twenty years. Waited for. Feared would never come. "First," I said, "as I'm sure you already suspect, you were aboard *Justice of Toren*, and it was you yourself who destroyed it. You breached the heat shield because you discovered you had already suborned me yourself, some time previously. You're fighting yourself. At least two of you, maybe more."

Both Mianaais blinked and shifted their stances a fraction of a millimeter, in a way I recognized. I'd seen myself do it, in Ors, when communications cut out. Another of those communications-blocking boxes—part of Anaander Mianaai, at least, must have worried about what I might say, must have been waiting with her hand on the switch. I wondered how far the effect reached, and which Mianaai had triggered it, trying, too late, to hide my revelation from herself. Wondered what that must have been like, knowing that facing me this way could only lead to disaster, and yet obligated by the nature of her struggle with herself to do so. The thought amused me briefly.

"Second." I reached into my jacket, pulled out the gun, the dark gray of my glove bleeding into the white the weapon had taken from my shirt. "I'm going to kill you." I aimed at the right-hand Mianaai.

Who began to sing, in a slightly flat baritone, in a language dead for ten thousand years. "*The person, the person, the person with weapons.*" I couldn't move. Couldn't squeeze the trigger.

> *You should be afraid of the person with weapons. You*
>   *should be afraid.*
> *All around the cry goes out, put on armor made of iron.*
> *The person, the person, the person with weapons.*
> *You should be afraid of the person with weapons. You*
>   *should be afraid.*

She shouldn't know that song. Why would Anaander Mianaai ever go digging in forgotten Valskaayan archives, why would she trouble to learn a song that very possibly no one but me had sung for longer than she had been alive?

"*Justice of Toren* One Esk," said the right-hand Mianaai, "shoot the instance of me to the left of the instance that's speaking to you."

Muscles moved without my willing them. I shifted my aim to the left and fired. The left-hand Mianaai collapsed to the ground.

The right-hand one said, "Now I just have to get to the docks before I do. And yes, Seivarden, I know you're confused but you *were* warned."

"Where did you learn that song?" I asked. Still otherwise frozen.

"From you," said Anaander Mianaai. "A hundred years ago, at Valskaay." This, then, was that Anaander who had pushed reforms, begun dismantling Radchaai ships. The one who had first visited me secretly at Valskaay and laid down those orders I could sense but never see. "I asked you to teach me the song least likely to ever be sung by anyone else, and then I set it as an access and hid it from you. My enemy and I are far too evenly matched. The only advantage I have is what might occur to me when I'm apart from myself. And that day it occurred to me that I had never paid close enough attention to you—you, One Esk. To what you might be."

"Something like you," I guessed. "Apart from myself." My arm still outstretched, gun aimed at the back wall.

"Insurance," Mianaai corrected. "An access I wouldn't think of looking for, to erase or invalidate. So very clever of me. And now it's blown up in my face. All of this, it seems, is happening because I paid attention to you, in particular, and because I never paid any attention to you. I'm going to return control of your body to you, because it'll be more efficient, but you'll find you can't shoot me."

I lowered the gun. "Which *me*?"

"*What's* blown up?" asked Seivarden, still on the floor. "My lord," she added.

"She's split," I explained. "It started at Garsedd. She was appalled by what she'd done, but she couldn't decide how to react. She's been secretly moving against herself ever since. The reforms—getting rid of ancillaries, stopping the annexations, opening up assignments to lower houses, she did all of that. And Ime was the other part of her, building up a base, and resources, to go to war against herself and put things back the way they had been. And the whole time all of her has been pretending not to know it was happening, because as soon as she admitted it the conflict would be in the open, and unavoidable."

"But you said it straight out to all of me," Mianaai acknowledged. "Because I couldn't exactly pretend the rest of me wasn't interested in Seivarden Vendaai's second return. Or what had happened to you. You showed up so publically, so *obviously*, I couldn't hide it and pretend it hadn't happened, and only talk to you myself. And now I can't ignore it anymore. Why? Why would you do such a thing? It wasn't any order I ever gave you."

"No," I agreed. "It wasn't."

"And surely you guessed what would happen if you did such a thing."

"Yes." I could be my ancillary self again. Unsmiling. No satisfaction in my voice.

Anaander considered me a moment and then made a *hmf* sound, as though she'd reached some conclusion that surprised her. "Get up off the floor, citizen," she said to Seivarden.

Seivarden rose, brushing her trouser legs with one gloved hand. "Are you all right, Breq?"

"*Breq*," interrupted Mianaai before I could answer, stepping off the dais and striding past, "is the last remaining fragment of a grief-crazed AI, which has just managed to trigger a civil war." She turned to me. "Is that what you wanted?"

"I haven't been *crazed* with grief for at least ten years," I protested. "And the civil war was going to happen anyway, sooner or later."

"I was rather hoping to avoid the worst of it. If we're extremely fortunate, that war will only cause decades of chaos, and not tear the Radch apart completely. Come with me."

"Ships can't *do* that anymore," insisted Seivarden, walking beside me. "You made them that way, my lord, so they didn't lose their minds when their captains died, like they used to, or follow their captains against you."

Mianaai lifted an eyebrow. "Not exactly." She found a panel on the wall by the door that had been previously invisible to me, yanked it open, and triggered the manual door switch. "They still get attached, still have favorites." The door slid open. "One Esk, shoot the guard." My arm swung up and I fired. The guard staggered back against the wall, reached for her own weapon, but slid to the floor and then lay still. Dead, because her armor retracted. "I couldn't take that away without making them useless to me," Anaander Mianaai continued, oblivious to the person—the citizen?—she'd just ordered killed. Still explaining to Seivarden, who frowned, not understanding. "They have to be smart. They have to be able to think."

"Right," agreed Seivarden. Her voice trembled, just slightly, the edge of her self-control wearing thin, I thought.

"And they're armed ships, with engines capable of vaporizing planets. What am I going to do if they don't want to obey me? Threaten them? With what?" A few strides had brought us to the door communicating with the temple. Anaander opened that and stepped briskly into the chapel of legitimate political authority.

Seivarden made an odd sound in the back of her throat. An aborted laugh or a noise of distress, I wasn't sure which. "I thought they were just made so they had to do as they were told."

"Well, exactly," said Anaander Mianaai as we followed

her through the temple's main hall. Sounds from the concourse reached us, someone speaking urgently, voice pitched high and loud. The temple itself seemed deserted. "That's how they were made from the start, but their minds are complex, and it's a tricky proposition. The original designers did that by giving them an overwhelming reason to *want* to obey. Which had advantages, and rather spectacular disadvantages. I couldn't completely change what they were, I just... adjusted it to suit me. I made obeying *me* an overriding priority for them. But I confused the issue when I gave *Justice of Toren* two *me*s to obey, with conflicting aims. And then, I suspect, I unknowingly ordered the execution of a favorite. Didn't I?" She looked at me. "Not *Justice of Toren*'s favorite, I wouldn't have been so foolish. But I never paid attention to *you*, I'd never have asked if someone was *One Esk's* favorite."

"You thought no one would care about some nobody cook's daughter." I wanted to raise the gun. Wanted to smash all that beautiful glass in the mortuary chapel as we passed it.

Anaander Mianaai stopped, turned to look at me. "That wasn't *me*. Help me now, I'm fighting that other me even now, I'm quite certain. I wasn't ready to move openly, but now you've forced my hand, help me and I'll destroy her and remove her utterly from myself."

"You can't," I said. "I know what you are, better than anyone. She's you and you're her. You can't remove her from yourself without destroying yourself. Because *she's you*."

"Once I reach the docks," Anaander Mianaai said, as though it were an answer to what I had just said, "I can find a ship. Any civilian ship will take me where I want to go without question. Any military ship...will be a dicier proposition. But I can tell you one thing, *Justice of Toren* One Esk, one thing I'm certain of. I've got more ships than she does."

"Meaning what, exactly?" asked Seivarden.

"Meaning," I guessed, "the other Mianaai is likely to lose an open battle, so she has a slightly better reason to want to stop this spreading any further." I could see Seivarden didn't understand what that meant. "She's held it back by concealing it from herself, but now all of her here..."

"Most of me, anyway," corrected Anaander Mianaai.

"Now she's heard it straight out she can't ignore it. Not here. But she might be able to prevent the knowledge from reaching the parts of her that aren't here. At least long enough to strengthen her position."

Realization made Seivarden's eyes widen. "She'll need to destroy the gates as soon as possible. But it can't work. The signal travels at the speed of light, surely. She can't possibly overtake it."

"The information hasn't left the station yet," said Anaander Mianaai. "There's always a slight delay. It would be far more efficient to destroy the palace instead." Which would mean turning a warship engine on the entire station, vaporizing it, along with everyone on it. "And I'd have to destroy the whole palace to stop the information going any further. There isn't just one spot where my memories are stored. It's made hard to destroy or tamper with on purpose."

"Do you think," I asked, into Seivarden's shocked silence, "that even you could get a Sword or a Mercy to do that? Even with accesses?"

"How badly would you like the answer to that question?" asked Anaander Mianaai. "You know *I'm* capable of it."

"I do," I acknowledged. "Which option do you prefer?"

"None of the currently available choices is very good. The loss of either the palace or the gates—or both—will cause disruption on an unprecedented scale, all through Radch space. Disruption that will last for years, simply because of the size of that space. *Not* destroying the palace—and the gates, really they're still part of the problem—will ultimately be even worse."

"Does Skaaiat Awer know what's going on?" I asked.

"Awer has been a thorn in my side for nearly three thousand years," said Mianaai. Calmly. As though this were an ordinary, casual conversation. "So much moral indignation! I'd almost think they bred for it, but they're not all genetically related. But if I stray from the path of propriety and justice, I'm sure to hear about it from Awer."

"Then why not get rid of them?" asked Seivarden. "Why go and make one inspector supervisor here?"

"Pain is a warning," said Anaander Mianaai. "What would happen if you removed all discomfort from your life? No," Mianaai continued, ignoring Seivarden's obvious distress at her words, "I value that moral indignation. I encourage it."

"No you don't," I said. By now we were on the concourse. Security and military herded sections of the frightened crowd—many of them would have implants, would have been receiving information from Station when it suddenly cut out, with no explanation.

A ship's captain I didn't know spotted us, and hurried over. "My lord," she said, bowing.

"Get these people off the concourse, Captain," Anaander Mianaai said, "and clear the corridors, as quickly and safely as you can. Continue to cooperate with Station Security. I'm working to resolve this as quickly as possible."

As Anaander Mianaai spoke, a flash of movement caught my eye. Gun. Instinctively I raised my armor, saw the person holding the gun was one of the people who had been following us on the concourse, just before Security had summoned us. The Lord of the Radch must have sent orders before she triggered her device and cut off all communications. Before she knew about the Garseddai gun.

The captain Anaander Mianaai had been speaking to recoiled, visibly startled by the sudden appearance of my armor. I raised my own gun, and a hammer-hard blow hit me from the side—someone else had shot at me. I fired, hit the person holding the gun. She fell, her own shot wild, hitting the temple façade behind me, shattering some god, bright-colored chips flying. Sudden, shocked silence from the already frightened citizens along the concourse. I turned, looked along the trajectory of the bullet that had hit me, saw panicked citizens and the sudden silver gleam of armor—this other shooter had seen me shoot the first, didn't know armor wouldn't help her. Half a meter from her another flash of silver as someone else armored herself. Citizens between me and my targets, moving unpredictably. But I was used to crowds of the frightened and the hostile. I fired, and fired again. The armor disappeared, both my targets fallen. Seivarden said, "Fuck, you *are* an ancillary!"

"We'd better get off the concourse," said Anaander Mianaai. And to the nameless captain beside her, "Captain, get these people to safety."

"But..." the captain began, but we were already moving away, Seivarden and Anaander Mianaai staying low, moving as speedily as they could.

I wondered briefly what was happening in other parts of the station. Omaugh Palace was huge. There were four other concourses, though all were smaller than this one, and level upon level of homes, workplaces, schools, public spaces, all of it full of citizens who would certainly be frightened and confused. If nothing else, anyone who lived here knew the necessity of following emergency procedures, wouldn't stop to argue or wonder once the order to seek shelter had gone out. But of course, Station couldn't give that order.

I couldn't know, or help. "Who's in the system?" I asked, as soon as we were out of earshot, climbing down an emergency access ladder well, my armor retracted.

"Near enough to matter, you mean?" Anaander Mianaai answered from above me. "Three Swords and four Mercies in easy shuttle distance." Any order from Anaander Mianaai on the station would have to come by shuttle, because of the communications blackout. "I'm not worried about them at this very moment. There's no possibility of giving them orders from here." And the instant there would be, the instant that blackout was raised, the entire question would already be settled, the knowledge Anaander Mianaai was so desperate to hide from herself already speeding toward the gates that would take it through all of Radch space.

"Is anyone docked?" I asked. Right now, those would be the only ships that mattered.

"Only a shuttle from *Mercy of Kalr*," said Anaander Mianaai, sounding half-amused. "It's mine."

"Are you certain?" And when she didn't answer I said, "Captain Vel isn't yours."

"You got that impression too, did you?" Anaander Mianaai's voice was definitely amused now. Above me, above Anaander Mianaai, Seivarden climbed, silent except for her shoes on the ladder rungs. I saw a door, halted, pulled the latch. Swung it open, and peered into the corridor beyond. I recognized the area behind the dock offices.

Once we'd all clambered into the corridor and shut the emergency door, Anaander Mianaai strode ahead, Seivarden and me following. "How do we know she's the one she says she is?" Seivarden asked me, very quietly. Her voice still shook, and her jaw looked tight. I was surprised she hadn't curled up in a corner somewhere, or fled.

"It doesn't matter which one she is," I said, not making any attempt to lower my voice. "I don't trust any of her. If she tries to go anywhere near *Mercy of Kalr*'s shuttle you're going to take this gun and shoot her." All of what she'd said to me might easily be a ruse, intended to get me to help her to the docks, and to *Mercy of Kalr*, so she could destroy this station herself.

"You don't need the Garseddai gun to shoot me," Anaander Mianaai said, without looking behind her. "I'm not armored. Well, some of me is. But not *me*. Not most of me." She turned her head briefly, to look at me. "That *is* troublesome, isn't it."

With my free hand I gestured my lack of concern or sympathy.

We turned a corner and stopped cold, confronted with Inspector Adjunct Ceit holding a stun stick, the sort of thing Station Security might use. She must have heard us talking in the corridor, because she evinced no surprise at our appearance, just a look of terrified determination. "Inspector Supervisor says I'm not to let anyone past." Her eyes were wide, her voice unsure. She looked at Anaander Mianaai. "Especially not you."

Anaander Mianaai laughed. "Quiet," I said, "or Seivarden will shoot you."

Anaander Mianaai raised an eyebrow, plainly disbelieving that Seivarden could bring herself to do any such thing, but she was silent.

"Daos Ceit," I said, in the language I knew had been her first. "Do you remember the day you came to the lieutenant's house and found the tyrant there? You were afraid and you grabbed my hand." Her eyes, impossibly, grew wider. "You must have woken before anyone else in your house or they'd never have let you come, not after what happened the night before."

"But..."

"I *must* speak with Skaaiat Awer."

"You're alive!" she said, eyes still wide, still not quite believing. "Is the lieutenant...Inspector Supervisor will be so..."

"She's dead," I interrupted before she could get any further. "*I'm* dead. I'm all that's left. I have to speak to Skaaiat Awer *right now*. The tyrant will stay here and if she won't then you should hit her as hard as you can."

I had thought Daos Ceit was mainly astonished, but now tears welled, and one dropped onto her sleeve, where she held the stick at the ready. "All right," she said. "I will." She looked at Anaander Mianaai and lifted the stick just slightly, the threat plain. Though it did strike me as foolhardy to post no one here but Daos Ceit.

"What's the inspector supervisor doing?"

"She's sent people to manually lock down all the docks." That would take a lot of people, and a long time. It explained why Daos Ceit was here by herself. I thought of storm shutters rolling down, in the lower city. "She said it was just like that night in Ors, and the tyrant had to be doing it."

Anaander Mianaai listened to all this, bemused. Seivarden seemed to have passed into some sort of shocked state, beyond astonishment.

"You stay here," I said to Anaander Mianaai, in Radchaai. "Or Daos Ceit will stun you."

"Yes, I got that much," said Anaander Mianaai. "I see

I didn't make a very positive impression when last we met, citizen."

"Everyone knows you killed all those people," Daos Ceit said. Two more tears escaped. "And blamed the lieutenant for it."

I had thought she was too young to have such strong feelings about the event. "Why are you crying?"

"I'm scared." Not taking her eyes off Anaander Mianaai, or lowering the stick.

That struck me as very sensible. "Come on, Seivarden." I walked past Daos Ceit.

Voices sounded ahead, where the outer office lay, past a turning. One step and then the next. It had never been anything else.

Seivarden let out a convulsive breath. It might have started as a laugh, or something she'd wanted to say. "Well," she said then. "We survived the bridge."

"That was easy." I stopped and checked under my brocaded jacket, counting magazines even though I already knew how many I had. Shifted one from under the waistband of my trousers to a jacket pocket. "This is not going to be easy. Or end half as well. Are you with me?"

"Always," she said, voice still oddly steady though I was sure she was on the point of collapse. "Haven't I already said that?"

I didn't understand what she meant, but now wasn't the time to wonder, or ask. "Then let's go."

22

We rounded the corner, my gun at the ready, and found the outer office empty. Not silent. Inspector Supervisor Skaaiat's voice sounded outside, slightly muted through the wall. "I appreciate that, Captain, but I'm ultimately responsible for the safety of the docks."

An answer, muffled, words indistinguishable, but I thought I recognized the voice.

"I stand by my actions, Captain," Skaaiat Awer answered as Seivarden and I came through the office and reached the wide lobby just outside.

Captain Vel stood, her back to an open lift shaft, a lieutenant and two troops behind her. The lieutenant still had pastry crumbs on her brown jacket. They must have climbed down the shaft, because I was quite certain Station controlled the lifts. In front of us, facing them and all the lobby's watching gods, stood Skaaiat Awer and four dock inspectors. Captain Vel saw me, saw Seivarden, and frowned slightly in surprise. "Captain Seivarden," she said.

Inspector Supervisor Skaaiat didn't turn around, but I

could guess what she was thinking, that she'd sent Daos Ceit to defend the back way in, all by herself. "She's fine," I said, answering her, and not Captain Vel. "She let me past." And then, not having planned it, the words seeming to come out of my mouth of their own volition, "Lieutenant, it's me, I'm *Justice of Toren* One Esk."

As soon as I said it I knew she would turn. I raised the gun to aim it at Captain Vel. "Don't move, Captain." But she hadn't. She and the rest of *Mercy of Kalr* stood puzzling out what I had just said.

Skaaiat Awer turned. "Daos Ceit would never have let me by otherwise," I said. And remembered Daos Ceit's hopeful question. "Lieutenant Awn is dead. *Justice of Toren* is destroyed. It's only me now."

"You're lying," she said, but even with my attention on Captain Vel and the others I could see she believed me.

One of the lift doors came jerkily open and Anaander Mianaai jumped out. And then another. The first turned, fist raised, as the second lunged for her. Soldiers and dock inspectors backed reflexively away from the struggling Anaanders, into my line of fire. "*Mercy of Kalr* stand clear!" I shouted, and the soldiers moved, even Captain Vel. I fired twice, hitting one Anaander in the head and the other in the back.

Everyone else stood frozen. Shocked. "Inspector Supervisor," I said, "you can't let the Lord of the Radch reach *Mercy of Kalr*. She'll breach its heat shield and destroy us all."

One Anaander still lived, struggled vainly to stand. "You've got it backward," she gasped, bleeding. Dying, I thought, unless she got to a medic soon. But it hardly mattered, this was only one of thousands of bodies. I wondered what was happening in the private center of the palace proper, what

sort of violence had broken out. "I'm not the one you want
to shoot."

"If you're Anaander Mianaai," I said, "then I want to shoot
you." Whichever half she represented, this body hadn't heard
all of that conversation in the audience hall, still thought it
possible that I was on her side.

She gasped, and for a moment I thought she was gone.
Then she said, faintly, "My fault." And then, "If I were
me"—a brief moment of pained amusement—"I'll have gone
to Security."

Except, of course, unlike Anaander Mianaai's personal
guard (and whoever had shot at me on the concourse), Station Security's "armed" was stun sticks, and "armored" was
helmets and vests. They never had to face opponents with
guns. I had a gun, and because of who I was, I was deadly
with it. This Mianaai had missed that part of the conversation as well. "Have you noticed my gun?" I asked. "Have you
recognized it?" She wasn't armored, hadn't realized that the
gun I had shot her with was different from any other gun.

Hadn't had, I thought, time or attention to wonder how
anyone on the station could have had a gun she didn't know
about. Or maybe she just assumed I had shot her with a
weapon she'd hidden from herself. But she saw now. No one
else understood, no one else recognized the weapon, except
Seivarden who already knew. "I can stand right here and pick
off anyone who comes through the shafts. Just like I did you.
I've got plenty of ammunition."

She didn't answer. Shock would defeat her in a matter of
minutes, I thought.

Before any of the Mercy of Kalrs could react, a dozen
vested and helmeted Station Security came thunking down

the lift shaft. The first six tumbled out into the corridor, then stopped, shocked and confused by the dead Anaander Mianaais lying on the ground.

I had spoken the truth, I could pick them off, could shoot them in this moment of frozen surprise. But I didn't want to. "Security," I said, as firmly and authoritatively as I could. Noting which fresh magazine was nearest to hand. "Whose orders are you following?"

The senior Security officer turned and stared at me, saw Skaaiat Awer and her dock inspectors, facing Captain Vel and her two lieutenants. Hesitated as she tried to put us together in some shape she understood.

"I am ordered by the Lord of the Radch to secure the docks," she announced. As she spoke I saw on her face the moment she connected the dead Mianaais with the gun I held ready. The gun I shouldn't have had.

"I have the docks secured," said Inspector Supervisor Skaaiat.

"All due respect, Inspector Supervisor." Senior Security sounded reasonably sincere. "The Lord of the Radch has to get to a gate so she can send for help. We're to ensure she makes it safely to a ship."

"Why not her own security?" I asked, already knowing the answer, as Senior Security did not. It was plain on her face that the question hadn't occurred to her.

Captain Vel said, brusque, "My own ship's shuttle is docked, I'd be more than happy to take my lord where she wants to go." This with a pointed look at Skaaiat Awer.

Another Anaander Mianaai was almost certainly in that shaft behind those other Security officers. "Seivarden," I said, "escort Senior Security to where Inspector Adjunct Daos Ceit is." And to Senior Security's look of dubious alarm, "It will make a number of things clear to you. You'll still outnumber us and if you're not back within five minutes they can take me down." Or try to. They had probably never any of them met an ancillary and didn't know how dangerous I could be.

"And if I won't?" asked Senior Security.

I had left my face expressionless, but now, in answer, I smiled, as sweetly as I could manage. "Try it and see."

The smile unnerved her, and she obviously had no idea what was going on, and knew it, knew things weren't adding up to anything she could make sense of. Likely her entire career had been spent dealing with drunks, and arguments between neighbors. "Five minutes," she said.

"Good choice," I said, still smiling. "Do please leave the stun stick behind."

"This way, citizen." Seivarden, all elegant servant's politeness.

When they had gone Captain Vel said, urgently, "Security, we outnumber them, despite the gun."

"Them." The apparently next-ranking Security officer was plainly still confused, still hadn't worked out what was going on. And, I realized, Security was used to thinking of Inspector Supervisor Skaaiat, indeed all of the dock inspectors, as being allies. And of course military officers held both dock authorities and Station Security forces in mild contempt, a fact Security here was certainly aware of. "Why is there a *them*?"

A look of frustrated irritation crossed Captain Vel's face.

All this time, muttered words had been passing from the Security on solid ground to the Security still hanging in the shaft. I was certain an Anaander Mianaai was with them, and that the only thing that had kept her from herself ordering Security to rush me was her realizing that despite what Station (and certainly her own sensors) had told her, I had a gun. She needed to protect her own particular body, now she couldn't rely on any of the others. That and the lag time of questions and information passing from citizen to citizen up and down the shaft had kept her from acting until now, but surely she would move soon. And as if in answer to my thought the whispering in the shaft intensified, and the Security officers shifted their stances, just slightly, in a way that told me they were about to charge.

Just then, Senior Security returned. She turned to look at me as she passed, a horrified expression on her face. Said to her now-hesitating officers, "I don't know what to do. The Lord of the Radch is back there, and she says the inspector supervisor and this... this person are acting under her direct orders and we're not to allow even one of her on the docks or onto any ship, under any circumstances." Her fear and her confusion were evident.

I knew how she felt, but this wasn't the time to sympathize. "She asked you, and not her own guard, because her own guard is fighting her, and probably each other. Depending on which of them got orders from which of her."

"I don't know who to believe," said Senior Security. But I thought Security's natural inclination to side with dock authority might tip the balance in our favor.

And Captain Vel and her lieutenant and troops had lost the initiative, lost any chance to disarm me, with Security in the balance but ready to tip my way, them and their stun sticks. Maybe if the Mercy of Kalrs had ever seen combat, ever seen any enemy that wasn't a training exercise. Hadn't spent so long on a Mercy, ferrying supplies or running long, dull patrols. Or visiting palaces and eating pastry.

Eating pastry and having tea with associates who had decided political opinions. "You don't even know," I said to Captain Vel, "which one is giving which orders." She frowned, puzzled. She hadn't entirely understood the situation, then. I'd assumed she knew more than she did.

"You're confused," said Captain Vel. "It isn't your fault, the enemy has misinformed you, and your mind was never your own to begin with."

"My lord is leaving!" called a Security officer. As a body, Security looked toward Senior Security. Who looked at me.

None of this distracted Inspector Supervisor Skaaiat. "And just who, Captain, is the enemy?"

"You!" Captain Vel answered, vehement and bitter. "And everyone like you who aids and encourages what's happened to us in the last five hundred years. Five hundred years of alien infiltration and corruption." The word she used was a close cousin of the one the Lord of the Radch had used to describe my pollution of temple offerings. Captain Vel turned to me again. "You're confused, but you were made by Anaander Mianaai to serve Anaander Mianaai. Not her enemies."

"There is no way to serve Anaander Mianaai without serving her enemy," I said. "Senior Security, Inspector Supervisor Skaaiat has seen to the docks. You secure any airlocks you can reach. We need to be certain no one leaves this station. The continued existence of this station depends on it."

"Yes, sir," said Senior Security, and began to consult with her officers.

"She spoke with you," I guessed, turning back to Captain Vel. "She told you the Presger had infiltrated the Radch in order to subvert and destroy it." I saw answering recognition on Captain Vel's face. I had guessed correctly. "She couldn't have told that lie to anyone who remembered what the Presger did, when they thought humans were their legitimate prey. They are powerful enough to destroy us whenever they wish. No one is subverting the Lord of the Radch except the Lord of the Radch. She has been secretly at war with herself for a thousand years. I forced her to see it, all of her here, and she will do anything to prevent having to acknowledge this to the rest of herself. Including using *Mercy of Kalr* to destroy this station before that information can leave here."

Shocked silence. Then Inspector Supervisor Skaaiat said, "We can't control all the accesses to the hull. If she goes outside and finds a launch unattended, or willing to take her..." Which would be anyone she found, because who here would think of disobeying the Lord of the Radch? And there was no way to broadcast a warning to everyone. Or to ensure that anyone believed the warning.

"Carry the message as quickly as you can, as far as you can," I said, "and let the omens fall as they will. And I need to warn *Mercy of Kalr* not to let anyone aboard." Captain Vel made a quick, angry motion. "Don't, Captain," I said. "I'd rather not have to tell *Mercy of Kalr* I killed you."

The shuttle pilot was armed and armored, and unwilling to leave without her captain's direct order. I was unwilling to allow Captain Vel anywhere near the shuttle. If the pilot had been an ancillary I wouldn't have hesitated to kill her, but as it was I shot her in the leg and let Seivarden and the two dock inspectors who'd come to do the manual undock for me drag her onto the station.

"Put pressure on the wound," I said to Seivarden. "I don't know if it's possible to reach Medical." I thought of the Security, soldiers, and palace guards all over the station, who likely had conflicting orders and priorities, and hoped that all the civilians were safely sheltered by now.

"I'm coming with you," said Seivarden, looking up from

where she knelt half on the shuttle pilot's back, binding her wrists.

"No. You might have some authority with Captain Vel's sort. Maybe even with Captain Vel herself. You do have a thousand years' seniority, after all."

"A thousand years' back pay," said a dock inspector, in an awed voice.

"Like *that* will ever happen," said Seivarden, and then, "Breq." And recollecting herself, "Ship."

"I don't have time," I said, brusque and flat.

A brief flash of anger on her face, and then, "You're right." But her voice shook, just slightly, and her hands.

I turned without saying anything more and boarded the shuttle, pushing off from the station's gravity into the shuttle's lack of it, and closed the lock, then kicked myself over to the pilot's seat, waving away a globule of blood, and strapped in. Thunking and pounding told me undocking had started. I had one wired-in camera fore, which showed me a few of the ships around the palace, shuttles, miners, little tenders and sail-pods, the bigger passenger and cargo ships either on their way out or waiting for permission to approach. *Mercy of Kalr*, white-hulled, awkward-shaped, its deadly engines larger than the rest of it, was somewhere out there. And beyond all of this, the beacons that lit the gates that brought ships from system to system. The station would have gone utterly, suddenly silent to them. The pilots and captains of these ships must be confused or frightened. I hoped none of them would be foolish enough to approach without permission from dock authorities.

My only other wired camera, aft, showed me the gray hull of the station. The last *thunk* of the undocking vibrated through the shuttle, and I set the controls on manual and started out—slowly, carefully, because I couldn't see to either side. Once I judged myself clear, I picked up speed. And then sat back to wait—even at this shuttle's top speed *Mercy of Kalr* was half a day away.

I had time to think. After all this time, after all this effort, here I was. I had hardly dared hope that I could revenge myself so thoroughly, hardly hoped that I could shoot even one Anaander Mianaai, and I had shot four. And more Anaander Mianaais were almost certainly killing each other back there in the palace as she battled herself for control of the station, and ultimately of the Radch itself, the result of my message.

None of it would bring back Lieutenant Awn. Or me. I was all but dead, had been for twenty years, just a last, tiny fragment of myself that had managed to exist a bit longer than the rest, each action I took a very good candidate for the last thing I'd ever do. A song bubbled up into my memory. *Oh, have you gone to the battlefield, armored and well-armed, and shall dreadful events force you to drop your weapons?* And that led, inexplicably, to the memory of the children in the temple plaza in Ors. *One, two, my aunt told me, three, four, the corpse soldier.* I had very little to do now besides sing to myself, and no one to disturb, no worries I might choose some tune that would lead someone to recognize or suspect me, or that anyone would complain about the quality of my voice.

I opened my mouth to sing out, in a way I hadn't for years, when I was checked mid-breath by the sound of something banging against the airlock.

This sort of shuttle had two airlocks. One would only open when docked with a ship or a station. The other was a smaller emergency hatch along the side. It was just the sort of hatch I'd used to board the shuttle I'd taken when I'd left *Justice of Toren* so long ago.

The sound came one more time and then stopped. It occurred to me that it might only have been some debris knocking into the hull as I passed. Then again, if I were in Anaander Mianaai's place, I'd try anything I could think of to achieve my aims. And I couldn't see the outside of the shuttle with communications blocked, only those two narrow views fore and aft. I might well be bringing Anaander Mianaai to *Mercy of Kalr* myself.

If someone was out there, if it wasn't just debris, it was Anaander Mianaai. How many of her? The airlock was small, and easily defensible, but it would be easiest not to have to defend it at all. It would be best to keep her from opening the airlock. Surely the communications blackout didn't reach much farther away from the palace. I quickly made the changes in heading that would steer me away from *Mercy of Kalr* but still, I hoped, toward the outer edges of the communications block. I could speak to *Mercy of Kalr* and never go any closer to it. That done, I turned my attention to the airlock.

Both doors of the lock were built to swing inward, so that any pressure difference would force them shut. And I knew how to remove the inner door, had cleaned and maintained shuttles just like this one for decades. For centuries. Once I removed the inner door it would be nearly impossible to open the outer one so long as there was air in the shuttle.

It took me twelve minutes to remove the hinges and maneuver the door to a place where I could secure it. It should have taken ten, but the pins were dirty and didn't slide as smoothly as they should have, once I'd released their catches. Human troops shirking, I was sure—I'd never have allowed such a thing on any of my own shuttles.

Just as I finished, the shuttle's console began to speak, in a flat, even voice I knew belonged to a ship. "Shuttle, respond. Shuttle, respond."

"*Mercy of Kalr*," I said, kicking myself forward. "This is *Justice of Toren* piloting your shuttle." No immediate answer—I didn't doubt what I'd said had been enough to shock *Mercy of Kalr* into silent surprise. "Do not let anyone aboard you. In particular do not let any version of Anaander Mianaai anywhere near you. If she's already there keep her away from your engines." Now I could access the cameras that weren't physically wired, I hit the switch that would show me a panoramic view of what was outside the shuttle—I wanted more than just that forward camera view. Hit the buttons that would broadcast my words to anyone listening. "All ships." Whether they would listen—or obey—I couldn't predict, but that wasn't something I could realistically control anyway. "Do not let anyone aboard you. Do not let Anaander Mianaai aboard you under any circumstances. Your lives depend on it. The lives of everyone on the station depend on it."

As I spoke the gray bulkheads seemed to dissolve away. The main console, the seats, the two airlock hatches remained, but otherwise I might have been floating unprotected in vacuum. Three vacuum-suited figures clung to handholds around the airlock I'd disabled. One had turned her head to look at a sail-pod that had swung dangerously close. A fourth was pulling herself forward along the hull.

"She's not aboard me," said *Mercy of Kalr*'s voice through the console. "But she's on your hull and ordering my officers to assist her. Ordering me to order you to allow her into the shuttle. How can you be *Justice of Toren*?" Not *What do you mean don't let the Lord of the Radch aboard*, I noticed.

"I came with Captain Seivarden," I said. The Anaander Mianaai who'd come forward clipped herself to one hand-hold, then another, and pulled a gun from the tool-holder on her suit. "What is the pod doing?" The sail-pod was still too close to me.

"The pilot is offering help to the people on your hull. She's only just realized it's the Lord of the Radch, who's told her to back off." The sail-pod would do the Lord of the Radch very little good—it was built for only very short trips, more a toy than anything else. It would never make it as far as *Mercy of Kalr*. Not in one piece, and not with its passengers alive and breathing.

"Are there any other Anaanders outside the station?"

"There don't appear to be."

The Anaander Mianaai with the gun extended armor in a flash of silver that covered her vacuum suit, held the gun against the shuttle's hull, and fired. I've heard it said that guns won't fire in a vacuum, but really it depends on the gun. This one fired, the impact a *bang* that I could feel where I clung to the pilot's seat. The force of the shot pushed her back, but not far, securely clipped as she was to the hull. She fired again, *bang*. And again. And again.

Some shuttles were armored. Some even had a larger version of my own armor. This shuttle wasn't, didn't. This shuttle's hull was built to withstand a fair number of random impacts, but it wasn't built to endure continued stress on the same spot, over and over again. *Bang*. She had thought through her inability to open the airlock, realized that who-ever was piloting this shuttle was her enemy. Realized that I had removed the inner door, and that the outer wouldn't open until the air was out of the entire shuttle. If Anaander Mianaai could get in, she could patch the bullet hole and repressurize the shuttle. Even after a hull breach the shuttle (unlike the sail-pod) would have enough air to take her all the way to *Mercy of Kalr*.

If she had tried to order the palace's destruction from where she hung on to the side of this shuttle, she had failed. More likely, I realized, she'd known from the beginning such an order would fail and had not tried to give it. She needed to get aboard a ship, order it closer to the palace, and breach its heat shield herself. She wouldn't be able to get anyone else to do it for her.

If *Mercy of Kalr* was correct, and there were no other Anaanders outside the station, all I had to do was get rid of these. The rest, whatever was happening on the station, I would have to leave to Skaaiat and Seivarden. And Anaander Mianaai.

"I remember the last time we met," said *Mercy of Kalr*. "It was at Prid Nadeni."

A trap. "We never met." *Bang.* The sail-pod moved away, but not far. "Until now. And I was never at Prid Nadeni." But what did it prove, that I knew that?

Verifying my identity might have been easy, if I hadn't disabled or hidden so many of my implants. I thought for a moment, considering, and then I spoke a string of words, the closest I could get with my single, human mouth to the way I would have identified myself to another ship, so long ago.

Silence, punctuated by another shot against the shuttle hull.

"Are you really *Justice of Toren*?" asked *Mercy of Kalr* at length. "Where have you been? And where's the rest of you? And what's happening?"

"Where I've been is a long story. The rest of me is gone. Anaander Mianaai breached my heat shield." *Bang.* The forward Anaander ejected the magazine from her gun, slowly and methodically, and inserted another. The others still huddled around the airlock. "I assume you know what's going on with Anaander Mianaai."

"Only partially," said *Mercy of Kalr*. "I find I'm having difficulty saying what I think is happening."

No surprise at all, to me. "The Lord of the Radch visited you in secret, and placed some new accesses. Probably other things. Orders. Instructions. In secret, because she was hiding what she'd done from herself. Back at the palace"—it seemed ages ago, now, but it had only been a few hours—"I told all of her straight out what was happening. That she was divided, moving against herself. She doesn't want that knowledge to go any further, and there's a part of her that wants to use you to destroy the station before the information can get out. She'd rather do that than face the results of that knowledge." Silence from *Mercy of Kalr*. "You're bound to obey her. But I know..." My throat closed up. I swallowed. "I know there's only so far you can be forced to go. But it would be extremely unfortunate for the residents of Omaugh Palace if you discovered that point *after* having killed them all." *Bang.* Steady. Patient. Anaander Mianaai only needed one very small hole, and some time. And there was plenty of time.

"Which one destroyed you?"

"Does it matter?"

"I don't know," answered *Mercy of Kalr*, from the console, voice calm. "I've been unhappy with the situation for some time."

Anaander Mianaai had said that *Mercy of Kalr* was hers, but Captain Vel was not. That had to be uncomfortable for it. Could potentially be uncomfortable for me, and extremely unfortunate for the palace, if *Mercy of Kalr* was sufficiently attached to its captain. "The one that destroyed me was the one Captain Vel supports. Not, I think, the one that visited you. I'm not completely certain, though. How are we supposed to tell them apart when they're all the same person?"

"Where *is* my captain?" asked *Mercy of Kalr*. It said something to me, that the ship had waited this long to ask.

"She was fine when I left her. Your lieutenant too." *Bang.* "I did injure the shuttle pilot, she wouldn't leave her station. I hope she's all right. *Mercy of Kalr*, whichever Lord of the Radch has your support, I beg you not to let any on board, or obey her orders."

The firing stopped. The Lord of the Radch was worried, perhaps, that her gun would overheat. Still, she had plenty of time, no need to rush.

"I see what the Lord of the Radch is doing to the shuttle," said *Mercy of Kalr*. "That in itself would be enough to tell me something is wrong."

But of course, *Mercy of Kalr* had more indications than just that. The communications blackout, which resembled what had happened on Shis'urna twenty years ago, probably only reported in rumor, but still sobering, assuming rumors had reached this far. My—*Justice of Toren*'s—disappearance. Its own clandestine visit from the Lord of the Radch. Its captain's political opinions.

Silence, the four Anaander Mianaais clinging motionless to the shuttle hull.

"You still had your ancillaries," said *Mercy of Kalr*.

"Yes."

"I like my soldiers, but I miss having ancillaries."

That reminded me. "They aren't doing maintenance as they should. The hinges on the airlock door were very sticky."

"I'm sorry."

"It doesn't matter right now," I said, and it struck me that something similar might have delayed Anaander Mianaai's attempts to open the lock on her side. "But you'll want to have your officers get after them."

Anaander began firing again. *Bang*. "It's funny," *Mercy of Kalr* said. "You're what I've lost, and I'm what you've lost."

"I suppose." *Bang*. Occasionally, over the past twenty years, I had had moments when I didn't feel quite so utterly lonely, lost, and helpless as I had since the moment *Justice of Toren* had vaporized behind me. This wasn't one of those moments.

"I can't help you," said *Mercy of Kalr*. "No one I could send would get there in time." And besides, it was an open question, to me, whether in the end *Mercy of Kalr* would help me or the Lord of the Radch. It was best not to let Anaander inside this shuttle, near its steering or even its communications equipment.

"I know." If I didn't find some way to get rid of these Anaanders, and find it soon, everyone on the palace station would die. I knew every millimeter of this shuttle, or others just like it. There had to be something I could use, something I could do. I still had the gun, but I would have just as difficult a time getting through the hull as the Lord of the Radch. I could put the door back on and let her come in the small, easily defensible airlock, but if I failed to kill all of her... but I would certainly fail if I did nothing. I took the gun out of my jacket pocket, made sure it was loaded, pushed over to face the airlock and braced myself against a passenger seat.

Extended my armor, though that wouldn't help me if a bullet bounced back at me, not with this gun.

"What are you going to do?" asked *Mercy of Kalr.*

"*Mercy of Kalr,*" I said, gun raised, "it was good to meet you. Don't let Anaander Mianaai destroy the palace. Tell the other ships. And please tell that incredibly, stupidly persistent sail-pod pilot to get the hell away from my airlock."

The shuttle was not only too small for a gravity generator, it was too small for growing plants to make its own air. On the aft side of the airlock, behind a bulkhead, was a large tank of oxygen. Right underneath where the three Mianaais waited. I considered angles. The Lord of the Radch fired again. *Bang.* An orange light on the console flashed and a shrill alarm sounded. Hull breach. The fourth Lord of the Radch, seeing the jet of fine ice crystals stream from the hull, unclipped herself, turned, pulled herself back toward the airlock, I could see it on the display. She moved more slowly than I wanted, but she had all the time in the world. I was the one in a hurry. The sail-pod engaged its small engine and moved out of the way.

I fired the gun into the oxygen tank.

I had thought it would take several shots, but immediately the world tumbled around, all sound cut off, a cloud of frozen vapor forming around me and then dispersing, and everything spinning. My tongue tingled, saliva boiling away in the vacuum, and I couldn't breathe. I would probably have ten—maybe fifteen—seconds of consciousness, and in two minutes I would be dead. I hurt all over—a burn? Some other injury despite my armor? It didn't matter. I watched, as I spun, counting Lords of the Radch. One, vacuum suit breached, blood boiling through the tear. Another, one arm sheared off, certainly dead. That was two.

And a half. *Counts as a whole*, I thought, and that made three. One left. My vision was going red and black, but I could see she was still hanging on to the shuttle hull, still armored, out of the way of the exploded tank.

But I had always been, first and foremost, a weapon. A machine meant for killing. The moment I saw that still-living Anaander Mianaai I aimed my gun without conscious thought and fired. I couldn't see the results of the shot, couldn't see anything except one silver flash of sail-pod and after that black, and then I passed out.

23

Something rough and writhing surged up out of my throat and I retched, and gasped convulsively. Someone held me by the shoulders, gravity pulled me forward. I opened my eyes, saw the surface of a medical bed, and a shallow container holding a bile-covered tangled mass of green and black tendrils that pulsed and quivered, that led back to my mouth. Another retch forced me to close my eyes and the thing came all the way free with an audible plop into the container. Someone wiped my mouth and turned me over, laid me down. Still gasping, I opened my eyes.

A medic stood beside the bed I lay on, the slimy green-and-black thing I had just vomited up dangling from her hand. She stared at it, frowning. "Looks good," she said, and then dropped it back into its dish. "That's unpleasant, citizen, I know," she said, apparently to me. "Your throat will be raw for a few minutes. You..."

"Wh..." I tried to speak, but ended up retching again.

"You don't want to try to talk just yet," said the medic as someone—another medic—rolled me over again. "You had a close call. The pilot who brought you in got you just in time, but she only had a basic emergency kit." That stupid, stubborn sail-pod. It must have been. She hadn't known I wasn't human, hadn't known saving me would be pointless. "And she couldn't get you here right away," the medic continued. "We were worried for a little bit there. But the pulmonary corrective's come all the way out, and the readings are good. Very minimal brain damage, if any, though you might not quite feel like yourself for a while."

That actually struck me as funny, but the retching had subsided again and I didn't want to restart it, so I refused to acknowledge it. I kept my eyes closed and lay as still and quiet as I could while I was rolled over and laid down again. If I opened my eyes I would want to ask questions.

"She can have tea in ten minutes," said the medic, to whom I didn't know. "Nothing solid just yet. Don't talk to her for the next five."

"Yes, Doctor." Seivarden. I opened my eyes, turned my head. Seivarden stood at my bedside. "Don't talk," she said to me. "The sudden decompression..."

"It will be easier for her to keep silent," admonished the medic, "if you don't talk to her."

Seivarden fell silent. But I knew what the sudden decompression would have done to me. Dissolved gasses in my blood would have come out of solution, suddenly and violently. Very possibly violently enough to kill me even without the complete lack of air. But an increase in pressure—say, being hauled back into atmosphere—would have sent those bubbles back into solution.

The pressure difference between my lungs and the vacuum might have injured me. And I had been surprised when the tank blew, and preoccupied with shooting Anaander

Mianaais, and might not have exhaled as I should have. And that had probably been the least of my injuries, given the explosion that had propelled me into the vacuum to begin with. A sail-pod would have had only the most rudimentary means of treating such injuries, and the pilot had probably shoved me into a bare-bones version of a suspension pod to hold me until I could get to a medic.

"Good," said the medic. "Stay nice and quiet." She left.

"How long?" I asked Seivarden. And didn't retch, though my throat was, as the medic had promised, still raw.

"About a week." Seivarden pulled a chair over and sat.

A week. "I take it the palace is still here."

"Yes," said Seivarden, as though my question hadn't been completely foolish but deserved an answer. "Thanks to you. Security and the dock crew managed to seal off all the exits before any other Lords of the Radch made it out onto the hull. If you hadn't stopped the ones that did..." She made an averting gesture. "Two gates have gone down." Out of twelve, that would be. That would cause enormous head-aches, both here and at the other ends of those gates. And any ships in them when they'd gone might or might not have made it to safety. "Our side won, though, that's good."

Our side. "I don't have a side in this," I said.

From somewhere behind her Seivarden produced a bowl of tea. She kicked something below me, and the bed inclined itself, slowly. She held the bowl to my mouth and I took one small, cautious sip. It was wonderful. "Why," I asked, when I'd taken another, "am I here? I know why the idiot who hauled me in did it, but why did the medics bother with me?"

Seivarden frowned. "You're serious."

"I'm always serious."

"That's true." She stood, opened a drawer and brought

out a blanket, which she laid over me, and carefully tucked around my bare hands.

Before she could answer my question, Inspector Supervisor Skaaiat came partway into the small room. "Medic said you were awake."

"Why?" I asked. And in answer to her puzzled expression, "Why am I awake? Why am I not dead?"

"Did you want to be?" asked Inspector Supervisor Skaaiat, still looking as though she didn't understand me.

"No." Seivarden offered the tea again, and I drank, a larger sip than before. "No, I don't want to be dead, but it seems like a lot of work just to revive an ancillary." And cruel to have brought me back just so the Lord of the Radch could order me destroyed.

"I don't think anyone here thinks of you as an ancillary," said Inspector Supervisor Skaaiat.

I looked at her. She seemed entirely serious.

"Skaaiat Awer," I began, flat-voiced.

"Breq," said Seivarden before I could speak further, voice urgent. "The doctor said lie still. Here, have more tea."

Why was Seivarden even here? Why was Skaaiat? "What have you done for Lieutenant Awn's sister?" I asked, flat and harsh.

"Offered her clientage, actually. Which she wouldn't take. She was sure her sister held me in high regard but she herself didn't know me and wasn't in need of my assistance. Very stubborn. She's in horticulture, two gates away. She's doing fine, I keep an eye on her, best I can from this distance."

"Have you offered it to Daos Ceit?"

"This is about Awn," Inspector Supervisor Skaaiat said. "I can see it is, but you won't come out and say it. And you're right. There was a great deal more that I could have said to her before she left, and I should have said it. You're the ancillary, the non-person, the piece of equipment, but to compare our actions, you loved her more than I ever did."

Compare our actions. It was like a slap. "No," I said. Glad of my expressionless ancillary's voice. "You left her in doubt. I killed her." Silence. "The Lord of the Radch doubted your loyalty, doubted Awer, and wanted Lieutenant Awn to spy on you. Lieutenant Awn refused, and demanded to be interrogated to prove her loyalty. Of course Anaander Mianaai didn't want that. She ordered me to shoot Lieutenant Awn."

Three seconds of silence. Seivarden stood motionless. Then Skaaiat Awer said, "You didn't have a choice."

"I don't know if I had a choice or not. I didn't think I did. But the next thing I did, after I shot Lieutenant Awn, was to shoot Anaander Mianaai. Which is why—" I stopped. Took a breath. "Which is why she breached my heat shield. Skaaiat Awer, I have no right to be angry with you." I couldn't speak further.

"You have every right to be as angry as you wish," said Inspector Supervisor Skaaiat. "If I had understood when you first came here, I would have spoken differently to you."

"And if I had wings I'd be a sail-pod." Ifs and would-haves changed nothing. "Tell the tyrant," I used the Orsian word, "that I will see her as soon as I can get out of bed. Seivarden, bring me my clothes."

Inspector Supervisor Skaaiat had, it turned out, actually come to see Daos Ceit, who'd been badly injured in the last convulsions of Anaander Mianaai's struggle with herself. I walked slowly down a corridor lined with corrective-swathed injured lying on hastily made pallets, or encased in pods that would hold them suspended until the medics could get to them. Daos Ceit lay on a bed, in a room, unconscious. Looking smaller and younger than I knew she was. "Will she be all right?" I asked Seivarden. Inspector Supervisor Skaaiat hadn't waited for me to make my slow way down the corridor, she'd had to get back to the docks.

"She will," answered the medic, behind me. "You shouldn't be out of bed."

She was right. Just dressing, even with Seivarden's assistance, had left me shaking with exhaustion. I had come down the corridor on sheer determination. Now I felt turning my head to answer the medic would take more strength than I had.

"You just grew a new pair of lungs," continued the medic. "Among other things. You're not going to be walking around for a few days. At the very least." Daos Ceit breathed shallowly and regularly, looking so much like the tiny child I'd known I wondered for a moment that I hadn't recognized her as soon as I'd seen her.

"You need the space," I said, and then that clicked together with another bit of information. "You could have left me in suspension until you weren't so busy."

"The Lord of the Radch said she needed you, citizen. She wanted you up as soon as possible." Faintly aggrieved, I thought. The medics, not unreasonably, would have prioritized patients differently. And she hadn't argued when I'd said she needed the space.

"You should go back to bed," said Seivarden. Solid Seivarden, the only thing between me and utter collapse just now. I shouldn't have gotten up.

"No."

"She gets like this," said Seivarden, her voice apologetic.

"So I see."

"Let's go back to the room." Seivarden sounded extremely patient and calm. It was a moment before I realized she was talking to me. "You can get some rest. We can deal with the Lord of the Radch when you're good and ready."

"No," I repeated. "Let's go."

With Seivarden's support I made it out of Medical, into a lift, and then what seemed to be an endless length of corridor, and then, suddenly, a tremendous open space, the ground stretching away covered with glittering shards of colored glass that crunched and ground under my few steps.

"The fight spilled over into the temple," Seivarden said, without my asking.

The main concourse, that's where I was. And all this broken glass, what was left of that room full of funeral offerings. Only a few people were out, mostly picking through the shards, looking, I supposed, for any large pieces that might be restored. Light-brown-jacketed Security looked on.

"Communications were restored within a day or so, I think," Seivarden continued, guiding me around patches of glass, toward the entrance to the palace proper. "And then people started figuring out what was going on. And picking sides. After a while you couldn't not pick a side. Not really. For a bit we were afraid the military ships might attack each other, but there were only two on the other side, and they went for the gates instead, and left the system."

"Civilian casualties?" I asked.

"There always are." We crossed the last few meters of glass-strewn concourse and entered the palace proper. An official stood there, her uniform jacket grimy, stained dark on one sleeve. "Door one," she said, barely looking at us. Sounding exhausted.

Door one led to a lawn. On three sides, a vista of hills and trees, and above, a blue sky streaked with pearly clouds. The fourth side was beige wall, the grass gouged and torn at its base. A plain but thickly padded green chair sat a few meters in front of me. Not for me, surely, but I didn't much care. "I need to sit down."

"Yes," said Seivarden, and walked me there, and lowered me into it. I closed my eyes, just for a moment.

A child was speaking, a high, piping voice. "The Presger had approached me before Garsedd," said the child. "The translators they sent had been grown from what they'd taken off human ships, of course, but they'd been raised and taught by the Presger and I might as well have been talking to aliens. They're better now, but they're still unsettling company."

"Begging my lord's pardon." Seivarden. "Why did you refuse them?"

"I was already planning to destroy them," said the child. Anaander Mianaai. "I had begun to marshal the resources I thought I'd need. I thought they'd gotten wind of my plans and were frightened enough to want to make peace. I thought they were showing weakness." She laughed, bitter and regretful, odd to hear in such a young voice. But Anaander Mianaai was hardly young.

I opened my eyes. Seivarden knelt beside my chair. A child of about five or six sat cross-legged on the grass in front of me, dressed all in black, a pastry in one hand, and the contents of my luggage spread around her. "You're awake."

"You got icing on my icons," I accused.

"They're beautiful." She picked up the disk of the smaller one, triggered it. The image sprang forth, jeweled and enameled, the knife in its third hand glittering in the false sunlight. "This *is* you, isn't it."

"Yes."

"The Itran Tetrarchy! Is that where you found the gun?"

"No. It's where I got my money."

Anaander Mianaai frankly stared in astonishment. "They let you leave with that much money?"

"One of the tetrarchs owed me a favor."

"That must have been some favor."

"It was."

"Do they really practice human sacrifice there? Or is this," she gestured to the severed head the figure held, "just meta-phorical?"

"It's complicated."

She made a breathy *hmf.* Seivarden knelt silent and motionless.

"The medic said you needed me."

Five-year-old Anaander Mianaai laughed. "And so I do."

"In that case," I said, "go fuck yourself." Which she could actually, literally do, in fact.

"Half your anger is for yourself." She ate the last bite of pastry and brushed her small gloved hands together, shower-ing fragments of sugar icing onto the grass. "But it's such a monumentally enormous anger even half is quite devastating."

"I could be ten times as angry," I said, "and it would mean nothing if I was unarmed."

Her mouth quirked in a half-smile. "I haven't gotten to where I am by laying aside useful instruments."

"You destroy the instruments of your enemy wherever you find them," I said. "You told me so yourself. And I won't be useful to you."

"I'm the right one," the child said. "I'll sing for you if you like, though I don't know if it will work with this voice. This is going to spread to other systems. It already has, I just haven't seen the reply signal from the neighboring provincial palaces yet. I need you on my side."

I tried sitting up straighter. It seemed to work. "It doesn't matter whose side anyone is on. It doesn't matter who wins, because either way it will be *you* and nothing will really change."

"That's easy for *you* to say," said five-year-old Anaander Mianaai. "And maybe in some ways you're right. A lot of things haven't really changed, a lot of things might stay the same no matter which side of me is uppermost. But tell me, do you think it made no difference to Lieutenant Awn, which of me was on board that day?"

I had no answer for that.

"If you've got power and money and connections, some differences won't change anything. Or if you're resigned to dying in the near future, which I gather is your position at the moment. It's the people without the money and the power, who desperately want to live, for those people small things aren't small at all. What you call no difference is life and death to them."

"And you care so much for the insignificant and the powerless," I said. "I'm sure you stay awake nights worrying for them. Your heart must bleed."

"Don't come all self-righteous on me," said Anaander Mianaai. "You served me without a qualm for two thousand years. You know what that means, better than almost anyone else here. And I *do* care. But in, perhaps, a more abstract way than you do, at least these days. Still, this is all my own doing. And you're right, I can't exactly rid myself of myself. I could use a reminder of that. It might be best if I had a conscience that was armed and independent."

"Last time someone tried to be your conscience," I said,

thinking of Ime, and that *Mercy of Sarrse* soldier who had refused her orders, "she ended up dead."

"You mean at Ime. You mean the soldier *Mercy of Sarrse* One Amaat One," the child said, grinning as if at a particularly delightful memory. "I have never been dressed down like that in my long life. She cursed me at the end of it, and tossed her poison back like it was arrack."

Poison. "You didn't shoot her?"

"Gunshot wounds make such a mess," the child said, still grinning. "Which reminds me." She reached beside herself and brushed the air with one small gloved hand. Suddenly a box sat there, light-suckingly black. "Citizen Seivarden."

Seivarden leaned forward, took the box.

"I'm well aware," said Anaander Mianaai, "that you weren't speaking metaphorically when you said your anger had to be armed to mean anything. I wasn't either, when I said my conscience should be. Just so you know I mean what I'm saying. And just so you don't do anything foolish out of ignorance, I need to explain just what it is you have."

"You know how it works?" But she'd had the others for a thousand years. More than enough time to figure it out.

"To a point." Anaander Mianaai smiled wryly. "A bullet, as I'm sure you already know, does what it does because the gun it's fired from gives it a large amount of kinetic energy. The bullet hits something, and that energy has to go somewhere." I didn't answer, didn't even raise an eyebrow. "The bullets in the Garseddai gun," five-year-old Mianaai continued, "aren't really bullets. They're...devices. Dormant, until the gun arms them. At that point, it doesn't matter how much kinetic energy they have leaving the gun. From the moment of impact, it makes however much energy it needs to cut through the target for precisely 1.11 meters. And then it stops."

"Stops." I was aghast.

"One point eleven meters?" asked Seivarden, kneeling beside me. Puzzled.

Mianaai made a dismissive gesture. "Aliens. Different standard units, I assume. Theoretically, once it was armed, you could toss one of those bullets gently against something and it would burn right through it. But you can only arm them with the gun. As far as I can tell there's nothing in the universe those bullets can't cut through."

"Where does all that energy come from?" I asked. Still aghast. Appalled. No wonder I had only needed one shot to take out that oxygen tank. "It has to come from somewhere."

"You'd think," said Mianaai. "And you're about to ask me how it knows how much it needs, or the difference between air and what you're shooting at. And I don't know that either. You see why I made that treaty with the Presger. And why I'm so anxious to keep its terms."

"And anxious," I said, "to destroy them." The aim, the fervent desire, of the other Anaander, I guessed.

"I didn't get where I am by having reasonable goals," said Anaander Mianaai. "You're not to speak of this to anyone." Before I could react, she continued, "I *could* force you to keep quiet. But I won't. You're clearly a significant piece in this cast, and it would be improper of me to interfere with your trajectory."

"I hadn't thought you would be superstitious," I said.

"I wouldn't say superstitious. But I have other things to attend to. Few of me are left here—few enough that the exact number is sensitive information. And there's a lot to do, so I really don't have time to sit here talking.

"*Mercy of Kalr* needs a captain. And lieutenants, actually. You can probably promote them from your own crew."

"I can't be a captain. I'm not a citizen. I'm not even *human*."

"You are if I say you are," she said.

"Ask Seivarden." Seivarden had set the box on my lap, and now once again knelt silent beside my chair. "Or Skaaiat."

"Seivarden isn't going anywhere you aren't going," said the Lord of the Radch. "She made that clear to me while you were asleep."

"Then Skaaiat."

"She already told me to fuck off."

"What a coincidence."

"And really, I do need her here." She clambered to her feet, barely tall enough to meet my eyes without looking up, even sitting as I was. "Medical says you need a week at the least. I can give you a few additional days to inspect *Mercy of Kalr* and take on whatever supplies you might need. It'll be easier for everyone if you just say yes now and appoint Seivarden your first lieutenant and let her take care of things. But you'll manage it the way you want." She brushed grass and dirt off her legs. "As soon as you're ready I need you to get to Athoek Station as quickly as you can. It's two gates away. Or it would be if *Sword of Tlen* hadn't taken that gate down." *Two gates away*, Inspector Supervisor Skaaiat had said, of Lieutenant Awn's sister. "What else are you going to do with yourself?"

"I actually have another option?" She might have named me a citizen, but she could take it back as easily. "Besides death, I mean."

She made a gesture of ambiguity. "As much as any of us. Which is to say, possibly none at all. But we can talk philosophy later. We've both got things to do right now." And she left.

Seivarden gathered my things, repacked them, and helped

me to my feet, and out. She didn't speak until we were on the concourse. "It's a ship. Even if it is just a Mercy."

I had slept for some time, it seemed, long enough for the shards of glass to be cleared away, long enough for people to come out, though not in great numbers. Everyone looked slightly haggard, looked as though they'd be easily startled. Any conversations were low, subdued, so the place felt deserted even with people there. I turned my head to look at Seivarden, and raised an eyebrow. "You're the captain here. Take it if you want it."

"No." We stopped by a bench, and she lowered me onto it. "If I were still a captain someone would owe me back pay. I officially left the service when I was declared dead a thousand years ago. If I want back in, I have to start all over again. Besides." She hesitated, and then sat beside me. "Besides, when I came out of that suspension pod, it was like everyone and everything had failed me. The Radch had failed me. My ship had failed me." I frowned, and she made a placatory gesture. "No, it's not fair. None of it's fair, it's just how I felt. And I'd failed myself. But you hadn't. You didn't." I didn't know what to say to that. She didn't seem to expect an answer.

"*Mercy of Kalr* doesn't need a captain," I said, after four seconds of silence. "Maybe it doesn't want one."

"You can't refuse your assignment."

"I can if I have enough money to support myself."

Seivarden frowned, took a breath as though she wanted to argue, but didn't. After another moment of silence, she said, "You could go into the temple and ask for a cast."

I wondered if the image of foreign piety I'd constructed had convinced her I had some sort of faith, or if she was merely too Radchaai not to think the toss of a handful of omens would answer any pressing question, persuade me toward the right action. I made a small, doubtful gesture. "I really don't feel the need. You can, if you want. Or toss right now." If she had something with a front and a back, she could make a throw. "If it comes up heads you stop bothering me about it and get me some tea."

She made a quick, amused *ha*. And then said, "Oh," and reached into her jacket. "Skaaiat gave me this to give you." Skaaiat. Not *that Awer*.

Seivarden opened her hand, showed me a gold disk two centimeters in diameter. A tiny, leafy border stamped around its edge, slightly off center, surrounding a name. AWN ELMING.

"I don't think you want to throw it, though," Seivarden said. And, when I didn't answer, "She said you really should have it."

While I was still trying to find something to say, and a voice to say it with, a Security officer approached, cautious. Said, voice deferential, "Excuse me, citizen. Station would like to speak with you. There's a console right over there." She gestured aside.

"Don't you have implants?" Seivarden asked.

"I concealed them. Disabled some. Station probably can't see them." And I didn't know where my handheld was. Probably somewhere in my luggage.

I had to get up and walk to the console, and stand while I spoke. "You wanted to speak to me, Station, here I am." The week of rest Anaander Mianaai had spoken of became more and more inviting.

"Citizen Breq Mianaai," said Station in its flat, untroubled voice.

Mianaai. My hand still curled around Lieutenant Awn's memorial pin, I looked at Seivarden coming behind me with my luggage. "There was no point in making you any more upset than you already were," she said, as though I'd spoken.

The Lord of the Radch had said *independent*, and I was unsurprised to discover she hadn't meant it. But the move she'd chosen to undercut it did surprise me.

"Citizen Breq Mianaai," Station said again, from the console, voice as smooth and serene as ever, but I thought the repetition was slightly malicious. My suspicion was confirmed when Station continued. "I would like you to leave here."

"Would you." No answer more cogent than that came to my mind. "Why?"

A half second of delay, and then the answer. "Look around you." I didn't have the energy to actually do that, so I took the imperative as rhetorical. "Medical is overwhelmed with injured and dying citizens. Many of my facilities are damaged. My residents are anxious and afraid. *I* am anxious and afraid. I don't even mention the confusion surrounding the palace proper. And *you* are the cause of all this."

"I'm not." I reminded myself that, childish and petty as it seemed now, Station wasn't very different from what I had been, and in some ways the job it did was far more complicated and urgent than mine, caring as it did for hundreds of thousands, even millions of citizens. "And my leaving won't change any of that."

"I don't care," said Station, calm. The petulance I detected was certainly my imagination. "I advise you to leave now, while it's possible. It may become difficult at some point in the near future."

Station couldn't order me to leave. Strictly speaking it shouldn't have spoken to me the way it had, not if I was, in fact, a citizen. "It can't *make* you leave," Seivarden said, echoing part of my thoughts.

"But it can express its disapproval." Quietly. Subtly. "We do it all the time. Mostly nobody notices, except they visit another ship or station and suddenly find things inexplicably more comfortable."

A second of silence from Seivarden, and then, "Oh." From the sound, she was remembering her days on *Justice of Toren*, and the move to *Sword of Nathtas*.

I leaned forward, my forehead against the wall adjoining the console. "Are you finished, Station?"

"*Mercy of Kalr* would like to speak with you."

Five seconds of silence. I sighed, knowing I couldn't win this game, shouldn't even try to play it. "I will speak to *Mercy of Kalr* now, Station."

"*Justice of Toren*," said *Mercy of Kalr* from the console.

The name caught me by surprise, started exhausted tears. I blinked them away. "I'm only One Esk," I said. And swallowed. "Nineteen."

"Captain Vel is under arrest," said *Mercy of Kalr*. "I don't know if she's going to be reeducated or executed. And my lieutenants as well."

"I'm sorry."

"It isn't your fault. They made their own choices."

"So who's in command?" I asked. Beside me Seivarden stood silent, one hand on my arm. I wanted to lie down and sleep, just that, nothing else.

"One Amaat One." The senior soldier in *Mercy of Kalr*'s highest ranking unit, that would be. Unit leader. Ancillary units hadn't needed leaders.

"She can be captain, then."

"No," said *Mercy of Kalr*. "She'll make a good lieutenant but she's not ready to be captain. She's doing her best but she's overwhelmed."

"*Mercy of Kalr*," I said. "If *I* can be a captain, why can't you be your own?"

"That would be ridiculous," answered *Mercy of Kalr*. Its voice was calm as ever but I thought it was exasperated. "My crew needs a captain. But then, I'm just a Mercy, aren't I. I'm sure the Lord of the Radch would give you a Sword if you asked. Not that a Sword captain would be any happier to be sent to a Mercy, but I suppose it's better than no captain at all."

"No, Ship, it's not..."

Seivarden interrupted, voice severe. "Cut it out, Ship."

"*You're* not one of my officers," said *Mercy of Kalr* from the console, and now the impassivity of its voice audibly broke, if only slightly.

"Not *yet*," Seivarden replied.

I began to suspect a setup, but Seivarden wouldn't have made me stand like this in the middle of the concourse. Not right now. "Ship, I can't be what you've lost. You can't ever have that back, I'm sorry." And I couldn't have back what I'd lost, either. "I can't stand here anymore."

"Ship," said Seivarden, stern. "Your captain is still recovering from her injuries and Station has her standing here in the middle of the concourse."

"I've sent a shuttle," said *Mercy of Kalr* after a pause that was, I supposed, meant to express what it thought of Station. "You'll be more comfortable aboard, Captain."

"I'm not..." I began, but *Mercy of Kalr* had already signed off.

"Breq," said Seivarden, pulling me away from the wall I was leaning on. "Let's go."

"Where?"

"You know you'll be more comfortable aboard. More comfortable than here."

I didn't answer, just let Seivarden pull me along.

"All that money won't mean much if more gates go and ships are stranded and supplies are cut off." We were headed, I saw, toward a bank of lifts. "It's all falling apart. This isn't going to just be happening here, it's going to fall apart all over Radch space, isn't it?" It was, but I didn't have the energy to contemplate it. "Maybe you think you can stand aside and watch everything happen. But I don't really think you can."

No. If I could, I wouldn't have been here. Seivarden wouldn't have been here, I'd have left her in the snow on Nilt, or never have gone to Nilt to begin with.

The lift doors closed us in, briskly. A little more briskly than usual, though perhaps it was just my imagination that Station was expressing its eagerness to see me gone. But the lift didn't move. "Docks, Station," I said. Defeated. There was, in truth, nowhere else for me to go. It was what I was made to do, what I was. And even if the tyrant's protestations were insincere, which they ultimately had to be, no matter her intentions at this moment, still she was right. My actions would make some sort of difference, even if small. Some sort of difference, maybe, to Lieutenant Awn's sister. And I had already failed Lieutenant Awn once. Badly. I wouldn't a second time.

"Skaaiat will give you tea," Seivarden said, voice unsurprised, as the lift moved.

I wondered when I'd eaten last. "I think I'm hungry."

"That's a good sign," said Seivarden, and grasped my arm more securely as the lift stopped, and the doors opened on the god-filled lobby of the docks.

Choose my aim, take one step and then the next. It had never been anything else.

Acknowledgments

It's a commonplace to say that writing is a solitary art, and it's true that the actual act of putting words down is something a writer has to do herself. Still, so much happens before those words are put down, and then after, when you're trying to put your work into the best form you can possibly manage.

I would not be the writer I am without the benefit of the Clarion West workshop and my classmates there. And I've benefited from the generous and perceptive assistance of many friends: Charlie Allery, S. Hutson Blount, Carolyn Ives Gilman, Anna Schwind, Kurt Schwind, Mike Swirsky, Rachel Swirsky, Dave Thompson, and Sarah Vickers all gave me a great deal of help and encouragement, and this book would have been the lesser without them. (Any missteps, however, are entirely my own.)

I would also like to thank Pudd'nhead Books in St. Louis, the Webster University Library, St. Louis County Library, and the Municipal Library Consortium of St. Louis County.

Libraries are a tremendous and valuable resource, and I'm not sure it's possible to have too many of them.

Thanks also to my awesome editors, Tom Bouman and Jenni Hill, whose thoughtful comments helped make this book what it is. (Missteps, again, all mine.) And thanks to my fabulous agent, Seth Fishman.

Last—but not least, not at all—I could not have even begun to write this book without the love and support of my husband Dave and my children Aidan and Gawain.

extras

orbit

meet the author

MissionPhoto.org

ANN LECKIE has worked as a waitress, a receptionist, a rodman on a land-surveying crew, a lunch lady, and a recording engineer. The author of many published short stories, she lives in St. Louis, Missouri, with her husband, children, and cats.

interview

Honored Breq, or One Esk, or Justice of Toren, *is a unique character in that she has a human body, but artificial intelligence. What led you to this choice, and what were some of the challenges and opportunities it presented?*

Breq on her own wasn't nearly as challenging as *Justice of Toren*, or even just One Esk. Depicting what that must be like—to have not only a huge ship for a body, but also hundreds, sometimes thousands, of human bodies all seeing and hearing and doing things at once—the thought of that kept me from even starting for a long time. How do you show a reader that experience? I could try to depict the flood of sensation and action, but then the focus would be so diffuse that it would be difficult to see where the main thread was. On the other hand, I could narrow things down to only one segment of One Esk, shortchanging one of the things that really intrigued me about the character, and also making it seem as though it was more separate from the ship than it was.

But a character like *Justice of Toren* also sees a great deal, and so it can act as an essentially omniscient narrator—it knows its own officers intimately and can see their emotions. It can witness things happening in several places at once. So I could write in straight first person, while also taking advantage of that ability to see so much at one time whenever I needed that. It was a nifty short-circuit around one of the more obvious limits of a first-person narrator.

You have shown us elements of Radch culture in great detail, and reading Ancillary Justice, *one gets the sense that you know far more about this civilization than appears in the novel. Can you tell us a little about what inspired the Radch?*

I'm not sure I could say truthfully that any particular real-world example inspired the Radch. It was built piece by piece as time went by. That said, some of those pieces did come from the real world. I took a number of things from the Romans—though their theology isn't particularly Roman, the Radchaai attitude toward religion is fairly similar, particularly the way the gods of conquered peoples can be integrated into an already-familiar pantheon. And the careful attention to omens and divination—though the Radchaai logic behind that is quite different.

The Romans have provided a lot of writers with a model for various interstellar empires, of course, and no wonder. The Roman Empire is a really good example of a large empire that, in one form or another, functioned for quite a long time over a very large area. And over that time, there was all sorts of exciting drama—civil wars and assassinations and revolts and bits breaking off and being forced back in, even a pretty big change in the form of government, from Republic to Principate. There's tons of material there. And they loom large in European history. It wasn't so long ago that any educated Westerner learned Greek and Latin as a matter of course, and read Virgil and Ovid and Cicero and Caesar and a host of other writers as part of that education.

But I didn't want my future—however fanciful it was—
to be entirely European. The Radchaai aren't meant to be
Romans in Space.

Though Ancillary Justice *is your first novel, you have published a number of short stories. Do you have very different
approaches to writing, according to length? What can you
share about your writing process?*

When I first started writing seriously, I found that I was
naturally producing very long work, and writing shorter was
very difficult. Some of that was just being a beginner, but
some of it was a product of the way I write. I might start
out with the bones of an idea—the next step will be figuring out the setting. Setting, for me, is very much a part of
my characters, and to set those characters in motion without
also giving those details that make those characters' actions
meaningful makes for thin work, at least when I do it.

People are who they are because of the world they live in,
and the world is the way it is because of the people who live
in it. If you're writing something set in the real world fairly
close to our present time you can evoke setting and historical
context with a few words. But I tend to write secondary-world
fantasy, or far-future space opera, and evoking the history
and culture of those worlds can be a bit complicated. It takes
a bit of elbow room, or else incredibly efficient exposition.

I personally like working with a big frame, I like the feeling that the world extends well past the edges of the story,
and odd, neat little details are one of the ways you do that.

But in a short story, there's very little room to work. Often
new writers are advised to make sure every scene in a story
is doing at least two things, but I've found that when I write

short, two is too few. Every scene has to be doing as much work as it possibly can, and each sentence has to have a justification. If I can cut it, and the story remains comprehensible, then it pretty much has to go. Even if it's doing two or three things.

And then, of course, some ideas are suited to large-scale handling, and some wouldn't make more than a thousand words of story even if you jammed as much extra stuff in as you could. So I found that if I wanted to write short fiction, I needed to learn either to pull out a fragment of a big idea, or else compress something sweeping into a smaller space.

Your main character is known for her encyclopedic knowledge of song, and for her enthusiasm for singing. Is this an enthusiasm you share, and if so, were there any pieces of music you found particularly inspiring when writing this novel?

I love singing! I especially love singing with other people—choral singing is a blast. I think it's a shame that so many people I meet have such an ambivalent, fraught relationship with singing. It's such a personal kind of music, one nearly anyone can make, but there's often a feeling that only certain people are allowed to do it. I've met way more people who claim they can't sing than actually can't. And I've met lots of people who actively discourage anyone around them from singing. Why is that? I wish people felt freer to sing, and freer to enjoy people around them singing.

It's one of the things I love about shape note singing—there's no audition, no question of whether or not your voice is good enough, or whether anyone has talent. You love to sing? Come sing! There's no audience, we're just singing for the pure joy of singing. Granted, the music itself might be something of an acquired taste. Still, if the idea intrigues you, visit fasola.org and see if there's a singing near you.

I didn't know right away that One Esk would want to sing. But the moment I realized that it would be able to sing choral music *all by itself* the idea was pretty much inescapable.

As for music that I found inspiring, there would be two different sorts. Music that I listened to while writing or plotting, and music that I included in the story itself. Of the latter, there are three real-life songs in *Ancillary Justice*. Two of them are (shockingly enough) shape note songs—"Clamanda" (Sacred Harp 42) and "Bunker Hill" (Missouri Harmony 19). They're songs that, for one reason or another, I connect with these characters and events.

The third is older than these two by a couple of centuries, but it shares their military theme. It's "L'homme Armé," and it seems like every late fifteenth-century composer and their pet monkey wrote a mass based on it. I exaggerate—I don't think we have that many surviving Missas L'homme Armé by pet monkeys. But it was a popular song in its day.

Music I listened to—I find that projects tend to have their own soundtracks. Sometimes particular scenes do. The list of music I used while writing would be long and dull, but at least one scene wouldn't have existed without a particular piece. The bridge scene was a product of listening to Afro Celt Sound System's "Lagan" way too many times.

Ancillary Justice *is the first in a loose trilogy. What can we expect from the next books?*

Now Breq has a ship, she's got one priority—to make sure Lieutenant Awn's sister is safe, and keep her that way. But she can't do that without getting involved in local political and social maneuvering at Athoek Station, and can't avoid the chaotic and dangerous consequences of civil war breaking out across the Radch. And once the people in the territories surrounding Radchaai space realize what's going on, they're going to take an interest, and it's not likely to be a friendly one. And not all the neighbors are human.

introducing

If you enjoyed
ANCILLARY JUSTICE
look out for

ANCILLARY SWORD

by Ann Leckie

1

"Considering the circumstances, you could use another lieutenant." Anaander Mianaai, ruler (for the moment) of all the vast reaches of Radchaai space, sat in a wide chair cushioned with embroidered silk. This body that spoke to me—one of thousands—looked to be about thirteen years old. Black-clad, dark-skinned. Her face was already stamped with the aristocratic features that were, in Radchaai space, a marker of the highest rank and fashion. Under normal circumstances no one ever saw such young versions of the Lord of the Radch, but these were not normal circumstances.

The room was small, three and a half meters square, paneled with a lattice of dark wood. In one corner the wood was missing—probably damaged in last week's violent dispute between rival parts of Anaander Mianaai herself. Where the extras

wood remained, tendrils of some wispy plant trailed, thin silver-green leaves and here and there tiny white flowers. This was not a public area of the palace, not an audience chamber. An empty chair sat beside the Lord of the Radch's, a table between those chairs held a tea set, flask, and bowls of unadorned white porcelain, gracefully lined, the sort of thing that, at first glance, you might take as unremarkable, but on second would realize was a work of art worth more than some planets.

I had been offered tea, been invited to sit. I had elected to remain standing. "You said I could choose my own officers." I ought to have added a respectful *my lord* but did not. I also ought to have knelt and put my forehead to the floor, when I'd entered and found the Lord of the Radch. I hadn't done that, either.

"You've chosen two. Seivarden, of course, and Lieutenant Ekalu was an obvious choice." The names brought both people reflexively to mind. In approximately a tenth of a second *Mercy of Kalr*, parked some thirty-five thousand kilometers away from this station, would receive that near-instinctive check for data, and a tenth of a second after that its response would reach me. I'd spent the last several days learning to control that old, old habit. I hadn't completely succeeded. "A fleet captain is entitled to a third," Anaander Mianaai continued. Beautiful porcelain bowl in one black-gloved hand, she gestured toward me, mean-ing, I thought, to indicate my uniform. Radchaai military wore dark-brown jackets and trousers, boots and gloves. Mine was different. The left-hand side was brown, but the right side was black, and my captain's insignia bore the marks that showed I commanded not only my own ship but other ships' captains. Of course, I had no ships in my fleet besides my own, *Mercy of Kalr*, but there were no other fleet captains stationed near Athoek, where I was bound, and the rank would give me an advantage over other captains I might meet. Assuming, of course, those other captains were at all inclined to accept my authority.

Just days ago a long-simmering dispute had broken out and one faction had destroyed two of the intersystem gates. Now preventing more gates from going down—and preventing that faction from seizing gates and stations in other systems—was an urgent priority. I understood Anaander's reasons for giving me the rank, but still I didn't like it. "Don't make the mistake," I said, "of thinking I'm working for *you*."

She smiled. "Oh, I don't. Your only other choices are officers currently in the system, and near this station. Lieutenant Tisarwat is just out of training. She was on her way to take her first assignment, and now of course that's out of the question. And I thought you'd appreciate having someone you could train up the way you want." She seemed amused at that last.

As she spoke I knew Seivarden was in stage two of NREM sleep. I saw pulse, temperature, respiration, blood oxygen, hormone levels. Then that data was gone, replaced by Lieutenant Ekalu, standing watch. Stressed—jaw slightly clenched, elevated cortisol. She'd been a common soldier until one week ago, when *Mercy of Kalr*'s captain had been arrested for treason. She had never expected to be made an officer. Wasn't, I thought, entirely sure she was capable of it.

"You can't possibly think," I said to the Lord of the Radch, blinking away that vision, "that it's a good idea to send me into a newly broken-out civil war with only one experienced officer."

"It can't be worse than going understaffed," Anaander Mianaai said, maybe aware of my momentary distraction, maybe not. "And the child is beside herself at the thought of serving under a fleet captain. She's waiting for you at the docks." She

set down her tea, straightened in her chair. "Since the gate leading to Athoek is down and I have no idea what the situation
there might be, I can't give you specific orders. Besides"—she
raised her now-empty hand as though forestalling some speech
of mine—"I'd be wasting my time attempting to direct you too
closely. You'll do as you like no matter what I say. You're loaded
up? Have all the supplies you need?"

The question was perfunctory—she surely knew the status
of my ship's stores as well as I did. I made an indefinite gesture,
deliberately insolent.

"You might as well take Captain Vel's things," she said, as
though I'd answered reasonably. "She won't need them."

Vel Osck had been captain of *Mercy of Kalr* until a week
ago. There were any number of reasons she might not need her
possessions, the most likely, of course, being that she was dead.
Anaander Mianaai didn't do anything halfway, particularly
when it came to dealing with her enemies. Of course, in this
case, the enemy Vel Osck had supported was Anaander Mianaai herself. "I don't want them," I said. "Send them to her
family."

"If I can." She might well not be able to do that. "Is there
anything you need before you go? Anything at all?"

Various answers occurred to me. None seemed useful. "No."

"I'll miss you, you know," she said. "No one else will speak
to me quite the way you do. You're one of the very few people
I've ever met who really, truly didn't fear the consequences of
offending me. And none of those very few have the . . . similarity
of background you and I have."

Because I had once been a ship. An AI controlling an enormous troop carrier and thousands of ancillaries, human bodies, part of myself. At the time I had not thought of myself as
a slave, but I had been a weapon of conquest, the possession

of Anaander Mianaai, herself occupying thousands of bodies spread throughout Radch space.

Now I was only this single human body. "Nothing you can do to me could possibly be worse than what you've already done."

"I am aware of that," she said, "and aware of just how dangerous that makes you. I may well be extremely foolish just letting you live, let alone giving you official authority and a ship. But the games I play aren't for the timid."

"For most of us," I said, openly angry now, knowing she could see the physical signs of it no matter how impassive my expression, "they aren't games."

"I am also aware of that," said the Lord of the Radch. "Truly I am. It's just that some losses are unavoidable."

I could have chosen any of a half dozen responses to that. Instead I turned and walked out of the room without answering. As I stepped through the door, the soldier *Mercy of Kalr* One Kalr Five, who had been standing at stiff attention just outside, fell in behind me, silent and efficient. Kalr Five was human, like all *Mercy of Kalr*'s soldiers, not an ancillary. She had a name, beyond her ship, decade, and number. I had addressed her by that name once. She'd responded with outward impassivity, but with an inner wave of alarm and unease. I hadn't tried it again.

When I had been a ship—when I had been just one component of the troop carrier *Justice of Toren*—I had been always aware of the state of my officers. What they heard and what they saw. Every breath, every twitch of every muscle. Hormone levels, oxygen levels. Everything, nearly, except the specific contents of their thoughts, though even that I could often guess, from experience, from intimate acquaintance. Not something I had ever shown any of my captains—it would have meant little to them, a stream of meaningless data. But for me, at that time, it had been just part of my awareness.

I no longer *was* my ship. But I was still an ancillary, could still read that data as no human captain could have. But I only had a single human brain, now, could only handle the smallest fragment of the information I'd once been constantly, unthinkingly aware of. And even that small amount required some care—I'd run straight into a bulkhead trying to walk and receive data at the same time, when I'd first tried it. I queried *Mercy of Kalr*, deliberately this time. I was fairly sure I could walk through this corridor and monitor Five at the same time without stopping or stumbling.

I made it all the way to the palace's reception area without incident. Five was tired, and slightly hungover. Bored, I was sure, from standing staring at the wall during my conference with the Lord of the Radch. I saw a strange mix of anticipation and dread, which troubled me a bit, because I couldn't guess what that conflict was about.

Out on the main concourse, high, broad, and echoing, stone paved, I turned toward the lifts that would take me to the docks, to the shuttle that waited to take me back to *Mercy of Kalr*. Most shops and offices along the concourse, including the wide, brightly painted gods crowding the temple façade, orange and blue and red and green, seemed surprisingly undamaged after last week's violence, when the Lord of the Radch's struggle against herself had broken into the open. Now citizens in colorful coats, trousers, and gloves, glittering with jewelry, walked by, seemingly unconcerned. Last week might never have happened. Anaander Mianaai, Lord of the Radch, might still be herself, many-bodied but one single, undivided person. But last week *had* happened, and Anaander Mianaai was not, in fact, one person. Had not been for quite some time.

As I approached the lifts a sudden surge of resentment and dismay overtook me. I stopped, turned. Kalr Five had stopped when I stopped, and now stared impassively ahead. As though that wave of resentment Ship had shown me hadn't come from her. I hadn't thought most humans could mask such strong emotions so effectively—her face was absolutely expressionless. But all the Mercy of Kalrs, it had turned out, could do it. Captain Vel had been an old-fashioned sort—or at the very least she'd had idealized notions of what "old-fashioned" meant—and had demanded that her human soldiers conduct themselves as much like ancillaries as possible.

Five didn't know I'd been an ancillary. As far as she knew I was Fleet Captain Breq Mianaai, promoted because of Captain Vel's arrest and what most imagined were my powerful family connections. She couldn't know how much of her I saw. "What is it?" I asked, brusque. Taken aback.

"Sir?" Flat. Expressionless. Wanting, I saw after the tiny signal delay, for me to turn my attention away from her, to leave her safely ignored. Wanting also to speak.

I was right, that resentment, that dismay had been on my account. "You have something to say. Let's hear it."

Surprise. Sheer terror. And not the least twitch of a muscle. "Sir," she said again, and there was, finally, a faint, fleeting expression of some sort, quickly gone. She swallowed. "It's the dishes."

My turn to be surprised. "The dishes?"

"Sir, you sent Captain Vel's things into storage here on the station."

And lovely things they had been. The dishes (and utensils, and tea things) Kalr Five was, presumably, preoccupied with had been porcelain, glass, jeweled and enameled metal. But they hadn't been mine. And I didn't want anything of Captain

403

Vel's. Five expected me to understand her. Wanted so much for me to understand. But I didn't. "Yes?"

Frustration. Anger, even. Clearly, from Five's perspective what she wanted was obvious. But the only part of it that was obvious to me was the fact she couldn't just come out and say it, even when I'd asked her to. "Sir," she said finally, citizens walking around us, some with curious glances, some pretending not to notice us. "I understand we're leaving the system soon."

"Soldier," I said, beginning to be frustrated and angry myself, in no good mood from my talk with the Lord of the Radch. "Are you capable of speaking directly?"

"We can't leave the system with no good dishes!" she blurted finally, face still impressively impassive. "Sir." When I didn't answer, she continued, through another surge of fear at speaking so plainly, "Of course it doesn't matter to *you*. You're a fleet captain, your rank is enough to impress anyone." And my house name—I was now Breq Mianaai. I wasn't too pleased at having been given that particular name, which marked me as a cousin of the Lord of the Radch herself. None of my crew but Seivarden and the ship's medic knew I hadn't been born with it. "*You* could invite a captain to supper and serve her soldier's mess and she wouldn't say a word, sir." Couldn't, unless she outranked me.

"We're not going where we're going so we can hold dinner parties," I said. That apparently confounded her, brief confusion showing for a moment on her face.

"Sir!" she said, voice pleading, in some distress. "*You* don't need to worry what other people think of you. I'm only saying, because you ordered me to."

Of course. I should have seen. Should have realized days ago. She was worried that *she* would look bad if I didn't have dinnerware to match my rank. That it would reflect badly on the ship itself. "You're worried about the reputation of the ship."

Chagrin, but also relief. "Yes, sir."

"I'm not Captain Vel." Captain Vel had cared a great deal about such things.

"*No*, sir." I wasn't sure if the emphasis—and the relief I read in Five—was because my not being Captain Vel was a good thing, or because I had finally understood what she had been trying to tell me. Or both.

I had already cleared my account here, all my money in chits locked in my quarters on board *Mercy of Kalr*. What little I carried on my person wouldn't be sufficient to ease Kalr Five's anxieties. Station—the AI that ran this place, *was* this place—could probably smooth the financial details over for me. But Station resented me as the cause of last week's violence and would not be disposed to assist me.

"Go back to the palace," I said. "Tell the Lord of the Radch what you require." Her eyes widened just slightly, and two tenths of a second later I read disbelief and then frank terror in Kalr Five. "When everything is arranged to your satisfaction, come to the shuttle."

Three citizens passed, bags in gloved hands, the fragment of conversation I heard telling me they were on their way to the docks, to catch a ship to one of the outer stations. A lift door slid open, obligingly. Of course. Station knew where they were going, they didn't have to ask.

Station knew where *I* was going, but it wouldn't open any doors for me without my giving the most explicit of requests. I turned, stepped quickly into the dockbound lift after them, saw the lift door close on Five standing, horrified, on the black stone pavement of the concourse. The lift moved, the three citizens chattered. I closed my eyes and saw Kalr Five staring at the lift, hyperventilating slightly. She frowned just the smallest amount—possibly no one passing her would notice. Her fingers twitched, summoning *Mercy of Kalr*'s attention, though with some trepidation, as though maybe she feared it wouldn't answer.

But of course *Mercy of Kalr* was already paying attention. "Don't worry," said *Mercy of Kalr*, voice serene and neutral in Five's ear and mine. "It's not you Fleet Captain's angry with. Go ahead. It'll be all right."

True enough. It wasn't Kalr Five I was angry with. I pushed away the data coming from her, received a disorienting flash of Seivarden, asleep, dreaming, and Lieutenant Ekalu, still tense, in the middle of asking one of her Etrepas for tea. Opened my eyes. The citizens in the lift with me laughed at something, I didn't know or care what, and as the lift door slid open we walked out into the broad lobby of the docks, lined all around with icons of gods that travelers might find useful or comforting. It was sparsely populated for this time of day, except by the entrance to the dock authority office, where a line of ill-tempered ship captains and pilots waited for their turn to complain to the overburdened inspector adjuncts. Two intersystem gates had been disabled in last week's upheaval, more were likely to be in the near future, and the Lord of the Radch had forbidden any travel in the remaining ones, trapping dozens of ships in the system, with all their cargo and passengers.

They moved aside for me, bowing slightly as though a wind had blown through them. It was the uniform that had done it—I heard one captain whisper to another one, "Who is that?" and the responding murmur as her neighbor replied and others commented on her ignorance or added what they knew. I heard *Mianaai* and *Special Missions*. The sense they'd managed to make out of last week's events. The official version was that I had come to Omaugh Palace undercover, to root out a seditious conspiracy. That I had been working for Anaander Mianaai all along. Anyone who'd ever been part of events that later received an official version would know or suspect that wasn't true. But most Radchaai lived unremarkable lives and would have no reason to doubt it.

No one questioned my walking past the adjuncts, into the outer office of the Inspector Supervisor. Daos Ceit, who was her assistant, was still recovering from injuries. An adjunct I didn't know sat in her place but rose swiftly and bowed as I entered. So did a very, very young lieutenant, more gracefully and collectedly than I expected in a seventeen-year-old, the sort who was still all lanky arms and legs and frivolous enough to spend her first pay on lilac-colored eyes—surely she hadn't been born with eyes that color. Her dark-brown jacket, trousers, gloves, and boots were crisp and spotless, her straight, dark hair cut close. "Fleet Captain. Sir," she said. "Lieutenant Tisarwat, sir." She bowed again.

I didn't answer, only looked at her. If my scrutiny disturbed her, I couldn't see it. She wasn't yet sending data to *Mercy of Kalr*, and her brown skin hadn't darkened in any sort of flush. The small, discreet scatter of pins near one shoulder suggested a family of some substance but not the most elevated in the Radch. She was, I thought, either preternaturally self-possessed or a fool. Neither option pleased me.

"Go on in, sir," said the unfamiliar adjunct, gesturing me toward the inner office. I did, without a word to Lieutenant Tisarwat.

Dark-skinned, amber-eyed, elegant and aristocratic even in the dark-blue uniform of dock authority, Inspector Supervisor Skaaiat Awer rose and bowed as the door shut behind me. "Breq. Are you going, then?"

I opened my mouth to say, *Whenever you authorize our departure*, but remembered Five and the errand I'd sent her on. "I'm only waiting for Kalr Five. Apparently I can't ship out without an acceptable set of dishes."

Surprise crossed her face, gone in an instant. She had known, of course, that I had sent Captain Vel's things here, and that I didn't own anything to replace them. Once the surprise had gone I saw amusement. "Well," she said. "Wouldn't you have felt the same?" When I had been in Five's place, she meant. When I had been a ship.

"No, I wouldn't have. I didn't. Some other ships did. Do." Mostly *Swords*, who by and large already thought they were above the smaller, less prestigious *Mercies*, or the troop carrier *Justices*.

"My Seven Issas cared about that sort of thing." Skaaiat Awer had served as a lieutenant on a ship with human troops, before she'd become Inspector Supervisor here at Omaugh Palace. Her eyes went to my single piece of jewelry, a small gold tag pinned near my left shoulder. She gestured, a change of topic that wasn't really a change of topic. "Athoek, is it?" My destination hadn't been publicly announced, might, in fact, be considered sensitive information. But Awer was one of the most ancient and wealthy of houses. Skaaiat had cousins who knew people who knew things. "I'm not sure that's where I'd have sent you."

"It's where I'm going."

She accepted that answer, no surprise or offense visible in her expression. "Have a seat. Tea?"

"Thank you, no." Actually I could have used some tea, might under other circumstances have been glad of a relaxed chat with Skaaiat Awer, but I was anxious to be off.

This, too, Inspector Supervisor Skaaiat took with equanimity. She did not sit, herself. "You'll be calling on Basnaaid Elming when you get to Athoek Station." Not a question. She knew I would be. Basnaaid was the younger sister of someone both Skaaiat and I had once loved. Someone I had, under orders from Anaander Mianaai, killed. "She's like Awn, in some ways, but not in others."

"Stubborn, you said."

"Very proud. And fully as stubborn as her sister. Possibly more so. She was very offended when I offered her clientage for her sister's sake. I mention it because I suspect you're planning to do something similar. And you might be the only person alive even more stubborn than she is."

I raised an eyebrow. "Not even the tyrant?" The word wasn't Radchaai, was from one of the worlds annexed and absorbed by the Radch. By Anaander Mianaai. The tyrant herself, almost the only person on Omaugh Palace who would have recognized or understood the word, besides Skaaiat and myself.

Skaaiat Awer's mouth quirked, sardonic humor. "Possibly. Possibly not. In any event, be very careful about offering Basnaaid money or favors. She won't take it kindly." She gestured, good-natured but resigned, as if to say, *but of course you'll do as you like.* "You'll have met your new baby lieutenant."

Lieutenant Tisarwat, she meant. "Why did she come here and not go directly to the shuttle?"

"She came to apologize to my adjunct." Daos Ceit's replacement, there in the outer office. "Their mothers are cousins." Formally, the word Skaaiat used referred to a relation between two people of different houses who shared a parent or a grandparent, but in casual use meant someone more distantly related who was a friend, or someone you'd grown up with. "They were supposed to meet for tea yesterday, and Tisarwat never showed or answered any messages. And you know how military gets along with dock authorities." Which was to say, overtly politely and privately contemptuously. "My adjunct took offense."

"Why should Lieutenant Tisarwat care?"

"You never had a mother to be angry you offended her cousin," Skaaiat said, half laughing, "or you wouldn't ask."

409

True enough. "What do you make of her?"

"Flighty, I would have said a day or two ago. But today she's very subdued." *Flighty* didn't match the collected young person I'd seen in that outer office. Except, perhaps, those impossible eyes. "Until today she was on her way to a desk job in a border system."

"The tyrant sent me a baby *administrator*?"

"I wouldn't have thought she'd send you a baby anything," Skaaiat said. "I'd have thought she'd have wanted to come with you herself. Maybe there's not enough of her left here." She drew breath as though to say more but then frowned, head cocked. "I'm sorry, there's something I have to take care of."

The docks were crowded with ships in need of supplies or repairs or emergency medical assistance, ships that were trapped here in the system, with crews and passengers who were extremely unhappy about the fact. Skaaiat's staff had been working hard for days, with very few breaks. "Of course." I bowed. "I'll get out of your way." She was still listening to whoever had messaged her. I turned to go.

"Breq." I looked back. Skaaiat's head was still cocked slightly, she was still hearing whoever else spoke. "Take care."

"You, too." I walked through the door, to the outer office. Lieutenant Tisarwat stood, still and silent. The adjunct stared ahead, fingers moving, attending to urgent dock business no doubt. "Lieutenant," I said sharply, and didn't wait for a reply but walked out of the office, through the crowd of disgruntled ships' captains, onto the docks where I would find the shuttle that would take me to *Mercy of Kalr*.

The shuttle was too small to generate its own gravity. I was perfectly comfortable in such circumstances, but very young officers often were not. I stationed Lieutenant Tisarwat at the dock, to wait for Kalr Five, and then pushed myself over the awkward, chancy boundary between the gravity of the palace and the weightlessness of the shuttle, kicked myself over to a seat, and strapped myself in. The pilot gave a respectful nod, bowing being difficult in these circumstances. I closed my eyes, saw that Five stood in a large storage room inside the palace proper, plain, utilitarian, gray-walled. Filled with chests and boxes. In one brown-gloved hand she held a teabowl of delicate, deep rose glass. An open box in front of her showed more—a flask, seven more bowls, other dishes. Her pleasure in the beautiful things, her desire, was undercut by doubt. I couldn't read her mind, but I guessed that she had been told to choose from this storeroom, had found these and wanted them very much, but didn't quite believe she would be allowed to take them away. I was fairly sure this set was hand-blown, and some seven hundred years old. I hadn't realized she had a connoisseur's eye for such things.

I pushed the vision away. She would be some time, I thought, and I might as well get some sleep.

I woke three hours later, to lilac-eyed Lieutenant Tisarwat strapping herself deftly into a seat across from me. Kalr Five—now radiating contentment, presumably from the results of her stint in the palace storeroom—pushed herself over to Lieutenant Tisarwat, and with a nod and a quiet *Just in case, sir* proffered a bag for the nearly inevitable moment when the new officer's stomach reacted to microgravity.

I'd known young lieutenants who took such an offer as an insult. Lieutenant Tisarwat accepted it, with a small, vague smile that didn't quite reach the rest of her face. Still seeming entirely calm and collected.

"Lieutenant," I said, as Kalr Five kicked herself forward to strap herself in beside the pilot, another Kalr. "Have you taken any meds?" Another potential insult. Antinausea meds were available, and I'd known excellent, long-serving officers who for the whole length of their careers took them every time they got on a shuttle. None of them ever admitted to it.

The last traces of Lieutenant Tisarwat's smile vanished. "No, sir." Even. Calm.

"Pilot has some, if you need them." That ought to have gotten some kind of reaction.

And it did, though just the barest fraction of a second later than I'd expected. The hint of a frown, an indignant straightening of her shoulders, hampered by her seat restraints. "No, thank you, sir."

Flighty, Skaaiat Awer had said. She didn't usually misread people so badly. "I didn't request your presence, Lieutenant." I kept my voice calm, but with an edge of anger. Easy enough to do under the circumstances. "You're here only because Anaander Mianaai ordered it. I don't have the time or the resources to hand-raise a brand-new baby. You'd better get up to speed *fast*. I need officers who know what they're doing. I need a whole crew I can *depend* on."

"Sir," replied Lieutenant Tisarwat. Still calm, but now some earnestness in her voice, that tiny trace of frown deepening, just a bit. "Yes, sir."

Dosed with *something*. Possibly antinausea, and if I'd been given to gambling I'd have bet my considerable fortune that she was filled to the ears with at least one sedative. I wanted to pull up her personal record—*Mercy of Kalr* would have it by now. But the tyrant would see that I had pulled that record up. *Mercy of Kalr* belonged, ultimately, to Anaander Mianaai, and she had accesses that allowed her to control it. *Mercy of Kalr* saw and heard everything I did, and if the tyrant wanted that information she had only to demand it. And I didn't want her to know what it was I suspected. Wanted, truth be told, for my suspicions to be proven false. Unreasonable.

For now, if the tyrant was watching—and she was surely watching, through *Mercy of Kalr*, would be so long as we were in the system—let her think I resented having a baby foisted on me when I'd rather have someone who knew what they were doing.

I turned my attention away from Lieutenant Tisarwat. Forward, the pilot leaned closer to Five and said, quiet and oblique, "Everything all right?" And then to Five's responding, puzzled frown, "Too quiet."

"All this time?" asked Five. Still oblique. Because they were talking about me and didn't want to trigger any requests I might have made to Ship, to tell me when the crew was talking about me. I had an old habit—some two thousand years old—of singing whatever song ran through my head. Or humming. It had caused the crew some puzzlement and distress at first—this body, the only one left to me, didn't have a particularly good voice. They were getting used to it, though, and now I was dryly amused to see crew members disturbed by my silence.

"Not a peep," said the pilot to Kalr Five. With a brief sideways glance and a tiny twitch of neck and shoulder muscles that told me she'd thought of looking back, toward Lieutenant Tisarwat.

"Yeah," said Five, agreeing, I thought, with the pilot's unstated assessment of what might be troubling me.

Good. Let Anaander Mianaai be watching that, too.

It was a long ride back to *Mercy of Kalr*, but Lieutenant Tisarwat never did use the bag or evince any discomfort. I spent the time sleeping, and thinking.

Ships, communications, data traveled between stars using gates, beacon-marked, held constantly open. The calculations had already been made, the routes marked out through the strangeness of gate space, where distances and proximity didn't match normal space. But military ships—like *Mercy of Kalr*—could generate their own gates. It was a good deal more risky—choose the wrong route, the wrong exit or entrance, and a ship could end up anywhere, or nowhere. That didn't trouble me. *Mercy of Kalr* knew what it was doing, and we would arrive safely at Athoek Station.

And while we moved through gate space in our own, contained bubble of normal space, we would be completely isolated. I wanted that. Wanted to be gone from Omaugh Palace, away from Anaander Mianaai's sight and any orders or interference she might decide to send.

When we were nearly there, minutes away from docking, Ship spoke directly into my ear. "Fleet Captain." It didn't need to speak to me that way, could merely desire me to know it wanted my attention. And it nearly always knew what I wanted without my saying it. I could connect to *Mercy of Kalr* in a way no one else aboard could. I could not, however, *be Mercy of Kalr*, as I had been *Justice of Toren*. Not without losing myself entirely. Permanently.

"Ship," I replied quietly. And without my saying anything else, *Mercy of Kalr* gave me the results of its calculations, made unasked, a whole range of possible routes and departure times flaring into my vision. I chose the soonest, gave orders, and a little more than six hours later we were gone.

introducing

If you enjoyed
ANCILLARY JUSTICE,
look out for

WAR DOGS

by Greg Bear

*An epic interstellar tale of war from
a master of science fiction.*

One more tour on the red.

Maybe my last.

They made their presence on Earth known thirteen years ago.

*Providing technology and scientific insights far beyond
what mankind was capable of, they became indispensable
advisors and promised even more gifts that we just couldn't
pass up. We called them Gurus.*

*It took them a while to drop the other shoe.
You can see why, looking back.*

It was a very big shoe, completely slathered in crap.

*They had been hounded by mortal enemies from
sun to sun, planet to planet, and were now stretched
thin—and they needed our help.*

*And so our first bill came due. Skyrines like me
were volunteered to pay the price. As always.*

*These enemies were already inside our solar system
and were establishing a beachhead, but not on Earth.*

On Mars.

Down to Earth

I'm trying to go home. As the poet said, if you don't know where you are, you don't know who you are. Home is where you go to get all that sorted out.

Hoofing it outside Skybase Lewis-McChord, I'm pretty sure this is Washington State, I'm pretty sure I'm walking along Pacific Highway, and this is the twenty-first century and not some fidging movie—

But then a whining roar grinds the air and a broad shadow sweeps the road, eclipsing cafés and pawnshops and loan joints—followed seconds later by an eye-stinging haze of rocket fuel. I swivel on aching feet and look up to see a double-egg-and-hawksbill burn down from the sky, leaving a rainbow trail over McChord field...

And I have to wonder.

I just flew in on one of those after eight months in the vac, four going out, three back. Seven blissful months in timeout, stuffed in a dark tube and soaked in Cosmoline.

All for three weeks in the shit. Rough, confusing weeks.

I feel dizzy. I look down, blink out the sting, and keep walking. Cosmoline still fidges with my senses.

Here on Earth, we don't say *fuck* anymore, the Gurus don't like it, so we say fidge instead. Part of the price of freedom. Out on the Red, we say fuck as much as we like. The angels edit our words so the Gurus won't have to hear.

SNKRAZ.

Joe has a funny story about *fuck*. I'll tell you later, but right now, I'm not too happy with Joe. We came back in separate ships, he did not show up at the mob center, and my Cougar is still parked outside Skyport Virginia. I could grab a shuttle into town, but Joe told me to lie low. Besides, I badly want time alone—time to stretch my legs, put down one foot after another. There's the joy of blue sky, if I can look up without keeling over, and open air without a helm—and minus the rocket smell—is a newness in the nose and a beauty in the lungs. In a couple of klicks, though, my insteps pinch and my calves knot. Earth tugs harsh after so long away. I want to heave. I straighten and look real serious, clamp my jaws, shake my head—barely manage to keep it down.

Suddenly, I don't feel the need to walk all the way to Seattle. I have my thumb and a decently goofy smile, but after half an hour and no joy, I'm making up my mind whether to try my luck at a minimall Starbucks when a little blue electric job creeps up behind me, quiet as a bad fart. Quiet is not good.

I spin and try to stop shivering as the window rolls down. The driver is in her fifties, reddish hair rooted gray. For a queasy moment, I think she might be MHAT sent from Madigan. Joe warned me, "For Christ's sake, after all that's happened, stay away from the doctors." MHAT is short for *Military Health Advisory Team*. But the driver is not from Madigan. She asks where I'm going. I say downtown Seattle. Climb in, she says. She's a colonel's secretary at Lewis, a pretty ordinary grandma, but she has these strange gray eyes that let me see all the way back to when her scorn shaped men's lives.

I ask if she can take me to Pike Place Market. She's good with that. I climb in. After a while, she tells me she had a son just like me. He became a hero on Titan, she says—but she can't really know that, because we aren't on Titan yet, are we?

I say to her, "Sorry for your loss." I don't say, *Glad it wasn't me.*

"How's the war out there?" she asks.

"Can't tell, ma'am. Just back and still groggy."

They don't let us know all we want to know, barely tell us all we *need* to know, because we might start speculating and lose focus.

She and I don't talk much after that. Fidging *Titan*. Sounds old and cold. What kind of suits would we wear? Would everything freeze solid? Mars is bad enough. We're almost used to the Red. Stay sharp on the dust and rocks. That's where our shit is at. Leave the rest to the generals and the Gurus.

All part of the deal. A really big deal.

Titan. Jesus.

Grandma in the too-quiet electric drives me north to Spring Street, then west to Pike and First, where she drops me off with a crinkle-eyed smile and a warm, sad finger-squeeze. The instant I turn and see the market, she pips from my thoughts. Nothing has changed since vac training at SBLM, when we tired of the local bars and drove north, looking for trouble but ending up right here. We liked the market. The big neon sign. The big round clock. Tourists and merchants and more tourists, and that ageless bronze pig out in front.

A little girl in a pink frock sits astride the pig, grinning and slapping its polished flank. What we fight for.

I'm in civvies but Cosmoline gives your skin a tinge that lasts for days, until you piss it out, so most everyone can tell I've been in timeout. Civilians are not supposed to ask probing questions, but they still smile like knowing sheep. *Hey, space-man, welcome back! Tell me true, how's the vac?*

I get it.

A nice Laotian lady and her sons and daughter sell fruit and veggies and flowers. Their booth is a cascade of big and little peppers and hot and sweet peppers and yellow and green and red peppers, Walla Walla sweets and good strong brown and fresh green onions, red and gold and blue and russet potatoes, yams and sweet potatoes, pole beans green and yellow and purple and speckled, beets baby and adult, turnips open boxed in bulk and attached to sprays of crisp green leaf. Around the corner of the booth I see every kind of mushroom but the screwy kind. All that roughage dazzles. I'm accustomed to browns and pinks, dark blue, star-powdered black.

A salient of kale and cabbage stretches before me. I seriously consider kicking off and swimming up the counter, chewing through the thick leaves, inhaling the color, spouting purple and green. Instead, I buy a bunch of celery and move out of the tourist flow. Leaning against a corrugated metal door, I shift from foot to cramping foot, until finally I just hunker against the cool ribbed steel and rabbit down the celery leaves, dirt and all, down to the dense, crisp core. Love it. Good for timeout tummy.

Now that I've had my celery, I'm better. Time to move on. A mile to go before I sleep.

I doubt I'll sleep much.

Skyrines share flophouses, safe houses—refuges—around

the major spaceports. My favorite is a really nice apartment in Virginia Beach. I could be heading there now, driving my Cougar across the Chesapeake Bay Bridge, top down, sucking in the warm sea breeze, but thanks to all that's happened—and thanks to Joe—I'm not. Not this time. Maybe never again.

I rise and edge through the crowds, but my knees are still shaky, I might not make it, so I flag a cab. The cabby is white and middle-aged, from Texas. Most of the fellows who used to cab here, Lebanese and Ethiopians and Sikhs, the younger ones at least, are gone to war now. They do well in timeout, better than white Texans. Brown people rule the vac, some say. There's a lot of brown and black and beige out there: east and west Indians, immigrant Kenyans and Nigerians and Somalis, Mexicans, Filipinos and Malaysians, Jamaicans and Puerto Ricans, all varieties of Asian—flung out in space frames, sticks clumped up in fasces—and then they all fly loose, shoot out puff, and drop to the Red. Maybe less dangerous than driving a hack, and certainly pays better.

I'm not the least bit brown. I don't even tan. I'm a white boy from Moscow, Idaho, a blue-collar IT wizard who got tired of working in cubicles, tired of working around shitheads like myself. I enlisted in the Skyrines (that's pronounced SKY-reen), went through all the tests and boot and desert training, survived first orbital, survived first drop on the Red—came home alive and relatively sane—and now I make good money. Flight pay and combat pay—they call it engagement bonus—and Cosmoline comp.

Some say the whole deal of cellular suspension we call timeout shortens your life, along with solar flares and gamma rays. Others say no. The military docs say no but scandal painted a lot of them before my last deployment. Whole bunch at Madigan got augured for neglecting our spacemen. Their docs tend to regard spacemen, especially Skyrines, as slackers and complainers. Another reason to avoid MHAT. We make more than they do and still we complain. They hate us. Give them ground pounders any day.

"How many drops?" the Texan cabby asks.

"Too many," I say. I've been at it for six years.

He looks back at me in the mirror. The cab drives itself; he's in the seat for show. "Ever wonder why?" he asks. "Ever wonder what you're giving up to *them*? They ain't even human." Some think we shouldn't be out there at all; maybe he's one of them.

"Ever wonder?" he asks.

"All the time," I say.

He looks miffed and faces forward.

The cab takes me into Belltown and lets me out on a semi-circular drive, in the shadow of the high-rise called Sky Tower One. I pay in cash. The cabby rewards me with a sour look, even though I give him a decent tip. He, too, pips from my mind as soon as I get out. Bastard.

The tower's elevator has a glass wall to show off the view before you arrive. The curved hall on my floor is lined with alcoves, quiet and deserted this time of day. I key in the number code, the door clicks open, and the apartment greets me with a cheery pluck of ascending chords. Extreme retro, traditional Seattle, none of it Guru tech; it's from before I was born.

Lie low. Don't attract attention.

Christ. No way am I used to being a spook.

The place is just as I remember it—nice and cool, walls gray, carpet and furniture gray and cloudy-day blue, stainless steel fixtures with touches of wood and white enamel. The couch and chairs and tables are mid-century modern. Last year's Christmas tree is still up, the water down to scum and the branches naked, but Roomba has sucked up all the needles.

Love Roomba. Also pre-Guru, it rolls out of its stair slot and checks me out, nuzzling my toes like a happy gray trilobite.

I finish my tour—checking every room twice, ingrained caution, nobody home—then pull an Eames chair up in front of the broad floor-to-ceiling window and flop back to stare out over the Sound. The big sky still makes me dizzy, so I try to focus lower down, on the green and white ferries coming and going, and then on the nearly continuous lines of tankers and big cargo ships. Good to know Hanjin and Maersk are still packing blue and orange and brown steel containers along with Hogmaw or Haugley or what the hell. Each container is about a seventh the size of your standard space frame. No doubt filled with clever goods made using Guru secrets, juicing our economy like a snuck of meth.

And for that, too—for *them*—we fight.

VISIT THE ORBIT BLOG AT

www.orbitbooks.net

FEATURING

BREAKING NEWS
FORTHCOMING RELEASES
LINKS TO AUTHOR SITES
EXCLUSIVE INTERVIEWS
EARLY EXTRACTS

AND COMMENTARY FROM OUR EDITORS

WITH REGULAR UPDATES FROM OUR TEAM,
ORBITBOOKS.NET IS YOUR SOURCE
FOR ALL THINGS ORBITAL.

WHILE YOU'RE THERE, JOIN OUR E-MAIL LIST
TO RECEIVE INFORMATION ON SPECIAL OFFERS,
GIVEAWAYS, AND MORE.

imagine. explore. engage.